IMMORTAL *Awakening*

IMMORTAL EVOLUTION SERIES
BOOK ONE

A NOVEL BY
KC RANDALL

OMNIFIC PUBLISHING
DALLAS

Omnific Publishing
P.O. Box 793871, Dallas, TX 75379
www.omnificpublishing.com

First Omnific eBook edition, September 2010
First Omnific trade paperback edition, September 2010

The characters and events in this book are fictitious.
Any similarity to real persons, living or dead,
is coincidental and not intended by the author.

Library of Congress Cataloguing-in-Publication Data

Randall, KC.
   Immortal Awakening / KC Randall – 1st ed.
   ISBN 978-1-936305-35-3
   1. Supernatural—Fiction. 2. Love—Fiction. 3. Vampire—Fiction.
   4. Immortal—Fiction. I. Title

10 9 8 7 6 5 4 3 2 1

Cover Design by Coreen Montagna and Micha Stone
Interior Book Design by Coreen Montagna

Printed in the United States of America

Dedicated to my Hubby,
who was so sure of the success of my book
that he had a dozen copies sold before anyone agreed to publish it.

PROLOGUE

Blood-red polish glistened against pale flesh as she tightened her grip on the poor girl's throat. "I find your answer unsatisfactory, Cassandra," she chastised. She smiled at the strangled sounds made in response. Loosening her vise-like grip, she allowed the girl to speak.

"Please, my Queen," Cassandra gasped, her voice cracked and hoarse. "I live but to serve you. I tell you all I see!"

The Queen cut her off by once again crushing her windpipe. "What good is a Seer who cannot see what I ask?" she said, her voice quiet as silk but sharp as a dagger.

In the silence of the crowded room, her voice rang clear. In one swift movement, the Queen pulled the Seer off her feet and slammed her down on the large stone table centered in the square room. As her talons closed on the unfortunate Cassandra's throat, small beads of dark crimson were added to the Queen's glittering nails.

"Poor Cassandra," she whispered into the ear of her prey. "In mortality your family failed you by refusing to believe in your visions." Reaching her free hand up, she pulled a slender wooden stick from the many used to hold her jet black hair. Cassandra's eyes widened in panic and fear, but no sound could make its way to her lips.

"Now your visions fail you, and you are left without purpose." With the speed of lightning and the power of thunder, the Queen stabbed Cassandra straight through the heart. There was not a sound in the cement room as those assembled held their breath in fear of inadvertently catching a stray blow from the Queen's fury. Cassandra lay motionless, her eyes staring up at nothing.

"Time is running out," the Queen said, turning her fierce violet eyes on her audience. Though no one moved, one could almost feel them cower before her gaze. "I can feel The Prophecy is upon me. I am Queen, Mother Eve to all Immortals. Should I fall, all would be lost."

Queen Eve stepped behind the table displaying Cassandra's small frame, prone upon the stone. "Say it!" she cried.

A cacophony of voices rose and echoed in the cement chamber. Several languages made hearing the words nearly impossible. Yet through the discord, a steady rhythm was felt as many voices of many nations repeated the same words. The words which, upon "invitation" to join the Queen in this room, they had written in their own blood on the stone floors and walls a thousand times, assuring they would indeed never forget them.

> "Let it be written that the Children of Adam will rise up against Eve, restoring all that has been lost. She shall not see them come, but shall know betrayal by her own blood. No sword can defend against my righteous vengeance. Though Eve shall rise and reign with violence, she shall be brought low with mercy."

"Know it," Queen Eve commanded. "Find it." Her penetrating gaze devoured each soul in its presence. "End it," she finished in a whisper, stroking Cassandra's hair softly. "You are my most trusted council, my Inner Court," the Queen mused. "You alone, of all my children, know of The Prophecy and its danger to me, to our way of life." Her hand trailed from the soft, silky strands of hair to the wooden shaft jutting out of the chest. "If you do not find the solution," she warned, gripping the stake firmly, "I have no choice but to assume you are part of the problem," she finished, twisting her hand sharply, causing the body to twitch once before again lying quite still.

"My son Lazarus will be joining you in the world," she said casually. A dark figure seemed to materialize and step away from the wall. Though the Queen called all her subjects her children, Lazarus shared her same raven hair and violet eyes. He also shared her passion for violence. The already tense atmosphere in the room jumped several notches. The fear of the Queen's secret assassin was exceeded only by the fear of the Queen herself. "Report to him any suspicious behavior. He will deal with those threats he deems worthy." She tenderly put a hand to his cheek, and he closed his eyes as he savored the contact. She then turned abruptly, leaving Lazarus leaning into the air. She crossed the room and stood over a stone podium, her back turned to them. Upon it lay an ancient page of script, The Prophecy.

"We will reconvene at the appointed time next year," she decreed. "I assume it will be to celebrate the end of this black cloud that threatens us. Until then, you are all dismissed." The room emptied quickly and Queen Eve was left alone with Cassandra's body and the page proclaiming her doom, blood still dripping from her fingernails.

CHAPTER ONE

Immortality is a bore. Years turn into decades, which turn into centuries, which turn into millennia, all of which blur together in a vast circle of sameness. Add to it self-sustained solitude and it's incredible we don't go mad. Though I suppose some of us have.

I've had my doubts about Jenny's sanity, certainly. But she was one of the small group of Immortals I could tolerate interacting with more than once a year. She was currently trying to hack me to pieces on the roof of my warehouse. There was no chance she'd ever land a blow, but that didn't stop her from trying.

Even at my medium height of five feet, ten inches, I towered over her small frame, which she'd repeatedly insisted was five foot even. Again, I had my doubts, but didn't care enough to argue. My slender build was far stronger, but her svelte little body had the reflexes of a cat. Her short, deep red hair and sultry brown eyes pointed more precisely towards a fox.

And so, to be fair, I tested her with my speed instead of my muscle. It was never a challenge, but entertaining enough that I didn't mind the occasional spar. Jenny took it very seriously. Being prepared to fight was one of her obsessions.

"You need a haircut," she said, interrupting what had been an hour of silence broken only by the ringing of steel blades. "It's distracting to have you leering at me from behind bangs with those cold green eyes."

She was probably right. My brown hair was shoulder length with a few layers to keep it lying mostly flat, and it was just starting to curl at the ends. Not that I was going to agree with her.

"I was under the impression you thought my eyes were penetrating," I answered, but ran my free hand through my hair to move it out of the way. No sense giving her an excuse to complain, though she would surely find another.

"That was a long time ago, Gregory," she said, continuing to dance in and out of my sword's range. "Though we could always get reacquainted after we finish this."

"I think not." While Jenny was pleasant to look at, and highly skilled, I had learned her "acquaintance" wasn't worth having her around that long, or that often.

"Your loss," she said, unaffected. Jenny was nothing if not resilient. "I told Rob I would come over later anyway."

"Tell him I'm taking another class," I said, stepping neatly away from her flashing blade. "I found one that is studying two of my personas at once— 'Classic Literature and Its Influence on Modern Prose.'"

"I thought you were through with all of that," she replied. "Especially after your last little stunt."

"An author's pen can never be stilled," I said nobly. "His voice never silenced."

She gave me a scathing look and an especially nasty jab, which I blocked.

"While I understand the need for diversions," she said with a knowing look, "you crossed the line. Getting famous and dying off as an author every century or so is one thing. Getting famous for writing vampire books borders on the insane."

She had a point. Bringing attention to ourselves was viewed with very little tolerance. Bringing attention to our "condition" was usually met with a swift death, in the best case scenario.

"You're lucky you weren't executed," she went on.

I simply looked at her. The truth was I'd been half-hoping for that exact reaction. I had long ago lost any zest for life, but suicide for an Immortal was … complicated, and therefore entirely too much trouble.

Jenny stopped sparring to stare at me. "That's what you were hoping for, wasn't it?"

I didn't answer her.

"You would so easily throw your life away?"

When I still didn't respond, she stepped back and returned her blade to its scabbard. Under her trendy cardigan wrap, it almost disappeared, looking like nothing more than a fashionable belt. She and Lance were constantly harping on me that it only took a little creativity to conceal a decent sized sword.

Stalking away in disgust, she paused to turn around. "If you find Immortality a bore, Gregory, perhaps it is because *you* are boring." She stepped off the roof and disappeared from view. I could hear her motorcycle rev and peel off before I reached the door.

I entered my loft apartment, if you chose to call it that; I had refurbished half of the top floor of an old warehouse. There was a large main room that contained a few comfortable leather chairs I used for reading, a large desk for my writing, and my bed. The walls were lined with books. I only kept the ones I really liked to read, but I had been around long enough that the collection was still vast. Aside from these few furnishings, the room was sparse.

I had spent a great deal of time and money on the architecture of my room. I shut the door behind me and held my breath. The result was absolute blackness accompanied by the sweet music of utter silence. I savored the abyss for a moment, and then reached over to flick on the light.

Walking over to my desk, I retrieved a soft cloth and oil. I proceeded to clean and care for my sword, slowly wiping along its blade with my long fingers. Unlike the rest of my fleeting possessions, I had not bought or stolen it. It was one of a pair, a *daishō*—"the big and small." They had been a gift, the only one I'd received in my very long life.

I'd had to replace the hilts a few times over the centuries, but I'd done so with great care and exactness to detail. The blades were in the tradition of the samurai and were nearly five hundred years old. Their age, no doubt, made them a valuable artifact. I smirked at that thought. When I'd received the swords, they had been new. I had thought them priceless then. Though my age was greater than even these swords', by millennia even, I was pretty sure no one thought of me as priceless. Tolerable maybe, entertaining perhaps, but not so important.

I shook my head at my melancholy thoughts. It wasn't as though I felt any different about the world than it felt about me. I sighed as I slid the sword into its sheath and returned it to its mount above my bed. Most Immortals felt as Jenny and Lance did, keeping themselves armed at all times, or at least like Rob, keeping a blade within arm's reach for protection. My blades, however, had taken up permanent residence on display.

I stood gazing at the beautiful tribute to death it made. While my peers thought my choice about personal armament either foolhardy or over-confident, I actually had very solid reasons for choosing not to carry. In fact, they correlated directly with the reasons most had to carry. The first reason for a sword is offense. I didn't care enough about the thoughts or opinions of anyone else to take offense and didn't interact with enough of my kind to create offense. The second reason would be defense. I happened to be faster, stronger, and smarter than everyone I know. That was not conceit talking, it was just fact. Adding a weapon to that just makes things ridiculous.

The only Immortal that could really do me damage is Queen Eve herself, and she seemed to have some kind of mental block when it came to me. She never spoke to me, unless absolutely necessary. In fact, she generally ignored my existence and expected those around her to do the same, which is most likely why I'd gotten away with the vampire books. The only thing more irritating than her lack of response when I'd been published was the response I got from her at the next Immortal Gathering. She had broken her own precedent by making eye contact with me from her throne. She gave me a look similar to that of a parent gazing upon a favored child who was acting impudently. It was confusing and belittling at the same moment. If I was so careless with my own life, gambling recklessly with it for mere entertainment, what could there possibly be worth protecting? And so the swords became decoration.

I turned away from them with a deep sigh. It was more in defeat than fatigue, but I decided to sleep for a while. The day was only now beginning to dawn, and my class didn't start until tonight. I didn't own a clock, and no light could get through the lined windows, but my body kept track of the passing time like a metronome. It would be good to rest my hyper-aware senses before I went out again.

I undressed so my body would have no distracting clothing rubbing against it and turned off the light. I lay down upon the king-sized waterbed attaining a certain degree of weightlessness. While some of my kind actually submersed themselves in water, I preferred the dry softness of lying on silk sheets. I closed my eyelids, resting them as well.

The seal that kept out light and sound was also airtight, so I had eight hours to rest before I would have to turn on the air conditioner and circulate fresh air into the room. My body could go much longer essentially holding my breath, but it would be uncomfortable and that would defeat the purpose.

My body relaxed as the strain of responding to so much stimuli was eased. I lay perfectly still for a few hours, not wanting even the soft rustle of the sheet to interrupt my perfect solitude. But even when there is no light, no sound, nothing to smell, nothing to taste, no movement to feel, the brain will find stimuli. As my physical senses shut down to rest, my mind came alive. I never lost consciousness, but rather, detached myself from reality.

Many Immortals used this time to sift through memories, organizing them as humans would a box of photos. I had lived so many memories, so many minutes and seconds, that I had long ago given up on keeping track of any but the most recent. So my mind had come up with a new way to entertain itself while I rested—I began to dream. My dreams were always the same. They came in variations, but the central theme remained.

Darkness. I was still as I listened to my prey. Its heartbeat was alone. It knew I was dangerous and that it stood no chance of survival on its own. We began to run, pressing through the wet, hot plants, making a terrible noise in our frantic race and startling other animals, including the birds that fled screeching into the sky above the dense forest. This brought our chase up into the trees, but there was no escape, and I could hear my large paws cracking branches as I closed in on my kill. Suddenly there was silence. I was alone in the dark, hot, green damp. Then I heard the roar and was bathed in blood, my fangs and claws drenched, satisfying my need and thirst. I bellowed again, claiming my prize and announcing my victory. But there were no ears left to hear. I was alone as it began again to rain.

I opened my eyes in the darkness, taking a deep breath, and shook my head, trying to rid myself of the lingering feelings the dreams brought. I didn't mind so much seeing myself as a predator bathed in blood. Although I was a much tidier killer, I was otherwise no different than the beast in my dream. I lived on blood and had no regrets about it. The strong preyed on the weak. Immortals preyed on man. It was the way of things.

What bothered me was the absolute reality of the sensations in the dream. It was as though my nose remembered the damp smell, my hands and feet remembered the dark, fertile earth, my lungs remembered the heavy air, my ears remembered the jungle sounds. But I had no access to the actual memories. With each dream it felt as though my body was trying to remind me of something I had lost, something I should be searching for.

It was a disturbing feeling because, while I had limitless memories of my Immortal life, I had none of being human. This seemed a unique phenomenon among my kind. While most eventually forgot much of their human memories over the centuries, they still had lingering, yet vivid recollections of what it was to be mortal. For me, there was nothing before my Immortality.

I rose from my bed. It would still be light and I would have to travel at mortal speed to avoid attracting attention. That left me with a walk that would take a few hours to get to the college campus. I didn't have a car. I had never seen the need for one. I quite literally had all the time in the world. I was never in a rush to get anywhere. I had gone through a phase a long time ago in which I fought against time as it eroded and decayed everything, stubbornly leaving me alone. Then I had come to embrace it, realizing it was the only thing I would be left with in the end. So now I used it as I saw fit, and today it was fitting to walk for a few hours.

Entering the vast closet that led to the bathroom, I pulled out some silk boxers and a pair of comfortable jeans. I would usually go for a lighter pair of cotton or linen slacks, but it would be cool this evening as I walked home.

With the same thought, I pulled on a tan cashmere sweater. It was a little warm for it now, but I would be glad for it later, and it was also softer than any of my T-shirts. It wasn't as though the heat or cold could actually hurt me in any way, but my sensitive skin could definitely feel it, and it could make me very uncomfortable.

I chose a pair of sandals for my feet, since, apparently, my toes preferred breathing to warmth. I don't analyze why I dress the way I do, I just wear whatever is comfortable against my skin. There were no mirrors in my loft as I had looked exactly the same for a few millennia now and didn't need one. I simply ran my hands through my hair and left, knowing the door alarm would lock behind me.

I walked down the abandoned street in front of my warehouse. The air was stale, as though even the wind had forgotten this neighborhood. Too soon, however, I came around a corner teeming with human life. My nostrils were instantly bombarded with the smell. Rotting corpses walking around. How they could stand to live with dead skin clinging to their bodies, I would never understand. The smell of their sweat, their breath bringing with it remnants of what they had last eaten. It was a wonder we could feed on them at all. Occasionally, one would walk by that had managed to mask the stink of death that naturally surrounds all mortals. However, the perfume or cologne mixed with countless sprays and lotions was just as overpowering, if not quite as unpleasant. The younger ones were always easier to be around, but the infantile ones were annoying.

And yet, as a whole, they were fascinating. Though I avoided contact with any of them, touching or otherwise, I couldn't help but watch. It was like observing an ant farm from the inside. The mortals ran every which way trying to live their short lives as fast as possible. To them, life is full of choices. Every day these mortals make choices about everything from what they will wear, to where they will live, to whom they will marry. Some believe the choices they make are important, life altering. They spend a lot of time choosing carefully. They believe that, while life is full of choices, there is but one right choice. Such is the belief of idiots. In fact, they are so foolish, they have it backwards. There is only one choice: Life or Death. Nothing else matters. Yet after having chosen life for so long, I can't really say it's the better choice.

Chapter Two

When I arrived at the college building, I chose a seat near the back of the small classroom. I was here mainly for observation. There were several empty chairs around me, which was no great surprise as humans tended to shy away from people like me. They could unconsciously sense my "differentness." I spoke too softly, moved too gracefully, stared just a little too long. Added to this natural aversion was the request of the professor to "scoot" as close together and to the front as possible.

"Get comfy and get familiar," he had said with a sappy smile. "We're about to embark on a fantastic trip, and it's no fun to travel alone." I had almost smiled at that one, but instead there was a small twitch at the corner of my lips. I had also ignored his request. Then he had insisted that everyone call him Tony instead of Professor Pierce. It was an attempt to be hip for the younger students. With his fifty-plus years behind it, it had come off as sad and pitiful.

As "Tony" droned on about the syllabus and testing schedules, I studied my fellow students. The combination of my classic romance author persona, Martha Vinegross, and my urbanely gothic author persona, Jerry Mack, had brought together a wide range of humans. There were older "alternative" students who preferred the classics, but probably wanted to understand their kids, or grandkids even. There were the young kids themselves, fresh from high school, wanting to look sophisticated, so they took a literature class. But they didn't want to be bored to death, so they had chosen one featuring a newly popular author. And there were a few students nearing graduation, who were mature, yet young and comparatively bright. These students would provide the most interesting views on my works. I nearly smiled again. They were invariably wrong, but still the most interesting.

Twenty minutes into the class I remembered why I never came the first day. It was all business, rules, and formats for essays. I should have skipped the Tuesday class and come Thursday instead. I began counting the stitches on the elbow patches of Tony's tweed jacket and contemplating making an early departure. It was just entertaining enough, with him swinging his arms around constantly so I could almost never keep his elbows in my direct sight. The door behind me opened, sending a fresh sea breeze through the stuffy room. Some frat boy or soccer mom was running late. A moment later my peripheral vision caught a young woman sitting down in the chair right next to me. Obviously she was flustered about being late and had simply sat in the first available chair she saw. I didn't let her distract me from my studious inventory of stitches on leather.

"What did I miss?" she asked in a soft voice.

I glanced at her, annoyed and determined not to lose count. I was startled by her round face, as it was mere inches from mine. Nothing had surprised me in a very long time. It must have been the counting. I had been distracted and hadn't felt her lean in so close. The hair falling over her shoulders was nearly touching my desk. I stared at her without answering. Finally she gave up, withdrew, and turned her attention to Tony. A few minutes later, I too returned my attention to the aging professor. But I had most certainly lost count. I had also lost the desire to start again. I was still disturbed that she had surprised me. No one surprised me, most especially not a mortal. They were all alike. Completely predictable.

"Apparently, I didn't miss much, just the regular first day drudgery." Her clear voice came to me again.

I turned to her in disbelief that she would speak directly to me again. I instinctively leaned back as she was, again, only inches away from me. As I eyed her derisively, she smiled at me and leaned back slightly.

"Sorry," she apologized. "I have notoriously little personal space. But yours seems to make up for it." She laughed quietly to avoid Tony's attention.

The small sound was packed with mirth. I stared at her, again bewildered by her behavior.

"I'm Nikki," she said, sticking out her hand with such earnest vigor, I had no choice but to take it. "Nicole, actually, but my friends call me Nikki, and that's pretty much everyone." She continued shaking my hand with enthusiasm.

I blinked at her. She laughed again.

"Didn't your mother ever tell you it's not polite to stare?" she asked. With no memory of a mother, I had no response. She smiled, finally released my hand, and turned her eyes back to the front of class.

I continued staring at her, trying to analyze her every movement. She was otherwise an utterly normal human. Her heart rate was normal. The pace of her breathing was normal. She smelled like a human, of sweat and blood and decay. She even had normal human habits, like tapping her pencil against her lips, and bouncing one leg up and down to create movement while sitting still. There was absolutely nothing to differentiate her from the rest of humanity. So why had her behavior toward me been so strange for a human? After twenty minutes of staring, I had gotten no closer to finding the reasoning behind her actions. Tony dismissed the class, and the girl went to the front to gather the papers she had missed from her late arrival.

I stood and walked swiftly out into the brisk night air, breathing in the freshness after being trapped with the smell of death for so long. During my walk, I contemplated whether perhaps the endless parade of sameness that was my existence had finally begun to dull my senses. How else could a mortal have surprised me in any way? By the time I got home, however, I had dismissed such a ridiculous thought and forgotten about the girl entirely.

When Thursday night came, I was expecting the class to be a little more entertaining. Tony would surely start to lecture, and I would find out just how ludicrous his ideas about my writing were. I already knew he was not the most insightful man, but perhaps some of his students would give me some sport.

I arrived early and took the same seat in the back of the class. The humans all remembered Tony's request and automatically sat front and center. I chuckled cynically at their sheep-like obedience and could almost hear them bleating to each other. Just before class started, the door opened, sending a breeze across my desk. The same insolent little blond girl sat in the chair next to me. I was incredulous.

"I think we're about ready to start, so let's all get nice and cozy," Tony began. There were only two people currently in the back of the room. He had to be talking to us. "Feel free to come forward, there's plenty of room," he continued. I, of course, ignored him and expected the girl to quickly move. Much to my surprise, however, she didn't. She looked from me to Tony and stayed right where she was. I stared at her, wondering why she would act this way.

Tony gave up on involving us and began class.

"I hate when teachers use false kindness to manipulate impressionable students." Her voice came to me quietly. I glanced at her, but her eyes were forward, not wanting to bring attention to her comment. I had to agree with her assessment of Tony. He wasn't as interested in his students' education as he was in their adoration. But I kept that agreement to myself. I turned my attention back to the aging professor.

"We have only two authors on our itinerary this semester," he began grandly. "Would anyone care to chance a guess as to why I chose them?" It was obvious his question was rhetorical and he was trying to gather momentum for some grand revelation. That didn't stop the girl next to me from raising her hand, causing her curls to bounce gently.

"Ah, so now you'd like to participate," Tony said coolly. "And your name, Miss?"

"Nikki," she replied, "Nikki Christian."

"The famous Nikki Christian!" the professor exclaimed. I wondered briefly what he meant. "I've heard so much about you in the English department, Ms. Christian." I didn't particularly care for his tone of voice. "Please enlighten the class with your views."

It looked like she shared my opinion of his tone, but now she had little choice but to go on. "I thought, perhaps, that you chose these two authors for their striking similarities," she offered. I turned my head to look at her.

Tony kept his face a careful mask. "You find them similar?" he asked.

The girl was a little embarrassed to be addressing the entire class, but was sure of her opinions. "Yes, very. They have a different genre and were written in different eras, but their style is much the same."

"Their style?" Tony asked.

"Yes, it's like…" She searched for words for a moment, her brow slightly creasing. Then her face lit up. "Have you ever watched a really bad movie on purpose?"

"I'm afraid not," Tony said with that same careful tone.

"Oh, well you should," she recommended. "My family and I sometimes rent a truly horrible film, just to make fun of it. It becomes less about the movie itself and more about how smart and funny you are with your commentary about it."

"Of course," Tony said, with obvious disdain this time, but by now the girl was on a roll.

"I get the feeling both of these authors have done just that, only instead of taking something really bad and mocking it, they created something beautiful and mocked it anyway."

I turned my head to stare at her. That was exactly what I had done. How could she know that? No mortal could be so observant.

Then she continued, "In fact it feels to me like Mr. Mack is emulating Ms. Vinegross. He must have studied her for a long time in order to write with such a recognizably similar voice in such a different genre of work. If I didn't know better, I would say he knew her, that they were perhaps even related." As she finished, my hands were clenching the sides of my desk. This human girl had come far too close to the truth. And she was dangerously close to revealing it to a class full of other mortals. But before I had to do something drastic, Tony spoke up.

"But you do know better, I would hope," he said. "In fact, I would hope that the rest of this class would know better than to agree with your long and erroneous theories."

The girl lowered her head in embarrassment, but the squint in her eyes was from anger.

"Is there anything else you would care to add?" Tony asked, sensing his victory in humiliating the girl.

"No," she said humbly, "but I do have one more question."

"By all means," Tony gushed. "How may I enlighten you?"

"Why did you ask me to go on and explain my theories if you assumed them to be wrong? It seems to me that a professor interested in teaching the truth would correct erroneous statements at once instead of encouraging students to prattle on and on about them," she finished, looking Tony straight in the eye.

I couldn't help but be amused by her victory. Not only had she gotten the last word in what should have been an uneven fight, but she had called Tony out on his motivation. She had also warned the rest of the class not to cross him, and not to respect him.

Tony decided to completely ignore her last comment and began lecturing as if the whole incident had never happened. The class went along with him, but it was obvious by the side glances the girl got that she had made an impression, some positive, most not.

As Tony rambled on about the many differences between Ms. Vinegross and Mr. Mack, I continued to stare at the girl next to me. There must have been something more to her, but what? What made her so observant? And if she was so observant, how did she not see how different I was?

I watched as every move of her head sent her large blond curls swaying gently. But blond wasn't the right word, her hair was so much more than blond. There were a hundred different shades from pale gold to deep auburn, which together created something rather like harnessed sunshine. It had to be natural, not even the most skilled colorist could put that many hues together and have it look perfect. The length was just past her shoulders, and every time she leaned forward to write something in her notebook, soft curls would fall forward, partially hiding her face.

At first I couldn't see why she didn't pull it back or do something with it to keep it out of her way. Then I realized she was probably trying to hide the pock marks that sprinkled her face. A mortal would probably assume they were acne scars, but my eyes could see there was something off about that assumption. They were too old to be acne scars and had once been much worse than they were now.

I became frustrated that her hair was obscuring my scrutinizing and before I could think, I spoke to bring her face around.

"You never told me you were famous," I said, my voice low so I wouldn't interfere with Tony's entrancing monologue.

As I had hoped, her head came up at my voice. I was not prepared, however, for the brilliant smile she flashed me, her lips framing white teeth too perfect for anything but braces to be responsible for.

"And here I thought you were either deaf or mute after yesterday," she replied. Her tone was teasing and her eyes twinkled. They were as blue as the sky.

"Neither," I responded. "But I have been told I'm rude."

"And a quick wit, too," she laughed softly. "Perhaps this class won't be a total waste of my time. Though you're more curious than rude, I'd dare to guess."

I actually smiled a little in response to the sound of her laugh and found myself wanting to hear it again. "I guess that would explain my inquiry of your undisclosed fame," I agreed.

She smiled again and my gaze was drawn to the cupid's bow of her upper lip which, paired with the fullness of her lower one, created a perfect blend of sultry innocence.

"Well," she said, "I'm an English Lit major and so I've taken classes from pretty much every professor in the department. What 'Tony' said about my being famous was only half true." Her fingers made sarcastic quotation marks in the air as she said the professor's name, and I couldn't help but smirk at her obvious contempt for him.

"The department is divided into two camps; in one I'm famous, in the other I'm infamous." As she said the last word, I could tell she was prouder of it than the more positive one. Something about that appealed to me as well. It was probably because I was so contrary by nature myself. "On one side we have 'team traditionalist,' and on the other 'team,' shall we say, 'free thinkers,'" she said, indicating each team with her hands.

"And which team are you on?" I inquired.

"You have to ask?" she cried, a little too loudly. Tony shot her a glance and she lowered her head, soft curls bouncing on her desk.

"I guess not," I acquiesced.

She glanced sideways at me, smirking. "I should have known better about Tony," she whispered, her voice as soft as velvet. "He's only been teaching here two years, so I haven't had a class from him before. I wasn't sure which camp he was in," her eyes narrowed, "until now."

She sighed heavily and I could smell her breath. It was surprisingly sweet. "Really, I knew that first day. I guess I was just giving him the benefit of the doubt."

I had also known that first day just who Tony was, but I was more observant than a mortal. "How did you know?" I wondered.

She turned to face me again, and her captivating eyes were now open and honest as she leaned forward. "I can read people," she said frankly. "I'm really good at it, actually. It's one of the reasons I'm infamous. Some people have a hard time believing I can tell who a person is by what they write."

I was momentarily startled. Was she saying that she knew I had written these books? Then I came back to myself and realized there was no way she could know. "And that is why you think Jerry Mack is emulating Martha Vinegross?"

"Yes," she agreed immediately. She apparently had no fear of my baiting her like Tony had. "They have such similar voices. If I didn't know better I would say they were the same person, writing under two different pen names." My eyes widened at her statement and she rushed on. "But that would just be crazy. I mean they lived a hundred years apart! So I'm left hypothesizing." She sighed again, this time it was sadder. "Which is why I took this class. I was hoping I had finally found someone as crazy as I am."

I couldn't bear the forlorn tone to her crystal voice. "I don't think you're crazy," I said, instantly regretting it. I couldn't exactly tell her she was right.

"Really?" she asked, looking up at me with hope shining in her eyes. I couldn't help but smile, but I didn't respond. She continued looking at me, waiting for more. Then she smiled and shook her head, sending the golden curls dancing. As she turned back to Tony, she quietly muttered, "Curiouser and curiouser."

I smiled and continued my inventory of her, wondering if that made me the White Rabbit, or the Cheshire Cat. She was dressed comfortably in generic jeans cut off at the knees and a black T-shirt proclaiming the name of a local band. She had brought a soft sweater that was the same robin's egg blue as her eyes. That, along with the fact that her sneakers were high quality, implied she would likely be walking at least partway home in the cool night air. I also noticed in the next twenty minutes while watching her write notes with her left hand, and nearly speak up again a few times at some of Tony's more inane comments, that she didn't seem to mind my staring. As soon as Tony dismissed the class, I stood and was out the door.

Chapter Three

s I strode across campus, I decided to pay a visit to Lance and Rob. Their apartment was near the college, so I wouldn't have to go out of my way. It was obvious it had been Rob's turn to choose where they were living this go round. The building they lived in was loud and cheap, which I knew was sure to irritate Lance. But the location gave them an ample selection of food from the college coeds and was close enough to the beach for endless surfing. The whole set up was Rob through and through.

I shook my head, wondering again why they were so set on staying together when they were so incompatible. Of course, things didn't exactly go well for them when they tried living separately, and old habits die hard. I smirked at my own joke. Old indeed; ancient habits really. Their friendship pre-dated even their Immortality. I occasionally wondered if I had ever experienced such a bond during my forgotten mortal life.

I scaled the fire escape and stood outside the window of their apartment. I despised going through the inside of the building. The smell of too many humans living together was rank indeed. I rapped gently on the window, knowing they would hear it, and waited for them to call for me to enter. I knew I was welcome at any time, but this was one of our oldest habits. We were very territorial by nature. Simply walking into another person's dwelling was basically the same as declaring war.

I didn't wait long before I heard Lance's strong bass voice call out, "Enter, my sword is drawn." I knew he hadn't actually armed himself; this was simply the customary response. It let whoever was coming know you were ready, whether it be to fight or to converse. Immortals are a fairly tense group, especially when we get together.

And yet there was no tension in the atmosphere of the apartment. I found Lance and Rob playing a video game in their den. It was some military strategy game, obviously Lance's choice. Rob preferred cartoon games where you could beat your opponent while making funny faces and ludicrous noises.

Even their physical appearances were polar opposites. Lance had wide shoulders and a chest like the trunk of a tree. The rest of him was just as heavily muscled, with only his six feet, three inches of height keeping him from looking out of proportion. His sharp jaw was square, accentuated by a cleft chin and a dominant, straight nose. His slate gray eyes were on constant alert, his black hair cut short to tame the tight curls. He dressed in clothes that gave him an excuse to demand respect, usually slacks and a button up, sometimes even with a jacket. To humans he always looked like he was just coming from or leaving for an obviously important corporate job. You could take the Legionnaire out of Rome…

Rob, on the other hand, was even shorter than me. He was barely five foot, eight. Though tiny compared to Lance, he wasn't as willowy as me. He had a strong build, especially his upper body. He seemed to take his latest persona of "eternal beach bum" to heart. His sandy blond hair fell haphazardly into hazel eyes that seemed to always be laughing at some private joke. His skin was a few shades darker than Lance's pale ivory, but not as dark as mine. His clothes usually consisted of baggy shorts with too many pockets to count and a variety of novelty tees. He generally looked like he was about to get into mischief of one kind or another.

"Bit of a surprise to see you here, Gregory," Lance said without taking his eyes from the screen. It looked like the two of them were playing online with several other live people. Lance was commander, of course.

"Yes, it's rare you grace us with your presence more than once a month." Jenny's voice came from the hallway leading to the bedrooms. She was refastening the belt across her runway ready attire. She had impeccable taste and looked as though she belonged in the houses on celebrity row, which is probably why she lived there.

Jenny only took her sword off for one thing. Apparently she and Rob were, in fact, on again. Every fifty years or so, they would get together. It generally lasted a year or two before Jenny would get bored or restless and break it off again.

Being solitary creatures, we don't have mates. We generally can't get along with each other long enough to make cohabitation possible. But I've heard of some Immortals who find a preference in a specific person and return to them when so inclined. Jenny was the only Immortal I knew who would actually keep up the pretenses of a relationship. I theorized it has something to do with her talent. She had an incredible sense of smell.

Over the course of her long life, Jenny had learned what the combination of different chemical smells in the body meant. In essence, she could smell emotions. She was fascinated by the fact that humans seemed to have an unending variation. She was constantly trying to convince me we must be capable of the same emotions, having the same chemicals. I told her that when she smelled an Immortal that had anything in common with a mortal to let me know. That would be something to see.

As a side effect to this talent for reading smells, Jenny was more empathetic to the mortal plight. She fed only often enough to stay strong, because she hated the taste of fear from them. I believed her charade with Rob was an attempt to emulate the feelings she could smell in the humans around her. I sometimes wondered if she had ever been successful in recreating similar chemical reactions, but had never asked.

Rob was the perfect partner for Jenny's experiments. He had a natural love of life and anything fun. He was also laid back enough that he wasn't put off when Jenny would suddenly decide she needed to be independent again. Jenny and I had not been together in that way for probably five hundred years. And she knew better than to go anywhere near Lance with such advances.

"You're the only one I've seen recently," I reminded her. "And I didn't really expect to find you here."

"But you're not surprised," she replied.

"Indeed not," I agreed. I turned my attention to Rob. "I thought I'd stop by on my way home to tell you about my class."

"Oh yeah!" Rob said, indicating Jenny had in fact told him about it. He was still watching the game while speaking to me. He absently flipped his hair out of his eyes. "So, how do you compare to you? Do you 'measure up,' or 'fall short'?" He winked at Jenny and she smiled indulgently.

"Is it already showing signs of a promising diversion?" Jenny asked as she preened her auburn hair in the large mirror mounted on the wall.

"I really enjoyed it when people thought you were a chick," Rob declared. "Are you the ultimate role model to this old lady, too? Or is she crushing on your bad boy dark side?"

"Actually the professor is a male and an imbecile, but there is this strange girl—" I stopped short as three pairs of eyes suddenly focused on me. "What?"

"You noticed a mortal?" Lance asked.

"A mortal girl?" Jenny added.

"She's rather hard to miss," I replied, irritated by their unexpected response.

"Wow," Rob said eloquently.

"What I mean by that is she insists on sitting right next to me and tries to engage me in conversation," I explained. "She has the most fascinating views on my books, but I can't see why she would go to such great lengths to talk to me."

Jenny took my jaw in her hand and turned me to the mirror. "That's why she would talk to you, obviously."

I looked at my reflection. I had brilliant green eyes. My white teeth were framed by full lips and stood out against skin that couldn't decide if it had a California tan or was ethnic in some way, Greek or Hispanic perhaps. I unconsciously ran a hand through my soft brown locks.

"Most humans still avoid me," I countered.

"That's because you're scary as the devil when you scowl," Jenny explained.

"And you're generally scowling," Lance reminded me.

"What does she look like?" Jenny asked.

"She must be HOT to feel like she can approach an Immortal," Rob said, waggling his eyebrows at me.

"She's average. Average height, average build. She's a blue-eyed blonde." Their eyes bugged out again. "What now?" I asked, the volume of my voice increasing.

"You know what color her eyes are?" Jenny asked, incredulously.

"Yes, well, when she insists on getting within inches of my face to speak to me, I can't really *not* see her eyes," I responded sarcastically.

"And you didn't kill her?" Lance asked. I didn't understand his question.

"You've almost killed me for much less than getting in your face," Rob supplied.

Suddenly Jenny grabbed my shoulders and drew her nose from my chest to my ear, inhaling deeply. "I beg your pardon!" I cried, stepping back and removing myself from her grip.

"You smell different," she said, almost accusing.

"What are you talking about?" I asked. This visit was not going according to plan. I was getting ready to leave.

"You smell different," she repeated. "You haven't smelled different in, well, ever." Lance and Rob looked at Jenny then back to me, their game long forgotten.

"I already told you she had some fascinating views on my writing. She doesn't believe it herself, but she knows the two authors are the same person. You must smell my surprise at finding a mortal so observant. I'm not often surprised," I explained.

"Hmm," Jenny said. "I have to meet her."

"What?" I said, shocked. I didn't want Jenny anywhere near this girl. I didn't know why, but it seemed like a very bad idea. "Absolutely not. This is my class, and if you suddenly show up, it will draw attention to both of us."

"Then you'll have to find out more about her," she insisted.

"Why?" I asked, feeling defensive.

"Because there must be something to this mortal for her to not only catch your attention, but get your respect," Jenny insisted. Rob and Lance's eyes widened as they decided she was right.

"I didn't say I had respect for her, and she is utterly normal in every way," I argued.

"You said she was 'observant,' which is more than you'll say for most Immortals," she countered. "She may be too observant."

"Fine, I will find out what she really knows," I agreed. I wanted to leave and I wanted Jenny to stay away from this girl, which meant I would have to give in.

"Perfect," Jenny said brightly, as if that had been her plan all along. Rob and Lance just shook their heads and finally returned to their game. "Would you like a ride home?"

"No," I all but growled. "I'm going hunting." Jenny smiled smugly at me as she sauntered out the door and I went out the window.

Chapter Four

Lazarus was frustrated. Mother's Inner Court was useless. Not one of them had found something worth investigating. It had been several months since he left home, and he knew he could not return until his assignment had been fulfilled. While that was standard procedure, in the past it had also been standard to know exactly who he was being sent to destroy. Even on the rare occasion when they had known he was coming and foolishly decided to run, he'd found them in a matter of days. He had never been separated from his Queen for more than a few weeks.

Picking another name from his list of agents, he dialed the number on his cell. He was not surprised when it was answered after the first ring. They knew better than to keep him, and by extension Queen Eve, waiting.

"Hello?" came the unsure female voice.

"What have you found?" Lazarus asked without preamble.

"I … I don't have anything to report," she answered.

"You have failed then?"

"No!" she cried. "I have been searching, and I may have something, but nothing is sure yet."

"Would my assistance help you to become more expedient?" he offered.

"No. No, that's not necessary. Give me a few more weeks and I'll have a report for you, whether it's something for you to look into or not."

"I have been disappointed several times recently," Lazarus noted. He did not add that the Queen had unfortunately not allowed him to eliminate said disappointments, yet.

"If I could have a month…" she began.

"I make no promises, but I will give you more time," he glanced at his list, "Guinevere."

"*You are most gracious, as is Mother Eve,*" *she pandered.*

He clicked his phone shut and considered his options. He had no business left in Paris. In fact, he was fairly bored with the entire continent of Europe. Guinevere was in the United States. While he had told her he would give her time before he called again, there was no reason to stay where he was.

Stepping over the body at his feet, he decided to find another mortal to take with him on his plane. It was a long flight to America.

CHAPTER FIVE

It was only midnight when I came to a bar that had what I needed. There was a shadowy alley near the exit, and it was in a fairly questionable part of town. I would have cover for my attack, and there would be plenty of excuses for a dead body in the area. While there were some who hunted for the sport, I had long since found there was no sport in hunting mortals. It was too easy. They were too easy to stalk, too easy to seduce, too easy to manipulate. So I had given up on trying to make it a challenge and made it as easy as possible. This was also why I had chosen a bar. As easy as it was to overtake a normal mortal, a drunk wouldn't know what was happening until they were already dead. Lance sometimes said this was cheating. I considered it less contact with a feeble and unworthy race. The alcohol made for less appetizing blood, but it would still quench the thirst and I could be on my way. Human blood was usually tainted by one thing or another these days anyway. Between the drugs, diseases, herbs, and vaccinations, blood just wasn't as sweet as it had been in times past.

I settled into my perch on the roof across the street from the bar. It was still too early for the mortals inside to be drunk enough to call it a night and come stumbling out into the street. I didn't mind waiting. I had all the time in the world. As I waited, my mind began to wander. Not surprisingly, after the conversation I'd just had with Jenny, I found myself thinking of that girl. I could see the curve of her petal pink lips as she smiled. Remembering the long brown lashes framing her wide eyes, I took note that she didn't wear much make-up. There had been enough to accentuate her naturally beautiful features, but she hadn't bothered trying to cover the scars. I found this contrary to the observation I had made about her trying to hide them with her hair. This girl was proving to be stranger by the minute. "Curiouser and curiouser," I thought to myself, a small smile coming to my lips as I thought of the girl as Alice falling down the rabbit hole.

Just then, a brunette came stumbling out of the bar. I watched her intently, but something seemed off. She would not be the one tonight. She leaned against the brick wall, apparently trying to get some fresh air. Moments later, a large man came out and leaned next to her. I could tell by her body language she not only knew him, but had been hoping for this very thing. As I watched, he put a hand to her neck and pulled her into a rough kiss, which she returned enthusiastically. The two of them stumbled into the alley, booze and lust doing nothing for their natural lack of coordination. The man pressed the girl against the wall again and they really started to enjoy themselves. It was like watching gorillas mating at the zoo. I wondered again what made Jenny think humans had deep emotions. I had written about human love, but from what I had seen, it was the same for them as it was for me, just words. The primates finished their tryst and headed back for the bar. Their distance and posture told me neither of them planned on calling the other. I didn't even think they would spend the rest of the evening with each other.

Humans came and went from the bar, and about an hour later, another girl exited alone. She was obviously more drunk than the first girl had been. She stumbled and fell against the wall. Pulling a phone from who knows where in the outfit she was sporting, she pushed one on her memory dial. I heard a male voice answer. A very sad conversation followed. Apparently her boyfriend had forgotten about meeting her. When she asked him to come for her because she was too drunk to get home, he told her to call a cab and hung up. The girl dropped the phone and began to cry. Strike two for human compassion. Suddenly her body stiffened and she ran into the alley, where she promptly vomited. She was too far gone to even pull her long blond hair out of the way. This was truly a pitiful creature. Perfect.

Before she could even straighten up, I was standing behind her. As she stood, she noticed me and jumped.

"Oh!" she cried. "I didn't know you were there, sorry." Her speech was so slurred it was hard for even me to understand.

I locked her eyes onto my own, staring deep. She swooned a little. I brushed her hair behind her shoulder with one hand, carefully avoiding the mess at the ends.

"I think I vomited in my hair," she whispered distractedly.

I put one hand to her cheek and she closed her eyes, leaning into it. I put my lips to her throat and she sighed. Too easy, I thought. Then I sliced through her flesh with teeth so sharp, she barely felt it, and pulled strongly of the blood that came gushing from her neck. With my lips secured to her skin, not a drop was wasted. Her body stiffened against me, and I could hear her make small sounds of shock and pleasure. Many of my kind made feeding into some kind of "experience," be it sensual, exciting, or what have you. As the girl's blood left her body and filled my stomach, I had no such feeling. I was simply feeding and she was simply dinner. Once I had sucked her as dry as possible without inflicting more wounds, I let her body fall to the asphalt. Her blond hair fell all around her and over her face. Licking my lips to clean the last of her life from them, I turned and started the long walk home. The sensation of being full was already fading as her blood passed into my own.

As the night enveloped me, I decided I'd had enough darkness for the time being. Perhaps tomorrow I would go to the beach. I was definitely in need of some sun.

Chapter Six

The sun rose the next morning into a clear, blue, endless sky. It was indeed the perfect day to go to the beach.

I donned the typical beach wear of a black tank top, a pair of dark green board shorts, and my trusty sandals. I threw a towel over one shoulder and was just about ready to go. I needed to put on one more thing—my contacts. My skin didn't need sun block because I couldn't get sunburned, or rather, if I did I would heal before I knew I had been burned. However, my eyes needed protection. Being able to see in the dark made sunlight fairly painful. Usually sunglasses would do, but when I knew I would be outside for a long period of time, the contacts were better. They were tinted to protect my sensitive eyes from the glare. The drawback was that I could feel them sitting on my eyes as long as I wore them. Not painful, but certainly not comfortable, which is why I usually went for sunglasses. But at the beach, with the sun reflecting brightly off the water, it would be well worth the small discomfort.

Because I was surrounded by mortal observers, I had to walk at a mortal speed. It took an hour to reach the beach, and until I got within a mile of it, my attire got more than a few second glances. Of course, after that, I was still stared at, but for different reasons than looking out of place. I couldn't help that I was beautiful.

Once at the beach, I slipped off my footwear and wiggled my toes around in the hot sand. The only thing my toes liked better than breathing through my sandals was feeling the sand rub between them. I realized it was too hot and that a mortal would wonder why I wasn't hopping down to the water like everyone else, so I headed for the ocean. I refused to do any hopping, but for the sake of humans watching I winced and walked quickly to the cooler sand. I removed my shirt and left it with my towel and sandals on the beach, then continued on. At the water's edge, I stopped and let my toes have a little more fun. I let the lapping water bury them in the thick wet granules. I could feel each one as they rubbed against my skin. I smiled for a moment.

Then with a loud sucking sound, I freed my feet and walked into the cool ocean. The combination of the hot sun and the cold and grainy salt water was delightful. I continued walking out to sea until the waves were finally crashing over my head. With almost no body fat, I sank like a rock. I kicked off the now softer sand at the bottom and began to swim. I stayed under the water so I could use my speed and be free. Streaking through the water was almost like flight, or at least what I imagined it to be. I was soon a mile or more away from shore.

I swam slowly now, just enough to stay afloat and drifted, feeling the swells rise and fall. The sun began to dry my skin, spreading delicious warmth through my chest and over my face. My back remained cool in the water and my arms would occasionally ripple refreshing ocean across my torso. I wondered why it had been so long since the last time I went swimming. I had been so morose lately, wrapped up in my own apathy.

Then I heard a loud horn blow, bringing me out of my reprieve. I dove beneath the surface hoping the boat hadn't seen me. The last thing I wanted right now was a bunch of mortals trying to save me from drowning. Swimming deep enough to be invisible from the surface, I looked up. An enormous cruise ship was passing over head. I watched as it noisily cut through the water, churning up the peacefulness I had briefly achieved.

This is why I didn't go swimming often. Why I didn't do anything fun very often. Mankind was everywhere. Like a blight on the face of the Earth, you couldn't go anywhere without running into him in one form or another. It was this constant reminder of his futile struggle against mortality that had me spending so much time in isolation. Having to look at death at every turn, sometimes wishing you could know what it was like, isn't a pleasant existence. Finally the ship passed. I waited until the last of its wake had settled and there was no sign of it ever having been before I resurfaced.

I swam along as I had before, pretending to float. But the spell was broken. I decided to give up on getting back my feeling of peace and head home. Then I was splashed in the face. I was startled into losing my rhythm and sank.

I quickly came back up and looked around. A pod of dolphins was swimming near me. I ignored them and went back to swimming on my back, but the dolphins splashed me again and again, refusing to give me any peace. In my irritation, I lashed out at one, but they were swimming just out of my reach. Smart little mammals. Finally, I gave up and returned to shore.

When I got back to the beach it was nearing sunset. I was nowhere near where I had entered the ocean. In fact, it would be faster to head for my loft than to go back and retrieve my things. I sighed, not looking forward to walking home barefoot. The streets would be filthy. There were several fire pits getting started by groups of humans already starting to drink and use other recreational substances. Their laugher and talking was loud and rough after my day away from such nuisances. I was definitely ready to head back to my loft.

Cars spewed noxious fumes at me, filling my lungs. Every time I passed a bar or restaurant, I was covered in a cloud of nicotine laced smoke. By the time I got home, my feet were black and I was covered from head to foot in grime. As the hot water from my shower sprayed me from every direction, I remembered now why I never went out. Humanity was disgusting.

Having had quite enough interaction with mortals for a while, I spent Saturday and Sunday at home in my loft reading Shakespeare. He was one of my favorites. I read his complete works, in chronological order. I could have read them in one day, but I was in no hurry. I took my time and contemplated his complex language and subtle innuendos. People just didn't write like this anymore. I mourned a little for the English language while I was at it. It was tragic what people had done to it. Once I finished his entire library, I started again with the tragedies. They were by far the most entertaining. I found myself snickering at his rendition of the mortal plight.

And yet I had to admit The Bard was one of the few mortals who seemed to understand. He knew there was but one question: To be or not to be. Yet, for humans there is but one answer to the one question: death. From the day they are born, they are dying. Twenty years, fifty years, eighty years, it all ends in death. Not only are they doomed from the moment they begin to breathe, they have pitifully short lives. One cannot learn much in a hundred years, and humans learn even less. They spend all their time devoted to their bodies. First, they learn how to use it, then they abuse it, then they ignore it. Then, when it's far too late, they try to save it. It is little wonder the human race as a whole is foolish and weak. If I cared, it would be tragic that they spend so much of their brief existence yearning to make the right choices, when the only choice that matters is made for them. They will die. It is only a matter of when.

As dawn broke on Monday morning, I was in a speculative mood. After such a deep delve into the depravity of man through the fiction of Shakespeare, I began again to ponder my own writings and their portrayal of the dismal creature. These thoughts led me inevitably to the class I had decided to observe, which lead me inexplicably to thoughts of the strange girl I had encountered there. Remembering my coerced promise to Jenny, I decided to do some research. I would write out all I had observed about this girl and see what conclusions I reached. I pulled an empty journal from the shelf and, sitting at my desk, took a pen from the drawer. I began to list everything I knew about this annoying little girl.

Hours and pages later, I was nowhere closer to understanding her. I had plenty of details, thanks to my extraordinary skills of observation. I had even sketched her face, captured from the side with her curls falling forward as I often saw her in class. The proportions and representation of her face were perfect, yet I was not satisfied with it as a likeness of her. I had failed to truly expose her.

I knew nothing of what went on in her mind. I didn't understand her motivation. I could list the words she said, but not comprehend why she said them. Therein lay the mystery. There may not be anything extraordinary about her as a mortal, but there was something wrong with her mind. She saw and thought things differently than she should. How could I get information like that? Perhaps by comparing her behavior to that of other mortals, I could see the exact difference and pinpoint what it meant.

And so I went for a walk, once again immersing myself in the sea of humanity, which is much less pleasant than the Pacific Ocean. I watched as men and women conversed. Listened to what they said and how they responded. I took note of their tone of voice. Were they flirting with or dismissing each other? One couple claimed to be in love. I then followed the male to another encounter with a different female, whom he also loved. I even tried watching children, thinking perhaps the girl had never matured. They avoided me even more than adults generally did. When night fell, I'd had quite enough and gotten nowhere. I returned home to once again wash off the stink of human life that had collected on my clothing and settled in my hair. After my shower, I put several classical CDs into the player and hit shuffle. I lay on my bed in the dark and let the music and my soft breathing wash my mind clear from the cacophony of humanity as the water had washed my body. It was tragic how far man had fallen, really. Perhaps he had once been noble, capable of great literature and moving music. But as the mortal body was doomed to decay, so was its race. I wondered how much longer man could hold out, walking around in the corpse that had once been full of vitality.

Chapter Seven

$\mathcal{A}$s Tuesday night came, I decided to try something different. It had occurred to me that what made this girl's behavior different from what I had come to expect from mortals was how she was reacting to me. Perhaps I was the x-factor. And so I waited outside the building, out of view from any human until class had started and I saw the girl enter. Then I casually walked in and took a seat a few rows away from her. Perhaps I could concentrate better if she weren't so oppressively close. Practically in the corner, I was even farther from Tony than before. I sat and smugly turned my attention to the professor, studiously ignoring the girl completely.

That was until, to my complete shock, she quietly gathered her things and moved. I had a brief hope she had given in and was moving to the front to be with the rest of the sheep. It was very brief, however. She slid over as inconspicuously as possible, in a vain attempt to avoid the very irritated glare she was getting from Tony, and sat in the chair directly to my right. I turned to glare at her myself, but was distracted by the design on her bright red shirt. Across her chest was a fuzzy green caterpillar, and underneath it read, "but he was still hungry." Fortunately, I quickly recovered and turned away from her to stare forward. Unfortunately, this wasn't very subtle considering Tony was also to my right and in order to look at him, I would have to look past her.

She smiled at my inept attempt to ignore her. I was delighted to see it, and was then immediately irritated at my own reaction, causing me to scowl. How was it possible for this insignificant mortal to have such an effect on me?

"What did you do?" she asked. My eyes involuntarily flicked toward the sound of her soft voice, adding to my irritation. "It must have been something horrible if you had to put yourself in the corner," she continued.

I turned my head and forced my eyes to look past the large soft curls framing her angelic face to stare at Tony.

"I'm sure if you asked him, he must have a 'dunce cap' around here somewhere," she whispered conspiratorially. "He stashed it away with his youth and his sense of humor." The corners of my lips twitched, itching to smile at her apt joke. This made my temper flare and I was unthinkingly honest.

"I killed someone this weekend," I said without looking into her eyes. In my peripheral vision, I could see her studying me.

"Did they deserve it?" she asked quietly.

I was bewildered by both her question and her tone. She obviously believed me. I made the mistake of focusing on her fathomless blue eyes. I became lost in them, drowning in the mixture of concern, confusion and compassion I found there. Finally, she blinked and I resurfaced, but with the intense desire to explain myself. "It was them or me," I half-lied. I had needed the blood to survive.

This answer seemed to appease her and the confusion disappeared, leaving me looking into pools of compassion and understanding. I couldn't stand it and quickly looked away, back at the wall, not trusting myself to see past her. She seemed to sense my discomfort and turned away from me, looking back at Tony. After a few moments, I was able to relax enough to look at the back of her head.

What had just happened? I didn't recognize any of the feelings this girl elicited in me. Was she some sort of witch? I knew that was ridiculous, but so was the fact that I had just tried to defend my behavior, to a mortal no less. Suddenly, she turned around and caught me staring. She smiled brightly at me.

"I feel like I should warn you," she said quietly. My lips twitched again, threatening to smile at the irony of her statement. "In addition to my radical literary views and lack of personal space—" she paused and I smirked despite myself. She smiled in return and continued. "—I am also infamous for my uncanny ability to free people from self-imposed emotional prisons."

My smirk dissolved and I blinked at her, the look on my face conveying the impression she had suddenly started speaking Swahili. Her smile only grew at my reaction. "And you, my friend, are a turtle in desperate need."

"Why would you bother?" was the only one of my hundred questions that came out.

"Because I can," she said simply.

"Most people don't even talk to me," I responded.

"I've learned you can't tell who a person is by how they look." She winked at me and my heart beat coincidentally. "Even if they are beautiful." She abruptly turned back around and began taking notes on Tony's lecture.

She thankfully didn't turn around again for the rest of class, and I was able to watch her properly. Once Tony opened a discussion, I noticed with some humor that he seemed unable to see her hand whenever it rose into the air to participate. After fifteen minutes of being ignored, she decided to forego asking permission and began simply calling out her comments, much to Tony's chagrin.

I knew Jenny was right. I needed to know more about her. I decided following her home might give me more insight into who she was. You can tell a lot about a person by where they live.

When class ended, I was again out the door before the girl could move. I returned to my invisible position and waited for her to emerge. She came out and walked a few steps past me. Then she stopped and turned around in a circle, as if searching for someone. I closed my eyes, knowing that without their shine, she would not be able to see me in the shadows. I heard her make a small sound of confusion and begin walking again. I reminded myself to be especially cautious while following her. She seemed unnaturally observant.

It was not as hard as I first thought, however. The girl stayed on the well-lit walkway, making it easy for me to stay well covered by the shadows of the buildings. Near the edge of campus, she came to a fork in the pathway. One choice was as brightly lit as the path she had been following, the other had several bulbs out and the light was patchy at best. Assuming she would continue in the same manner, I had already moved onto the dark path. I was hiding in one of the shadows, waiting for her to turn so I could resume my stalking.

As she stared down the obviously safer choice, I caught a whiff of something foul. From the smell of sweat, alcohol, and worse, I could tell there were three men waiting just around the corner of the brightly lit pathway. I listened more carefully and could hear drunken whispers arguing about how much longer they would have to wait for some coed to come by and make their night. I knew the girl could neither smell nor hear the human waste that lay in wait for her.

Before I could wonder if I should do something, she turned away from them and started walking down the path I was on, forcing me to press tightly against the building. Her step faltered for a moment as she passed me, but then she continued on. She seemed completely unaware of any type of danger and began humming some tune to herself. I shook my head at her luck.

After following her for the next half hour, I began to wonder if it was indeed luck. She was walking in an area of town that had once been a nice neighborhood, but was rapidly in decline. She had twice more turned abruptly from her obvious path to avoid dangerous men that she could not have been aware of. The final straw, so to speak, was at an intersection. As she got to the corner, the crosswalk was green, indicating she could simply proceed across the street. Instead, she inexplicably took several steps back, once again sending me deeper into the shadows. This time I nearly had to jump over a hedge to get out of her way.

My jaw actually dropped as a sedan came barreling out of nowhere, the driver talking on her cell phone and blowing right through the red light. The girl simply shook her head mumbling to herself about women drivers, which made me smile despite myself.

Finally she walked up the steps of a small house. It was older, but well kept. Parked in the drive was an "old school" Volkswagen bug. It was a faded yellow and I smiled at how very well it fit the girl. It seemed overly cheerful, but without being loud, like the neon yellow cars were painted these days. It was soft and warm, like sunshine. I chuckled, realizing that was just what I had thought of her golden curls.

I decided I had seen enough for one night and didn't cross the street to investigate further. My mind was reeling with the oddity of this human girl. She seemed to have some kind of sixth sense about danger. There was only one flaw. Each time she had changed her path to avoid danger, she had come within inches of me. If she could sense danger, why couldn't she sense me?

Chapter Eight

*K*nowing it was useless to try avoiding her, on Thursday I returned to my customary seat in the back near the door. It opened just as Tony stood to begin class, sending a breeze across my desk, and the girl was once again by my side.

"Am I to assume you've already given in?" she asked quietly as Tony began to lecture on my most recent story. I held my tongue and pretended not to have heard her. She watched me for a few moments, an impish smile on her perfect lips as she raised an eyebrow.

"Surely you're not here to listen to that," she said incredulously, turning her hand upside down to point with one finger at Tony. With great effort, I continued to ignore her. "Ahhh," she said as if suddenly understanding. "And so returns the Mysteriously Brooding, Tragically Deaf, Devastatingly Handsome, Mute Stranger." The corners of my lips twitched up. "I saw that," she teased.

And so I gave up. I would learn more about this strange human by talking to her anyway, so she may as well think of me however she wanted, a friend even. I raised an eyebrow at the girl. "You think I'm devastatingly handsome?"

She laughed merrily in triumph, earning her a glare from Tony. The sound also made my heart beat and brought another involuntary smile to my lips. I knew that it was a sound I would never grow weary of, no matter how many times I heard it.

"Yes," she whispered in response to my question, keeping her voice low to avoid more glares. "But don't worry, I won't hold it against you." She smiled brightly at me, and it was like the sun itself was beaming. Her whisper took on a mockingly concerned tone as did her sweet face. "It's the Mysteriously Brooding I'm more concerned with." She paused momentarily and then smiled again. "Now that the spontaneous deafness seems to be under control."

I felt my lips turn into an impish grin of their own. "Yes, it seems I've been cured," I said.

"However did you manage that?" she asked in wonder. I shook my head at her teasing.

"Self-preservation techniques are only productive so long as they work." I leaned back a little, taking on the air of a lecturer, and she played along by leaning forward, resting her elbow on her knee, her face in her hand. Her face was rapt with attention. "Say, for instance, you are trying your best to preserve your grade in a class by blocking out distractions." I leaned forward again and our faces were suddenly very close. "It only works if said distractions aren't irresistibly and persistently stubborn about being a distraction."

She laughed again, her breath blowing across my face. I was surprised by its pleasant sweetness. "Lucky you, then. If I weren't so stubborn, you'd be stuck listening to Tony for the rest of the semester." Her whispering was conspiring again. "And it would be tragic for a wit like yours to be dulled by such a pedagogue as that," she said, gesturing again at Tony.

I took note that she had focused on my calling her "stubborn" as opposed to "irresistible" and that she had used the word pedagogue. It was the very kind of word Rob loved to tease me for using. I chuckled, and her blue eyes danced. "My savior," I whispered.

She laughed again. "Oh, I wouldn't go so far as that." She smirked and continued, "Hero maybe, but not so far as 'savior.'"

I laughed right out loud at that, getting a glare from Tony myself. "Fine then, my hero," I whispered. The girl was looking at me strangely. "What?" I asked.

"You have a wonderful laugh," she said softly. Her eyes trapped me again in their clear blue skies. "You should use it more often. Your smile, too." Her lips curled into a delicious smirk. "It's what takes you from 'handsome' to 'devastating.'" She finally blinked, releasing me from her smoldering gaze. I then realized how very close we were, and that I had stopped breathing.

I instinctively leaned back again. "I don't find many things that funny anymore," I said honestly. How did she get the truth from me so easily? Then I smiled. "Besides, I wouldn't want to go around devastating the female population."

She smiled in return. "I'm not sure it would only be the female population, and it is definitely easier to look at you when you're scowling." Then she winked at me and my heart beat again. "I'm one who enjoys a challenge, however, so grin away."

In response, I found myself unleashing a smile I had not used in centuries. My lips spread wide, one side slightly higher than the other, most of my teeth visible. I saw the immediate effect it had on her. Her eyes widened and went slightly glassy. I returned her wink, and her breath caught momentarily. I could also hear her heartbeat race. I found myself delighted by her reaction.

She shook her head slightly as if to clear it, and her own smile grew as well. "You might want to be careful with that one," she said and giggled. It was a new sound, and I loved it as much as, maybe even more than her hearty laugh. I reined my smile in a little, and we simply stared at each other for a moment.

"Is that why you laugh so much?" I asked. "Because you know the effect it has on people?"

She looked slightly confused. "I laugh a lot because the world is a funny place."

If she could get to me like this, I could only imagine the effect she had on mortal men. Could she really not know that? "I thought you said you could read people," I said.

She smiled. "I can."

I was quiet for a while, thinking about that. It was quite an anomaly if she could read people and still not realize how she personally affected them. She was patient as I thought. "What is it, exactly, that you read?"

"All kinds of things, really," she began. "I told you about the writing being able to tell me about the author. When I'm with someone in person, I can generally tell if they're lying." My eyes widened a fraction. "And if it's for a good reason or a malicious one," she finished. I remained silent, so she went on, "I can tell if someone is sad, or lonely, happy or angry, that sort of thing."

"Do you have to be in direct contact with them?" I asked, thinking of the men she had avoided on campus the other night.

"For emotional readings, yes, but I'm not sure about intentions." She took a moment to arrange her thoughts. "I seem to have a sixth sense for danger, and perhaps that's an extension of it or something, but I'm pretty good at steering clear of trouble."

"Lucky you," I murmured. Was I the exception to her sixth sense? "What do you read from me?" I asked, half-hoping she had no idea what I was, half-hoping she knew entirely.

She smiled again, but thoughtfully this time. "You believe me?" she asked.

"I believe there are more things in heaven and earth than are known in the philosophies of man," I responded.

"Shakespeare," she muttered to herself, "of course." Then she smiled brightly at me again, and I couldn't help but return it. "Are you sure you want to know? I'm brutally honest," she warned.

I smiled. "I can take it," I said reassuringly. She looked a little hesitant, but began.

"From you I get an immense loneliness, worse than I've ever seen. Like you've been alone, literally forever." She was watching me closely so I put a careful mask over my features to hide my shock. "And boredom, also bigger than I've ever seen. In fact, most of what I get from you is stronger and deeper than anything I've ever felt." She paused a moment, still watching me. "It's like you've been feeling this way for a very long time." She paused again. "It would take most people hundreds of years to get this mired in apathy and sadness." Her eyes were burning with compassion and pity. It was as if she could see right to the depths of my black soul. She smiled sadly at me. "And I can tell you were not always this way." My mask finally cracked, and I blinked at her.

"What?" I whispered.

"Once upon a time, you were happy, mirthful even. I can see that too." Her smile brightened some. "Which is why I'm so persistent in trying to help you."

I swallowed and had to look away for a moment. None of this was what I expected to hear. Yet I found myself believing her. But it wasn't what I needed to know. How to ask her without suggesting an answer? I steeled myself and looked back into her captivating blue eyes, which were now filled with understanding. "Do you read anything else from me?"

It was as if she knew exactly what I was asking. "You're dangerous," she said simply.

I stared at her for a long moment. "But I don't frighten you." It was a statement, not a question.

"No," she whispered. "Should you?"

"Yes," I replied.

This time she looked at me for a long while. Then she shook her head, curls flying wildly. "No," she said vehemently. "I don't believe it."

"You should," I said seriously. "I'm deadly."

"I know that," she insisted, "but I don't believe you're dangerous to me." I stared at her incredulously. She sighed and then clarified. "There are a lot of dangerous people in the world, but that doesn't mean they're all out to get me, personally. Army Rangers, Navy SEALs, CIA assassins, what have you. People trained to kill." She took a breath, then looked me straight in the eye.

"It's not that I don't think you capable of violence, I just feel like you would never aim it at me."

I was completely speechless. What could I possibly say to that? She was right, of course. I knew deep within my being that I could never harm her. But she equated that to mean I was one of the "good guys." She didn't understand that I would kill another human without a second thought. And I couldn't tell her. So I stared. She met my gaze for a long while, emotions streaming across her blue eyes—hope, fear, wonder, and finally, sadness.

"I told you I would be honest," she whispered, looking away. It wasn't an accusation. It was acceptance of a truth she had seen time and again. I was obviously not the first person to be disturbed by her "reading." The look on her face made me ache in a way I didn't understand.

"And I wanted it," I reminded her. She looked at me with a dim hope in her eyes. "I'm not angry." I paused, knowing she would see any deception. "I'm just surprised you were so accurate." I smiled at her, and she responded with a small smile of her own. "For not knowing anything about what I am, you seem to know an awful lot about me. It was just … disconcerting, that's all."

"You keep a lot of secrets," she said.

"Some even from myself," I said, smiling again. This time her smile returned in force.

"Perhaps I can help with that," she suggested.

I arched an eyebrow. "I highly doubt it, but something tells me that won't stop you from trying." She laughed and I thrilled to the musical sound. It was like an angel dancing in the clouds, carefree and innocent.

Tony dismissed the class with a reminder about an assignment due soon. The girl turned away to write the reminder in her date book, apparently she did care at least a little about her grade, and I slipped out the door and into the shadows. I would follow her home, once again in secret.

As the girl came out of the building, she paused, again looking for someone. Then she smiled a small secret smile to herself and took off for home. The walk was uneventful tonight. Apparently, danger was taking a break. But she did take a slightly different route home, and it kept bringing her closer and closer to me. Each time she would stop at an intersection, I would watch, using my gift to know which way she would turn. And every time, I would have only seconds to hide before she walked by. In the end, I gave up on staying ahead of her as I usually did with my prey, and simply followed behind.

Once she entered the house, I made a quick circuit around the perimeter. The blinds were drawn in every room. I would have to actually go inside to learn more. As I sat on the porch, contemplating how to do just that without her feeling like a prowler was trying to get in, I heard the front door knob turning. I dove silently into the bushes before the door opened. The girl came out tucking a slip of paper with what looked like a shopping list written on it into her purse. She walked to the driveway and got into her little bug of sunshine and drove away.

Smiling, I got back onto the porch. Now I would be free to enter without feeling like I was invading. I looked around, knowing a girl like her would need to hide a spare key for when she inevitably locked herself out. I spotted a plastic rock tucked in among the stones by the hedges I had just been hiding in. Picking it up, I slid open the false bottom. It was empty. Decoy. You're not the only one who likes a challenge, I thought. I took another, closer look at her front door and the surrounding area.

There was a large and ancient bronze sun attached to the wall next to the door. I stared at it then reached behind it and, laughing, pulled out the magnetic hide-a-key. I slid the key in the lock, turned it, and then replaced the key. I was still chuckling to myself as I entered.

It was dark inside, but there was plenty of light for me to see. The house had been built sometime in the 1950's. It looked as though the last remodeling had been done sometime in the late 70's. If the floors hadn't all been wood, there would probably still be shag carpeting. The decor was eclectic. There were knickknacks that looked like they belonged to an eighty-year-old woman next to fresh cut flowers in asymmetrical vases. It was obvious the furniture was only replaced when it was beyond repair. There was an antique rocking chair and an overstuffed and well-worn easy chair next to a much newer wicker futon. The TV and DVD/VCR were obviously much newer than the stand they were perched on.

Covering every inch of flat surface, walls and tabletop alike, were framed photographs. I began to study these and could easily pick the girl out in each one. They ranged from her birth to some very recent. People I assumed to be her family were with her in the majority of the photographs. As I compared them, I found answers to the questions about the decor and the fact that a grown woman would have baby pictures of herself on display. There were several pictures taken with a very old woman. Every picture with the old woman had been taken in this very house, or in the yard around it. The house had obviously been hers.

It must be the girl's inheritance, which would explain why she would change so little about it and also why she could afford to live here without roommates. She, or her family at least, probably owned it free and clear. Once that fact had been established, it was easy to see what had come with the house and what the girl had added.

Passing through the front room, I could see the house was divided into two parts. On one side was the living room and behind it, the kitchen. The other side consisted of two bedrooms, divided by the small bathroom. Entering the kitchen, I could see even in the dark that it was a light and cheery place. There were a few dishes stacked in the sink, but aside from that it was clean and tidy. Grandma would be proud, I thought, smirking to myself. There were a few snapshots and reminders on the fridge, but nothing really interesting, so I moved on from the kitchen and glanced into the bathroom.

The room was so small it had no choice but to be cluttered. A hair dryer was perched precariously on the edge of the tiny sink. A multi-compartment bag hanging over the back of the door contained several items of human hygiene. I was glad not to have to worry about such things. Our bodies are so efficient we don't even sweat. We only have to wash the stink of the world off, not worry about creating it ourselves.

I moved on to a bedroom. It was obvious that while she had left the front room and kitchen as partial memorials to her grandmother, she had made this room entirely her own. There were books everywhere. Shelving stacked from floor to ceiling was covered in an astonishing array of literature. At first I could not see how she had organized them. Then I realized she had organized them chronologically. Fiction was mixed in with nonfiction, subject matter was ignored, but they were meticulously ordered by the printing date. The original printing date, I noted.

A large table was serving as a desk in the center of the room. It had several stacks of books, notebooks, paper, and note cards on it. There was barely enough room for the laptop to sit untouched by the clutter. Looking closer, I could tell she was in the middle of three papers for her classes and a thesis. Two of the papers and the thesis had to do with Shakespeare. I smiled, remembering her reaction to my quoting him earlier. I left the library to see the last room, which I assumed must be her bedroom.

Opening the door, I smiled again. This room was not nearly as tidy as the rest of the house. There were several articles of clothing strewn randomly across the floor. The double bed was unmade. One of the drawers in the dresser was hanging half open. The library had her mind written all over it. This room was brimming with her personality.

There were a few prints of Van Gogh flowers on the wall. To either side of the bed were night stands. On one was a glass half full of water and a box of cookies. I chuckled at that. On the other stand were three books. I wasn't sure how I felt when I saw two of them were mine, one from each pen name. The third was a journal with a pen inside, marking the latest entry. Obviously this piqued my interest, and I picked it up to read a few pages. Just as I cracked it open, however, I heard a car slowing outside. Headlights turned into the drive. I replaced the book where I had found it.

I swiftly went through the house again, adjusting the blinds. I opened them enough to be able to see, but not enough for her to notice I had moved them. It was also not enough for some random sociopath to see through. I didn't want to rob her of her privacy. Once that was finished, I slipped out the back door, locking it behind me. As I clicked the door shut, the front door opened. I could hear her clearly from outside the house.

"Hello?" she called. "Is anybody here?" Of course no one answered. Perching on the roof, I peered down into the kitchen. She was shaking her head at herself as she put away her groceries. "Paranoid," she mumbled to herself.

She flipped on the small stereo on the counter and set it to a modern rock station. Singing along to most of the songs, she danced around as she finished putting her groceries away. Her curls were bouncing in all directions. I had to bite my lip to keep from laughing aloud. As it was, my body shook with silent humor. Once she was done in the kitchen, she went into the bathroom, the only window I couldn't see through. I could hear the water run as she brushed her teeth and completed other human routines.

I crossed the roof and peered down into her bedroom. She came in soon after, her hair pulled back from her freshly scrubbed face with a soft head band. She began peeling clothes off as she crossed to the closet. I could see now that the piles of clothing weren't random after all. Sweaters went in one direction, pants in another, her shirt and socks went into a hamper next to her closet door. I smiled at the turquoise and purple paisley pattern on her bra and underwear.

Suddenly she stopped humming the song she was repeating and crossed her arms across her chest, looking around. She peered for a long moment at the blinds on the window, but couldn't see through them. "Paranoid," she muttered to herself again. She crossed the room to her dresser and pulled a long T-shirt and boxers from the top drawer. Once she was in the T-shirt she removed the bra and tossed it into the hamper as well. I chuckled to myself, wondering if perhaps she was getting a less than noble "reading" from me.

Turning off the overhead light, she crawled over the bed and turned on the table lamp. Propped up on her pillows she wrote in her journal for thirty minutes, occasionally talking aloud to herself as she wrote. "Stranger than I thought … Like I'm being watched … groceries … safe." I still had no idea what she had written about when she closed the book and picked up both of my novels. She seemed to be reading them simultaneously, underlining and making notes in the margin. I wasn't sure I liked the look of that. Then I decided to attribute it to the assignment Tony had talked about being due in class.

After an hour of study, she glanced at the clock, yawning hugely. I found myself smirking again as she stretched and put out the light. My eyes quickly adjusted to the new darkness, and I watched as she tossed and turned for ten minutes until she found a comfortable position. She was sprawled across the bed, one arm under her pillow, the other hand by her face. The girl was entirely adorable. She was obviously not accustomed to sharing her bed. I found myself smiling at that thought and wondered why. There seemed to be many thoughts and feelings I was having about this girl that needed to be explained. I watched her sleep for a long time, but went home long before sunrise.

Chapter Nine

Friday morning, I reviewed the two books the girl was studying, trying to decipher what she might be able to draw from them. I was at a loss and ended up reading through all of my works searching for similarities. As Martha Vinegross, I had been a woman writing during the Romantic Era. Her stories were full of hope and wonder, tinged with the sadness and drama that made books worth reading. Jerry Mack had been a much darker persona, writing books full of blood and gore, Gothika at its finest, really. I found myself actually agreeing with Tony in that there was nothing remotely alike between the two personas. Apparently, I couldn't recognize my own "voice" as the girl had called it. Perhaps I should have the others read them and see if they could perceive what I was missing.

I decided to first update my notes on this bizarre and entrancing human. Saturday morning found me compiling detailed notes of my latest observations. When I finished, I read through the whole notebook, searching for connections. I now had nearly half the journal full of her. I had inventoried everything from the books in her library to the toothpaste in her bathroom. Every word she had uttered, to me or to herself, had been carefully recorded. Yet, in the end, I was no closer to understanding her or the fascination I had for her.

I needed an outside perspective on my writing and on the girl. Sunday I went, once again, to the apartment entrenched in humanity. Upon entering, I found Lance surrounded by brightly colored, voluminous material. Sitting on the floor where the dining table would have been, he was scrutinizing the fabric inch by inch.

"Sky diving?" I questioned, already knowing the answer.

Lance grinned at me. "Want to come? If you flew the plane, I could finally get away with ditching the parachute."

"Says the man meticulously searching for pin-sized holes, 'just in case,'" taunted Rob from across the room.

Rob was also seated on the floor, but his area was covered in beach towels and he had his long board on his lap. Like most surfers, he was nearly obsessive about cleaning and replacing the sticky wax. Stepping towards him, I finally viewed Jenny reclining on the couch. She was apparently going to accompany Rob to the beach, wearing a swimsuit that could be best described as a technicality. While she was on prominent display for Rob, her voluptuous and highly visible curves were hidden from Lance by the back of the couch. I was gratified to note she still had some modicum of decorum.

"Back so soon, Gregory?" she purred. "Did you find your pet human isn't as fascinating as you first thought?" I didn't care for the tone she was using with me, so I ignored her.

"Have either of you ever read my books?" I asked Lance and Rob. They both looked at me apprehensively. Not knowing where I was going, they were afraid to give the wrong answer.

"I don't care, either way," I answered honestly. Their opinions had never mattered before and so I had never concerned myself with whether or not they read my work. "I just need an outside opinion." The apprehensive looks turned sheepish, and it was obvious neither could help me.

"I've read your books," Jenny said, surprising me.

"You have?" I asked.

"Of course I have, Gregory. You're brilliant, why wouldn't I read them?" Then she looked at me closely. "Why are you asking about them? Does this have to do with your human?"

"She's not *my* human," I said. "But yes, she claims to see similarities in them. I read through them all again and I can't see it. I thought perhaps it was simply because I was too close to the work. So I came for a second opinion."

There was silence.

"You want an opinion other than your own?" Rob finally asked.

I gave him a quick glare, and he went back to his surf board. Turning back to Jenny I asked, "Did you notice any similarities between the two personalities of the writers? Similar tone or styles?"

Jenny thought about my question for a minute. I was glad because it meant she was taking me seriously.

"Not when I first read them, no," she replied. "But I wasn't looking for any."

"Was Jenny right in thinking that this human may be too observant?" Lance asked. His parachute was now being neatly packed. "Perhaps this particular diversion has run its course. If she's a threat, she should be eliminated."

"She's not a threat," I said adamantly. My tone shocked them all. "No one believes her theories. Even *she* thinks she's half-crazy," I explained. None of them looked convinced.

"This is your game, Gregory," Lance said carefully. "We know you're in control of it."

And I was. I was always in complete control. So, why was this human able to distract me so? How could I be surprised? How was it possible she could know so much about me? It was all very disconcerting, and as I headed home, I realized I not only didn't feel better, but had planted seeds of paranoia in the others as well.

I decided to try to think of something else for a while, anything else. Sitting at my desk, I took a new notebook and began to write. Any story would do really; I just needed to get my mind somewhere else. There were several false starts that were immediately torn out and thrown away. Finally I got wrapped up in a story about a man trapped in a labyrinth trying to escape from various snares. The snares, however, turned into different human vices, and in the end he was seduced into staying in the maze to live the rest of his days as a slave to the succubus living there. The graphic love scenes were straight from a Harlequin romance novel. It was not what I had been aiming for at all. In fact, I was fairly disgusted with myself. Perhaps it had been too long since my last coupling. It had been nearly two hundred years. Shaking my head at the sad product I had yielded, I stood up and took it with me to the roof. Tossing it into the rubbish bin, I planned to burn it, erasing it from existence. I struck six different matches trying to get it to light, but each time I touched flame to the book, a breeze would blow in and put it out.

By this time I was frustrated, irritated, and in a generally foul mood. I decided a bit of oblivion was in order. I turned out the lights, turned off the air, stripped, and by concentrating on the rhythm of my breathing was able to blissfully shut down. I didn't even dream. I felt much better when I rose from my bed, doubting that even being able to actually sleep would have refreshed me anymore. I remembered once again that I was an Immortal and even if I never solved the riddle of this mortal girl, she couldn't plague me forever. If necessary, I could wait this irritation out. With that pleasant thought, I found myself once again looking forward to my next class. This girl had no bearing on my life. It was just the same as it had always been, the same as it always would be. I couldn't remember what had convinced me otherwise.

CHAPTER TEN

*H*eading to class Tuesday night, I was sure the girl would be frustrated with my complete lack of interest in her, but I was wrong. She was utterly distracted by something. She didn't comment on even the most ridiculous remarks the professor made. What could have captured her attention so completely? I found myself feeling dissatisfied, and wondered why, considering that last week I would have been thrilled if she had ignored me. Perhaps I would discover more clues as I followed her home tonight. Then I decided I didn't want to wait.

"Are you all right?" I asked quietly. She seemed startled to see me sitting next to her.

"What? Oh, yeah, I'm fine." She smiled at me and suddenly it was easier to breathe, which was ridiculous. "My thoughts are just a little muddled is all."

I waited, expecting her to continue, but she didn't. I wanted to know more, but decided not to press. It really would be better if she didn't consider me a confidant, for many reasons.

When Tony dismissed the class, it took her a moment to realize it. Then she shook her head and began to gather her things. I stood up to wait outside for her.

"Excuse me, but could I have a moment of your time?" Tony was standing near us and I thought at first he was talking to the girl. But when she didn't hear him through her own thoughts and left in a hurry, he didn't stop her. I moved to follow her, but Tony stepped directly in front of me.

"Yes?" I asked, annoyed that I would be delayed.

"I had a question concerning your assignments," he said. I stared at him. I hadn't submitted any assignments.

"Excuse me?" I said.

"Well, I've been trying to place the assignments to the students' faces to get to know everyone better," Tony went on. "And it seems someone hasn't submitted any."

"That would be me," I stated, wanting to be done with this mortal and on my way.

"Right," the aging professor said, a little surprised at my ready confession. "Well, I can't find you on my roster either," he said.

"I'm auditing the class," I lied.

"But you would still be on my roster," Tony insisted. I swallowed a growl of frustration.

"I'm sure there was simply some mistake at the registrar's office. I'll rectify the situation tomorrow," I assured him. Of course Tony would be the one out of a hundred college professors that actually looked at his roster.

"Well, yes that would be good," he fumbled. He seemed to be flustered by my complete lack of respect.

"I'll see you Thursday then," I said and promptly left him standing there. I had run out of patience. Now I would actually have to do some tracking to find her. I had never tried tracking a specific mortal before.

I stepped out into the cool night, walked a few yards from the building and then stopped. Standing perfectly still, I opened my senses. One of them would find the girl. I scanned the campus for a glimpse of her golden hair. She was nowhere to be seen between the campus buildings. I closed my eyes to sharpen my other senses. I listened and heard a few human foot falls from different directions. They were all accompanied by voices in hushed conversations. The girl would be alone. Lifting my face, I felt the breeze coming in from the ocean gently swirl my hair. Its salty, damp air brought with it the many scents it had gathered along its way. It was heavy with the smell of asphalt and exhaust from the freeway it had crossed, and tainted with the stench of countless dying mortals. There was also the sharpness of the palm trees and holly bushes, and the sweetness of jimson weed and California lilacs. Then I smelled something enticing and familiar. The scent of jasmine brought forth a vision of flowing blond curls, bouncing on her shoulders and the scent of almond brought to mind her arms as she rested her face on them, her legs crossing beneath her desk.

I opened my eyes in shock. I knew Nikki's scent? The combination of her jasmine scented hair products and her almond scented body lotion would take me right to her. I opened my eyes and headed into the breeze. I followed the walkways, as Nikki usually did. Every now and then I would get a stronger taste of almond from a rail she had touched or jasmine from a tree branch that had brushed her hair. I picked up my pace as the scent became increasingly stronger. Nikki would soon be in sight. Then I caught a whiff of something that stopped me in my tracks.

It was the smell of life, new skin, clean and crisp, another Immortal. Not one that I could immediately identify. Fear began to bloom in me as I continued on Nikki's path and found that the other's scent seemed to be following her as well. I began to run, fearing the worst. What were the odds that one mortal woman could have two Immortals stalking her on the same night? Then I heard Nikki's voice cry out in pain and fear. And I could smell fresh blood.

As I flew around the corner I saw Nikki cowering on the ground, her knees scraped and bleeding from a fall. Over her stood the other Immortal. He was tall, with long black hair pulled back at his neck. He bent down and pulled Nikki to her feet. She was frozen in fear and shock. He pulled her head back by her hair exposing her long throat.

I was already charging at them as he bent down, and I threw a fist at his jaw that knocked his head sideways with a sharp crack. He dropped Nikki and she crumpled to the ground. I desperately wanted to make sure she was all right, but there was no time.

The other Immortal had straightened and was glaring at me. I took a protective stance in front of Nikki's prone form. "She's mine," I snarled, hoping it would stave off further struggle. I was not one to fight unless I had to.

His lip curled into a sneer, his violet eyes full of contempt and malice. "My apologies, my brother, I had no idea I was trespassing." His accent was thick, he didn't often speak English.

My response was a low and menacing growl. He smiled at my attempt at intimidation. He was slight of build, but seemed supremely confident.

"She does smell so delicious, though," he went on. "Surely you wouldn't mind sharing?" He was taunting me. I lowered my stance and narrowed my eyes. "Perhaps not, then," he said, turning away.

I watched him warily, knowing he had no intention of giving up so easily. As I thought, he spun and was suddenly leaping at me. I reached out and caught his shoulders, using his momentum to take us both flying away from Nikki. We hit the ground and slid for a few feet, both grappling for control. Finally we both let go and sprang to our feet. He tried to circle around me, but I kept my body between him and Nikki.

"So protective of your territory," he hissed. "She must be one of your favorites."

He was trying to provoke me. I was distracted by his reference to Nikki being a regular on my diet, but I was still ready when he came at me. I leapt and met him in the air with my feet, knocking him back five feet. I had not used all my strength. I had no desire for a war with this Immortal. I just wanted him to know Nikki was off limits. His violet eyes showed annoyance and surprise as he stood and brushed at his black clothing.

"I know you can do better than that, Gregory," he said. My eyes must have registered the shock at his calling me by name. "Yes, I know you," he said with a sly grin. "I know a great many things, my brother. And because I know of the Queen's preference for you, I shall overlook this offense." He gave Nikki a disturbing glance. "Enjoy your evening." He turned and was gone. I watched the direction he'd run off for a moment, but it was obvious he wasn't coming back.

While I was confused and more than a little bothered by the encounter, it was not in the forefront of my mind. I turned and found Nikki still lying prone on the cement. Her blue eyes were wide as saucers and full of immobilizing panic. I walked toward her very slowly.

"It's all right Nikki, he's gone," I said, trying not to frighten her further. I reached her side and was relieved to see that she had no apparent injury other than her scraped knees. "Nikki, you're going to be all right. I'm here, you're safe," I whispered, trying to calm the wild look in her eyes. She finally focused on my face, then her eyes rolled back and she fainted.

I caught her before she could bash her head on the hard ground. Since I couldn't ask her, I gently checked her for broken bones and other less obvious injuries. She didn't make a sound of pain and seemed to be intact. Ignoring the tantalizing smell of bloody knees, I gathered her into my arms. The smell of jasmine and almonds enveloped me. I ran swiftly to her home, keeping her pressed tightly to my chest.

Using her key, I entered through the front door and took her to her bedroom. I laid her down on her soft bed. Nikki looked peaceful, as if she had just fallen asleep. As I stood staring at her, the phone began to ring. She stirred slightly and her brow creased in a frown. I was in the kitchen instantly and pressed the automatic answer button on her machine. The phone stopped mid-ring and I listened for sounds from the bedroom. From her breathing, I could tell she was still asleep. Then the machine finished its message and the caller began leaving his.

"Nikki? Are you there?" a deep male voice asked. I felt a strange sensation in my gut. "Huh, well I was going to apologize for calling so late, but I guess you're not home..." His voice trailed off for a moment. "I was hoping you could meet me for coffee or something tomorrow. It's been a while since we got together." He paused again, and the sick feeling I was having did not ease up. "I miss you," he said quietly. "Call me. It's Rich," he said almost as an afterthought. As if it was more out of politeness than that she wouldn't recognize his voice.

I left the house, locking the door behind me. I didn't understand the sick knot in my stomach. I didn't understand why I had felt such an intense need to keep Nikki alive, as if my own survival depended on it. I didn't understand the comfort I felt holding her close as I ran her home. And who the hell was Rich?

CHAPTER ELEVEN

My thoughts raced in dizzying circles. I couldn't seem to concentrate on any one thing. My emotions were even more disconcerting, specifically because I was still feeling them. I needed to calm down and clear my head. Back at my loft, I closed the door and welcomed the silent dark. The fight, such as it was, had really left me on edge. I had never been in a fight like that before. No, that wasn't it. I'd been in plenty of fights with other Immortals. We weren't exactly peaceful by nature.

I had never *felt* like that during a fight before. I had been afraid—not for myself, but for Nikki. Still, the fear was there. And it was lingering. I sat down on the edge of my bed without turning the lights on. I wasn't used to feeling so off center. I wanted to understand, but there was too much. Too many thoughts were pulling at my attention. I needed to turn them all off and start fresh.

Ah, turn it all off. Brilliant idea. I lay back on my bed and closed my eyes. Holding my breath for total silence, I waited patiently for oblivion to take me. In my haste to avoid the thoughts I was presently drowning in, I momentarily forgot the dream that could be waiting.

Darkness. I was alone in the dark. I could hear sounds. They were dangerous. Alone, I had no chance of survival. I began to run, pressing through the wet, hot plants, and in my panic I was faster than I should be, so I matched pace with the other fleeing prey, and when the noise of pursuit sent birds crying into flight, I wanted to join them, so I flew up a tree, climbing to escape the predator behind me, but he was a giant and I could hear his enormous paws cracking branches in the darkness. I held very still. I heard no sound. There was nothing. I was utterly alone in the dark, hot damp. Then I heard the roar and saw two glittering eyes soaring at my face, and by instinct I reached out, caught the great cat by the throat and in one swift movement snapped its neck, letting its body crash to the ground below as I stared at the hands at the ends of my arms. They weren't mine. I had no such strength. There was no pride or satisfaction in victory, only horror. It was unnatural for me to have bested the feline predator. It was a greater hunter than I. I leaped from the tree landing on my impossibly graceful feet and, still terrified, I ran again, trying now to flee from the awful truth. But I could not outrun it and I was left alone with the deadly stranger that was me.

Gasping, I sat up and shook my head, scattering the thoughts of my dream. My hands fisted the sheet as I took shaking breaths, trying to refuse what had just happened. My dreams were vague impressions, a type of déjà vu that was easily dismissed. But this had been different. This had been so much more. My mind was dredging up fractured memories that were better left forgotten. I rejected the image of myself fleeing from some unknown danger. I had always been the predator. I had always been strong. I had always been alone. It was the way of things. My muscles were wound tight, and my mind was even more muddled.

Obviously, resting had been a bad idea. But there was more than one way to meditate. I grabbed both of my blades from the *daishō* and escaped to the fresh air on the roof. Taking a deep breath, I started the *Nitō-ryū*. It was an exercise that used every muscle in my body, but required no thought as the procession had long ago become as natural as breathing.

After a few minutes, I closed my eyes and began to increase my speed. This was one of the few ways I could truly push myself physically. When I was the only one involved in an activity, I was free to reach my limits. Soon, I was moving faster than sight, looking like nothing more than a blur of movement to anything other than the most ancient of Immortals. As my body relished the challenge and became mesmerized by the rhythm, my mind took me back nearly half a millennium.

I was living in Japan then. My features and skin color were such that any race would see me as at least half native. That, combined with the perfect accent I had in any language I heard and subsequently learned, allowed me to blend in just about anywhere. Or rather, just as well one place as another, since there was nowhere I actually looked at as home.

One evening around twilight, I was hunting near a rural farm on my way from one city to the next. I came upon the smell of old, rotting flesh. In those days, I would not have hunted such a pathetic meal, but it was accompanied with the sweet smell of strong blood and I was very thirsty. Peering across the expanse of a plowed field, I saw a hunched and ancient man, bent over tending to his garden. Expecting him to be near deaf with his age, I made no effort to cover the sound of my approach. I still made no more sound than the whisper of the wind. As my hand reached out for him, he suddenly whirled around, knocking my arm away with the plow in his hand.

I was momentarily frozen with shock. Not only had the old man heard me, he had landed a blow. While I was distracted, he took a step forward and jabbed me hard in the chest.

"We are poor farmers with nothing worth stealing, move on and torment someone else," the old man hissed. I realized he thought me a bandit and was deeply offended he could take me for something so common.

"I am no bandit, old man," I replied indignantly. He eyed me suspiciously.

"Then what are you here for?" he asked.

"I came to take your life," I said calmly. His eyes widened and flicked briefly toward the tree line. It was only an instant, but drew my gaze there nonetheless. Sleeping at the edge of the trees were three children, the strong blood I had smelled. "After I take you, I will have no need of them," I assured him. I wasn't entirely sure why I would say such a thing, but something had struck me about this old man.

"Their parents will not return until the end of the summer for them. They will die alone," he whispered.

"What is that to me?" I responded, sparing their pathetic lives was one thing, caring if they died was something far beneath me. His wrinkled faced hardened, and he drew himself up as best he could.

"I will not die as easy as you think," he said.

"Such as I am cannot be found within your thoughts," I replied. Then I reached for him again, and again he struck me. He was much faster than he should be, but it was more than that. This old man had piqued my curiosity. I didn't allow him to land another blow, but I didn't simply overpower him either. I began to watch how he fought. I was fascinated by the beauty he brought to the violence. It was much different from the style I had grown accustomed to in Europe. If I could learn what this old man was doing, I would not only be lethal, I would be unstoppable.

I put an end to the fight by snatching and breaking his plow, then dashing to the tree line and standing two feet away from the children he cared for. The old man froze instantly.

"Please," he begged.

"I have found something worth sparing your life for," I told him.

"I have nothing to give."

"Teach me how you move when you fight, and I will spare your life until the small ones are gone," I offered.

"It is more than simple actions you can mimic," he said hesitantly.

"I can learn anything you can teach, old man," I replied snidely. "Take my offer quickly or I kill all four of you, starting with them," I said, indicating the children near my feet.

"Yes, all right, I will teach you," he agreed. "But if you are going to learn it, you must allow me to teach you properly. You must never let the little ones know the danger they are in. They see more than they should. You will have to treat me as your master, with respect."

A barking laugh escaped my throat. "Surely you jest! How could I treat you as a master?"

"There is no other way to learn, for I know of no other way to teach," he replied.

"Fine, but know this, old man, if I lose my patience with the façade, or tire of your teachings, you will not be able to stop me from killing you, or them."

And so began the time I spent learning how to fight from an old and broken samurai. In the beginning, he treated me as harshly as he would have any apprentice. Soon, however, he took note of how I not only learned quickly and thoroughly, but that even holding myself back from him, I moved faster than I should, my untrained muscles stronger than they should be. He eased up on the belittling and I, in turn, found it easier to address him with respect, even when the children were not present. A month into my training the old man could no longer hold his peace.

"What are you?" he asked me quietly one night as we shared a pot of tea, from which I did not drink.

"I am your most devoted and humble pupil, master," I said with the trace of a smile on my lips.

"You may be learning a great deal from me," he agreed, "but you are not capable of humility and I could never be master to one such as you."

I remained silent, but he knew I agreed with his words.

"I know you are no man, not such as I have seen in all my many years," he said. My faint smile came back as he mentioned his age. I had seen many more years, and many more things. "I ask only that you tell me if a creature such as yourself, one who would take the life of an old man, but spare that of his grandchildren … is such a creature good or evil?"

I considered his question at great length. Eventually I answered, "Do you remember what I said when you warned me that you would not die as easily as I thought?"

"Of course I do, I am old, not stupid," he chastised me. "You said, 'Such as I am, is not held in your thoughts.' Which I now see is true. My thoughts cannot explain you."

"If I am such a creature as you say I am, and cannot be held by the thoughts of such a man as you are, could I be defined by the morals such a mind believes?" We were both silent as my question hung in the air.

"What do you learn from me?" he finally asked.

"I learn the art of death, the dance of swords," I replied.

"Nothing more?" he pressed.

"What more would you have me learn than mastery of how you fight?"

"I would have you learn why I fight."

"There are many reasons to fight."

"There are a few things worth fighting for," he corrected me. "But there are many more reasons not to."

After that conversation, I found myself listening to more than just his instruction in technique. I learned about things like honor, duty, and family. These concepts touched something familiar in the back of my mind. It was the first, and last, time I knew a mortal who seemed truly wise indeed.

The sun began to rise over the roofline, the light pulling me back from my memories of the past. I tried to apply them to my present. What reason did I have to fight for Nikki? I went into my apartment and replaced the blades. My journal full of notes was sitting on my desk. I added to it the events of the night. I decided to add another drawing as well. This time I tried charcoal, hoping to get a better result than my first attempt. I drew Nikki's face surrounded by her curls as it lay resting on her pillow. She looked so peaceful as she slept, so fragile and so human. It still wasn't right. I shook my head and put the notebook away.

I had obviously become too involved in my observations of Nikki to see her objectively. I was once again in need of a second opinion. I would go see the others. I wouldn't go so far as to call them wise, but we all have to work with what we've got.

Chapter Twelve

The afternoon sun was still shining when I got to the apartment building, so I couldn't, per normal, scale the wall to climb through the window. I had to settle for wading through the overwhelming scent of mortality as I passed through the hall and knocked on the door. After the customary greeting and response, I let myself in. Unlike me, most Immortals had little use for locks.

Lance and Rob were once again involved in a video game. This time it was one of Rob's choosing. It was always amusing to watch Lance use the same intensity when making a cartoon monkey dance as when he was commanding Special Forces. It was not amusing, however to watch Rob as he waited for his next turn. He was presently indulging in his most disgusting habit—eating Twinkies.

Rob insisted they helped him stay "full" between feedings. The sickly sweet cream cakes could stay in his stomach for weeks without rotting. As he once eloquently put it, "they're non-biodegradable!" I had once pointed out that if he swallowed them whole, there wouldn't be as much mess when he had to regurgitate them later, but he insisted that chewing was "part of the experience." He also insisted there really wasn't that much mess, since he realized waiting a few days after his last feeding would ensure there was no blood left for the cakes to absorb. I shuddered at the very idea.

While I generally avoided him when he was doing it, I never tried to convince him to stop. It was his way of compensating for his lost mortality, much like Jenny's sexual exploits and Lance's extreme sports. Their weakness was one I could not identify with, as I had no memories of being human to grieve, or in Jenny's case, fester over.

"This is becoming a habit, Gregory," Jenny's sultry voice said, breaking my train of thought. She was perched on the back of the couch, her small legs to either side of Rob's back, her hands running through his sandy-blond hair. I wondered briefly at her recent need for such contact. Tenderness wasn't really her forte. It generally meant she was worried about something and was seeking comfort. Before I could take note of it, Rob reminded me why I was here.

"How's 'Operation Hot Human Honey' going?" he asked with a smirk.

"Is she just a simple diversion or does she know enough to be a threat?" Lance asked, restating Rob's question with more tact.

"I'm still not sure what she knows. In fact, I came to get your advice on how much she should know."

The game was forgotten. I now had everyone's attention.

"You want advice?" Rob asked. "From us?"

"This really is getting to become a habit," Jenny repeated. It was a joke none of them seemed to find funny.

"She shouldn't know anything," Lance said, his gray eyes flashing like steel. "She's mortal."

"We may already be past that point," I replied. I paused as they watched me curiously. "Last night I saved Nikki's life." In unison, they blinked. Rob's jaw fell slightly, giving me a nauseating view of a half-chewed Twinkie. "I saved her from another Immortal," I finished.

Their response was instantaneous.

"You what?!" came from Rob, cake spraying everywhere.

"What did she see?" Lance asked, standing up from the couch.

"What Immortal?" Jenny questioned.

I decided to answer all of their questions. "I saved her from another Immortal when he attacked her after class on Tuesday. I don't know what she saw, she passed out and I haven't spoken to her since. I'm not familiar with him, but he sure seemed to know me."

Rob continued to stare at me in astonishment. I could see the gears turning in Lance's head as he thought over my next move. Jenny looked perturbed.

"Most Immortals know who you are, Gregory. Being so adamantly ignored by the Queen is about as inconspicuous as writing vampire books." She had a point. "Can you be more specific about him?" she asked.

"Not really," I answered dismissively. I didn't think the identity of Nikki's attacker was really the issue. I turned to Lance. "I don't think she saw much, and if she did, she may dismiss it all as a dream."

"She won't make a connection between a dream and waking up in an alley somewhere between the campus and her house?" Lance asked skeptically.

"I took her home," I corrected. "She'll wake up in her own bed."

Rob started to laugh. "Dude! You tucked her in?"

"I couldn't just leave her where she was," I responded indignantly.

"You totally took her to bed!" Rob went on. "I knew this wasn't just about what she thought about your books. Triple H strikes again! Seriously, I have got to meet this girl!"

"Absolutely not," I refused.

"A little protective of your new pet?" Jenny teased me. I raised my eyebrow at her and glanced at the hand she was presently "petting" Rob with. She smirked, ruffled his hair once more and then pulled her hand away.

"You know, Greg, humans are really hard to keep alive," Rob said sympathetically. "You might need help if you're going to watch her around the clock."

I began to wonder why I had come in the first place.

"I could take over watching her house," he offered. "You know, to make sure she didn't trip and fall in the shower," he said waggling his eyebrows.

"It isn't very wise for the butcher to fall in love with his cow," Lance said quietly.

"Who said anything about love?" I yelled, a sudden memory of Rich's voice causing my temper to flare. "You're all being ridiculous. This is why I don't come around here."

"You save a mortal from death, a fate she can't escape, expose yourself and another Immortal in the process, bring danger to us all, and we're being ridiculous?" Jenny asked snidely. She stalked over to me and took a deep whiff of my scent. I waited for her proclamation, but she simply studied me, quietly smiling. It was even more irritating than being told how I felt.

"Perhaps now would be the time to take her yourself," Lance suggested. I glared at him with an intensity that caused him to step back.

"I didn't save her simply to kill her myself," I snarled.

"Then why did you save her?" he asked.

A damn good question, I thought to myself. That was the reason I'd come, but obviously I would find no answers here. My associates noted my silence. I had to give them some reason.

"I haven't finished my investigation into what she knows. She's told several people about her theories on my books. I need to find out what exactly she's said and who believed her." There, that made sense. In fact, it made a lot of sense. That was exactly why I had saved her. The looks I was faced with on the Immortals before me, however, told me they were skeptical.

"She's nothing to me," I insisted. "I will find out how much of a threat she is, and how much light she has cast on us." I paused and looked the three of them square in the eye. "Then I will take care of her." I turned and walked out.

Chapter Thirteen

Lazarus pulled the brim of his hat further down. Even with the contacts, it was too bright outside. After all this time away he still missed the green darkness of the jungle. He was making one phone call before retiring for the day. It almost rang three times before she answered.

"Hello?"

"Have I disturbed you in something important, Guinevere?" Lazarus asked pointedly.

"Nothing is more important than my work for the Queen," came the smooth voice. "I apologize for keeping you waiting."

Lazarus noted the change in her tone from their last conversation. "Have you made significant progress?"

"I have found more information, but nothing that requires your immediate presence."

He didn't like how confident she sounded. "Perhaps you should not presume to know how I should fulfill my duties."

"No, of course not," she replied, her tone more appropriately shaken. "I simply meant that your time is so valuable to the Queen, I would not dare waste it."

"I see," he said. "Perhaps I should call again later."

"As you wish."

Lazarus snapped his phone shut. He watched as Guinevere slipped down the side of the building and straddled the fiery-red street bike. The little fox was hiding something from him. He would spend some time following her around. She gunned down the street, but he leisurely started the car. She was probably headed home and he could catch up to her there tonight. For now, he wanted to get out of this blinding sun, though perhaps he would stop for a bite on the way.

Chapter Fourteen

What had I been thinking, hoping to get decent input from those three imbeciles? They never took anything seriously. I had hoped Lance, at least, would give some rational advice. Instead, he had joined with them in insinuating I had feelings for a mortal. Of all the asinine assumptions! I don't have feelings, period. I haven't in centuries. And most especially not for one of the walking dead! That would be like plucking a rose from the bush because it was beautiful, then weeping when it withered away. Suddenly, the image of Nikki as a wrinkled old woman burst into my vision, stopping me in my tracks.

I needed a drink. I turned back from the road home and headed straight for campus. It was now late afternoon, early evening. It was the break between day and night classes. The campus would not be flooded with witnesses, but there would be plenty of warm-blooded bodies wandering around.

Hunting during the day was risky. I would have to put some effort into it. I looked forward to the challenge. I was feeling the need to reconnect with the hunt. As I stepped onto campus, I scanned the buildings for a suitable site. Aaahh. The library, perfect. Rob had described his escapades there in detail. At the time I had been bored, but slightly amused. Now I was glad for the information.

I passed quickly through the lobby and went into the stairwell, having no patience to wait for the elevators. It was a quick walk up to the third floor. This was where the "really boring stuff," as Rob put it, was shelved. The ceiling was low, the area having been converted from a storage attic. There were a few tables for study set up near the elevator, with lamps spread across them. The rest of the large room was lit with dim fluorescent light. In the back corner, near the stairwell, there were a few faulty wires and the lights flickered annoyingly.

The rows of shelving crammed with ancient textbooks created wall upon wall of privacy. These poorly lit, rarely used enclaves of paper and ink were called "The Stacks." Almost no one came up here, and when they did, it generally wasn't for academic research.

Quickly forming a plan, I took note of the numbers on a few of the books using a stray scrap of paper and bit of pencil that had been long forgotten. Then I headed in the direction of the elevators. If I was lucky, I wouldn't have to go far to find "a willing participant," as Rob would have put it.

As I reached the elevators, I saw there was actually someone studying at one of the tables. How very convenient. Her dirty blond hair was pulled into a messy bun on top of her head, strands of it falling limply about her. I came up behind her and cleared my throat.

"Oh!" She cried, jumping in her chair and putting one hand to her flat chest. "I didn't even hear the elevators," she said, turning to blink at me through her wire-rimmed glasses. There was something almost familiar about her blue-gray eyes. I quickly brushed it off and smiled brightly at her.

"Sorry," I apologized. "I didn't mean to startle you. I was hoping you could help me with something."

She surveyed me from head to toe, then blinked again as if confused that I was talking to her.

"I'm looking for a book, but I've never been up here before," I paused to let her collect herself a bit. She was completely flustered. It was obvious she wasn't used to dealing with men. "Perhaps you could help me?" I asked again, handing her my slip of paper.

She took it and read what I'd written. Her eyes flicked up to me and then down again. She giggled nervously. Apparently she was familiar with "The Stacks," though I doubted she had ever used them.

"These books are over there," she said, pointing, "In the back, near the stairs."

I almost wanted to laugh at the poor creature. Instead, I bent my knees, lowering myself to her eye level. "Do you think you could show me, personally?" I whispered, tucking some wiry hair behind her ear. She giggled nervously again.

"Well, I …" she stuttered, looking at the elevators as if expecting someone to step out. I stood up again, taking one of her hands and bringing it with me.

"Please?" I asked, my voice dripping with saccharine. This was much more fun than drunks in an alley. Who did those three whelps think they were, questioning me? I was ancient before they were ever born. The butcher and the cow, indeed.

The girl giggled nervously again, but allowed me to pull her to her feet. She hesitated, waiting for me to move.

"Which way?" I asked, reminding her I had never been here before. She stole a quick glance at the elevator, and I realized she really was expecting someone to step out. How exciting.

I smiled at her and squeezed her hand a little. She smiled shyly back at me and started to walk toward the back corner. When we reached the end of the aisle leading to the stairs, she stopped and turned around. I continued walking, forcing her backward, down the aisle and up against the wall of books. She looked at me like a deer in the headlights of a car. Or perhaps it would be more apt to say like a rabbit in the hunter's spotlight.

I released her hand and brought my hands up to her face. She was trembling from head to toe, her heart beating erratically. She couldn't seem to catch her breath. I smiled again, probably looking just like the Cheshire cat.

"Wh-what's your name?" she asked, her voice cracking.

"Does it matter?" I responded. She opened her mouth to speak, but I began to trace her lips with my thumb, my other hand sliding down, gripping her neck. She stopped breathing completely.

I ran my nose down her neck, inhaling the scent of her blood rushing just below the surface. It was clean, no drugs of any kind. It would taste better than I'd had in a long while. When I pressed my lips to her throat, she let out a shuddering breath.

As my teeth sank into her thin skin, she gasped and her hands gripped my shoulders weakly. Her blood began to pool in my mouth, and I drank deeply. I was right; she tasted much better than the club girls I had been settling for recently. I relished it as I continued to gnaw at her to keep the wound from healing. I looked forward to sucking this one completely dry.

A sharp ding sounded as the elevator doors slid open at the far end of the room. Perhaps they would see the girl was gone and just leave.

"Clara?" a female voice called. I could hear footsteps and another heartbeat coming toward us. I refused to be chased off and instead opted for camouflage. I had not chosen my spot randomly.

Keeping her neck secured to my lips with one hand at her throat, I used my other hand to begin pulling up her knee length skirt. To my amused surprise, she reacted by raising her leg and wrapping it around my waist. She may not be drunk, but her lack of experience was keeping her just as oblivious. She still had no idea I was slowly killing her.

"Clara?" the other one called again, closer this time. But she was too late; my dinner's heartbeat was already beginning to fail. By the time she reached us, the girl would be passed out.

Just as I predicted, as the footsteps neared our aisle, her eyes rolled back in her head and she moaned loudly. She went limp and I leaned slightly to the side, so her leg would remain draped over my hip. The footsteps paused. I took the extra time I was given to ensure the façade was complete. Letting one of her arms arm rest against my unoccupied hip, I raised the other one back up and draped it around my neck. By wrapping my arm around her back, I held her in place. The blood was coming much slower now and I had to suck much harder to get all of it out.

"*Oh!* Oh, I'm so sorry, I was … Clara?!" the voice behind us was clearly shocked. "I, uh … I'll call you later." And then there was a rapid retreat to the elevators. After a moment, the doors slid open and closed, and there was silence broken only by the hum of fluorescent lighting. Even my victim's heart was now still. Now I had only to dispose of the body.

I put one arm under the corpse's neck and swept its legs up with the other. The heart had stopped beating before the wound had healed, so I had to cover it with my hand. It was an awkward position, but much less suspicious than simply slinging the thing over my back.

Because most humans are too lazy to use the stairs, I went unseen from the third floor to the basement. The library was one of the oldest buildings on campus. The decrepit furnace had already been lit for the season, though the fire was burning low at the moment. I tossed the body in and turned up the heat. By the time anyone realized it was too hot, the remains would be long gone. I licked the hand that had been covering the wound clean and headed home very satisfied. I had hunted as Immortals should: without fear, in broad daylight, and with complete disregard to being witnessed.

Feeding followed by a nice long walk did wonders to clear my head. Mortals were simple creatures. Easy to fool and manipulate. Nikki had no idea what I really was. Still, if she were even close to the truth, it could start people thinking. And that's when things got dangerous. I needed to know what theories she had confided in others.

To do that, I needed to get her to confide in me. Perhaps if I convinced her to trust me, I could get the information I needed from her. It would be easy. I had just saved her life hadn't I? But that left the question of what she had seen. Did she consider me a hero, or a nightmare? I would find out tomorrow.

CHAPTER FIFTEEN

When Thursday night came, I was still determined in my new plan. But I'd had time to think, which is not always helpful when all you have is questions. As I sat in my accustomed seat, apprehension began to seep into my gut. I was glad for my distance from the fluster of the human students arranging themselves for class.

The questions continued to fly in and out of my head by the dozens. Would she be in class tonight? Would she expect me to be here? Would she wish I wasn't? What had she been aware of Tuesday night? Did she see enough to know she should be terrified of me? Was she glad I had saved her? Did she know that both I and the monster that attacked her were inherently the same?

My useless fretting was interrupted by the door pulling open. The breeze that blew in carried with it the scent of jasmine and almonds. My head spun around. Nikki was entering while trying to end a conversation with someone.

"Really, I'm fine. You don't have to—" her words died in her throat as her blue eyes met mine.

But the connection was brief as my gaze was drawn to the person following closely behind her. He was a tall, well-built man about Nikki's age. His hair was nearly black, his eyes were brown and alert, his skin was darker than a sun induced tan. My eyes narrowed at the sight of him and his proximity to Nikki. I barely held a low growl from rolling from my throat. I was slightly surprised by my reaction.

"I'm not letting you walk home alone at night anymore, Nikki. I told you it was dangerous," he said, not noticing why she had stopped talking.

"Look, Rich, I know you mean well," Nikki went on. When I heard his name from her lips, I had to redouble my efforts not to threaten him. I didn't know what was wrong with me. Intimidating her friends was surely not the way to keep her from being afraid of me. "But really, I don't need you to walk me home. It was a total fluke. I'm usually perfectly safe." She said this while looking directly at me. I pulled my eyes away from the pouting Rich and looked into hers. Had she known I was following her home?

"You can't possibly know that, Nikki. There are all kinds of weirdos out there," Rich said, now also looking at me, glancing up and down. I ignored his comment as Nikki's eyes held mine fast. They were asking for something.

"Rich, this is—" she paused, realizing I had never actually told her my name.

"Gregory," I supplied quickly. "It's nice to finally meet you," I said, taking his hand and firmly shaking it. He was momentarily taken aback, but recovered quickly and returned the hand shake with enough force behind it to make me smirk a little. He was trying to mark his territory. I suddenly found it amusing.

"I was just telling Rich that while I appreciate him escorting me to class, I don't need one home," Nikki said, her eyes still boring into mine as if trying to speak directly to my brain. Then I got it. She didn't want Rich to accompany her home, and she was asking me to rescue her, again. As the realization came, my smile grew and Nikki's posture relaxed.

"I assure you, Rich, that Nikki is perfectly safe when she walks home," I said.

Now it was Rich's eyes that narrowed. "And how would you know that, Gregory?"

"Because I ensure it," I answered honestly. I found myself wanting to avoid lying in Nikki's presence. How strange.

"Do you now," Rich said. His tone was that of someone who had just tasted something foul.

"Yes, actually," Nikki broke in before the two of us could speak to each other again. "Gregory has been making sure I get home safe since the second day of class," she said to Rich. I turned to her in momentary surprise, but recovered before Rich could notice. She had known I was following her. How was that possible? No human knew when I was tracking them. Before I could ponder it properly, however, Rich spoke up again.

"Then where were you Tuesday night when some creep attacked her?" he demanded. Nikki was quiet. She must have wondered the same thing.

"Tony kept me after class to blather on about some assignment," I said softly, looking directly at Nikki and ignoring Rich completely. "I'm sorry I was late."

Nikki smiled up at me from beneath her long lashes. It made my heart beat. "I'm just glad you came when you did."

Rich turned to Nikki. "I thought you said you didn't remember anything," he said. I didn't like his tone. Before I could say so, Nikki answered.

"Well, Rich, I told you I ended up at home, safe and sound except for the scrape from my fall, so someone must have helped me get there. Apparently it was Gregory," she said. Her voice was dripping with sarcasm, but I could tell it was to cover her inept lying. She obviously remembered much more than that.

Rich's narrowed eyes took me in again. He seemed to know something was wrong, but didn't want to accuse Nikki of lying. I waited with a smug grin on my face to see how he would proceed. "I don't like the idea of a stranger knowing where you live," he finally said.

"I trust Gregory with my life. And it isn't exactly your business who knows where I live, now is it?" Nikki stated. Rich took a step back as if she had physically slapped him. I could see by the look on her face she knew he would take it that way. It was also obvious she hated to hurt him. Perhaps I could give her another option. Not that I cared if Rich got hurt, but I didn't want Nikki to be so upset.

"Tell you what, Rich," I said, bringing his gaze back to me. "Nikki has already agreed to let me walk her home tonight, but I'm sure she'd be more than happy to give you a call the minute she leaves me at the door." I was lying now, but it was for Nikki because she was so bad at it. I also swallowed something nasty in order to play to his ego by dropping the hint that Nikki would be entering her house alone. I hoped it would get him to back off and leave her alone.

It seemed to work. Rich's ruffled feathers smoothed some as he looked at Nikki and asked, "You'll call the second you get home?"

"If everyone would take their seats, we can get started," Tony's voice came to us from the front of the room. Nikki and I turned to look, and saw we were the only ones left standing. I knew we had been talking too quietly for anyone to really hear, but Nikki sat quickly, obviously embarrassed. I calmly took my seat next to her. Rich didn't move.

"Promise me," he insisted.

"I promise, Rich, okay? Just go!" Nikki whispered harshly. I was tempted to say something along similar lines, but decided to hold my tongue. Rich nodded tensely and left.

I didn't really hear much of the lecture during class. Now that I knew Nikki wasn't afraid of me, I spent the time deciding how to proceed. I wasn't ready to confront her about the attack. A few more days may make her memory even hazier. The sooner I could get her to trust me, the sooner she'd be likely to dismiss anything she had seen as fantasy.

As we exited together into the crisp night air, I immediately took control of the situation. "You said you were an English Lit Major, right?" I asked pleasantly. She nodded, but I could tell she already knew I was avoiding talking about what happened Tuesday night. "What made you decide on that for a major?"

"You mean, why choose such an unpopular major that will only be useful if I plan on using it to teach English Lit classes?" she asked, smiling. "My dad asks me the same question about once a month." I returned her smile. She looked at me appraisingly. "Can I tell you a secret?"

"Of course," I answered automatically. She smiled at my quick response.

"I've been in love for, oh, ten years now," she said. My heart dropped into my stomach. Was she talking about Rich? "He's actually the reason for my major."

I held my breath, waiting for her to continue. Perhaps it was one of the professors? No, ten years ago she would have been . . .

"I was fourteen when my mom first introduced me to Shakespeare." My breath came out in a whoosh. "I had a broken leg and couldn't get around for weeks. She insisted that watching ten hours of TV a day would rot my brain, so she gave me a copy of *Much Ado About Nothing* and told me to read it. I've been in love with William ever since."

I tried to ignore the relief I felt. "I agree his work is some of the very best the English language has to offer. I read it just last weekend, actually."

She laughed, and I looked at her questioningly. "You make it sound like you read his entire works at once."

I remained silent.

She looked at me with her eyebrows raised. "You must do a lot of reading."

"I have a lot of spare time, and I read quickly."

She squinted at me as if she suddenly didn't believe me. "Give me your favorite quote," she demanded.

"What?" I asked, surprised.

"If you know Shakespeare so well, let's hear some," she insisted.

To ease her skepticism of me, I spouted off the first thing that came to my head.

> *"To-morrow, and to-morrow, and to-morrow,*
> *Creeps in this petty pace from day to day,*
> *To the last syllable of recorded time;*
> *And all our yesterdays have lighted fools*
> *The way to dusty death. Out, out, brief candle!*
> *Life's but a walking shadow, a poor player,*

That struts and frets his hour upon the stage,
And then is heard no more. It is a tale
Told by an idiot, full of sound and fury,
Signifying nothing."

"I see," she said. Then she was silent.

"See what?" I asked, my curiosity piqued.

"You can tell a lot about a person by the things they remember most. You say you're familiar with all of Shakespeare's work, and yet when I ask you to quote it, you not only choose a tragedy, but one of the most depressing speeches ever written … And yet …" She looked at me, her blue eyes capturing mine for a moment. Then she turned and watched the path in front of us again. "And yet it seems that you don't label yourself with that quote, but the rest of humanity."

Once again, Nikki was proving to be entirely too observant. I would have to be very careful what I said to her. "Do you have a favorite quote?" I asked in an attempt to steer the conversation back in the right direction.

"Does it have to be Shakespeare?" she asked.

"No, but I thought you *loved* him," I teased her. I sounded just like Rob.

She laughed, and I was glad I had said it. "I do love Shakespeare. He's brilliant, poetic, witty, and romantic. But he is also very dark. Even his comedies have such twisted plots." She shook her head. "While I'm drawn to his complex and shady nature, I'm nothing like that myself."

I took note of her attraction to his complex and shady nature. "Well then, no restrictions. Let's have your life's mantra."

"The sun shines today also."

I was struck silent. Five little words were all she lived her life by. And yet, when put together, they said everything about her. I had new respect for Ralph Waldo Emerson. I also had the perfect response.

"But the sun would burn me. I dare not step into its light lest it burn both my flesh and my soul, leaving me with nothing."

"My soul was ablaze with love, my flesh consumed by it."

I laughed out loud. I had quoted myself, as Jerry Mack, meaning to be ironic, and she had answered me with myself, as Martha Vinegross. Someone finally got the joke, after one hundred years of telling it. As we walked the remaining distance to her home, we continued our battle of words. I was impressed by both her wit and her repertoire. I also found myself reveling in her laughter. All too soon, we were standing in front of her door.

"You'd better get inside and call Rich before he starts to panic and come looking for you," I said a little snidely. I was uncomfortable knowing that's exactly what she was about to do. It bothered me for some reason.

"Can I do just one more?" she asked. I couldn't help but smile at the hopeful look on her face. Surely this was the look they deemed "puppy dog eyes."

"Of course," I replied.

"Okay, but this one's serious. I'm going to re-do your quote for you," she said. I questioned her with my eyes. "I have a Shakespeare quote, but it's for you."

I found myself once again intrigued. "By all means, let's hear it."

> *"To sleep—perchance to dream. Ay, there's the rub!*
> *For in that sleep of death what dreams may come…*
> *The undiscover'd country… puzzles the will,*
> *And makes us rather bear those ills we have*
> *Than fly to others that we know not of?*
> *Thus conscience does make cowards of us all…"*

I stared at her as she spoke to me of unknown dreams and puzzling conscience.

"I condensed it, to make it fit you better," she whispered as a confession.

"Yes, you did," I agreed, my own voice a whisper as well.

"Now I've offended you! Argh, I never know when to just shut up. I'm sorry, I wasn't saying I think you're suicidal or anything like that," she quickly began, but I held up a hand to stop her from saying out loud what she did think I was like.

"No, I'm not offended," I said, my voice still low. "Just surprised."

"Oh," she replied. There was an awkward silence.

"Goodnight, Nikki. I'll see you next Tuesday," I said, turning and walking down the steps.

"Goodnight, Gregory," she whispered. The sound of her sweet voice saying my name caused my heart to beat. I closed my eyes trying to get a grip on myself. What had I gotten myself into?

I needed to distance myself, immediately. I made a hasty retreat to my loft, planning to stay away from Nikki for a while. And yet, the breaking dawn found me hidden in the shadowy trees across the street, watching her house. I wanted to get closer, to see if she was awake yet. But I was afraid she would somehow sense my presence. I shook my head again in disbelief. I was afraid of a mortal. This could not be happening.

Around seven-thirty, she left the house and headed for campus. I thought she must have an early morning class, but she went straight into the library. The library. I was suddenly sick at the thought of her being inside. The image of her taking the elevator to the third floor flashed behind my eyes. She would sit at the same table to study. Or perhaps she was meeting someone... I quickly shut down that train of thought. She was obviously here to study. Only she didn't bring any books. I waited for her to come out.

Three hours later I admitted I needed an alternate theory. Perhaps she was tutoring other students? Or doing research for a paper? Or two? The possibilities were endless, and it was driving me insane trying to guess. Wait, why was I guessing? Why not just go in and see what she was doing? As far as she knew, I was a student here and had every right to be in the library. It would simply be a coincidence.

I stayed right where I was.

At one o'clock, Nikki went to the student center for lunch, then went right back to the library. Why would anyone spend the entire day in the library? By the time she left at six, my mind had come up with several increasingly outlandish theories. I had gone over everything from cleaning the bathrooms to turning tricks in "The Stacks." I even had a disturbing vision of her going into the basement to adjust the furnace and finding a gruesome surprise.

She seemed to be in a hurry to get home. She went inside and was back out again in less than thirty minutes. She got into her yellow Beetle and drove off. I was left staring in the direction she had gone. I couldn't exactly be subtle about running after a car. I let myself into her house to see if she had left any clues as to where she had gone.

From what I could see, she had simply come in and left again. If she had a date, she wasn't trying to impress him. Perhaps it was Rich. I smiled faintly at the thought of her not trying to impress Rich.

Despite wanting to stay inside among her things, I knew it would be smarter to wait outside. I had no idea where she had gone, and so no idea as to when she would be home. Catching me rifling through her drawers would definitely raise her suspicions.

Two hours later she was back. Either it was a really bad date, or she had just gone to get dinner. A really long dinner. Maybe she met up with some girlfriends and they spent the time gossiping. That's what females did, wasn't it? I sighed in frustration and admitted to the fact that I had no idea where she had been. Following someone around and knowing what they were doing were proving to be two different things. I had never needed to note the difference before.

That night I stayed to watch her go through her nighttime routine of showering, putting on comfortable pajamas, and reading before she went to sleep. My mind wandered a little more than necessary while I listened to the water falling in the shower. She was still reading and comparing my books. Again, she looked sweetly vulnerable in her sleep.

Saturday she was up at six-thirty and left at seven-thirty again to head back to campus. She couldn't have had classes today, because she went back to the library. I would not be spending the day in agonizing mystery again. I waited one hour, then went in myself. Trying to look inconspicuous, I began to walk around the edge of the first floor, searching for her.

I took two steps and spotted her behind the reference desk. Stepping behind a tall shelf of books, I looked through it at her. She was seated casually, speaking with someone. She pointed and smiled, and then the boy she was talking to headed off in the direction she had pointed. She worked here.

It was so obvious, it was painful. How could I have not thought of that? I was even tempted to smack myself in the head as Rob would have done, but just then a student walked by so I kept my hands at my sides.

The morning passed into afternoon as I watched Nikki work. She pulled her hair out of her face and braided the top of it together to hold in place. Her thick curls clung together loosely but she did not secure them with a band. Occasionally strands would fall out, but it was not enough to get in her way or even distract her. For the first time I was able to get an extended look at her whole face.

Even from a distance her beauty struck me. Her sweet and full lips would purse in distress every time she found damage done to a returned book. She would go about fixing them as if she were caring for history itself. Her brow creased slightly over her little nose as she concentrated on entering data into her computer, or when she was asked a difficult question. But she always came up with the answer, without looking in a single book.

The majority of the time, however, her face held a soft smile that was mirrored in the sky of her eyes. She was at peace here, at home. She belonged here, among the books. This was her space.

And I had defiled it. My nose twitched as if I'd smelled something rank as I recalled what I had done two stories up and what was probably still crammed in the furnace below. I had come to a place Nikki considered safe, and proved her infinitely wrong. What would she think of me if she knew?

I went outside for a moment to clear my rapidly clouding mind. Would it be any different if I had fed somewhere else? What did it matter who or where I killed? Any one of them could be someone she knew, in some place she frequented. It was a fact of my existence. I killed so I could live. No mortal could ever change that fact. Nikki would not make me feel guilty for surviving.

As I thought this, Nikki came out of the library and headed for home. It was only two o'clock. She must work a shorter shift on Saturdays. I followed her home, where she had lunch and then drove off in her car again. I growled in irritation. This was getting to be very inconvenient. Perhaps I needed to get a car, or borrow one.

I went inside and took my time going through her things again. I checked where she was reading in my books, what work she had done in her office. I even began an inventory of her DVD collection: a lot of romantic comedies, some historical dramas (one or two I'd seen with Lance), several Shakespeare adaptations (which I smiled at), and even some horror movies (though they were more of the suspense than gore variety). I wasn't surprised to find this evidence of an aversion to violence. Nikki didn't strike me as the Chainsaw Massacre type. Rob had made me watch that movie more than once.

Around seven, I began to feel like I was pushing my luck staying in the house, so I climbed onto the roof to wait. Nikki was home an hour later. She seemed a little drawn and tired. But she was smiling to herself as she sat down in the office and spent some time on her papers. Tonight she departed from routine by taking a bath instead of a shower, which sparked my imagination, and going to bed early. I found it fascinating that I never got bored watching her sleep.

Sunday morning she slept late, not leaving the house until almost ten. Unfortunately, she took her car when she left. I decided it was probably for the best. I was becoming far too engrossed in the life of this mortal. Trying to decipher her cryptic and overly observant remarks was one thing. Looking forward to watching her sleep was unhealthy. I needed a distraction. Watching the yellow Beetle disappear around a distant corner, an idea came. The sky was clear and crystal blue. I would go back to the beach and try again. You could never get enough sun.

CHAPTER SIXTEEN

On the way back to my apartment, I stopped to buy a cheap pair of flip-flops. They weren't the most comfortable footwear I'd ever owned, but I wouldn't care if they got lost. Not that I couldn't handle the expense of yet another pair of sandals. Nearly everything I owned was disposable in that sense, but my feet were just now getting used to, and fond of, my new pair.

I changed into my green swim trunks, but skipped the shirt. I put in my contacts and grabbed a towel while I was in the bathroom. Then I thought better of it and left it behind as well. I slipped my credit card into my Velcro pocket. Punching in the security code to my apartment, I left feeling much more prepared, though less equipped, for my trip to the beach.

My naked chest got even more stares than my tank top had garnered, but I ignored it. I pretty much ignored everyone, actually. I was already starting to feel much more like myself.

As soon as I reached the beach, I set my disposable shoes on the cement wall and wiggled my toes around in the hot sand. They were getting to quite enjoy the grainy texture. I left my shoes behind and headed for the ocean. I still refused to do any hopping, and instead walked quickly to the edge of the water where I again let my toes play in the wet sand before heading further out.

A few miles from shore I encountered something interesting. There was a school of small fish below being fed on by a group of blue sharks. I watched them as they circled and culled their prey—the ultimate aquatic predator. On a whim, I decided to test them.

I slowly closed in on the largest of the sharks, but it ignored me. I must have appeared as a man to it. How insulting. Once I was within inches of it, I gave it a rough pat on the head. It swung around, but I was already on its other side, giving its tail a pull. I wasn't going to hurt it, just annoy it a little to teach it some respect for a greater hunter.

The blue I had decided to pester seemed overly aggressive. Maybe it was still hungry. In either case, it charged at me. We spun around in a few circles. Then I darted away leaving it searching for me. In a flash I was back, tapping it on the nose. It really hated that. It snapped at me and advanced again. It came within centimeters of grazing my side with its rows of numerous and jagged teeth.

I decided I was done. While my skin was tougher than the average mortal, the iron jaw of a shark would certainly break through. And while I would heal from it, it would not be a pleasant way to spend the weekend.

I swam a mile or so away, giving the sharks a wide berth. Then I came to the surface and took a deep breath. The sun was beaming down brightly. Wanting to soak up its rays with my whole body, I rolled onto my back moving my arms and legs in long, slow movements. I smiled, thinking that from the sky it would look like I was trying to make snow angels on the surface of the ocean.

My reprieve was interrupted by a face full of water. I brought my head up in surprise, and received a second dose for my efforts. I had been accosted by dolphins, again. And it looked to be the same pod. Surely this had to be a coincidence.

I watched as they swam around me. Perhaps they hadn't noticed me and I was simply in their way. But just as I thought it, one of the males swam right next to me and smacked a flipper on the surface, splashing me in the face again.

"Did you just—" I cut myself off, realizing I was talking to an animal. The pod began to circle around me as if they were sharks. That image made me realize that just as the sharks had thought I was human, so did these mammals. Weren't dolphins known for playing with humans?

Then, almost as if they could read my mind, they all splashed me at once. I started to laugh. I splashed back at them and soon the water was churning white in all directions. I laughed harder than I had in a very long time.

Suddenly the male who splashed me first darted off and the rest followed. At first I thought they had tired of playing with me. Then he darted back and splashed me again. I splashed back, and he darted quickly away again. This happened twice more, and then, as he darted away the third time, he rose up in the water and called at me in the high chattering squeaks that sounded like laughing.

"Are you taunting me?" I asked him. He darted back, splashed and took off again. This time I went after him, and he swam even further and faster. I stopped, thinking I had scared it. But it stopped as well, then came back and splashed me again. I was bewildered for a moment. I watched his comrades looking for a clue to explain this behavior. They were darting quickly back and forth in the water, waiting for something. Then, all at once, it hit me.

"You want to race!" I realized. I wondered if it had any idea what a race with me would entail. I decided to play. The next time it came toward me, I splashed it before it could splash me and took off in the direction of his comrades. Instantly, the race was on. The dolphins pulled ahead of me, moving smoothly through the water. Not one to lose to an animal, no matter how smart, I put on some more speed and gained the lead again. To my surprise, the dolphins put on more speed as well and once again were winning this race to nowhere. I couldn't help smiling for an instant before sealing my lips against the salty water again.

Actually pushing myself a little, I pressed forward once again. The pod began falling behind, but not by much. Then I heard them start to jump in and out of the water. I slowed slightly to watch. The race had turned into a different game. They were trying, now, to best each other, jumping higher and turning this way and that before landing back into the water. I wasn't about to be left behind. Without a second thought, I sunk lower to gain some momentum, and then I used all my strength to streak toward the surface, aiming for a spot in the center of their midst.

I broke the surface and soared into the sky. Now I was really flying. At the peak of my jump I turned and spiraled back toward the ocean. I made six rotations before I sank below the surface. I immediately came up again, exhilaration written all over my face. I couldn't help but cry out from the joy and freedom of it. The pod was circling me, up on their tail fins chortling at me. I decided they were declaring me the winner and laughed, splashing at them. I continued to play with them for hours, until they became distracted by a school of fish, and I decided to head back for shore.

My original intention with this beach outing was to distract myself from my fixation with Nikki by isolating myself in the water to clear my head. Though I hadn't been isolated, and I was definitely not acting like myself, I had been distracted. I would have to do this again, soon.

Coming out of the water and onto the beach I saw that I was once again nowhere near my entry point. I smiled smugly at losing only a cheap pair of flip-flops instead of my favorite sandals. Across the street was a tourist shop. I stepped in and bought another pair. I shook my head with a smirk on my face, such a simple answer for something that had so perplexed me last time.

"Lose your … shoes?" The cashier asked me while staring at my still dripping chest.

"I'm afraid so," I replied. She pressed the keys on her machine without looking away. "You better hand me one of those, too," I said, motioning to one of the hideous T-shirts behind her. It was a cheap fabric, much rougher than I would normally wear, but at least I wouldn't be walking the streets half naked. And it would be just as disposable on my next trip as the foam sandals.

"If you say so," she said, handing me a bright yellow shirt with a turquoise shark that read, "San Francisco, C.A."

"Thanks," I said, handing her my card.

As I turned and put the shirt on while walking out the door, I heard her mutter, "Pity."

I walked through the city and was once again immersed in humanity. However, it was not quite as uncomfortable this time because I was not as naked. And I didn't have as many people staring blatantly at me. I think they were trying to avoid looking directly at my shirt. I had lived in this place long enough that all the buildings were familiar, but as I got closer and closer to my loft, I noticed something else. The people were familiar too.

That house was home to a divorced mother of three. This one belonged to a widower who hadn't had company in years. I was surprised by how much I knew about these mortals around me. I had observed far more than I thought while I was so earnestly ignoring them. I got to the last populated corner before the area my loft was in and passed the bum who served as sentinel. He had been there for at least a decade. I wondered briefly what his name was.

At home, I washed away the stink and filth easily. There was no mark left by mankind that could not be removed. They were all fleeting, temporary, which is why I had let all my observations of them go unnoticed. Standing there in the shower, watching the dirty water spiral down the drain, I realized what had happened, why Nikki had seemed to have such a strong effect on me.

I had gone decades without noticing humanity at all. When I started paying attention again, it was to one specific mortal. It was like I had closed the cover on a telescope until it was covered in dust. Then I had suddenly thrown it open and focused it tightly on one star. Of course I had been blinded. Now that I could see the rest of the sky, I would be able to put Nikki in her proper place.

Chapter Seventeen

$\mathcal{I}$ had given up any pretense of paying attention in class, and so Tuesday I spent the hour simply watching Nikki. I watched as she took notes. I chuckled quietly at her running commentary on Tony's bumbling lecture. I noticed she still didn't seem to mind having my undivided attention, though she pretended not to know.

After class I was ready to begin my quest to get Nikki talking. We left the building, and in my mind I ordered the questions I would ask once we were a little farther along the path.

However, two steps from the door, Nikki altered all my plans.

"I want to apologize," she said. I paused, midstep, for a millisecond.

"What did you say?" I asked, sure I had misheard her, superhuman hearing notwithstanding.

"I want to apologize," she repeated, "for what happened after class last Tuesday."

Her explanation only confused me more. "I don't understand."

She turned and studied my face for a moment as we continued walking. I was quiet, waiting for more explanation. The better I listened, the more she would talk. My silence was rewarded when she seemed to make a decision and spoke again.

"I can see you're not ready to talk about what happened, so I can't thank you for saving my life from," she glanced at me from the corner of her eye, and I could tell she chose her next words carefully, "someone only you could have saved me from."

She was quiet again as if to test her theory about my willingness to talk about the incident. I confirmed it by remaining quiet myself. She nodded in acceptance.

"So, I wanted to apologize for what happened after, for passing out like that." It was obvious she was embarrassed. This was ridiculous, witnessing what she had would have sent any normal person into shock. "I don't want you to think I was frightened."

I looked at her, my eyebrows raised a little.

"Well, yes, I was terrified, but not of you." She paused in her speech and her step to look me right in the eye, halting my movement as well. "I'm not scared of you," she said with conviction. It warmed my heart and chilled my spine at the same time, a most curious sensation.

"In fact, I think that's what got me into trouble in the first place," she admitted. Now she was finally making some sense. "I can usually avoid trouble. My 'Spidey-sense,' you know," she said tapping her temple. A brief smiled touched my lips.

"Last Tuesday I was … distracted. It was my friend's birthday. I had wanted to call him, but … it's a complicated friendship. I couldn't decide what the right thing to do was." She paused, refocusing her thoughts. "After class, I felt like something dangerous was following me, but I assumed it was you. I didn't notice the subtle difference in his motives until it was too late." By the end she was whispering, "I should have been paying better attention. I shouldn't have needed saving. So, I'm sorry."

I shook my head, surprised by her unorthodox logic. "Please, Nikki, don't be sorry. Everyone needs saving every now and then."

"I hate being a victim," she whispered, one hand coming up absently to rub her lightly dimpled cheek. This was definitely not the direction I had meant our conversation to go, but now I had a new question I hoped she would answer.

"What are they from?" I asked quietly.

"What?" she asked in response. Touching them had been automatic and unconscious.

"The scars on your face," I clarified simply. She flinched at my abruptness.

"It's a long story," she hedged.

"It's a long walk," I countered. She looked at my face, probably reading my earnest desire to know. She looked at her feet, and took a deep breath as if to steady herself. Then she began.

"When I was very young, a new family moved into our neighborhood. They had a little girl my age and I was so excited to have a new friend." She was speaking very softly, but I heard every word.

"How old is 'very young'?" I asked. I wanted to know everything. She glanced at me and smiled at my insistence for details.

"I was six," she clarified. "Her name was Kasha. She was quiet and sweet and we quickly became best friends. Our families got along as well. We shared dinners and had family activities together almost every weekend." As she was talking, her face softened and reflected the memories she was recalling. Then her smile fell and her eyes became pained.

"Sadly, not everyone appreciated our new neighbors. After about a month, even a child my age could see something was wrong. Kasha's parents were quieter, and they came to our house less and less." Nikki was quiet for a moment, lost in her own memories. I waited for her to go on, not wanting to intrude on her musings.

"Finally, I asked my mom why Kasha's family didn't come over anymore." She glanced up at me, trying to gauge my reaction again. "She told me they felt safer at home. I didn't understand what she meant, but I was still allowed to see my friend, so I didn't press for an explanation." I could tell she was leaving some crucial bit of information out. There was obviously something off about the situation, but I kept my questions to myself for once and let her tell her story.

"Then the calls started," she continued. "My mom and dad began letting the phone ring and ring and ring before they would answer it. I could tell the people calling were angry, but I couldn't think of what my parents would have done wrong." As we passed a bench, she sat down. I remained standing.

"Once again, I asked my mom what was going on. She was hesitant to explain at first, but she and my father decided I should know. Apparently, there were people who didn't like Kasha's family. So much so, that it made them angry that my family was nice to them." Nikki looked up into my face. "Kasha's family was black. I had never known racism before. Even after my parents tried to explain it, I didn't understand. I still don't, really." She looked back down at her delicate hands as she said this. There was a look of deep sorrow in her usually buoyant eyes. It felt so wrong to see them like that.

"One night, I was playing with Kasha in their living room. There was a great big picture window." Her face was once again lost in her memories as she looked into the past. This time I could see it was not a pleasant sight. "I was so young that when the crash came it was natural for me to look toward the sound. My face was sprayed with shattered glass," she paused and her voice became even softer, so that even I had to strain to hear. "The brick hit Kasha in the head. She died instantly."

My eyes went wide. I had been expecting something along these lines as her story had progressed, but nothing so tragic. I couldn't imagine someone as loving and kind as Nikki being witness to something so horrific. I wanted to reach out and touch her, to hold her and make the pain in her face go away.

I mentally checked myself. Why would a killer holding her make her feel better, less afraid? I remained where I was, watching as she struggled to compose herself. A few tears escaped and left trails that glistened in the light of the street lamp behind me. Its incandescent light somehow made her blond hair glow, and sitting before me was a weeping angel. Finally, I couldn't take it anymore. I reached one hand out to her, but she spoke again and I let it drop back. She never even saw it move.

"Kasha's family moved away right after the funeral. I was in the hospital and couldn't go. I felt like, when she really needed me to show people I loved her, I couldn't," she whispered.

"It wasn't your fault you were in the hospital," I said, my need to somehow comfort her overwhelming my ability to remain silent.

She rewarded me with a sad smile. "I know that now. But then I was too young to know much of anything. When I finally did go home, my mother hid all the mirrors in the house." I held my breath. The scars must have been truly terrible for her to resort to such drastic measures. "But I found one," she continued. "I went into my mother's purse and found her compact. Then I saw the scars. I dropped my mother's mirror, breaking it, and ran to my room. I threw myself onto my bed and wept for hours. My mother found the mirror and realized what had happened." Nikki stopped and looked up at me with emotion in her eyes. I wondered if she still saw her scars as they were then, if she didn't realize how much they had faded over time. I took a step towards her, but didn't want to interrupt the spell her memories were casting.

"My mother told me that I was still me, still her beautiful baby. Something terrible had happened, but nothing about our family had changed. We still had each other and that was a blessing I should try to see." Nikki's blue eyes turned hard and fierce, I could see strength that had nothing to do with physical superiority.

"I decided I had a choice to make. I could let what those people did change me, or I could refuse to let them win. There are horrible and terrifying evils in this world that one must be wary of." She looked me directly in the eye. I was once again left feeling like she could see my very soul. "Knowing that, we can either choose to see the world as dark and frightening, or beautiful and wondrous. I choose to cherish the things that are beautiful. Every time I do, I honor Kasha's memory." Now her brilliant smile returned to her face, making it shine in the dark. "And every time I share that beauty with someone, the people who hurt her lose all over again."

I stood, staring at her for a long while. I had thought Nikki was unusual before. Now I could see she was extraordinary. I was sure I could never explain to her how much it meant that she would share that story with me. I understood so much more now. Finally she sighed and her lips turned up in a smirk. I realized she was smiling at me for my "bad habit" of staring.

My lips twitched a smile in return, and I simply said, "I see." She stood up and we walked the rest of the way to her house in a comfortable silence, the rest of my questions forgotten. At her house, I stayed on the walk as she went up the front steps.

"Until Thursday," I said, giving her a small wave.

She smiled a knowing little smile and replied, "Yes, Gregory. I'll see you Thursday." She turned and walked into the house, leaving me once again with the impression that she had meant more than she said.

The next morning, Nikki was up early and headed to class on campus. I was still slightly in shock from her tragic story the night before. How could someone so sensitive even survive that sort of event? And yet, as I watched her interact with her friends while walking from one class to another, she seemed fine, completely well-adjusted.

I shifted my focus from Nikki to the people around her, remembering my goal of placing her among the rest of humanity. I saw faces light up as she entered a room. Every mortal she came in contact with left with a smile, looking lighter somehow. At lunch she sat at a table full of young people, joking and carefree. A sweet warmth spread through me each time her boisterous laugh rang out.

A girl ran though the room and out the far door. I could smell the salt of her tears from where I stood. She went unnoticed by everyone but Nikki, who politely excused herself and went after the weeping girl. I followed them through the exit.

The girl had gotten across a large expanse of grass before Nikki caught up to her. I couldn't get any closer without exposing myself. The noise of hundreds of students bustling back and forth kept me from hearing well, but I could see them clearly.

The girl was obviously distraught, gesticulating wildly with her arms while she spoke. Nikki was calm and compassionate, first helping the girl to calm down, then putting her arms around her when she broke down into tears again. Nikki began whispering in her ear. I cursed under my breath for not being able to hear. The girl gradually began to calm down, and then to my astonishment, she laughed. Nikki let her go and smiled benevolently at her. They each made a few more comments, and then they split up, heading in opposite directions.

The thing that astonished me most was the look about them. As they walked away, they wore matching countenances that shone like the sun. Having observed enough to make my mind spin, I headed home to add this day to my journal about Nikki.

After describing the extraordinary encounter in detail, I decided to attempt another drawing of Nikki. Using oil pastels this time, I hoped the vibrant colors would capture her better. In the end, I was left staring at the image of Nikki with her head thrown back in laughter. I was close. Just not close enough. There was more to her than this.

As I pondered that thought, I was drawn again to the effect she'd had on the weeping girl today. She had gone from despondent to radiant in a matter of minutes.

"As we let our own light shine, we unconsciously give other people permission to do the same." Nikki's voice floated through my mind. Her light was bright enough to catch my attention, and she had certainly taught that other girl to shine. Would it be possible for her to do the same for me?

I had spent most of my very long life imitating the humans around me. Observing and mirroring their behaviors, so as not to be noticed. Even my writing was only a reflection of what I had seen, nothing I had actually experienced. I was as the moon, stealing light and claiming it as my own. Could the sun teach even the moon to shine?

I put the notebook aside and went to lie down on my bed. I needed to know Nikki, but I now found myself needing her to know me, as well. Would it be possible for me to share myself with her, while keeping the nature of my existence a secret? It would be a difficult line to walk, a dangerous game to play. It was irresponsible to even entertain the thought.

I stood up and turned off the lights. I would rest for a time before tomorrow night's class and my next encounter with Nikki. But as my body relaxed, my mind continued to whirl with possibilities.

Chapter Eighteen

We left class Thursday night and strolled together across campus. It already seemed like we had been doing this for months, instead of weeks. Nikki seemed hesitant to start the conversation, and I realized I had no idea where to begin. There was so much I wanted to ask, and so much I couldn't say. So we were silent, but even that was somehow comfortably familiar.

She was right beside me, matching my stride. Every few minutes a breeze would touch her hair, and I would get a new dose of her scent washing over me. As we walked, I discovered an overwhelming urge to touch her, to draw her even nearer to me. This was in direct contradiction to my ever present desire to keep her safe. The two feelings should not coexist where humans are concerned.

When we reached the bench from Tuesday night, she sat down again. This time, I sat beside her and was closer than I had meant to be. Yet I couldn't bring myself to move away from her.

A gentle breeze floated over and past us, again stirring her hair. A strand of it was captured by her full lips. It tickled them and they twitched slightly. Once again I found myself unable to keep from staring at her. She was looking down into her hands, as if searching for something. Her lips twitched again, and I realized she didn't know there was a hair there, causing the discomfort. I smiled at her innocent beauty. Without thinking, I reached out and drew a finger down the side of her face, freeing the errant hair from her mouth. We both gasped at the unexpected sensation it brought.

"I'm sorry," I apologized, thinking I had scared her. "That was inappropriate." *Most inappropriate*, I thought.

"No!" she cried, enforcing my poor behavior. "I want you to touch me."

I stared at her, incredulous. Surely she wasn't saying what I thought she was saying.

"What I meant to say is," she said in a softer voice, embarrassed by her outburst, "I don't think it's inappropriate for you to touch me." She smiled shyly at me, her Cupid's bow mouth turning up adorably. "I told you the first day of class, I have a notoriously small personal space," she reminded me. I wondered why she brought it up.

"I'm used to a lot of touching, actually. Generally initiated by me." She looked into my eyes. "I could sense your discomfort, though, so I restrained myself. I assumed you would let me into your space when you were ready." She looked back into her lap again. "But you didn't, and I started to feel like you must think I have some sort of infectious disease or something."

I was stunned by her words. I had thought I was protecting her by keeping my distance. Instead, I had made her feel like I thought she was a monster. I mentally berated myself for being such an idiot, then I reached out and took her slender hand in mine. She looked up at me in surprise, her sapphire eyes searching mine for the truth.

"I don't think you're diseased," I said softly. "Infectious, yes, but diseased, no." I smiled and gently touched her face with my other hand. She closed her eyes. "My fear of touching you has nothing to do with you and everything to do with me," I explained.

She opened her eyes and reached up, covering my hand with her own. "Because you're dangerous." It was a statement, not a question.

"Yes," I whispered.

"Do you want to hurt me?" she asked.

"Of course not," I replied.

"Then you won't," she said, beaming at me as if it were as simple as that.

But it wasn't that simple, not by a long shot. I smiled in return briefly, then stood up, reclaiming my hands. "We'd better get you home."

Her beautiful smile fell, and she sighed sadly. "Yes, before I turn into a pumpkin." For a second I was puzzled. Then the meaning of her words struck me. She thought her time with me was a fairytale.

I smiled at her abstruse comment as well as the effect it had on me. I had the irrational urge to make sure she got her happy ending. But how could I do that and still keep her safe? It was not only danger from me that she faced. The more she knew, the more she was a threat to any of my kind. I searched silently for ideas until we got to Nikki's door. By then I was desperate to see her smile again.

"Can I see you tomorrow?" I asked as she turned the knob on her door.

She turned around, keeping her hand on the door. "I have to work tomorrow," she replied. My face fell in disappointment. Then, that all too familiar little smile that said "I know more than you think I know" came to her lips. "But I wouldn't be surprised if my favorite stalker happened to show up there as well." She pierced me through with those blue eyes and added, "again." Then she turned and walked into her house, shutting the door behind her and leaving me, once again, speechless.

I couldn't bring myself to spy on her bedtime routine after she so blatantly hinted at knowing when I was watching her, so I went home. I also waited until I knew she would be at work before returning the next morning to see her at the library.

Once I was there, I was inexplicably struck with anxiety. Instead of just walking right up to her, I fell into my habit of watching her work. She had pulled her hair up again, giving me the full view of her face. I was entranced as she made notes about the books she was working on, occasionally nibbling on the end of her pen. Eventually, she got up and put the books on a giant rolling cart. She pushed it around the library, re-shelving them.

After several books were put back, she paused, looking at the book in her hand. Then she smiled, laid it down flat on the shelf, and walked away. I was puzzled. Obviously she hadn't put it in its proper place. But she was meticulous about the other books, even shuffling some of the still shelved ones around to keep them in order. I walked over to the book and picked it up. *The Witches of Eastwick.* Why would she have left this here? Not wanting to lose track of her, I moved on, taking the book with me.

I caught up to her quickly and stopped at the end of the row she was on. She re-shelved a few books and then, with deliberate movements, she laid another book flat on the shelf. When she left, I quickly went to pick it up. *Frankenstein.* Could she be mocking me in some way?

Two rows down I caught up to her and, once again, she took a book from the cart and put it flat on the shelf. *The Wolf Within.* It was actually a self-help book for aggressive men, but I could see what she was getting at—werewolf. She was teasing me. She knew there was more to me than I'd admit, so she was taking wild guesses.

I waited for her to leave more books for me to find, highly amused now that I knew the game. But she didn't leave any more books until her cart was almost empty. Then she walked down an aisle and instead of taking a book from the cart, she began searching along the shelf. Finding what she wanted, she pulled the book from its place and laid it flat.

Now I was really curious. This wasn't a book she had seen and simply thought would amuse me. She had sought this one out and wanted me to see it. I strode over and picked it up. *Dracula*. I nearly dropped it. She wasn't guessing anymore. She knew, and she wanted me to validate it.

To really drive her point home, the next two books she left for me, both of which she had to pull from the shelves, were two of my own books. One of Martha's and one of Mack's. She knew. She knew everything. And she wanted me to admit it. But even as I swallowed the lump in my throat at being found out, I had to smile.

By leaving these books for me, she was telling me she knew, but she was also telling me I didn't have to talk about it. By not asking me directly, she was giving me a way out. And because she had given me the choice, I couldn't take it, at least not completely. I couldn't give her the entire truth, but I could give her something.

Taking the bundle of books with me, I went and sat at a table clearly visible from her desk. Then I divided them into two stacks, putting one on either side of me. When Nikki returned with her empty cart, she saw me and immediately walked over.

"What a coincidence!" she said, smiling brightly at me. "Imagine seeing you here at the library, and just when I happen to be working. Why haven't I seen you here before?"

"Generally, I just buy the books I want to read," I replied, chuckling at her sarcasm. "But I heard one of the librarians was a hottie, so I decided to come check her out." Rob would have been proud.

Nikki smirked at my lame line, as I had expected. "Maybe, if you're really smooth, she'll let you walk her home." I waggled my eyebrows at her and she laughed. "I see you found a few books to look at?" she asked, indicating my stacks.

"They were recommended by a friend of mine," I replied cryptically.

"And what do you think of them?" she pressed.

"I think they are all works of fiction," I informed her. She pursed her lips slightly; it was not the reply she was hoping for. "But that these are closest to the truth," I finished, pushing forward the stack that included my two books and *Dracula*.

Her shining smile returned. "I've heard those are pretty good."

"Why don't you have classes on Fridays?" I asked spontaneously, ready to change the subject.

She saw right through my tactic, but answered me anyway. "My Monday, Wednesday, Friday classes are all lit classes. And they all happen to be taught by professors that think I'm brilliant." She winked at me, and my heart beat, catching me by surprise. "I explained to them that I need to work to make money for things like food and electricity. They agreed to let me take off Fridays as long as I didn't fall behind."

Her professors sounded like reasonable men. Either that or they had also fallen prey to Nikki's charm. I smiled again. "What time are you done with work?" I asked as if I didn't know.

She rolled her eyes at my continuing denial of stalking her and answered, "Well, I usually get off at six, but I'm getting off early because I promised to meet Rich for dinner later..."

"Don't let me keep you then," I said abruptly cutting her off. Hearing that she had plans with Rich was disturbingly unsettling.

"That's not how I meant it," she tried, but I cut her off again.

"I wouldn't want to give him the wrong impression when he came to pick you up," I said snidely. Why had she all but told me to ask to walk her home if she was meeting Rich?

"I said I was meeting him for dinner, not that he was picking me up for a date," she corrected me, her tone cool and calm. It irritated me further.

"Don't let me keep you," I said again.

"I have to stay at work until five," she said, sounding like she was trying to explain it to a five-year-old, which is how I was behaving. I closed my eyes, feeling like a complete idiot. Why was I constantly making a fool of myself in front of this woman?

"Then I'll leave you to it," I said standing up fast enough that I had to grab the back of my chair to keep it from falling over. "I'm sorry for disrupting your day."

I left, leaving Nikki standing there looking confused and irritated. I was pretty confused and irritated myself. What had just happened? I needed to get some perspective, and quick. I ran, at mortal speed due to the daylight, to the first place I thought of.

Once I got there, however, I wasn't sure it was the best idea. I had yet to have a satisfying encounter here. I hesitated outside the door. But there was nowhere else to go. I couldn't exactly go to a bar and cry into my beer while telling my sorrows to the bartender. I wasn't even sure what my sorrows were anymore.

Just as I decided to go home and collect myself, Lance called from inside, "Come in or go away already! You're starting to give Rob the creeps!"

Sighing in defeat, I opened the door and stepped in. I was slightly disappointed to see Jenny once again draped over Rob as the boys virtually battled each other. Her brand of honesty wasn't what I wanted right now.

"You seem to be here a lot lately, Jen," I noted.

"I could say the same thing about you, Greg," she retorted, smirking at me.

"How's Triple H?" Rob asked, giving me a you-know-what-I-mean look.

"She has a name, Rob," I snapped.

"Ooooh, someone has his panties all in a bunch," Jenny sassed.

"No offense intended, bro," Rob said contritely, adding, "How is our friend Nikki?" I was momentarily startled that he remembered her name. Then with a huff of air, I dropped into a leather reclining chair, all pretenses falling away.

"She's confusing," I admitted. Once again the game was quickly forgotten and I was the center of attention.

"You can't get any information out of her?" Lance asked. "Or you don't understand what she's telling you?"

I leaned my head back against the chair and put my hands over my face. "I mean I'm getting all kinds of information out of her and I don't understand the effect it's having on me." It was very quiet for a moment. I pushed the heels of my hands into my eyes. "I find myself telling her things I shouldn't."

"What things, exactly?" Lance asked tensely. I recounted the scene at the library. When I finished I rubbed my hands down my face and looked at the three Immortals before me. Rob was shocked. Lance was furious. Jenny I couldn't read.

"You have to kill her," Lance said quietly.

"*No!*" I yelled sitting up in my chair.

"There's no other choice now! She knows too much!" he yelled back at me, standing in front of my chair. I stood to face him, refusing to cower, though he was several inches taller than me.

"I will not kill her! And neither will you!" I challenged him.

"You want her," Rob said with a touch of awe.

"Don't be an idiot! She's human!" I said, turning away from Lance. "Besides, she has a human boy, *Rich*." I couldn't stop the sneer from escaping with his name.

Jenny took two steps, but I put my hand over her face before she could reach my neck. I was not getting sniffed like a dog tonight.

"You're jealous," she said through my fingers. Lance gauged the look on my face, the tenseness in my body.

"She's right," he said falling back onto the couch in surprise and defeat.

"Not to worry," Rob said lightly as Jenny delicately pried my hand from her face. "No way could a boy compare to a fine specimen of Immortality such as you."

"I do not want her," I insisted, giving Jenny a look daring her to try smelling me again. She smirked condescendingly at me and went back to lying in Rob's lap.

"Hey, there's no shame in dabbling in mortal women, Gregory." Rob waggled his eyebrows. "Some of them are right sexy beasts."

Jenny shot him daggers from her eyes and tightened the grip she had on his knee. He flinched, but smiled sweetly at her. "That is, of course, if you don't have the sweet miracle of being with a true sex goddess." She smiled at his flattery and patted the knee she had just nearly crushed.

"This is ridiculous," I said, shaking my head. "You're ridiculous!" I turned and strode quickly to the window.

"Gregory," Jenny called softly. The tone of her voice caused me to turn around. Her next words made me wish I hadn't. "Jealously is only a heartbeat away from love."

With an aggravated growl, I went out the window. Instead of going straight home, I began wandering the streets. They were familiar. I had lived in this city for a hundred years now. Long enough to see it change. But it wasn't really the city that changed. It was the people, the atmosphere. The streets and buildings were in the right places, but everything felt wrong. That's what fickle humanity does to things. It changes them.

CHAPTER NINETEEN

Lazarus paced back and forth across the rooftop, waiting for Guinevere to exit again. Following her was worthless. The only thing out of the ordinary here was her penchant for spending time with multiple male Immortals. He wondered if she was unnaturally attached to them, or if they had something to do with her work in finding The Prophecy. Perhaps he would learn more by following one of the males. He was ready to try anything to make some progress. He was desperate with longing for Queen Mother.

Chapter Twenty

As dawn began to lighten the sky Saturday morning, I entered my apartment. I closed the door behind me and immediately sighed in relief. This was one place humanity hadn't touched. The technology was updated and replaced from time to time, but it never really changed. This was my home. It was mine. It always felt the same.

Stripping down, I crawled into my soft, welcoming bed. I closed my eyes and willed my body to relax, to let go. I concentrated on relaxing the tension in each of my muscles and then concentrated on thinking about nothing at all. It worked for a while. Then my mind began to wander.

The darkness was vast. The heat was pressing in on me, pushing wet, suffocating air into my lungs. I couldn't hear another living soul. No one breathing, no heart beating. The silence was deafening. I began to run, searching. But there is nothing to find, no one to look for. There is only me. And I am completely alone. Forever.

I sat up gasping, the memory of humid air fresh in my mind and lungs. As I struggled to gain normal breath, I blinked in rapid succession trying to focus on something, anything. Finally realizing where I was, I reached over and pulled the chain on the bedside lamp. The soft glow was immediately comforting. Since when was I afraid of the dark? Since when did I have dreams of being trapped in oblivion? I shook my head, vigorously trying to get rid of the lingering dread. But wisps of the dream held tight like cobwebs you can feel but can't see.

What was wrong with me? Had I somehow ingested some new strain of disease that my body was still adjusting to? Wait, how long had it been since I ingested anything? More than a week, and I recalled the girl's blood had been purer than most. Perhaps all the stress had simply depleted my blood faster than usual. Nikki had certainly triggered my fight or flight response more than once.

I just needed to feed. Then I would be able to think straight. And I could get some fresh air as well. By the time I got to the beach, it would be dark enough to hunt, but not so late that it would be completely deserted. I dressed and a macabre thought came to me. The beach was often where lovers went to rendezvous. Perhaps I would find a couple that had lingered a little too long and catch two birds with one stone, as they say. I knew I wasn't really that thirsty, but it still seemed a fine idea.

Once at the beach, I began stalking in the moonlit sand, and soon came upon two mortals. The male had dark hair, his female was blond, or rather pretending to be with an overdose of peroxide. They had covered themselves with a blanket, but it was still obvious that they were … occupied. I wouldn't even have to try to be quiet.

I could see something familiar in the male. In fact, he could be Rich's doppelganger. My lip unconsciously drew up into a sneer as I came closer to the edge of the blanket. Just as I tensed to pounce, the female tossed her blond hair. It broke my concentration and suddenly in my mind's eye, I was watching Rich and Nikki. Sighing, and kissing, and touching.

And then it was me, whispering into Nikki's ear, her soft hair in my hands, her warm mouth on my neck, her delicate hands …

"Dude! Do you like, mind?" The present came rushing back like a gale of wind with the voice of the male yelling at me. They had noticed me standing at the edge of the blanket.

Without answering, I turned and ran up the beach, the girl's voice following me, "What a, like, total perv!"

As I put physical distance between me and the debacle that had just happened, I tried to explain it mentally. I couldn't. Other than it was obvious my interactions with Nikki were far from healthy. Maybe Lance was right. Perhaps enough was enough.

I tried to convince myself I believed that. That getting rid of Nikki and getting back to normal was what needed to be done, then I heard a heartbeat coming. A female jogger that was out much too late. She should know better.

I turned my pace into a jog as well, to look less suspicious. As she came to me, I could see the bulge her mace was making in her pocket. She probably thought it would protect her. I would have to pin her arms down to keep her from using it. My vision would clear in seconds instead of debilitating me like it would a mortal, but it would still sting like hell.

I smiled and waved slightly as she was about to pass me. She returned the smile as we came side by side. Then I had my arms locked around her and she was bent over with her back pressed against my knee. I made the mistake of looking into her face. It was filled with terror and confusion.

It was the same look Nikki had when looking up at the Immortal that would have killed her. The memory hit my gut like a freight train and before I could snap back, the girl was screaming. My instinct should have been to rip out her throat, ending the sound and completing my goal. Instead, I dropped her into the sand, jumping back as if she had burned me. She scrambled backwards, continuing to scream. I turned and ran again.

This time I ran toward the street. I flew through the city. It took all my effort not to move faster than I should. Each time I nearly gave in, I would pass someone. This man could be Nikki's father. That girl could be her best friend. She could have sisters, brothers. Everywhere I turned, Nikki was staring back at me from the face of humanity. Finally, I gave in and took to the rooftops, leaping from building to building. I had to get home. Back to where the sky was up, the earth was down, and I was a blood-sucking Immortal.

I burst into my loft like the whirlwind I could feel churning inside me. I slammed the door, shaking the frame. My gaze was automatically drawn to the journal sitting on my desk. My fury suddenly had a focus. I snatched it up and threw it forcefully against the opposite wall. It bounced off, knocking several books to the floor and skidded halfway back to me.

In two long strides, I took it in my hands, ready to rip it to shreds. My fingers tightened on its covers, the tendons in my forearms straining. I took a deep breath and then…I stopped. I couldn't do it. After so many years of treasuring the world's literature, I couldn't destroy a book. Not even one that had infected me like a plague.

Instead, I turned it over in my hands, studying the outside. It certainly didn't look like the fourth horseman of the apocalypse. It looked like every other book I had on my shelves. That's how I should be treating it. I had become too emotionally wrapped up in the study of this human, Nikki. I shook my head as the thought echoed back…I had become emotionally involved. Obviously my writing had become tainted. That didn't mean my reading had to be. Nikki said she could tell a lot about an author by their work. Perhaps I could learn something about myself by reading the first true story I had ever written.

I took the tome and went to my rooftop. The night was clear, the air crisp. The stars and full moon gave me more than enough light to read by. I sat with my back against the wall, the book resting on my knees. This time I would not just be reading about Nikki. I would be reading how I had written about her.

I immediately saw words fraught with emotion, the kind I hadn't used for decades, centuries even, before I had meet Nikki; singularly the most infuriating…intriguing…unique…precious person. There was a similar pattern in how I described her features: eyes of crystal blue, captivating, pools of liquid sapphire; rose petal pink lips, sensuously innocent, perfect; hair like captured sunshine, soft curls bouncing, jasmine scented heaven; skin smooth as ivory, soft as satin, would taste like almonds.

These were words and phrases I had heard before. I had even used them myself in some of my books, but I had never known them as truth. I cautiously turned through the pages of portraits I had done of Nikki; the first time we met, watching her sleep, hearing her laugh. They were the same as the "notes" I had taken. The entire journal was the work of a man in love.

In love.

The realization lit up my soul like I was seeing the sun for the first time. "I'm in love," I murmured. Hearing the words from my own mouth spread warmth through my every pore, every atom in my being coming alive with fire. I had been in existence for millennia, and I was just now waking up to life. I was reborn into a world full of color, light, sounds, tastes, and, most overwhelming, feelings.

"I'm in love!" I shouted, leaping to my feet and calling to the moon. Suddenly there was meaning, there was purpose. I had not only the ability to live, but a reason to. And it was all because of Nikki.

Nikki. Just thinking her name brought a smile to my lips. I had to tell her. I had to tell her *everything*.

As I ran to Nikki's house, the sky darkened and then began to clean the city with life-giving rain. I laughed as it fell upon my face. When I arrived, I slid open her bedroom window and crawled in without a second thought.

In the darkness I could see Nikki's sleeping form. She lay sprawled across the bed, her covers twisted in disarray. It looked like she hadn't been sleeping well. Lightning flashed, followed almost immediately by a loud crash of thunder. Nikki stirred and rolled over, one arm falling over the side of the bed and her hair falling over her face.

Silently, I walked over and knelt beside her bed. Needing desperately to see her, I reached out and gently moved her hair, laying it behind her. Her eyes fluttered open, inches from my own. I froze.

I suddenly realized what I had done. I'd broken into her house in the middle of the night and was now kneeling beside her bed. I held my breath and waited for her to start screaming, perhaps even throw things.

"Mmmmm," she sighed. "Hello, Gregory." Hearing my name from her lips brought a grin to my own.

"Hello, Nikki," I whispered in return. She blinked dreamily at me, and I wondered if she was really awake.

Then Nikki rolled onto her back and reached over to the lamp by her bed. She closed her eyes against the light as she turned it on. Looking back at me, she opened them one at a time, still trying to wake up.

"You're wet," she said with her brow creased in confusion.

"What?" I asked. Most of my mind was still braced against screaming and flying objects.

"You're all wet," she said lazily waving a hand up and down at me. "Is it raining?"

"Oh!" I said, realizing now that I had left her window wide open. I turned and quickly shut it, but the floor was already drenched, adding to the mess I had made by dripping on it. "Yes, it's raining. Sorry about the carpet."

She yawned and smiled brightly at me. "Don't worry about it. I'll just send you the cleaning bill."

"You do that," I said, returning her smile. "What were you thinking leaving your window unlocked like that anyway?" I asked. "It's like you were just waiting for some psychotic monster to come murder you in your sleep."

"I'm pretty sure any psycho trying to sneak up on me would have their hands full with you," she retorted. "Besides, if I locked the window, how would you sneak in every night to watch me sleep?"

"I'm not here every night," I said, my stomach lurching at the thought of her being so vulnerable while she slept.

"I know that," she stated.

"And I've never actually come inside to watch you sleep," I added.

"Really?" she almost sounded disappointed.

"Really," I answered, leaving out the fact that I had been in her house, just not while she was asleep.

"Huh, and here I thought you were a first class stalker," she said, shaking her head and tsking me with her tongue in disappointment. I laughed, but couldn't let it go.

"Seriously, Nikki, you need to lock your windows and doors at night. Bad things happen in the world today," I insisted, probably sounding like her father. Not what I was going for at the moment.

Nikki sighed. "That's why I left it unlocked."

"What?" I asked, a little too loudly. "You want something bad to happen?"

"No! That's not what I meant!" She sat up in bed, then looked down. Her hands began to pick at the edge of her comforter. She closed her eyes and bit her lips as if trying to resolve herself to something. Then she looked up at me. "If I tell you something crazy, will you promise not to laugh at me?"

The earnest look in her clear blue eyes left me weak in the knees, and I could barely speak. "Of course," I whispered.

Without breaking eye contact, she began to speak softly. "Since the second week of class, I started getting this feeling when I would walk home." She was choosing her words carefully, knowing I wouldn't freely admit too much. "I've always been able to sense danger, so I could avoid it. But this feeling was different. It didn't feel like something I should avoid, or turn away from." She was watching my face intently, so I kept it a careful mask, not knowing what reaction she was looking for. "It felt safe. No, more than that, I felt protected. It followed me from school every Tuesday and Thursday night. And then I felt it other days as well. But it always stopped at my door. And then I would be alone again." She took a deep breath and gazed so deep into my eyes I was sure she could see my soul, if I only had one.

"I wanted it to follow me home, to come inside with me." My breath stopped, but I took an involuntary step toward her bed. With my movement something solidified in her eyes. "I wanted you to come inside, Gregory. I know when you're following me because you make me feel safe and protected. You feel like home in a world where bad things happen."

I was speechless. Part of me was still soaring. I make her feel safe. She wants me here with her. But the rest of me had become grounded by reality. I had come to tell her everything. I realized now that I couldn't. Not if I wanted to keep her safe. The more she knew about what I was, the more danger I put her in. I watched as a single glistening tear rolled down her cheek, and realized I'd been silent too long. I could at least tell her part of the truth.

"Nikki, I came here to tell you something," I said softly, taking one more step toward her bed. Her eyes were wide with anticipation. "You say I make you feel safe, that I feel like home." My voice caught in the emotion the phrase brought with it. "You talk about it like everyone knows what it is to feel as deeply as you do about life and everything in it. When the truth is, Nikki, I haven't felt anything for a very, very long time." Nikki's eyes were filling with tears and her bottom lip was trembling as she continued to bite it.

"And then I met you," I said, smiling down at her. "And suddenly the world was alive with emotions. Confusion, Irritation, Anger, Jealously, Joy, Love; they were coming at me from all sides and I never had a chance."

"Did you just say love?" Nikki asked, interrupting my rant.

My smile grew. "Yes, I did. Nikki Christian, I love you, with every atom of my being."

"Greg—," she started but I was kneeling by her bed with a finger to her lips before she could continue.

"Please don't, Nikki," I said. She nodded but looked confused. "I don't think I could stand it just now if you told me you didn't love me. But the truth is you don't know anything about who or what I am, so even if you said you do, I couldn't believe you. As much as I'd want to," I whispered, gently drawing my finger along her lips as I pulled it away and stepped back again.

"I just want, no I *need* you to know how I feel, to know that I would do anything for you, Nikki, to keep you safe, to make you happy." I was nagged briefly by the thought that the two may not always be compatible.

Nikki crossed her arms and narrowed her eyes. It was not the response I had been expecting. "Let me get this straight," she said, clearly irritated. "You get to break into my house, tell me that I've changed your life, that you love me, and I'm not allowed to say anything about it?"

"That sounds about right, yes," I replied. I couldn't help but smile at her. She was adorable when she was irritated.

"Doesn't exactly sound fair," she pouted, which was even cuter than irritated.

"Tell you what," I consoled her. "Next time you break into my house, you can be in charge." She rolled her eyes at me. "Speaking of breaking in, you really do need to keep your window locked at night."

She gave me an appraising look and I could tell she was plotting something. "I'll make you a deal," she offered.

"What kind of deal?" I asked hesitantly.

"I will promise to keep my doors and windows securely locked, if *you* promise that you will still let yourself in the next time you feel the need to visit at—" She glanced at the clock. "—three in the morning. I'll even give you a key."

"I know where you keep the spare," I said without thinking. She raised her eyebrows at me. "I said I had never come inside to watch you sleep, not that I had never been inside," I defended myself.

She smiled, but was quickly serious again. "Promise?"

"Nikki, I shouldn't have come this late in the first place," I said. "A normal person would come by during the day."

"I can't believe you just compared yourself to a normal person," she teased. "A fairly odd sentiment coming from a fairly accomplished stalker. Promise me you will let yourself in no matter what time it is, or I'll just end up leaving the windows unlocked in the hopes that the maniac crawling through is you."

I gave in, laughing. "Fine, I promise."

"You promise what?" she insisted.

"I promise to let myself in with the key you have hidden behind the sunshine sculpture hanging outside your front door whenever I feel so inclined, no matter the time, day or night," I said with a smirk.

My thorough promise finally got her to laugh again. "Thank you, and I promise to keep my windows locked," she agreed. "Though, if it's during the day, you could probably just knock."

"What fun would that be?" I asked with an innocent face. She laughed again. "Make sure you lock this behind me," I said, turning to go.

"Wait? Why are you leaving?" she cried. Then, embarrassed by her outburst, she finished, "You just got here."

"But as you pointed out, it's three in the morning, and being the fairly accomplished stalker I am, I know you have places to go on Sunday."

She smirked at me. "So you just came to love me and leave me?" she quipped.

I laughed. "Something like that, yes."

"I thought you'd do anything to help me," she said, smirking again.

"And you need help with?" I asked, my mind filling with a thousand things I would love to help her with, none of which I should.

"Well, you come in here, finally filling the place with that warm and cozy 'homey' feeling I was telling you about and now you're going to take it with you when you leave. It'll be all frigid and lonely in here by comparison. I'll never get back to sleep," she said. I wasn't sure where she was going with this.

"And so … You want me to help you sleep?" I asked.

"Yep," she replied.

"How, exactly?"

"You're the wizard of words aren't you? Mr. I've-been-a-best-selling-author-not-once-but-twice," she smiled at me, her eyes twinkling in the dim light. "Tell me a bedtime story."

I stared at her, which she was probably getting used to by now. "Are you serious?" I asked.

"Absolutely."

"All right, if you're sure," I relented.

She clapped her hands and scooted over in her bed to make room for me.

"Oh no, I'm not getting your bed as wet as your floor," I insisted. I smiled at the disappointed look on her face. "Wait there," I commanded. In a flash I was back, placing a chair by her bed.

"Is that the folding chair I keep stored in my closet?" Nikki asked.

"Yes, I didn't want to ruin the wooden ones in the kitchen, or risk your research by walking past it to get to the one in your den," I explained.

Nikki raised her eyebrows. "That definitely takes you past fairly accomplished and into the mad skills arena of stalking."

"I am very sneaky," I replied. She rewarded me with a laugh. "What kind of story would you like?"

She thought for a moment. "Tell me a true story," she said, innocent of the burden it placed on me.

"I'm not used to telling stories that are true," I hedged, trying to think of something I could tell her. Then I thought of the perfect story. It was true, it was ancient, and it had nothing to do with me. "Once upon a time," I began.

"True stories don't start with 'once upon a time,'" Nikki argued.

"They do when they're bedtime stories," I countered. She held her peace. I began again. "Once upon a time, there was a warrior. He was a most noble and fierce Samurai. He was trained very young and fought very well. He rose quickly in rank and honor. The time came when he was noticed by even the Emperor himself. He was chosen to be among the escort for the Emperor's youngest daughter as she traveled across the country to meet the man her father had agreed she would marry."

"Oooooh, I know where this is going!" Nikki whispered excitedly.

"Shhhh!" I scolded. "You're supposed to be going to sleep." She quickly lay down and closed her eyes. Then she opened one to peek at me. I laughed, but continued on.

I told her how, as the months of traveling passed, he fell in love with the princess, though he could never speak directly to her, or even look into her eyes. Then, when there was only a week left before they arrived and he would never see her again, he resolved to tell her. She had to know how he felt. He came to her that night in her tent and declared his love, expecting to be put to death for it. Instead she begged him to flee into the mountains, and to take her with him.

It was at this point I heard Nikki's breathing relax and her heartbeat change almost imperceptibly. She was asleep, or very close to it. I got up and put the chair away. I locked her bedroom window and made sure the rest of the windows were locked as well. Then I spent a few minutes watching Nikki sleep. Though the state of her sheets made it apparent she had been tossing and turning earlier, she seemed peaceful now.

I marveled at how easy it had been to tell her how I felt, how readily she'd accepted it. She was so open and honest, so trusting, even though her life could have made her a cynic. I loved her so much it ached. She said I felt like home. I knew that meant a lot to her, that she came from a warm, inviting home with a loving family. I had never known a home like that. But I knew about safe and protected. And I knew I would do anything to keep her from harm.

"Goodnight, Nikki," I whispered softly. "I love you." She sighed in her sleep and rolled toward the sound of my voice. I went out the front door and used the spare key to lock it behind me. As the first ray of sunlight came over the horizon, it touched a smile on my face I was beginning to think would never go away.

CHAPTER TWENTY-ONE

*S*unday night I was still flying high from my life-changing realization. I had to share it with the others. I rapped on the window and then impatiently opened it and entered without permission.

Lance and Jenny both jumped up, startled. Lance had already drawn his sword. Rob ended up on the floor after being dumped out of Jenny's lap. "Paranoid much?" He rolled his eyes at them.

"I have news for you," I said eagerly, even as I realized I wasn't sure if they would think it was good news, or bad.

"You've taken care of the mortal girl?" Lance asked with relief.

"I hope to," I answered cryptically. "For as long as she'll let me."

"What?" Lance asked, confused.

Jenny took two quick steps to me then paused, remembering my reaction to her last attempt to come near. I smiled and tilted my head to one side, offering her my neck. That made everyone's eyes bug out, but she seized the opportunity. Closing her eyes, she drew her nose from my shoulder to my ear, inhaling deeply. Then her eyes popped open and she gasped, backing up again.

"I didn't think... You really..." Her voice trailed off in shock. My smile grew.

"Dude, that look on your face is really starting to creep me out here," Rob said, looking from me to Jenny and back again. "A little help for those who aren't olfactory-enhanced?"

"I love her," I said bluntly.

"You what?" Lance asked, collapsing once again into his chair.

"I love the mortal, Nikki Christian," I repeated. It really felt good to say it out loud.

"Is that even possible for us?" Rob asked.

"Of course it's possible," Jenny said, her voice touched with awe. "At least I always hoped it possible. We can do everything else the mortals can do." She smiled at me. "Only better."

"Why are you telling us this?" Lance asked. His question struck me.

"Why wouldn't I be telling you this?" I asked peevishly.

"Oh, I don't know, maybe because you're breaking a few of the fairly important, if unwritten, laws of our society?" he responded.

"We don't have a 'society.' That would take people interacting with each other. We simply allow each other to live, provided we stay out of each other's way," I said snidely. "Besides, are you going to tattle on me?"

"Lance is only reminding you that you never know where the Queen has agents," Jenny said, trying to ease the tension.

"But he had to tell *us*," Rob said. "We already knew about Triple H, I mean Nikki. Besides, how totally uncool would it have been if we had accidentally made a meal of her?" Rob seized his chance to put in his request again. "Which is why he's going to let us finally meet her, right? So we can tell her apart from the other stock?"

I was most disturbed by Rob's comments, both because he was using them to defend me by comparing Nikki to cows, and because he actually had a point. "I'll think about it, Rob."

"He has a point, Gregory," Lance said. "What are you going to do? Watch her every second of every day?"

If that's what it takes to keep her safe, I thought. But before I could say it, Jenny spoke.

"He's going to convert her, of course," she said as if it were the simplest of things.

"Are you mad?" Lance yelled as I cried, "I most certainly will *not*!"

"Why not, Gregory? It makes perfect sense. If you love her, why not be with her forever instead of watching her grow old or die some horrible death?" she asked. The visions her words put in my mind chilled my soul.

"I will not bring her into our world, Jenny," I insisted. "To have her subject to the Queen? To make her into the blood-drinking monsters we are? It would change her very nature. She would never survive in a cold and heartless world like ours. Her humanity is what I love most about her."

The three of them just stared at me when I finished my little rant. Finally, Rob spoke, "All right, Gregory. She's your girl. We'll keep your secret."

I looked at the other two, who nodded mutely. "Thank you." I sighed in relief.

"You've changed, Gregory," Lance stated.

"Of course he's changed," Jenny commented. "He's in love."

"I, for one, think it's a good change," Rob added. "You're already a lot more fun to be around. I can't wait to see what Nikki can do for the rest of us."

I rolled my eyes at his choice of words, but smiled a little at his enthusiasm. I turned toward the window.

"Gregory," Jenny said, causing me to turn around. "Be careful with her."

"I will," I promised.

I was suddenly very tired. I wasn't used to the emotional roller coaster I was riding on. However much fun I was having, I needed to get off the ride, even if just for a little while. Back at my loft I showered and toweled off. Then I lay on my bed for some much needed down time. It was quiet and still.

It was so dark, and I could feel the air, thick and warm. I was afraid and looked wildly around me, thinking I was alone. But as I turned to my right, there was Nikki. Her face shone in the darkness, her eyes happy, her lips smiling. Then we heard the sound coming from the blackness. The content look on Nikki's face turned to one of absolute dread and fear. We took flight with the other animals running through the damp greenness, following them into the trees, wishing we could take flight, and I tried to keep Nikki safe. I pushed her up and up and up and away from the crashing limbs I could hear below us, but it was too late and it was here and I had to turn and face it. With a roar, I seized its great throat in my hands and snapped its neck, letting it fall to the ground, far below, then looking above me for Nikki. She was gone. I called for her, crying out into the darkness. I searched and searched, and finally I looked down. There on the forest floor lying utterly still by the body of the great cat was my Nikki. She was as white as death.

"No!!" I shouted, sitting up and fumbling for the light in my room. I shook my head, willing myself to get rid of the horrific image that had burned itself into the back of my retinas. It was a dream, just a dream. I kept repeating it to myself over and over.

After a while I was able to get my breathing back to normal. My heart rate had even sped up at the intensity of the dream. I knew it was a reaction to what the others had said. But the fact remained that they were right.

I was putting Nikki in danger simply by being near her. By allowing her to live and know I existed. But not being near her wasn't an option anymore. I couldn't live without being able to see her face, or hear her laugh. I needed her. I had never needed anyone or anything, but I needed her.

Nikki would want to know the truth. She would want to know all about me. But that wasn't possible. I had to keep Nikki as far from my world as possible. I could love her without exposing her to the ugliness that I came from, that I still had to live in. Couldn't I? A far more daunting question was, could Nikki love me if she didn't know the whole truth? And the most important, the one that I refused to even ask: could she love me if she did?

CHAPTER TWENTY-TWO

I had wanted to give Nikki some time to digest my late night confession before she had to see me again. The result was that my entire body was nearly buzzing with anticipation at seeing her again by the time Tuesday night came. Then, as I sat waiting for her to arrive, a sobering thought came. What if she didn't remember? It had been the middle of the night, and I had come and left while she was sleeping. Was it possible she wouldn't remember what happened in between?

Then, the scent of jasmine and almonds was carried in with the evening breeze. "Hey there, stalker-boy," Nikki said quietly as she sat down beside me.

"Hello, Nikki," it came out almost as a sigh of relief. She remembered, and she was smiling, a very good combination.

She tried very hard to pay attention to class. I was making no effort to pay attention to anything but her. Occasionally she would glance at me through the corner of her eyes. Invariably, I would be staring back at her, and a small smile would come to her perfect lips.

Once we were free of class and prying eyes and ears, Nikki began hesitantly.

"So, you played along with my game at the library." She looked at me to make sure I would admit it. I nodded once. I may not be able to tell her everything, but I wouldn't lie to her. "And you seem comfortable enough with me to break into my house in the middle of the night for a chat." I smirked at her description. "So, does that mean I can ask questions now?"

I was silent for a moment, contemplating how to answer. "Do you remember my telling you I wasn't used to telling true stories?" I asked.

"Yes," she answered, disappointed.

"I want to tell you the truth, Nikki, always, but some things are better left unknown." I paused, wanting to use the right words for her to understand. "Some truths are dangerous."

"I see," she whispered, staring down at her sneakers. The hopelessness being conveyed by her entire body broke me.

"Nikki." I sighed. "You can ask me anything you want. I'll always be truthful with you." The sudden change in her demeanor as she looked up at me, smiling brightly made me chuckle. "Just don't be upset if I tell you I can't answer."

"Sounds fair enough," she agreed. "True or false: you are both Martha Vinegross and Jerry Mack?"

"True," I answered without hesitation.

"Ha! I knew I wasn't crazy!" she said, pumping her fist in the air. I chuckled again. "Wait, that makes you … over a hundred years old?"

I laughed at the understatement. "Yes, very."

"Very over a hundred?" she questioned, raising her eyebrows. I nodded again, smiling. This game was getting too close, but she was just so eager.

"And you're not a wizard, or a werewolf, or a lab-grown monster?" she asked, already knowing the answer to that one.

"Correct again."

"But you are a being who lives for a really long time, is inhumanly beautiful, and dangerous to an innocent young woman like myself?"

I laughed again. "Aside from the 'inhumanly' part of beautiful, yes."

She looked at me incredulously. "Do you ever look in the mirror?"

"Actually, I don't very often," I answered honestly. "My reflection hasn't changed in so long, I don't see the need to."

"You have a reflection?" she asked, but when I really started to laugh, she retracted it. "Scratch that, apparently a stupid question. Do you know how green your eyes are?"

I was thrown off a bit by that one. "Green as the grass?" I asked lamely.

This time Nikki laughed. "I think not. Try taking all the emeralds in the world, and plant them in Ireland where they magically grow into glistening evergreens … Times ten."

I laughed. "A bit of a hyperbole, don't you think?"

"Maybe the times ten part," she acquiesced, "but I wasn't finished. The emerald encrusted isles are when you're happy. When you're angry, or annoyed," she smirked, recalling the many times she had annoyed me, "then they're more like a stormy sea that's been captured by an Amazon rainforest."

I shook my head at her ridiculous imagery. "And you say I am the wizard of words?" She smiled at me again, her blue eyes dancing with mirth.

"And your hair is like chocolate silk, and your skin is sun-kissed honey." She paused. "And now I've made you sound like a dessert."

"I admit, that's a first," I chuckled.

Slightly chagrined, she became serious again. "Okay, putting the subjective characteristic of beauty aside, that leaves us with a really old creature that preys on young women?"

I chuckled again. "Now you are getting too specific. I just happened to prefer young women." Then I stopped as we both realized what I had just said. So much for keeping the ugly side of my nature hidden.

"You're a vampire?" she asked innocently.

I smiled sardonically and paused for a moment before deciding to answer. "That is what humans call us, yes."

She, of course, picked up on my subtle inference.

"But you call yourselves something else?" She was nothing but curious, not a trace of fear.

"Yes," I said, still hesitant to tell her the complete truth. She was already in too much danger.

"What?" She looked at me with complete trust, and a desire to truly understand. How she could feel this way about me when she already knew so much of the truth, was incomprehensible. As she waited patiently for my response, I realized I would never be able to keep myself from her.

"We call ourselves, The Immortal," I answered, sealing both her Fate and my own.

"Immortal, as in you can't die?"

"Immortal, as in we don't age," I clarified.

"You're frozen in time?" she asked.

"Nothing so romantic; more like time has no meaning to us."

"But your body never changes?" she pressed. I sighed, knowing I was about to tell her much, much more than she should ever know.

"Actually, our bodies are in constant change," I corrected. She looked bewildered, watching me closely as if she could see what I was talking about. "We have regenerative powers that defy human understanding. We heal from every wound, and our body is constantly renewing itself, keeping all of its cells alive, rather than letting them die and casting them off."

"Wow," was her response. "So you're indestructible?"

"Not quite," I replied. "Bullets don't exactly bounce off my chest. They hurt like hell, in fact."

She smiled at my joke, but kept on. "But they wouldn't kill you?"

"No, my blood would heal me." I really should have been changing the subject.

"I know this will sound stupid, again, but what about sunlight? And silver crosses? And wooden stakes?" she asked with wide-open earnestness.

"Sunlight doesn't even give me a tan anymore. I'm not sure where silver crosses came from, that one's as bogus as not having reflections. And no, a stake through the heart wouldn't kill me," I responded to all her questions.

She peered at me closely. "You just edited something," she declared.

"Yes," I confessed, smirking. "But I was still honest."

She pouted a little, but let it go. "Okay, so you can get hurt, but you can't die, and you stay young forever?"

"Yes."

"You sound more like an elf than a vampire," Nikki stated in a scholarly tone, and I laughed. "Of the folklore variety, not the Santa variety," she clarified, making me laugh harder.

"I suppose there are some similarities between the legends of elves and vampires, which happen to apply to us."

"But you said I, as a human, would consider you a vampire," she noted. "Why not an elf?"

"Because from all the legends of what you consider to be fantastical creatures, there is one truth to the vampire legend that no other legend shares," I said quietly. "The most vital one."

"You have to drink human blood in order to survive," she stated. She kept her voice even, but I could still hear the tenseness in it, the tenseness in her whole body.

We continued toward her house in silence for a moment. "How often?" she finally asked. I glanced at her sideways. I really didn't want to be having this conversation.

"Every two weeks, more or less," I reluctantly replied. "Depending on how often I've had to push myself, or heal."

Nikki was quiet for another minute. Then she asked, "Is that the only downside?"

I was stunned into silence by her question. Then I thoughtlessly spat, "Is having to murder someone twice a month by sucking them dry the only downside to living for eternity?" I flinched the second the words were out of my mouth. So did Nikki.

"Yes."

I sighed deeply. What could I tell her? I wanted her to know me, but at what cost? She already knew I was a monster. Would it help or hinder to tell her just how dreary my existence was before her?

"Nikki, Immortality itself isn't really an upside," I started. She looked at me in surprise. "In the beginning, when everything is new, it seems wonderful. You have all the time in the world to do anything you want. It can be overwhelming and exhilarating all at once." I paused. "At least, that's what I'm told. It's been a very, very long time since my beginning."

We came to the steps of her house and I sat down heavily on them. I put my face in my hands and rubbed vigorously. Finally, I let one hand come to rest in my hair and tried to tell Nikki the truth. "How long have you lived in your grandmother's house?" I asked her.

"How did you know . . ." she started to ask, then dismissed it. "Four years."

"And before that, how often did you visit when your grandmother lived there?"

"At least once a week for as long as I can remember."

"So you are intimately familiar with it?"

"Yes."

"You know where every light switch is, every loose board, every chip in the wall?"

"I would suppose so."

"Because you've seen it so many times, you know it by heart."

"Yes."

I looked up at Nikki's eyes as they struggled to follow the point I was making. "Now, imagine you've seen the whole world that many times, Nikki. Every corner. Time and time again. Eventually, there's nothing left to see."

"But the familiarity of my Mam's house is part of what I love about it," she argued.

I smiled sadly at her limited understanding. "That's because, to you, it's still your Mam's house. Time has no effect on us, Nikki, but it continually erodes everything around us. People, places, everything fades away with time. How would you feel about your house a hundred years from now, when the block it's on is now an apartment building and has been for 20 years? When no one even remembers your Mam's house was ever there? After so long, Nikki, I've seen everything. The whole world is vaguely familiar, like déjà vu, only I've really been there before, a hundred times. Yet there is no consistency. Nothing to place value on that will last as time passes and human memories fade. The one constant in the world is that Immortals will continue to live, and mortals will continue to die."

I stood quickly and turned to go, trying to escape the futility of my own words. Nikki was right behind me, surprising me by reaching forward and catching my hand in hers, once again making my heart jump as I turned around to look at her.

"I understand, now," she whispered, her eyes capturing me in a gaze full of compassion. "You think time has no effect on you, Gregory, but it does. Instead of aging your body, causing wrinkles and decay, it's pulled you down in spirit. It's worn away the facets of a glittering soul until there was nothing left but a smooth, flat echo."

As her eyes continued to hold me captive in their grace, and her warm hands gripped mine tightly, I was stunned by her words.

"It's no wonder that your quote was Macbeth, Gregory, when the only thing you feel you have is a life full of tomorrows."

Reaching up, Nikki put her soft hand to my face, stroking my cheek. She smiled and my heart nearly burst. "But that's the best part of living. No matter how many yesterdays you've had, you never know what tomorrow will bring."

She walked up the steps, slowly letting go of my hand. "Just take a look at me. Yesterday I was an ordinary girl with an ordinary life. Today I have a love-struck vampire stalker-slash-protector." She got to her door and turned around with a bright smile. "Personally, I can't wait to see what happens tomorrow," she said before disappearing behind her front door.

As I walked home, the enormity of what just happened struck me. I had told Nikki the truth. She knew. And she understood. I was horrified and encouraged all at once. I was horrified at the thought of the wrong Immortal finding out about her. The more she knew, the more I spent time with her, the more likely it was for one of the Queen's agents to discover us. That would certainly go beyond whatever tolerance I had been granted in the past. Surely we would both be put to death.

Yet, I could not regret telling Nikki. I was encouraged by the fact that she had not run screaming from me at hearing the blunt and gory truth. Perhaps if she could accept that part of me it was possible, in time, for her to feel something more for me than the typical human reaction. They were so easy to seduce. But that's not what I wanted from Nikki. I wanted more than her adoration. I wanted her to *love* me. I wanted her to love *me*.

And that meant telling her the truth, all of it. If it was possible for her to love me at all, I would have that love be true. If all she could offer to me was friendship, I would gladly take it, knowing it was true. Even if knowing the truth turned her away from me, at least I would know it was real.

It had been a long time since I had dealt with truth. Sitting at the desk in my loft, I added to the journal about Nikki and realized it was the only true thing I had ever written. Opening the drawer in the desk, I pulled out a new book. On the opening page, I wrote "True Stories." I wasn't able to start with "In the Beginning" but I had millennia worth of "Once Upon a Times." They would fill hundreds of books. I knew simply bringing these books into existence would be considered madness in the Immortal court. The fact that I intended to give them to a mortal put me in a class of treason all my own. It was unheard of.

Then again, so was falling in love. And I truly loved Nikki with every beat of my heart. I would give her all of me and, should she decide to keep me, I would protect her from the consequences.

Chapter Twenty-Three

Contrary to what I was expecting, Nikki seemed completely at ease after class on Thursday.

"So, am I not as exciting on a Wednesday?" she asked, smiling at me.

"You had a lot to accept, after Tuesday," I answered, explaining why I had left her alone yesterday.

"It's amazing how easy the truth is to accept," she replied. "No matter how strange."

I smiled at her response, but couldn't believe she wasn't even a little bothered by what I was. "I thought you might not want a trained attack dog following you around, wondering if it would snap and eat your friends." I was still smiling, but watched her reaction carefully.

She laughed aloud, which took me by surprise. "Did you actually just compare yourself to something as mundane as a dog?" She laughed again. "Maybe a trained peregrine falcon, or a harpy eagle, but they're not pretty enough ..."

"A white Bengal tiger?" I suggested, going along with her somewhat.

"Exactly! Now you're talking: something rare, beautiful, and dangerous," she agreed. "With mad stalking skills," she added, laughing.

"That has been known to bite the hand that feeds it," I added, still trying to push a reaction from her.

"Correction," she said stubbornly. "That has been known to look like it was biting the hand that feeds it, while actually trying to protect it." I shook my head, chuckling at her. "Offense and defense come from the same skill set. You can't be a protector without knowing how to attack."

She had me there.

"Besides, the truth is, you're not a wild animal," she said, laughing when I raised my eyebrows to question her. "Your language skills and posh fashion taste prove it." I chuckled at her reasoning. "*And*, another truth is, given the right circumstances or pressure, anyone could snap. Haven't you ever heard of 'going postal'? For heaven's sake if a postman can go berserk... I'm well aware of the fact that I take my life in my hands every Tuesday and Thursday night."

I started and looked at her but recovered swiftly enough that she missed it and went on. "I just know one of these nights I will point out one too many flaws in poor Tony's thinking, driving him over the edge, and he'll end up stabbing me right in the eye with his antique fountain pen."

I started laughing, having to stop to collect myself. Hearing her graphically describe Tony going berserk was only topped by the fact that he actually did have an antique fountain pen on him at all times.

"What can I say? I'm a Lit major," she said with a straight face. "We like living on the edge."

"So I'm learning," I replied, after another laughing fit at her remark. I was glad she was in such a good mood tonight. Now that she knew the truth about me, there were some things I wanted to get straight about her. "All right, now it's your turn to tell the truth," I informed her. She looked at me with surprise in her pale blue eyes.

"I'm always honest with you, Gregory. I was joking," she said, sounding slightly offended. I smiled at her.

"I know that. Which is why, now that I've told you all my darkest secrets, I want to know yours," I said, wondering if she would really be willing to tell me what I wanted to know.

She laughed. "All my darkest secrets, huh? Sorry to disappoint you, but I don't have any."

"You may feel that's true, but there is still a lot I don't know about you," I reminded her.

"Ask me anything," she said openly. I shook my head, smiling at her endearing frankness. "What?" she asked.

"Nothing," I replied. Then I requested the information I was after. "Tell me about Rich."

Her eyes went wide as I surprised her by my sudden change in conversation. "We used to date, and now we're friends," she said quietly, looking down.

"I know that," I said. She remained quiet, and I waited patiently.

Finally she sighed and shook her head. "Do you have any idea how obnoxious that is?"

"What?" I asked, confused.

"Your utterly disarming amount of patience," she responded, smiling. "You would sit there, waiting for me to answer all night if I took that long wouldn't you?"

"Of course," I replied. What else was there for me to do?

She shook her head again. "I've never had someone so attentive. It really isn't fair, you know."

I was definitely missing something. Was she pleased or upset with me? "I'm sorry," I apologized for my slowness, "but what isn't fair?"

She gazed into my eyes, and I was drowning in crystal blue seas. "Knowing that you'll wait forever just to hear me speak, makes it so I have this overwhelming desire to tell you everything," she said, smiling brightly at me.

I returned the smile. "Good, then we're even," I said. "You've bewitched me into confessing my every sin. It's only fair you tell me everything as well."

"All right, fine." Nikki took a deep breath to prepare herself. "Rich and I were engaged," she blurted.

"To be married?" I asked, surprised into sounding like an idiot.

She smirked at me. "Yes, to be married," she answered. "In fact, we would have been married this Christmas."

"How long ago did you break it off?" I inquired.

"How do you know I'm the one who broke it off?" she countered.

It was my turn to smirk. "I only met Rich briefly, and though I can't say I like him much—" Nikki grinned softly at that. "—he didn't strike me as a complete idiot. Besides, if he had been the one to break the engagement, he wouldn't be so . . . persistent in pursuing you."

Nikki looked at me for a long moment. Then she caved. "Okay, I broke it off this summer."

Not too long ago. No wonder Rich was still so possessive of her. "Why?" I wondered aloud.

Nikki sighed deeply. "I don't know," she whispered. My heart dropped at the honest ring in her words. Did she still love him?

"Rich is . . . a great guy. I really loved him. I guess I still do, in a way." She was obviously struggling to find words. I was struggling with my patience. "I just knew something was wrong. Not with him, with me."

"There's nothing wrong with you," I argued, my patience losing the battle.

She smiled at me briefly, but continued. "I felt like something was missing. Like there was some vital part of my life I needed to find." She narrowed her eyes and pursed her lips as she searched for the words. "I couldn't promise to give my whole self to Richard when I wasn't whole. Does that make any sense at all?" she asked, looking up at me with hopeful eyes.

She had no idea how much sense that made to me. I had found a part of me I didn't even know was missing. "Yes," was all I said. It was a part I could never live without, now.

Nikki sighed again. "I should never have let it go so far." I briefly wondered exactly how far it had gone, then immediately reminded myself that was far beyond the boundaries of my business. "I knew when he asked me to marry him how I felt."

"Then why did you say yes?" I queried, unable to stay silent.

Her eyes looked off into the distance, away from my face. "I guess I was afraid of missing my opportunity," she answered. My confusion must have been apparent on my face, because she explained before I could ask. "I didn't date much, at all really in high school. And even in college there was no one serious before Rich." She got very quiet again. "I figured Rich was the only one able to see past my face and love me for me." Finally she looked at me again with a mixture of deep sadness and flickering hope warring in her eyes. "I thought he was my only opportunity for lasting love." I was momentarily spellbound by her gaze. Then she broke it by looking down at her hands again. "But I knew he deserved more than a partial wife. He deserves someone who can give him as much as he has to give."

I stared at her, knowing I needed to say something. But what do you say to convince an angel she's fallen from heaven? It was time for Nicole Christian to see herself clearly. If anyone could find the right words, I could. What good was my gift of language if I couldn't use it to help the woman I loved?

I took her hand in mine and used my other hand to tilt her chin up. "Nikki," I said firmly as I locked her gaze with my own. "I'm assuming you meant the scars when you said 'Rich was able to see past my face'?" She nodded weakly, trying to avert her gaze. I wouldn't have it and locked my eyes on hers. "You do realize that it is just as hard if not harder for men to talk to a beautiful woman as it is to one who is not?"

She didn't move, but pain flashed across her eyes. I pursed my lips. She was not understanding. "Nikki, your scars had little to nothing to do with boys and men not approaching you." She blinked. "Mortals are intimidated by two things: beauty and strength," I informed her. "You have both. That would overwhelm teenage boys as well as most college-age men."

She pulled her face from my grasp, and I let her turn away. "Gregory," she began.

I cut her off. "Nikki, do you believe I know what beauty is?" I asked.

"Yes," she whispered, her voice laced with pain. "I'm sure you've seen so much."

I leaned closer to her. "Do you believe me when I say I'm telling the truth?"

She glanced at me briefly. "Yes."

I leaned even further, cocking my head, trying to get around the soft curtain of curls to see her face. She kept it turned away from me, but looked sideways at me with her eyes.

"Nikki," I said, my voice softly pleading for her to believe me. "You are beauty. In every way. Your hair shines softly with a thousand colors of sunlight. Your body is strong and lithe, while still so enticingly feminine." She blushed at this, but I was far from done. "Your eyes are the color of the purest mountain lake and wide as the sky. Your lips, so full and perfectly sculpted are temptation incarnate. Your face," I paused and she brought said face around to mine. "Your face is that of an angel descending from heaven and allowing us the gift of looking upon it. All of that makes you beautiful. But there is even more," I whispered. I reached out and softly touched one of the faint scars on her cheek. "You are the only creature I have ever witnessed that is able to show how beautiful their spirit is on their skin. And that," I stressed, "makes you beyond exquisite."

Tears began to form and then fall down her sweet cheeks. Could I do nothing right by this woman? Here I tried to make her see how wonderful she was and all I did was bring her more pain. I should have let her alone. I should never have pursued her. I was about to apologize and tell her she would never have to see me again, when she moved.

Taking my face in her hands, she leaned forward and kissed me. My eyes opened wide in shock. I was so surprised I didn't have time to react before she pulled away. She still held my face in her hands and looked at me with questioning eyes. My brain finally caught up to what had happened and I grinned widely. She smiled in return and relaxed her tense expression.

I then did something that surprised even myself. Wrapping one arm around her waist, I pulled her close to me, as I had been aching to do for so long. Then, leaning forward, I pressed my lips to hers once more, touching her soft curls with my other hand. Now that we were both aware of what was going on, the kiss was much more. Electric currents ran from her lips through my body. I could hear her heart begin to race and was amazed to hear mine beat as well. Moving my lips against hers, I could feel their soft texture. I began to drown in their warmth.

Her hands tightened on my face and her lips parted, giving me permission to deepen the kiss further. As much as I yearned for this, it would not be a good idea. Instead, I pulled away before my body could overpower my mind and Nikki's safety. Nikki looked fairly disappointed and slightly confused that I had ended the kiss.

"I'm sorry," she apologized, feeling she had gone too far. "That was inappropriate."

I smiled at her, looking like an idiot, I'm sure. "That depends," I responded.

My goofy grin was contagious and she smiled in return. "On what?"

"On why you kissed me," I replied, not quite sure I was ready to know.

She looked at me for a long moment, her blue eyes searching my green ones. "You don't really want to know, yet," she said and began walking again. Her abruptness irritated me.

"Try me," I challenged.

She glanced at me and was quiet for a moment. Then she smiled. "I kissed you because I wanted to. Because you are the first person to ever make me feel beautiful *because* of my scars, not in spite of them." She smirked. "Then you kissed me."

"Because I love you," I said freely. She smiled brightly at my admission.

"And I kissed you back, because I enjoyed it." She shyly ducked her head a little. "A lot."

By this time we had reached her front door and I stopped at her steps. "Those sound like excellent reasons," I said. I reached up and stroked one of her soft curls again.

"Would you like to come in, Gregory?" she whispered. "While I'm actually home?" she finished, teasing.

"I should probably go," I replied, leaning closer to her, drawn in by her alluring lips.

Just as she began to move closer to me, her phone rang inside her apartment, halting both of us in our tracks. We stood there, with our faces inches apart, lost in each other. The phone rang again.

"Why is someone calling me this late?" she whispered, drawing my eyes to her lips as they moved.

"It must be important," I murmured. Then my own words came to my brain and I pulled slightly away. "You should probably answer it," I suggested as it rang again.

"Maybe they'll give up," she said, but the phone rang insistently.

"Or not," I said smiling. "I really should go anyway."

Nikki sighed deeply and took a step up the stairs. Then she quickly turned around and kissed the corner of my mouth. "Good night, Gregory."

"Good night," I replied. I watched her walk into the house and shut the door. I was still standing there, staring at it when I heard her answer the phone.

"Hello? Oh. Hi, Rich." There was a tenseness in her voice. Was she irritated that he'd called? I doubted it. She seemed to care for him. Hadn't she just said she still loved him? Was it guilt? Did she regret kissing me?

I walked swiftly away from her house to avoid any more accidental eavesdropping. Even if she did regret it, I couldn't. It had felt amazing. It felt natural and right, and I wanted to do it again. But at what cost? I loved Nikki, but I couldn't be intimate with her. Not without damming her to the same hell I had been living in for so long now. I couldn't, wouldn't turn her into a monster like me.

Perhaps it would be better for her to be with Rich. He obviously loved her, and didn't bring her danger with his every breath. And he could be with her in ways I couldn't. Or could I? The truth was, I had no idea. I had never even considered being with a mortal before. In any case, Nikki could probably use some space over the weekend to decide how she really felt about kissing a blood drinking demon.

But that didn't mean I wouldn't use the time to find out just how close I could get to Nikki, if she wanted me to. I recalled Rob making some comment about "dabbling in humans now and then." I wasn't dabbling with Nikki, but perhaps Rob actually knew something that could be useful. The question was, would his information be worth the grief he would undoubtedly give me for asking about it. The answer, if it let me get closer to Nikki, was a resounding *yes*.

Chapter Twenty-Four

The next afternoon, a wave of relief washed over me as I noted Jenny's absence from the apartment. "You finally reminded Jenny that she doesn't live here?" I asked.

"You don't live here either, Greg, but we still let you visit," Rob responded from the couch where he was, to my great disgust, eating Twinkies again. "And she is much more … entertaining … when she's here," he finished, wagging his eyebrows.

"She's been acting funny lately," Lance said from his customary staging area. It was littered with diving equipment: flippers, goggles, knife belt, full body steel mesh suit, and several other small items. The only thing missing was an oxygen tank.

I gave him an incredulous look. "Jenny's acting funny?"

Lance smiled wryly. "Weird, even for Jenny. I suspect she'll be scarce for a few days before she comes round again." He shrugged his shoulders nonchalantly.

"I see you're going diving," I noted dryly. "What's with the steel mesh?"

Lance smiled. "Sharks."

"Sharks?"

"You'd be surprised how much power those jaws have, not to mention the number of teeth. The steel mesh helps keep them from breaking the skin, which would put blood in the water, which would start a feeding frenzy," he explained. "Not pretty."

I remembered having similar thoughts recently. I smirked, unable to stop the comment. "I thought it was all about the danger."

"Danger yes, ugly, hard to forget and painfully embarrassing, no." He smiled at me and continued, "Don't worry, if they latch on tight enough they could keep me under for hours, maybe I'll drown." We laughed, both knowing it was highly unlikely, if not impossible for him to die that way.

"What brings you here?" Rob asked. "Finally decided to try some of my tasty cakes?"

I physically shuddered, which made him laugh. "I think not." I took a deep breath and tried very hard to make my next comment sound casual. "But, I was thinking of perhaps trying something else."

"Our honored and ancient Gregory has found something new to try?" Rob asked, mocking me, but honestly surprised. Then his quick spinning wheels clicked. "Or has he found some*one* new to try?"

"Knock it off, Rob. You know Gregory will trounce you if provoked," Lance said, coming to my aid. I wished I could accept it. But, crudely as he put it, Rob was right.

"You said something about being with mortals a few weeks ago," I prompted, trying to bring the conversation to a civil tone. Lance looked up at me in surprise. Then he pursed his lips, silently stood, and strode from the room.

Rob watched him go. "A bit of a sore subject still." He sighed.

"I can understand why, considering," I remarked.

Rob rolled his eyes. "It was one mistake, for crying out loud! He shouldn't hate himself forever."

"It probably doesn't help to have such a … permanent reminder," I noted.

"Probably not," he conceded. Then his face brightened. "But back to the matter at hand. I assume it's triple H we're talking about?"

"Yes," I replied. But I didn't know what else to say, or where to begin. "Her name is Nikki," I reminded him.

"I know that. I just thought, considering the subject of our conversation, I might get away with Hot Human Honey."

"You thought wrong," I informed him. I was already getting irritated.

"All right, all right, don't get all pissy on me," he said. He took a long look at my face. Whatever he saw there must have made an impression. He put the confections he was eating away and gestured for me to take a seat. "Tell me what you want to know, Gregory. It's only fair that I get to help you, after all you've done for us."

I was touched by both his honesty and his serious approach to a potentially awkward conversation. I sighed in relief and sat down in the leather recliner.

"Thank you," I said earnestly. I was silent for a moment as I tried to collect my thoughts. To my surprise, Rob waited patiently for me.

"I know it's not possible for us to actually have sex, but I've never thought about even kissing a mortal before. How much DNA does it take to turn them? I know letting it into the bloodstream is crossing the line, but exactly how far can I take it?" The words came out in a rush and Rob was silent as he processed my rapid speech. Then he bit his lip, trying unsuccessfully to suppress a laugh. "What?" I asked indignantly.

"I'm sorry, Greg. I'm really not making fun of you. I just had no idea how little you knew about yourself." When my gaze turned threatening, he hastened on. "I mean, you know everything there is to know about being an Immortal, and I'll never be out of your debt for teaching us what you have, but you apparently don't know much about how one becomes an Immortal."

"I've had no reason to," I defended myself.

"Of course not," Rob replied. "I'm just a little surprised by your lack of curiosity." Then, after a moment's thought, he amended, "Or perhaps I'm not surprised, considering the distance you keep from mortals, or did until you met Nikki."

"So why don't you enlighten me, so I can know everything about everything?" I asked sarcastically.

Rob ignored my tone, which I realized I was grateful for when he spoke earnestly. "First of all, you can't change someone by kissing them."

"But my saliva has my DNA in it," I argued.

"Yes, but Greg, it takes much more than that to actually trigger a change. Unless you were drooling excessively into her mouth for a month straight—" he paused, chuckling at the visual he'd just given himself. "Actually even then I doubt it would work. The worst you could do would be to heal a few cold sores, if she had any." He looked at me expectantly.

I rolled my eyes. "Her lips are perfect, you dolt. So, I can kiss her all I like." *If she'll let me*, I thought to myself. "But sex is crossing the line," I reiterating the obvious.

Rob smiled widely at me. "Gregory, this is where I'd like to welcome you to the twenty-first century," he chuckled again. "They've been around for a while, so even with your apathy for the human culture, you must have heard of condoms?" He smirked, waiting for my reaction. I didn't disappoint him.

I'm an idiot! I thought, literally slapping myself in the forehead.

Rob laughed openly at me. "Yeah, I thought maybe it hadn't occurred to you yet. The physical mechanics of it aren't anything you can't overcome."

Rob paused then and looked at me, as if afraid to continue. "But sometimes, how do I put this, styling can be a problem."

"What?" I asked, completely lost.

"Well, mortals and Immortals are different by nature," he began, obviously still trying to find the right words. I was surprised at his effort to be tactful. "We react differently to certain … stimuli." He looked at me again, as if waiting for me to start shouting.

"Rob, please just spit it out," I implored, my patience waning.

"The cravings and desires can get all mixed together," he tried, "all of them."

I gave him an exasperated look.

"Look, I've dabbled in human females from time to time, but I don't make a habit of it for a reason. And while it only discourages me from making it a regular habit, it may make you completely rethink having sex with Nikki." His words were rushed together.

"It's about more than sex," I bristled.

"Which is exactly my point!" Rob said, clearly as frustrated as me. "Hell, I tried being tactful, but I give up. Sometimes what starts out as a date ends up as a meal."

I stared at him, uncomprehending for a second. Then the mortification hit and showed clearly on my face.

"See? Now you know why I was trying to soften the blow," Rob defended himself.

"I could never," I stuttered, standing upright. "I would never hurt Nikki like that!"

"I sincerely hope not, Gregory, but I think knowing that it's a possibility will only help you control yourself," Rob stated. He had me there. It was better to know.

"What is it that triggers the need to feed?" I asked, a strange calm in my voice. "What stimuli changes the love to thirst?"

Rob sighed. "That's just it, Greg. I don't know. For me it never was love." He caught my disapproving look and added, "Nor was it for the girls, some of which do still live, by the way." He shook his head and got back to his point. "For me it was just lust from the very beginning, and if I gave into that lust too freely, or if I hadn't fed for a while … Lust for the body mingled and then was outweighed by lust for the blood."

I sat heavily in the chair again. I loved Nikki, but the very fact that I was having this conversation indicated I felt lust as well. "So, I don't have to worry about accidentally turning Nikki," I mourned, covering my face with my hands. "I'm just taking her life in my hands every time I touch her."

"Is that really any different than how things are now?" Rob asked quietly.

I looked up into his surprisingly sympathetic face. I didn't have an answer for him.

Walking home from my disconcerting talk with Rob, my newly opened eyes began to notice things. A man wearing a tank top and shorts that were barely there, and was most obviously using some illicit substance to boost his physique was holding a door open for a young mother with frazzled hair and her too-large stroller. He smiled kindly at her as she expressed her thanks. A greasy-haired teenager in baggy jeans offered his arm to a wizened old man who was struggling to cross the street. Similar acts of unsolicited compassion were occurring everywhere. Perhaps humanity was not lost after all. Perhaps it was simply broken and needed fixing. Not that I could affect the flow of human evolution. But perhaps they would somehow save themselves.

At the last inhabited corner before my loft, I felt something was off. I looked around, noting nothing different. And yet it was wrong somehow. Something permanent was missing. As if a tree or building had gotten up and walked away without anyone noticing. Then, with a surprising wave of regret, I realized what was gone. The vagrant, who had been living within human walking distance of my home for decades, whose name I had never bothered to learn, was absent. I closed my eyes in silent mourning for the stark reminder of just how broken humanity was. He had probably died cold, sick and alone, had probably been dead for days before anyone called the police to have him removed.

I entered my apartment feeling morose. It was not long, however, before my contemplation of humanity became more centralized. Not surprisingly, my thoughts returned to Nikki. Lying on my bed, I ran through my conversation with Rob over and over again in my mind.

Saturday morning came and all it brought me was a growing number of questions. I really didn't think I would be capable of hurting Nikki. I couldn't even hunt anymore because of my reaction to her. But at the same time, the longer I went without feeding, the weaker and thirstier I would get. It might only be a matter of time.

As much as my heart rejected that thought, my mind told me not to dismiss it. But my mind also told me there were ways around it. I simply needed to feed. Easier said than done these days. But then, I hadn't tried since that night on the beach. I was sure there was a way Nikki could be safe. I had multiple lifetimes of experience. I was extremely intelligent, even for an Immortal. I could solve this problem.

Which would become a moot point if Nikki didn't want me in the first place. My whole problem hinged on the assumption that she wanted me to want her. That may not be true. In fact, it made more sense for it not to be true. I made her feel safe, protected, yes, but her father probably made her feel the same way. She had said I felt like home. Which was a beautiful sentiment but did not, in itself, connote the kind of intimacy I wanted.

Or was that even what I really wanted? Isn't crossing that line what ruined the friendship in every tragic romance ever written? I could stay with Nikki, watching over her, caring for her for the rest of her life. She could not stay with me for the rest of mine. Did I really want to escalate this relationship and have a few years, decades at the most, of bliss, only to spend the rest of eternity mourning her loss?

Even as the thought of Nikki's inescapable mortality froze the blood in my veins, I knew in the core of my being, I wanted nothing more. If Nikki would let me, I would give her anything, everything, every part of me. I also realized that meant I would give her less if that's what she wanted. As long as she was happy and safe.

There was one thing I knew she wanted. The truth. And so I spent Saturday in the warehouse below my loft, sorting through remnants of my past. Rob considered me a pack rat. I argued that a pack rat hordes things in order to save them. I simply didn't discard things because I didn't care. It was easier to put some things in storage than to throw them out.

These same things also happened to be the type of remnant that turned into "antiques" if held onto for long enough. I generally went through my collection every couple hundred years or so, selling off the largest pieces to make room, and the most valuable pieces to make money. Each of us had our own method of financial ingenuity.

Occasionally, some items would make it through the bicentennial house cleaning. These often became too valuable. "Priceless" was actually a term that meant, "unable to sell without some plausible explanation for owning it in the first place." I couldn't exactly tell the auction house that I had a Louis XIV crystal wine set because it was given to me by Louis XIV. But it was just these things I was looking at now. Things that were old, ancient, that had layers of dust on them. They each had a story behind them, of where I was, when I was. Some told stories of the others as well. I smiled as I thought of the many stories we had been a part of throughout history. They were all stories Nikki would want to hear. And so I began a new kind of inventory, one that focused my mind and eased my troubled heart. I would be able to at least give Nikki something.

CHAPTER TWENTY-FIVE

I was ridiculously eager to see Nikki Tuesday night. At the same time, I was anxious to the point of sweating, if I were mortal. I had done a lot of thinking over the weekend. I knew what I wanted, but I had no idea if Nikki felt the same. I was sure she hadn't spent the weekend agonizing over every possible scenario our relationship could take as I had. I wondered if she had thought of me at all, of the kiss we had shared.

"Hey, Hot Lips," her soft voice brought a thrill to my nerves and a smirk to said lips. Apparently she had thought about it.

"Hello, beautiful," I replied turning to watch her sit down.

She looked at me with mild surprise on her face. Then she looked down, giving her head a little shake, sending her curls bouncing. She smiled a little smile.

"What?" I asked, confused by her actions.

"You calling me beautiful is … ironic," she said, with that same little smile, like she was enjoying a private joke.

"I mean it," I reiterated.

"I know," she said, turning toward Tony as he began his lecture. I couldn't tell if she was laughing at me, or pleased at what I'd said.

"How was your weekend?" I asked, ignoring the fact that class had started. I wondered if perhaps something had happened to put her in such a cryptic mood.

"Utterly mundane. Apparently it was a national holiday for vampire stalkers." She sighed dramatically.

I chuckled. "I thought you'd have plans," I said. *With Rich*, I thought.

"Just the usual," she replied as she began to take notes. I realized that still didn't tell me whether or not Rich was included. I decided to let it go. She would tell me if she wanted me to know. I let her pay attention to Tony for the rest of class. It was torture to sit so close without reaching out to touch her soft hair or skin.

After class, as she stood to leave, I reached over and took her backpack, putting it on my shoulder. The brief touch of her hand caused me to sigh in relief. I marveled again at the effect this woman had on me.

"Thank you," she said, smiling.

"My pleasure," I replied honestly. She smiled that little smile again.

As we walked out into the cool night air, Nikki became more serious.

"Not being able to feel you hanging around this weekend made me think about something," Nikki said, her tone hard to read. I knew what I had been thinking about all weekend.

"Would you like to share it with me?" I asked, trying to keep my tone even.

She rolled her eyes. "Of course. That's why I brought it up." She smiled briefly. Then, more somberly she asked, "How do I defend myself?"

Her question caught me off guard, as my thoughts had most assuredly not been focused on her protection at the moment. "What?"

"When you're not there, how do I defend myself against," she paused momentarily as a dark memory flashed over her eyes, "others."

I knew exactly what she meant. "You don't," I replied, suddenly realizing how vulnerable I had left her over the last few days. It made me sick.

"But even vam—Immortals must have some weakness," she persisted. "If not garlic, or silver, or stakes ..."

"Actually, stakes do work, just not like the legend says," I corrected her automatically, without thinking. Then I realized what I had revealed and checked my tongue. Nikki looked up at me, eyes wide and innocent, expecting me to continue. "A stake through the heart, wooden or otherwise, doesn't kill us, but it does leave us paralyzed," I finished haltingly.

"Completely unable to move?" she asked.

"Yes. Utterly defenseless."

"How?"

I looked at her. There was no hidden motive, no shadow in her curious face. She really wanted to know all there was to know. And I would tell her, though it wouldn't do her any good. "As I told you, our regenerative powers come from our blood. Our blood also does what yours does. We use it to move muscles, nourish the body, etcetera. Something lodged in the heart keeps it from beating, which keeps the blood from flowing, which results in paralysis."

"You have a heartbeat?" she asked in surprise, then winced. "Sorry, probably another stupid question."

I smiled at her. "None of your questions are stupid, Nikki. I just find some of them amusing. Consider it me laughing at an inside joke, not at you. It's not your fault we've carefully cultivated such erroneous myths." Her smile returned, though she was still a bit embarrassed. "And yes, I have a heartbeat. It's just much, much slower than yours."

"How much slower?" she asked. I found myself smiling at her insistence for details.

"It varies from one Immortal to the next, depending on their age and strength," I replied. "Mine beats about twice an hour."

Her jaw dropped as she stared at me. I kept from chuckling at her, but my smile widened. Then I saw a few gears click in her brain. "Wait, if you need a heartbeat to move, but it only needs to beat every half hour, why would a stake to the heart immediately paralyze you? Couldn't you just use the time you would have had until your next beat to pull it out?"

"A very good question," I said, trying not to sound patronizing. "Our muscle movement only needs the occasional beat of our heart, unless we are straining ourselves in some way, as in battle."

"So generally, if you're in the position to get a stake in the heart, your heart is already beating in double time?"

"Yes, but even if we were caught unaware, our blood is needed to heal our wounds. When the heart is pierced, the rest of our blood instinctively flows to it, trying to heal it."

"But it can't because the stake keeps the wound fresh, while your limbs are starved of the blood they need in order to remove it."

"Precisely," I said, impressed with her understanding.

"Nasty Catch-22," she said, shaking her head.

"Quite unpleasant, yes," I agreed.

Her head snapped up. "Have you ever been staked?" she asked in horror.

"No," I replied, touched by her concern. "I've yet to meet an Immortal stronger or faster than myself, and I'm too observant to be caught unaware," I said honestly.

Her small smile returned and I had a feeling she was laughing at me, though I couldn't fathom why. "Which brings us back to you being indestructible." I opened my mouth to contradict her, but she waved me off. "So a stake through the heart would paralyze, but you made it sound like there was something that would be more … final," she prompted.

"Yes," I replied. She again waited patiently for me to continue. I had another momentary struggle with paranoia over why she wanted to know how to kill me. It passed quickly as I remembered that she would never be capable of it, and if she were, I would have nothing to live for anyway.

"The brain instructs the heart to beat, the body to heal. It stores my memories and essentially everything I am. Without it, I would cease to exist." There was a sharp intake of breath from Nikki.

"Oh, I don't mean—" She looked sick. "Gregory, I wasn't trying to find out how to kill *you*." She paused again. "I just want to know all I can. To defend myself."

"In any case, killing the brain kills the Immortal," I replied, somewhat placated.

"So a bullet to the head would do it?" she asked hesitantly.

"If it did enough damage. If it simply went straight through, the brain would heal too quickly," I explained. Her eyes went wider as she shook her head in amazement. "Which is generally why we use decapitation. It severs the brain from the blood flow, but also destroys the synapses that would send messages to the body. Swift and sure."

Nikki was silent for a moment. "I really am defenseless," she said quietly.

"No," I said, taking her hand in mine. "You have me. I won't leave you alone again." She smiled a little and squeezed my hand, sending an electric current from her fingertips straight to my heart.

"How many Immortals are there?" she asked.

"We don't exactly take a census," I replied. She smiled again, but it wasn't reaching her eyes. I hated that I was terrifying her so. I was bringing such dreary darkness to her sunny existence.

"Take a guess," she said dryly.

"Well, there is a gathering every year, although not all of us go every year." I paused, again shocked at what I had just told her. This was information she didn't need and would most surely get her killed. She was looking at me expectantly. "Those at the gathering would fill a city the size of New York," I hastily finished. Her eyes widened in horror.

"Is that all?" she asked.

"What?" I responded, confused by her reaction.

"If the Immortals are so invincible, at least from a human standpoint, why are there not more of you?" she asked. "What keeps you all from just … running amuck?"

I chuckled at the image of Immortals running amuck. "Well some of us realize that, while you aren't a threat, you are necessary. Allowing ourselves to simply wipe you out would be our downfall as well."

"Yes, annihilating your food source would be bad," she agreed sardonically. I was taken aback by her casual attitude. "But you could have taken over the world by now."

"Who says we haven't? For all you know The President could be one of us," I teased, immediately regretting it as her eyes registered the possibility that her whole perception of reality could be false. Panic danced around the edges of her wide eyes. "I'm kidding, Nikki. We have some influence and generally get what we need and want done, but we aren't secretly running the world's governments." She pursed her lips, squinted her eyes, and ripped her hand from mine. Then she balled it into a fist and punched me in the arm, hard.

"Don't *do* that!" she yelled. "You had me completely freaked out!" But there was mirth in her eyes.

"Ouch," I said, rubbing my shoulder.

"Oh, shut up. I know that didn't hurt," she said, rolling her eyes.

"Just because you didn't injure me, doesn't mean it didn't hurt," I said petulantly. "I have highly developed senses that come with sensitive nerve endings."

"Did I really hurt you?" she asked, her eyes going wide again.

"No," I admitted, guilted into honesty by her concern. She hit me again. We looked at each other and began laughing. It felt that much sweeter after the morose conversation we had just had. We stopped in front of her house. She was breathless, tears streaming down her face. I hadn't laughed so hard in ... ever.

And then our eyes met. I was swept away into endless blue skies. There was suddenly a field of electric energy vibrating between us. I wanted to close the gap, take her in my arms, and kiss her into oblivion. Instead, I stood there, frozen in place.

Nikki's smile faltered a bit. The atmosphere got increasingly awkward. Could she tell how desperate I was to kiss her again? Of course she could, and it was upsetting her. I quickly took a step back, to give her space.

"Goodnight, Nikki," I said. *I love you*, I thought to myself.

The smile faded completely from her face. "I thought you weren't going to leave me alone."

"Immortals don't make a habit of breaking into houses to attack," I assured her. "You're safe at home. If you lock your windows," I added.

She didn't laugh. "Good night, Gregory," she said. She sounded so disappointed. It broke my heart that only seconds ago she had been laughing and carefree. Now she was distraught, and it was my fault, again.

"I'm sorry I scared you, Nikki," I apologized.

"The truth is hard to hear sometimes. That's not your fault," she replied, walking to her door. "I'd rather know I'm weak and insignificant, and be armed with the truth, than think myself invincible in my ignorance."

"You are not insignificant," I argued as she turned the knob. She smiled sadly back at me, then closed the door softly behind her. "You are everything," I whispered.

I had no idea what had just happened. I told her the truth, some horrible truths as a matter of fact. And as horrifying as they were, she seemed to accept them. She was even able to laugh. But then the whole atmosphere had changed. In my gut I knew it was my fault. She had been expecting something and I had disappointed her. As well as I captured humans in my stories, I was sadly inept at interacting with one in real life.

Compounding this was the realization I'd had about leaving her alone and, as she pointed out, defenseless. I had meant what I said about her being safe in her own home at night, but I had left her alone for days. I was sick with what could have happened to her. The Immortal that had attacked her could still be in the area. He didn't seem the type to simply fade away. And, of course, I knew of at least three other Immortals in the immediate vicinity. The others had heard of Nikki, but had no idea who she was. Any one of them could take her, having no idea she was the very mortal I was so consumed with.

I may not have any clue as to how to make her happy, but I could keep her safe. I wouldn't even have to cloud her bright life with my darkness. She seemed to almost enjoy having a "stalker." Stalking was something I was definitely good at.

Chapter Twenty-Six

was waiting across from Nikki's house bright and early Wednesday morning. I was hidden well out of sight, of course. She came out and crossed the street on the way to school. As soon as her foot touched the sidewalk again, she paused momentarily. Then she smiled that private little smile and went to class.

I followed her all morning. I quickly realized how foolish it was for me to have worried about her while she was at school. She was always surrounded by people, and it was broad daylight. Yet, I couldn't just let her be. Even if she was safe, I wanted to be near her. Even just to see her.

After lunch she came out of the student center and headed across campus. She walked straight across a large quad, and I started to edge around it. Then she stopped right in the middle. I stopped as well, not sure how to proceed.

She turned in a slow circle. When she stopped she was facing me, but I could tell by her searching eyes that she couldn't see me. You'd be surprised how many shadows one can find to hide in when the sun is shining. Nikki smiled and sat down on the grass.

"I know you're there, Gregory. And I know you can hear me," she said quietly while looking down at her feet. The mortals passing by wouldn't even know she had spoken. She smiled and looked up in my direction again. "Come out, come out, wherever you are."

Her little smile told me she wasn't upset with me for following her, but I was still chagrined that she would call me on it. Her eyes widened momentarily as I materialized from against the brick wall and crossed the field to where she sat. She patted the ground next to her and I joined her.

"So much for my mad skills," I said wryly. "You knew I was following you the second you came out your front door this morning, didn't you?"

She smiled at me, her eyes catching the sun and turning an almost transparent azure. "Not until I crossed the street, actually. And my knowing you were there has more to do with my freaky sixth sense than your expert stalking," she assured me. "How do you hide in plain sight like that? I was looking pretty hard, and I couldn't see you at all until you moved."

"Trade secret," I chuckled. "If I told you, I'd have to kill you." The words were out of my mouth before I could think and I silently cursed Rob for making me watch too many movies. But Nikki laughed.

"Of all your secrets, that's your most closely guarded one?"

"How would I impress you without cheap magic tricks?" I asked.

She laughed, her head falling back, golden curls bouncing around her shoulders, sunlight reflecting back to itself. "Yes, because being a dangerous, beautiful, ageless, indestructible knight in shining armor is so blasé."

"I told you, I'm not indestructible," I reminded her.

"For a mere mortal like me, you might as well be," she countered.

"You are no mere mortal, Nikki," I argued. "You have no idea the power you have over me," I finished softly.

"Tell me," she whispered, gazing intently into my eyes. I was lost, the noise of the busy college campus faded away, and all I could see was sapphire blue.

"I would do anything for you, Nikki," I breathed.

"How about you start with walking me to class instead of following me around like a stray puppy?" she said, smirking as she stood up and brushed off her jeans.

I stood up as well. "I thought you said I was more exotic than a dog," I said, pretending to be peeved. An excited puppy was exactly how I had been acting. "Besides, I thought you liked having a stalker." I reached down and picked up her backpack. She smiled at me again.

"Thank you. And while having a stalker may be thrilling in its own right, when you're hiding in the shadows, I can't do this," she said and took my hand in hers as she turned to walk toward her next class.

I was shocked by the sudden contact, not to mention the electricity her touch sent through my system. She noticed my hesitation and dropped my hand. I instantly felt the loss.

"I'm sorry," she said.

"No, Nikki, don't be sorry. I'm sorry. I just..." I struggled to explain my ineptitude. "Immortals are not exactly a caring bunch of individuals. I've never been in love before. Just holding your hand feels...intimate. I don't always know how to respond, what is considered appropriate." I hoped she would understand.

"Do you want to hold my hand?" she asked.

"Yes," I said a little too quickly. *I want to hold more than your hand*, I thought.

"Then do," she said with a smile. I reached out, taking her hand back in mine, lacing our fingers together. My heart beat, and I could breathe easier. "Gregory, I have yet to be offended by anything you've done, late night breaking and entering included. I promise to tell you if you cross the line," she said sweetly. "I won't even get mad, if you won't get mad either."

"I could never be mad at you, Nikki," I replied. Her smile brightened.

"Now that that's settled," she said, squeezing my hand, "you'd better get me to my next class, or I'll be late."

"We can't have that," I agreed, chuckling as we walked, our hands melded together.

She was a few minutes late anyway, and left me at the door to make as little amount of a scene as possible. Two people strolling hand in hand would cause a much bigger stir than one flighty blonde, as she put it. I leaned on the wall opposite her classroom and waited for her. After class, she quickly said goodbye to her friends then came to me, taking my hand again. I smiled, hoping that meant she had missed the contact as much as I did.

At her next class, she again had me wait outside. As she exited, I started toward the small group of friends she was with. She was again quick to extricate herself and meet me before I reached them. A shadow flitted across the back of my mind. She smiled brightly at me and took my hand, all thoughts momentarily drowning in her gleaming sapphire eyes. Then she turned fully away from the group of people behind us and started tugging me across campus. The shadow solidified into an outrageous question. Was she so eager to be walking home with me, or was she walking me home to get me away from all the people? I glanced at her through my peripheral vision. She seemed completely content, her face radiant, our hands swinging casually between us. But I had been a cynic too long.

"You didn't need to rush away from your friends so quickly, Nikki," I said, my voice bringing her face to mine. She seemed surprised by the expression she found there. "I am capable of having a five-minute conversion with a group of humans without going on a killing spree." I hadn't meant for it to sound so spiteful.

Her eyes widened in shock. "Gregory! Is that what you think I was doing? Protecting *them?*"

"You weren't?" I asked.

"No! Gregory, I wouldn't have asked you to walk me to class in the first place if I thought I was putting anyone in danger," she chastised me. "I didn't introduce you to anyone because you're ... Well, for lack of a better word, you're shy. I practically had to twist your arm to get you to talk to me when we first met," she reminded me. "And you have good reason to be. Obviously, there are a lot of secrets that need to remain secret. I won't be the one to put them at risk."

I was once again rendered momentarily speechless. Once I ordered my thoughts, I apologized. "Nikki, I'm sorry. I'm not accustomed to trusting others, or having them trust me. I should not have doubted your intentions but simply asked you what your behavior meant." I smirked even as I looked repentant. "I told you I'm not very good at this."

"I can be patient," she said. "Maybe not as patient as you, but I do pretty well for a mere mortal."

I gave her a stern look for her reference to herself as a "mere" mortal again. Then another thought occurred to me. "Did you want to introduce me to your friends?"

"Actually, it didn't even occur to me as a possibility," she said honestly. "You're so big on being sneaky and secretive."

"I have trusted you to keep my truth secret, Nikki. But that doesn't mean you have to keep me a secret," I said, reaching out with my free hand to brush her hair behind her shoulder so I could see her face better. "I want to know everything about you, including the important people in your life. If that's what you want."

She smiled at me, considering what I'd said. "Good to know." We walked the rest of the way to her house in amicable silence, the touch of her hand warming me much more efficiently than the sun shining down on us.

At her porch, however, it turned awkward again. Her face began to look irritated. Then she closed her eyes, took a deep breath and sighed it out again.

"You still have no idea what to do with me, do you?" she asked.

"You are quite the quandary," I agreed.

"Gregory," she breathed, leaning closer to me. "What do you want to do?" As her warm breath brushed my face, I was bombarded with graphic images of what I wanted to do for her, with her, to her. My breath came in a quick gasp between my teeth, sounding a lot like a hiss, my green eyes burning.

Nikki's eyes widened and she gave a nervous little laugh. "Okay, maybe not that just yet. Whatever thought you just had looked a little intense for my front porch."

I closed my eyes and ground my teeth, banishing the vivid fantasies, for now.

"For heaven's sake, Gregory, three hours ago you weren't even sure you wanted to hold my hand. Now you look like you're trying to avoid ravishing me right here in broad daylight!" Her imagery was not helping. "Is there no middle ground?"

I was struck by her words, probably because they were true. I tried to explain my poor behavior once again. "Nikki, please understand that I have so many conflicting desires when it comes to you." She blushed a little at my words, but I went on. "I want to protect you, but I put your very life in danger by telling you the truth. I want to be near you, touching your skin even, but I don't want to hurt you." I took a step closer to her so that we were inches apart.

"You are so very delicate," I whispered, reaching up to trace her cheek with the back of my hand, leaving it to hold her chin. Her heart fluttered in her chest. "I'm not accustomed to feeling intimate because Immortals are much more aggressive in their behaviors, all of their behaviors. We are traditionally only concerned with our own needs." She blushed again at my innuendos.

"I am trying to find my middle ground. Right now, all I know is that I love you, and when I touch you, I want you to feel that, not simply my desire for you."

My thumb lifted from her chin to trace her mouth, gently caressing the Cupid's bow and her full bottom lip. As much as I loved drowning in her eyes, I could not tear my sight from the spellbinding petal pink softness. I made another circuit with my thumb as I was drawn in, as if gravity were pulling me forward rather than down to the earth. I moved my hand along her jaw, my fingers sliding into her hair. My eyes closed when our lips were but centimeters apart. I paused for a millisecond, trying to sense if this was what she wanted too, but it was too late for me to stop now anyway. Our lips met, and though I kept my touch feather light, my body exploded in white hot flashes of light. My lips parted, a sigh escaping. Then Nikki's knees gave out, breaking our connection. I released her hand, catching her by the waist before she could fall, my other hand still lingering in her soft hair.

"Mission accomplished," she said dreamily. I smiled down at her.

"Mine or yours?" I smirked, still flying high. She smirked back at me.

"Both," she admitted, standing up again. "Now even my toes know you love me." One of her hands was gripping the arm I still had around her waist, the other came up to rest on my chest, over my heart. It beat at her touch.

"Your toes, huh?" I was very gratified to know the kiss had affected her similarly as it had me. Her heart was still hammering away in her chest, her breathing a little too fast. I was becoming increasingly aware of just how close her body was to mine.

"I should let you go," I suggested. "You have papers to write, books to read, things to do, I'm sure."

"That can wait," she replied with a smile, but I released her, which made her pout. I chuckled, delighted by her reaction. I took her hands in mine and she smiled at me again.

"I can wait longer. We have all the time in the world to be together, Nikki. You're assignments have due dates," I reminded her. "If I don't leave, I doubt you'll get any work done," I said, stroking her soft curls again. She smiled coyly at me from under her long lashes, and I nearly came undone. I closed my eyes to concentrate and took a deep breath. "I should go," I repeated. When I opened my eyes, there was a resigned smile on her face.

"All right," she sighed. "I'll see you … soon." She reached up and put a hand to my face.

"Soon," I agreed, leaning into the soft warmth. She released my face and my hand, opening her front door. I was suddenly cold and alone and fought the urge to reach out and snatch her back into my embrace. Instead, I went home, knowing if I watched her house tonight, I wouldn't be able to stay outside.

Chapter Twenty-Seven

The next twenty four hours took longer to pass than most centuries I'd known. After her encouragement, I found myself needing to be near her even more. I wasn't sure I could continue to leave her every night. Which brought me back to the fact that I still didn't know what was considered appropriate. She said she would tell me if I crossed the line. I longed to test the boundaries; but I didn't want to offend her, or scare her off by revealing what an animal I was. Though she did already know the worst there was to know about me.

When Nikki left her house for class Thursday night, I was sitting on her top step, waiting for her. She laughed when she saw me. "So much for my subtle stalker."

"You convinced me that this has better benefits," I said, slinging her backpack over my shoulder. Taking her hand in mine, I winked at her. Her heart skipped, and I smiled.

She sighed dramatically. "Yes, but being able to say I had a stalker felt so … dangerous," she said, raising one eyebrow with a smirk. She sighed again and began to walk away, hips swaying.

I reacted without thinking. I spun her back to me with the hand I was holding, pinning her arm gently behind her back. My other hand grabbed her neck and held her face to mine, my lips at her ear, "And this doesn't feel …" I drew my mouth down her neck to where it met her shoulder. Throwing caution to the wind I parted my lips and nipped at her jugular, just barely enough for her to feel the whisper of my teeth before placing a soft kiss against her pulsing skin. Drawing my nose back up to her ear I finished my sentence, "… dangerous?" Nikki's heart was thundering against my chest.

But she wasn't breathing.

I pulled back to see that her face was white and her eyes were the size of saucers. I immediately let her go, only to have to grab her again as she gasped and fell over. I wanted to give her some room, but I was afraid she was going to faint.

"Nikki, I am so sorry," I apologized lamely. "I didn't mean to frighten you so badly. That was in very poor taste." I mentally kicked myself repeatedly as I realized I had probably just given her flashbacks to the night she'd been attacked. So much for making her feel safe and protected.

Nikki's hands were clutching my shoulders. "Not scared," she managed to pant. She shook her head and blinked a few times. I looked at her in confusion. "That was—" she started, but faltered. Then her eyes focused on mine. The skies were burning. "Not. Scary," she finished, smiling sheepishly at me, even as I saw the wicked gleam in her eyes.

"Right," I teased her, part of me wanting to ask her exactly what she thought it was, if not scary. But I was able to restrain myself. Instead, I set her on her feet, took her hand again, and said. "Come on, Tough Stuff. We wouldn't want to damage Tony's ego by being late to his class." Her heart rate slowly returned to normal.

"I don't think rampaging elephants could damage Tony's ego," she retorted. I laughed. We arrived with plenty of time to keep Tony's ego intact, though our casual bantering throughout class probably didn't help it much.

It was as though some invisible weight had been lifted, or a barrier taken down. Our conversation was lighthearted, trivial. We spoke of many things, of shoes and ships and sealing wax, of cabbages and kings. But when we got back to Nikki's house, she surprised me.

"Why don't you come and meet my family this Sunday?" she asked brightly as we ascended her front steps. I nearly tripped on the top one.

"You want me to meet your family?" I asked incredulously.

"Well, you said you wanted to meet the important people in my life, and really they are the most important people in my life," she replied. "Do you not want to meet them?"

"Of course I do," I said, not sure just yet if I meant it. "But I thought you would want to protect them from, oh say, a blood sucking monster?"

"If you see one, let me know," she sassed. "It would make more sense for me to try to protect you from them. They're the ones who made me as loony tunes as I am, you know."

"How many of them are there?" I asked. "I don't want you to go to all that trouble," I tried, but Nikki cut me off.

"Relax," she laughed. "There's only three of them. And it's no trouble. They're only an hour away, and I go home every Sunday anyway. Besides, they'll want to meet you."

I supposed three didn't sound like too many … wait. "Why would they want to meet me?" I finally thought to ask.

"My parents generally encourage me to bring home the men I fall in love with," she said, then quickly added, "Not that that happens all the time; only once before, actually. And I'm starting to think I didn't even know what love was then," she started to ramble, but I put a finger to her lips.

"Nikki Christian," I whispered. "Did you just insinuate that you're in love with me?" She nodded against my finger. I moved it away and brought my other hand up to cup her beautiful face.

"I would love to meet your family," I breathed and then pressed my lips to hers tenderly. At least it started out as tenderly. As I kissed her, she brought her hands to my chest sliding them up to my neck and into my hair. My hands moved down her neck and around her back, bringing her as close as possible. Her heart was pounding against my chest again, my heart aching to keep up with it. My mouth grew hungry, reacting to the movement of hers. Our lips parted, our breath mingling. It was then I noticed how fast she was breathing. I drew back a little, so she could get some air.

"Gregory," she whispered, pressing her cheek to mine, her eyes still closed. "Come inside with me." My heart very nearly leapt out of my chest. But I hadn't thought this far ahead. I had never really believed Nikki would want this, want me. I didn't have anything with me to protect Nikki. She ran her hand back down my chest. I really wanted to go inside.

"Nikki, I …" I stopped and she heard the hesitation in my voice.

"Please," she begged, barely a whisper. My will power snapped like a twig at the pleading in her voice. Before she could blink we were inside the house and I had her pressed up against the front door. She gasped in surprise, and I traced her parted lips with my tongue. She trembled from head to toe. Her hands tightened in my hair, pulling on it. The hand I had between her shoulder blades gripped the material of her shirt, bunching it together. This accidentally brought my other hand in direct contact with the skin of her lower back. I felt an immediate jolt of electricity, but when she jumped as well, I could tell it was from a different kind of shock. My body was reluctant, but I pulled back and smoothed her shirt back over her back.

"Is that the line you were telling me about?" I asked softly.

"Yes, no, not really, it was just close, or well, seemed to be headed there, but I don't really know. I was just surprised, and it's really my fault because I mean, I did invite you in here like I did … and was kissing you like that and everything…" I stopped her nervous rambling, taking her by the shoulders and placing a soft kiss on her mouth, then kissing each corner.

"Nikki, it's all right," I said calmly while my animal side kicked, screamed, and pretty much threw a tantrum in the back of my head. I ignored it. "I just need to know where the line is."

"I'm sorry; I didn't mean to lead you on like that. And I don't want you to be upset with me or frustrated or anything…" I stopped her with another small kiss.

I gazed deep into her eyes and she stilled. "What *do* you want, Nikki?" I asked gently.

"I want you to hold me while I sleep," she blurted, then looked completely embarrassed. I didn't completely understand her request, but I wasn't about to argue over getting in her bed. I turned her and gently pushed her in the direction of her bathroom.

"Then you better go get ready for bed."

"Really? You're not mad, or think I'm strange or anything?" she asked cautiously.

"Nikki, I would be happy just to lie at the foot of your bed like a dog. Holding you in my arms while you dream is more than I could have hoped for," I assured her.

"Quit comparing yourself to a dog," she said, trying to scowl, but the smirk gave her away.

She gathered a few things and headed to the bathroom. Pulling my sweater over my head, I tried very hard not to conjure images to go along with the sound of falling water from the shower. I failed miserably. I had no practice trying to be chivalrous. I decided as long as I controlled my actions, I could work up to controlling my thoughts. I put my sandals at the foot of the bed and went to unbutton my jeans. Then I remembered her flustered look and decided to forgo getting completely comfortable.

I pulled the down comforter back from the pillows and chastised myself for the fluttering in my stomach. It wasn't as though I'd never been in a woman's bed before. I heard the shower stop. Leaning back against the pillows piled up at the headboard, I put my hands behind my head and closed my eyes. I was trying to focus my thoughts in order to calm down and slow my breathing.

Then the room was flooded with the scent of jasmine and I heard a small gasp from the doorway. I opened my eyes to find Nikki standing there, wide-eyed and slack jawed.

"Is this not what you wanted?" I asked, thinking perhaps I had misunderstood.

"No. Yes. I do. You just. Your chest, I mean your sweater, I mean, do you want me to see if I have anything that might fit you?" she spluttered.

I chuckled, realizing her reaction was to my bare torso instead of my being in her bed. "My sweater would be much too hot to sleep in. And I may be slender, and you're fairly tall, but I still doubt you own anything that would fit me. Am I making you uncomfortable?" I asked, my mouth twitching in an effort not to smirk. Nikki saw it, grabbed a pillow and smacked me with it.

"No you're not making me uncomfortable. I was just surprised is all," she defended. "I'm just making sure you're comfortable."

"Actually, I usually sleep in less than this, but thought you'd appreciate it if I kept my pants on," I teased, though it was the truth. Her eyes widened a little and she gave a nervous little laugh.

"Noted and appreciated," she said. "Do all Immortals have zero body fat and eight pack abs?"

I chuckled again. "It's not really zero, just close to it. And we're all shaped a little differently. While you lose any excess fat, you retain any muscle you had. I really am slender compared to most."

"You must have been a runner in your past life," she mused.

"Nice pajamas," I said, abruptly changing the subject. It was a T-shirt and pants set, bright yellow in color. The shirt was dominated by a brown monkey with the word "Curious" underneath. The pants had smaller versions of the same monkey printed all over them.

"Trust me," she replied. "It could be much worse."

"I like the flannel pants and holey T-shirt," I said, smirking again.

She looked surprised again, but this time it was only for a moment before she rolled her eyes at me and climbed onto the bed. Wrapping her arms around me, she laid her head on my chest. My left hand automatically came down from behind my head to stroke her hair.

"You're sure this is okay?" she asked quietly.

"This is fantastic," I clarified, my flesh tingling where she pressed against it. "Though I am curious," I admitted. She tilted her head up to smirk at me. I smiled, realizing what I'd said. "Really, why was this the first thing you thought of when I asked you what you wanted?"

"Do you remember when I told you that having you near made me feel safe?" she asked, still looking up at me.

"Of course," I replied. "You can't know what it meant to hear you say that."

"Well, I've been having nightmares. I haven't really slept well since…" she trailed off and looked down again.

"Since you met me?" I asked quietly. It hurt to know I had been giving her nightmares by telling her the truth.

"No!" she cried, putting a hand to my chest so she could sit up and look me in the eye. "No, Gregory. Since the other," she paused, terror fleeting across her eyes. I put my hand to her face, wanting to calm her. To my amazement, it actually worked. She closed her eyes, leaned into my hand and smiled. "That's why I kept leaving my windows unlocked," she said, opening her eyes again to gaze into mine. "I knew if… someone wanted to get in badly enough, the lock wouldn't hold them anyway. I kept hoping you would come in and make me feel safe again. I knew if you were here, I'd feel protected even in my dreams."

I had officially lost count of how many times this woman had left me speechless. Instead of trying to piece nonsense together, I leaned forward and kissed her tenderly. When I pulled away, I had found my words again. "I will always protect you, Nikki."

"I know," she replied confidently, her smile bright. She leaned across me, the scent of her damp hair enveloping me again, and turned off the bedside light. "Good night, Gregory." She sighed, snuggling back into my chest. "I love you."

My heart swelled to the point that it got caught in my throat. Hearing those words, in her voice, from those lips. I closed my eyes and concentrated on breathing again. Then I kissed the top of her head, gently squeezing the hip my hand rested on. "I love you too, Nikki," I managed to whisper as my hand went back to stroking her soft curls. "Goodnight."

I enjoyed listening to Nikki's heartbeat and breathing change as she drifted off to sleep. It was gradual at first, but then she must have reached deep sleep because her entire body relaxed at once, melting into me. It was really very pleasant. *I could spend every night like this*, I thought. Though if I did, I might have to bring a shirt to sleep in. My back was already starting to chafe from Nikki's rough cotton sheets. Then, she sighed in her sleep, warm breath escaping her lips and blowing across my bare chest. I closed my eyes as the tingles traveled down to my toes and back. Scratch the shirt. I'd just bring Nikki some silk sheets.

Chapter Twenty-Eight

watched as dawn crept lazily into Nikki's bedroom, gradually lighting up her face as it rested against me. Once the sun was fully up, but before it was very light, Nikki's alarm went off, sending rock music into the quiet room. Annoyed with the interruption of my tranquil state, I reached out and quickly shut it off. The room was silent once again. Nikki's eyes remained closed, but I could tell by her breathing that she was waking.

I stroked her hair from the top of her head down to her back, then left my hand there, rubbing gently. "Mmmm," she sighed, her lips curling into a smile.

"Good morning, beautiful," I whispered. Her eyes fluttered open and she turned to look up at me.

"A very good morning," she agreed. Then with a yawn, she stretched, her back pressing against my chest and her arms reaching up to sneak her hands behind my neck where her fingers laced together. She closed her eyes and relaxed again, without relinquishing her grip on my neck, as her head drifted to one side.

In her prone position, splayed across me, her small T-shirt left a gap of pale skin showing above her monkey covered bottoms. Unable to restrain myself, but not wanting to scare her again, I used a feather light touch to trace lines with my fingertips from one hip to the other and back again. This time she didn't jump. But I was leaving goose bumps, which brought a smile to my lips.

"I seem to be less scary first thing in the morning," I noted, leaning down to kiss Nikki's forehead while I gave her side a brief squeeze before returning to my circuit from hip to hip. "I'll have to remember that."

"Gregory, you're never scary," Nikki said, as she rolled over and sat up to look in my eyes. "At least not to me."

Her change in position forced me to cease the lazy trails I had been making on her stomach. But as she rolled, I kept my hand in contact with her skin, sliding it around to the small of her back. Still needing to feel the smooth texture, my thumb began to trace small circles on her hip.

She seemed to want to prolong the closeness as well. Even though she lifted her torso to see me better, her other hip was pressed against mine, her forearms rested on my chest, and her hands clasped my shoulders.

"Last night I was a little … overwhelmed, and the feeling of your hand on my skin … surprised me," she continued trying to explain. She looked away. "I'm sorry I freaked out like that. I just," her voice trailed off, and she gave her head a small, frustrated shake. I ran my free hand through her hair and gently traced her jaw, bringing her face back to mine.

"Just, what, Nikki?" I asked softly. She looked into my eyes briefly, then buried her face in my chest. Her behavior this morning was both fascinating and nerve-wracking. What could have her so flustered? I wrapped my arms around her and held her for a moment. Then my curiosity got the better of me. "Talk to me, Nikki," I urged. "I want to understand."

"I know," she mumbled against my skin.

"That tickles," I informed her. Finally, she lifted her face to smirk at me. With a deep breath and a great sigh, she tried again, still not looking me in the eye.

"I just … I haven't … I don't have …" She rolled her eyes at her rambling. "I don't have any idea how to tell you something you should probably know."

I looked at her with what was probably a baffled expression.

"I know. I'm not making any sense. Tell you what," she said. "I'm already running late, and this conversation would take a while even if I knew how to begin it, so how about I promise to tell you later, and maybe by then I'll have a clue how to start."

Not knowing what else to say, I went with, "Whatever makes you happy, beautiful." Apparently it was the appropriate response, because Nikki was now smiling brightly at me. I smiled in return, gratified that I had managed to cheer her.

"You have no idea what it means to me, when you call me 'beautiful,' and so obviously mean it," she whispered.

Then her mouth was on mine, pressing urgently. One of her hands slid up into my hair, the other tightening its grip on my shoulder. My body reacted before my brain could, my arms pulling her even closer, crushing her chest to mine. The slow-moving synapses finally fired, just in time to keep the first-response muscles from literally crushing her. Her lips parted, her warm tongue lightly caressing my upper lip. I sighed into her mouth and she took the opportunity to capture my lower lip and suck on it. My brain exploded in a thousand points of light and a moan marked its passing. Just as I was about to roll her over and really get things started, she backed off. Pulling slightly away, she kissed me twice more before looking me in the eyes. I happily drowned in crystal seas while trying to reassemble the scattered pieces of my mind. If she could have this effect on me while we were kissing, I was most looking forward to doing more than that.

"I think I'm beginning to have some idea," I breathed heavily. "Though you may need to get a little more specific," I suggested, sliding my hand further up the back of her shirt in an effort to bring her closer to me again. But my actions once again startled her. Though it was a much smaller reaction than last night, a mere hiccup, I noticed it and withdrew my hand, ready to apologize again.

She recovered quickly, however, running a reassuring hand through my hair. "As pleasant as that sounds," she said in a sultry voice, "I need to get in the shower. I'm already late as it is, and Gertrude does not tolerate tardiness, no matter how unbearably sexy the Immortal in your bed is."

A minute earlier I would have asked her if she wanted help getting into the shower, but her hesitation was fresh in my mind and I kept the comment to myself. She gave me one more kiss, then left me cold and alone in the bed. At the doorway she paused. With one hand on the frame, she turned halfway around to look at me for a moment.

"Thank you, Gregory," she said quietly, emotion weighing her voice. Then she was gone, and I was left staring at the open doorway.

I leaned my head against the headboard and rubbed my face with my hands. I left them covering my eyes as I tried to make sense of Nikki's erratic behavior. I started with the things I knew. Nikki loves me. Even as I thought the words, a smile crept across my face. She had said the words and I had no doubt she meant them. She wanted to introduce me to her family, of all things; that was proof. I shook my head at the image. Surely I was the first Immortal in history to be invited over for Sunday brunch with the folks.

I also knew Nikki wanted me, the fire of her lips still lingering on my mouth, the memory of her warm body making my chest ache with chill in its absence. But if that was the case, then why did she turn so skittish when I touched her? If she wanted to be with me, why were there boundaries at all?

If she wasn't scared of me, as she continuously claimed, what was she scared of? She had been trying to tell me something she found hard to talk about. Something she thought would initiate a lengthy discussion.

What could Nikki be afraid to tell me? Had something happened to her? Something worse than being scarred as a child? My mind began a downward spiral as I contemplated some of the horrible things humans did to each other that would cause Nikki to react the way she did. She was not afraid of touching people, of reaching out to embrace them. It was the more intimate contact that frightened her. Rage began building in my stomach, displacing the emptiness that had been nagging at the back of my mind.

Then I had a disturbing thought. Had that been why Nikki left Rich? Had he hit her? Gotten too rough? I'd kill him. I'd rip his head from his shoulders and tear him limb from limb. I'd...

My internal ranting was interrupted when the shower turned off and I could hear Nikki. She was singing. Her lilting voice carried through the walls and cooled my anger like rain on a wildfire. She was, in her core, a happy person. Nothing so horrific as what I was imagining could have left her so untouched. There must be a different explanation.

Someone knocked on the front door. I doubted Nikki could hear it in the bathroom with the door shut. Less than a minute later, they knocked again, more aggressively. Nikki turned on her blow dryer. I considered knocking on the bathroom door. Then the doorbell rang. The blow dryer turned off. The doorbell rang again.

"Who in the world?" Nikki asked herself. A minute later, as she opened the bathroom door, the knocking came again. "I'm coming!" she yelled. I realized only one person would be so rudely insistent about seeing Nikki.

Chapter Twenty-Nine

"Rich!" Nikki cried as she opened the door. I was already tense in anticipation, but hearing her say his name only wound me tighter.

"Surprise!" came the deep, cheery voice. "I brought bagels."

"What are you doing here?" Nikki exclaimed, her voice several pitches higher than normal.

There was a brief pause. "Let's try this again," Rich said with a little less cheer. "Surprise. I brought bagels." More silence. "This is where you say, 'Oh Rich, it's good to see you, you shouldn't have.'" His voice was getting increasingly irritated at Nikki's reaction, or lack thereof.

"Right, sorry," Nikki apologized. "Thanks for the bagels. I just wasn't expecting you."

"You were expecting someone else?" he asked in a tone I didn't appreciate. The awkward silence was palpable. I could feel it from the bedroom. "Well, since I'm here, you won't mind if I stay for a bit so we can have breakfast?" Rich asked.

"Rich, I—" Nikki started, but he cut her off.

"Nikki, I know you have to get to work in thirty minutes, and you're not even dressed yet. You can't really expect me to believe you're expecting someone before then."

I'd had enough. Rich was crossing the line in several places. Before Nikki could answer his accusation, I strode into the kitchen.

"Are you already done with the shower, Nikki?" I asked. Ignoring her shocked expression, I put my hands on her hips and kissed her gently on the lips. I knew that it was the animal in me essentially marking my territory, but

I couldn't bring myself to care. She blinked at me and then looked at Rich. I followed her gaze and pretended to notice him for the first time.

"Ah, I was wondering who would be dropping by unexpectedly so early in the morning," I said. I kept my tone overly courteous, making my point crystal clear. He wasn't welcome. I took a step forward and held out my hand. "It's Rich, isn't it? I think we met before class once."

Rich couldn't bring himself to shake my hand, and I let it dangle there in the air for a moment before lowering it again.

"I see," Rich said thickly, eyeing my bare torso like he was about to be sick. "No wonder you're running late," he continued to seethe, his eyes turning now on Nikki. I had expected him to be angry, but he looked … betrayed. "Guess it's a good thing I brought breakfast. You must be famished."

It was the kind of comment I would expect from Rob, and normally would have considered it harmless. But the look on his face and tremor in his voice told me it was far from harmless. So did Nikki's reaction.

She took one step forward and brought her hand across his face with a loud crack that echoed through the still air. As stunned as I was by her violence, I was even more confused by Rich's response. He actually looked relieved that she had slapped him.

"Nikki, I," he stuttered, but this time Nikki cut him off.

"Get out," she said quietly. Getting rid of Rich had been my intention when I came into the kitchen, but somehow my plan had gone terribly awry.

"Nikki, c'mon, what was I supposed to think when a half-naked man comes striding out of your bedroom?" Rich asked. Apparently it was the wrong question. The normally passive angel I knew lashed out again, this time leaving parallel lines of red across Rich's cheek.

"Get out," she repeated, her voice still quietly menacing. At this point I probably should have done something, but I was too stunned to do anything but stand there and watch the exchange.

Rich did take one step back before continuing, "Nikki, I'm sorry. You're right, I know better than that. I know *you* better than that." He lifted one hand pleadingly in her direction, but the flash of her piercing blue eyes gave him pause, and he dropped it again. "Nikki, please."

Clenching her jaw, Nikki walked past Rich and opened the front door. When he didn't move, she took a deep breath and her face softened, slightly. "Look, Rich. You and I both know that I am physically incapable of holding a grudge, and that I'm going to forgive you," she conceded. When he took a step towards her she held up her hand. "But it's not going to be today." She then waved her hand through the open door and raised her eyebrow. "Please go. Don't make me resort to asking Gregory to show you out."

Rich glanced back at me, and I felt like I should respond in some way, flex my pecs or some other intimidating gesture. I didn't. I felt like I was watching this melodramatic exchange of human emotions through a two-way mirror. I could see everything going on, but I was unable to interact with the images in front of me. Rich looked back at Nikki. He literally swallowed what he was about to say, lowered his head, and walked through the door.

Nikki closed it behind him and leaned on it with her back to me, her face pressed into the tight fists she had against the door. When silent sobs began to shake her slender frame, I was snapped back to reality. I crossed the room and reached out to touch her shoulder, not sure what she wanted. "Nikki," I said gently.

She turned and collapsed against my chest, weeping openly. I let her cry for a few moments, simply holding her. Then it became too much. "I want to understand," I whispered.

"I know," she sniffled. Then she looked up at me and smirked with the tears still streaming down her cheeks. "Having to deal with such an overwhelming amount of human emotion must be terribly obnoxious for you."

"Fascinating, maybe. Baffling, definitely. But not obnoxious," I corrected her, brushing at the rivers cascading down her face. "I admit I'm not used to seeing so much emotion on display. I'm still trying to understand *feeling* emotion myself. I need your help in translating what just happened." She smiled at my confession, sniffling again before taking a deep breath.

"It's complicated." She sighed, laying her head back down on my now damp chest.

"So am I," I replied, stroking her hair. She laughed softly.

"That's true," she agreed. She took another deep breath and looked up at me. "Let me get dressed and then we'll sit down and talk."

"You can't talk in a robe?" I asked, anxious to get an explanation.

"Yes, but," she blushed a little, "I'd be more comfortable if I had underwear on."

As I realized the bathrobe was the only thing she had on, I couldn't keep a sly grin from spreading across my face. "Right. Then I guess I'll go wait on the couch."

"I'll be right back," she promised.

When she returned in slacks and a cotton shirt under a lightweight blazer, I remembered she was supposed to be at work.

"What about Gertrude?" I asked as she sank down next to me on the aging sofa.

She smiled. "Gertrude loves me like the granddaughter she never had. I'm the only one who actually takes having a job at the library seriously. She won't mind if I'm late this one time."

I arched an eyebrow at her. "So you were lying earlier?"

"No," she defended. "Just trying to delay the inevitable with a convenient truth." She was quiet after that, still trying to find a starting point.

"So, my walking in without my shirt was a bad idea," I said, giving her an opening.

"Perhaps," she said. "But Rich overreacted."

"Actually, he didn't," I said cautiously. Nikki looked up at me in surprise. "I could have put my sweater on before I came out, Nikki. Rich got the message I was trying to imply. Men are men, mortal or not." I winced as I let the truth out. "I was telling him you were mine and to back off."

Nikki stared at me, open mouthed for a minute. Then she started to laugh. "You were jealous!" she cried incredulously.

I smiled at her happy face, but pressed on in the direction of the question I had. "Of course I was jealous. You've already told me you loved Rich once, that, in a way, you still do. I've never loved anyone but you."

Nikki stopped laughing and looked at me with a soft expression.

"Rich took the bait and assumed we'd had sex," I went on. Nikki was momentarily shocked at my frank wording, but recovered quickly.

"Yes," she agreed.

"And you slapped him for it."

"Yes."

"Is the idea of being with me so utterly repugnant?"

"No! Gregory, no, that's not it!" Nikki insisted. "The idea of being with you," she paused and looked down in embarrassment for a moment, then she looked to the side before finally looking me in the eye. "The idea of being with you is simply overwhelming. As I exhibited by my reactions last night ... and this morning."

I smiled at her response, but there was still a lot I didn't understand. "Rich wasn't mad you slapped him."

"No."

"He was relieved."

"Probably."

I raised an eyebrow and waited for her to explain.

"If Rich had come upon us while we were out to dinner, or walking to class, or in any other situation that would have made it obvious we were dating, he would have been hurt," she began. "But faced with a scenario that insinuated we had … been intimate, he felt betrayed."

"I'm confused," I admitted.

"That makes two of us," she said softly, mostly to herself. With a sigh she gave me more information. "Rich was raised in a very devout Catholic family. I grew up religious as well, though not as strictly, and Rich was really my first boyfriend, so when we talked about it, I agreed waiting was the right thing to do." She stopped and looked at me like I should understand what she had just said. For a few agonizing moments I didn't and we just stared at each other. Then it clicked.

"You're a virgin?" I blurted, she winced at my continuing lack of tact on the subject, then nodded, biting her lip nervously. "But … you're beautiful!" I said incredulously.

She rolled her eyes and laughed a little. "You're biased," she said. "Besides, there's more to it than that. Rich was my first love."

I was starting to get very frustrated with the fact that, while she was speaking English, I continued to struggle to understand her. It was probably apparent on my face because she took pity on me and tried again.

"When I … touch someone like that, I want them to know I love them, not just that I desire them," she said, nearly quoting my own words.

"Ah," I said as things finally started making sense. "I think I understand."

"I knew you would," she said, taking my hand, "eventually."

"So you think it's inappropriate to have," I stopped myself and edited, "to be intimate with someone if you're not married?"

She sighed deeply again. "Yes, well, that's where things get all kinds of confusing. My whole life, I thought and believed a certain way, and now I suddenly find myself in love with a man that defies conventional morality."

"Because what I am defies the very nature of the world you've known to be true," I suggested.

"Yes and no. You are different than any truth I've known, but your existence doesn't automatically disprove the rest," she responded. "I believe in God, Gregory. And I believe He created all living things and that everything has a soul, including you." I stared at her, stunned by this statement.

"But as obvious as it is that He would expect different things from wild animals as He would from human beings, He would just as obviously expect different things from Immortals than He would from mortals."

"And I fall in with the wild animals?" I asked quietly.

"Of course not, Gregory, don't be ridiculous. Animals live by instinct, you obviously have some choice in the way you live," she said gently. She gathered her thoughts for a moment, trying to make sense of a situation that was beyond reason. "I am absolutely sure of one thing." Gazing into my eyes, she locked me into the blue depths of her own. "I love you, Gregory. I'm just still trying to wrap my head around the details."

"That makes two of us," I replied, taking her face in my hand and kissing her gently. When I released her, she smiled sweetly at me.

"Are you coming to work with me today?" she asked happily.

"I would love to; unfortunately there are some things I need to attend to," I chuckled and kissed away her beautiful pout. "But I will see you later."

"You'd better," she threatened. Then she kissed me again in a way that sent sparks up through the ends of my hair and down through my toes. Reluctantly, we broke apart and finished getting dressed. I meant to only walk her to the campus, but it wasn't until we got to the library itself that I could let her go.

As she walked through the glass door, I could see an elderly woman in a tweed skirt and a severe bun look over her glasses critically at Nikki. Apparently, being thirty minutes late for work was stretching it even for Gertrude's favorite surrogate granddaughter. However, when Nikki went straight up to her and threw her arms around her in an exuberant hug, even the hardened old librarian couldn't keep the smile from sneaking up on her face. She began scolding Nikki, complete with wagging finger, but with a half-smile still on her face, it didn't look very scary.

Chapter Thirty

The walk back to my loft gave me ample time to think about the revelations I'd just received. It had never occurred to me that Nikki's boundaries had nothing to do with me. In this age, when humanity was at its most depraved, morality hadn't even factored into my thinking. Now I realized that a woman as pure in heart as Nikki would of course make such life choices. She had lived her life according to certain truths, and I had come along and twisted everything into a complicated and shadowy enigma. I knew without a doubt that she would have been better off if I'd never seen her. She would still be living in a world of black and white, where her choices were clear and easy. I was equally certain that I would never be able to let her go.

Whatever it took, I would stay with her. Any rules, or lines, or boundaries she thought up, I wouldn't question them. If I could simply be near her, kiss her, hold her close, it was more than I deserved to ask for.

In my loft, I went to shower, vaguely hoping to wash some of the conflict inside me away. As the hot water hit me, the last of Nikki's scent escaped from my skin into the steam, clinging to my nostrils. I was revisited by the images that had come to me while listening to Nikki shower. Knowing what I did now, I fought a little harder to reign in my imagination. Unfortunately, accepting the fact that I would only take what Nikki was willing to give, had no effect on changing what I wanted.

After toweling off, I collapsed onto my bed, utterly exhausted. The constant roller coaster of emotions had over stimulated my weary senses. And it had been too long since I last fed. As I lay in the dark, I tried to relax and slip away. But the shower had too thoroughly washed away Nikki's scent and without the overwhelming desire for her, my body was finally having a delayed reaction to being neglected. The walls of my stomach contracted, aching to be filled. My throat was dry and parched, causing me to swallow repeatedly. When my hands began to shake like an addict going into withdrawal, I knew it was useless to keep trying.

I rose from my bed, threw on some boxers and went to my desk. Perhaps thinking up new tales for Nikki would engage me enough to distract me. I opened my book of "true stories" and began writing. For a few hours, it worked. Then I noticed that the stories I was remembering were becoming increasingly dark and, more often than not, recounted times I had fed in a variety of ways. I realized my subconscious was taking my body's side in this personal battle and closed my book in disgust.

Noting the time, I realized Nikki would be getting off work soon. I had no reason not to go back to her place. I was getting nothing done here. I took a moment to daydream about her reaction to seeing me show up on her doorstep, or even waiting for her when she got home, if I hurried.

Her pink lips would smile, and I would capture them with my own. Her heart would speed up, sending her blood coursing through her delicate veins. Trailing kisses down her neck, I could feel it pulsing beneath my lips. How sweet it would taste when...

I stood up swiftly, my chair clattering to the ground behind me. Rob's words of warning came rushing back. *"If I gave into that lust too freely, or hadn't fed in a while..."* I couldn't go back to Nikki like this. I had to feed.

Dressing quickly, I went out into the quickly darkening night. As I stalked the streets of San Francisco, I continued to wage war against myself. I knew I was putting Nikki in danger if I didn't satisfy my thirst. But this one was too old, that one too young, too drunk, too much trouble. I knew I was just making excuses. Any of them would do. But even as my hands shook and my dry mouth watered as each mortal walked by, I couldn't bring myself to kill. How could I look Nikki in the eye knowing I was truly an animal, "ruled by my instincts" as she put it?

Stopping at the next intersection, I gaped across the street. I was standing in front of Nikki's darkened house. How had I gotten here? I cursed my traitorous body as it dragged my feet over the asphalt and to her bedroom window. Instinctively, I tried to pry it open. It was locked. I sighed, though I wasn't sure if it was from relief or disappointment. Even though I had seen her just this morning, I already ached for her. But being near her now could have disastrous results.

"I promise to let myself in with the key you have hidden behind the sunshine sculpture hanging outside your front door whenever I feel so inclined, no matter the time, day or night."

Before I could think, I was slipping the key into the lock with trembling hands and turning it. I'll just check on her, make sure she's okay. I'll just sit in the corner of her room and watch her sleep. I just need to be near her, to smell her scent.

Stepping into her front room, I breathed deeply. I followed the tantalizing smell of her warm blood blindly to her bedroom, then stood frozen and trembling in the doorway, my breath coming in shallow pants.

Nikki lay on her stomach, sprawled across her bed. One hand was tucked under her cheek, the other was hanging over the edge of the mattress. A sliver of moonlight broke through the blinds, falling across her tranquil face and making her soft skin glow as she smiled sweetly in her sleep.

I fell to my knees at her bedside, my face inches from her slender wrist. Tilting my head even closer to her skin, I inhaled greedily. The smell of her blood was strong and sweet. I sighed in delight and anguish, my breath blowing gently across her skin. Her hand twitched and my fingers automatically shot out and wrapped around her wrist before it could move further away.

Instead of waking up, screaming, and running away, which would have been most helpful to my present state of mind, Nikki simply sighed and smiled sleepily. She rolled backwards, pulling me into the bed by the arm I was latched onto. Then she returned to her previously splayed position, only now I was beneath her.

I tried to close my eyes against the warmth, the smell, but they flew open again as she turned her head and shook it a little to get the hair out of her face. Still getting comfortable, and oblivious to her peril, Nikki tilted her head back, exposing the length of her pale, perfect throat.

I was all but hyperventilating, vibrating from head to toe with the effort of my restraint. My jittery hand came up to her throat, my palm resting directly over the pulsing artery, feeling the blood rushing just under her skin. I closed my eyes and swallowed thickly, damning myself straight to hell for what I was about to do. As I leaned forward, Nikki came closer. Her lips met my neck before I reached hers.

"I love you," she whispered against my skin with a soft kiss.

Gravity shifted, and I stepped through the looking glass into a world where nothing was different, but everything had abruptly changed. I was suddenly hyper aware of the softness of her body pressing against my chest, her warm breath on my neck, the jasmine scented cloud drifting from her hair spread over my shoulder. I still had her wrist and brought it up to my nose, inhaling the sweet almond of her skin. Smiling, I placed a kiss on the palm of her hand and lowered it back to the bed.

I laid my head back on the pillows and closed my eyes. I could still smell her blood, and I could feel the deep ache that told me I was running on blood long past its expiration date. But they were background noises. Afraid that this might only be a temporary reprieve, I concentrated on Nikki's even breathing and the rhythmic beating of her heart, trying to hang on to her very essence.

It was a distinct pattern, one that I seemed intimately familiar with. It lulled my body, stilling the tremors, easing the tension. My lungs filled with her breath, inhaling in tandem with her sighs. My heart paced itself to the slow echo of hers, reaching out each time they beat together.

I realized it was not her blood that had drawn me, even unconsciously, to her tonight. It was simply her. Without her I was incomplete. She was the best part of me, the part that could feel love, compassion, and empathy, the part that I had been missing all my horrendously long life. I could never hurt Nikki, even at my most desperate and primal. Without her, I would cease to exist.

But with her, in my arms, I was whole. A deep sigh escaped my lips and the last of my muscles fully relaxed. I found the relief my body had been seeking tonight. I found the peace I had not known I was aching for over the countless years. As my senses shut down, entranced by the music of Nikki's body, and I slowly faded into the sweet oblivion, one word echoed through the caverns of my mind.

Home.

Chapter Thirty-One

The rest of the night passed without dreams, my consciousness completely spent. As dawn approached, the faint light broke through my trance and I came back to myself. I felt much better this morning. My newly refreshed senses and constitution made it much easier for me to ignore the gnawing hunger and bone-deep ache for blood. They were now simply reference points to highlight how utterly delicious and satisfying it felt to hold Nikki as she clung to me.

I smirked as I noticed the position we were now lying in. While my body and I had come to an agreement over Nikki's blood last night, it seemed we were still at odds over her virtue. My hands had drifted to places that surely would have made Nikki blush if she were conscious. The only reason I found it humorous instead of shameful, was that Nikki's body seemed to have had similar ideas in her sleep. Her legs had twined themselves with mine and one of her hands had somehow found its way under my shirt and was now resting against the skin of my chest.

As comfortable as I was, I knew this was not the position Nikki wanted to find herself in first thing in the morning—not *this* morning, anyway. So I carefully shifted my hands to her waist. I frowned at even the small loss of contact and, instead, wrapped my arms around her back, holding her closer to me. Much better. There wasn't much I could do about her position without waking her. She'd have to deal with that on her own.

It wasn't until the sun was fully up in the sky, filling the bedroom with golden light, that Nikki began to stir. I could hear her breathing change as she woke. She sighed deeply and snuggled up to me from head to toe, causing me to chuckle. She froze at the sound.

"Good morning to you, too," I said softly, humor coloring my voice.

She looked up at me, using her hands on my chest as leverage. All at once, she realized where all of her appendages were and she blushed furiously. "Why do you have your shirt on? I mean, why didn't you take it off? Wait, no." She stopped and collected herself while I raised an eyebrow at her "inappropriate" questions. "You weren't here when I fell asleep," she finally stated.

"Are you mad that I'm here now?" I asked. It hadn't occurred to me that she wouldn't remember last night at all. She had every right to be angry that I had snuck into her bed.

"No! Of course not, I'm always glad when you're here. I was just surprised is all," she said, smiling. "And a little embarrassed at the position I seem to have put you in," she added, removing her hand from my shirt and disengaging her legs.

"I didn't mind." I smirked, squeezing her shoulders. I then ran my hands down her back and squeezed her hips as well.

"Oh, well as long as I didn't make you uncomfortable," she said, rolling her eyes and shaking her head at me. She looked into my face again and smiled at me. Then she collapsed back onto my chest and wrapped her arms around my back, squeezing tight. "I missed you last night."

"Apparently so," I teased.

"Yeah, well, apparently you missed me too, seeing as I wake up and here you are," she retorted, lifting her head to glare at me.

I brought one hand up to cup her pouting chin. "Of course I missed you," I assured her. "You could simply step across the room and I would miss you. Any moment I'm not smelling your scent," I put my nose in her hair and breathed deeply, "touching your skin," I ran my hand up and down her bare arm, "tasting your lips," I breathed, coming inches from her mouth, "I ache for you," I finished, closing the gap and pressing my lips to hers.

She leaned forward into the kiss, her hands sliding up my chest and into my hair. I took that as an invitation and brought my hand up to the back of her head, securing her to me. My tongue flicked out, testing the waters so to speak. She parted her lips, and with a sigh, welcomed me into her mouth. For several minutes I blissfully drowned in a rising sea of desire. Then Nikki came up for air.

"I believe you," she said breathlessly. I kissed down her neck and back to her jaw before I could let go of her taste and lie back against the pillows again. She smiled down at me and I was struck senseless by the beauty of her blond curls falling wildly into her sapphire eyes.

"What should we do today?" she asked when she finally caught her breath. I smirked up at her, but wisely kept my first thought to myself.

"Don't you have to work today?" I asked instead.

"Nope," she said happily. "I'm all yours."

I grinned at that thought. What would I do with Nikki all day? Something wonderful. Something that could show her I'm not all gloom and doom. Something absolutely normal. My grin widened as the perfect idea came to me.

"How about we go to the beach?" I asked.

"Perfect," she agreed. "I'll go get my suit on."

I laughed at her exuberance. "Don't you need breakfast first?" I asked, even as her stomach growled.

"Right, breakfast first, then the beach," she laughed. She bounced off the bed and out the door with me following behind, wishing my hunger was as simple to satisfy.

An hour later we were climbing out of the sunshine bug and headed toward the sand.

"And why did we stop to buy new clothes instead of stopping by your house?" she asked me, indicating my new swimwear and flip-flops.

"Because my place isn't on the way here and the surf shop was," I pointed out reasonably.

She shook her head at me. "We weren't in that much of a hurry."

"Though from the looks of this bag, it looks like we're staying for a week," I teased, taking the enormous canvas sack from her as we walked across the sand.

"Oh stop, it's not even heavy," she protested. "All I put in there was the towels, my sunscreen, and some water. What do you usually bring your stuff in, a fanny pack?"

I laughed. "I usually don't bring anything at all."

She looked at me skeptically.

"I tend to lose things at the beach."

She raised an eyebrow. I shrugged my shoulders, and she laughed, letting it go. Nikki soon found a spot and spread out the towels. She then peeled off her shorts and T-shirt revealing her suit. It was a deep blue that very nearly matched her eyes. The top had a clasp at the neck and in back, with the material flowing down to meet the bottoms that were cut low, like little shorts. It was stylish, and modest, and very Nikki.

"Gregory," she said, raising an eyebrow, "You're staring."

"Yes, I am," I openly admitted, causing her to laugh and blush at the same time. "Do you need help putting on your suntan lotion?" I offered gallantly.

"You wish," she scoffed. "I put it on before we left." She laughed again at my pouting face.

"Then why did you bring it?" I wondered.

"I just keep this bottle in my beach bag, actually," she explained. "But I may have to reapply later," she admitted. I waggled my eyebrows at her in true Rob fashion and she rolled her eyes at me.

"Shall we swim?" I asked, standing up and reaching out for her hand.

"What a novel idea for the beach," she teased, lacing her fingers with mine as we strolled to the water.

The water was a little cold, but the weather was warm, so there were a lot of people about. They were noisy and rude, and I wanted Nikki all to myself.

"How long can you hold your breath?" I asked her.

"I don't know, a minute maybe?" she guessed.

"That's all?" I blurted thoughtlessly. She looked at me in shock, then her brows furrowed slightly. "I'm sorry. I just usually go further out to avoid the crowds, but to get out that far unnoticed I swim underwater for a mile or so." Her eyes widened again. "Here is fine," I finished.

We waded out far enough that every so often, the waves would pick Nikki up off the ocean floor. I, of course, sunk like a rock unless I took a small jump as the wave passed.

"This must be so frustrating for you," Nikki said quietly, "In so many ways."

"Being surrounded by humans? Most of them are closer to shore," I noted, glad that we had at least a little peace where we were.

She shook her head and smiled sadly. "No, well, yes, kind of… Being with me," she finally said, watching her hands as they floated back and forth in the water. "It has to be frustrating to deal with the human drama, emotion—" she paused for a moment, "—limitations."

"Nikki," I chastised her, taking one of her hands and pulling her around to face me. To my horror, her eyes were glistening with unshed tears. I reached my other hand out to gently touch her face. "Being with you … I feel so many things. Fear, hope, anger, jealously, love, compassion, and yes, sometimes I do get frustrated that there are things I want to share with you that I can't. But Nikki, don't you see? The fact that I can feel anything at all is amazing. You don't know what I was before I met you," I finished in a whisper.

I leaned forward and kissed her softly. When I pulled back she was smiling again. "Besides," I added, "you're not the only one with limitations."

She raised a skeptical eyebrow.

"Seriously," I insisted. "There are plenty of things you can do that I can't."

"Name one," she challenged.

"Float," I said, just as a new wave covered my head while she rode gracefully above it. When I came up I spit ocean water out of my mouth for effect. It worked. She laughed, and the sun started shining again.

"I suppose that would be inconvenient at times," she agreed once she could compose a straight face. "That's actually my favorite thing to do in the ocean. Just kick back and relax, watching the clouds."

She did just that and we spent a few lazy hours in the surf. It was completely mundane, ordinary, perfect. An hour or so after the sun had crossed directly overhead, I could tell Nikki would be hungry soon. I pulled her into my arms, feeling how the sun had warmed her skin.

"Time for lunch?" I asked, seconds before her stomach growled loudly.

She was obviously embarrassed but laughed. "Apparently so."

Back on the sand I asked her what she wanted to eat, wondering if we would be leaving. I didn't want our time at the beach to end just yet; I enjoyed feeling like a normal couple. It had been somewhat disappointing that I couldn't show her my favorite parts of the beach, but maybe another day we could rent a boat to go out further. Maybe even find those dolphins if they were still around.

"Beach food!" Nikki cried excitedly, cutting off my rambling thoughts.

"Beach food?"

"Yes."

I had to ask, "And what exactly is 'beach food'?"

"The kind of food that, while it's tasty at the beach, you would never eat it under normal circumstances," she explained. With a completely straight face she added, "It's in the same family as carnival food and theme park food, sharing many of the same options."

"And where does one go about procuring said beach food?" I asked, beginning to scan the sidewalk and nearby peer.

"Most often from someone yelling while standing behind, in front of, or near a big ol' box with wheels and an umbrella," she said. I turned to see where she might be looking, but found her digging through her bag.

"Need help with that?" I asked as she pulled out the bottle of sun block.

"I'm looking for my wallet," she mumbled absently.

"Why would you need your wallet?" I asked, raising an eyebrow. She looked up at me and raised one of hers in return.

"Beach food may not be quality nutrition, but it still costs money," she said dryly.

"I don't doubt that, but what kind of boyfriend would I be if I didn't buy you lunch?"

"The kind that isn't eating lunch," she retorted. Then she smiled. "Did you just say boyfriend?"

"Would it bother you if I did?" I returned.

"Nope," she said, her smile growing brighter. "Just checkin'."

"Is that what you were talking about?" I asked, pointing to a brightly striped umbrella shading a sweaty looking vendor that stood opposite his "big ol' box with wheels" from a line of people in bathing suits.

"That would be it," she said, moving to stand. I put a hand on her shoulder.

"You just relax and tell your boyfriend what to bring you," I suggested. Her face brightened at hearing the word again, making me chuckle.

"A soft pretzel dripping with mustard and some nachos drowning in molten cheese substitute, please," she requested. I couldn't help but wince a little at her choices.

"Really?" I asked.

"Beach food," she said by way of explanation.

I shrugged my shoulders. "Whatever makes you happy, beautiful." Before I could get up, she caught me in an embrace, pressing the still damp fabric of her top against my nearly dry chest. The chill spread goose bumps across my skin.

"I do love it when you say that," she whispered and kissed me soundly. Then she lay down on her back, closing her eyes and making a big show of relaxing.

I smiled crookedly at her antics and went to collect her food. It took longer than I thought, and when I got back she was closing the lid to her sun block and putting it back in her bag. She laughed at the pout on my face.

"You took so long I decided to do something productive," she said.

"I had some trouble with the vendor," I defended.

She raised her eyebrows. "What kind of trouble?"

"He refused to take a credit card," I replied indignantly.

She laughed. "I should have warned you about that. Don't you carry any cash?"

"Not since 1951," I stated. She blinked at my exactness, then laughed again, shaking her head.

"How did you end up with my food, then?" she wondered while taking it from me.

"The person behind me took pity and paid for it," I explained without elaboration.

"Wow, that was nice. I should thank him. Where is he?" she asked, looking around as she took a bite of the enormous pretzel.

"I don't think that's necessary, and she's right over there," I replied, pointing vaguely toward the cement barrier blocking the beach from the street.

Nikki turned and suddenly her eyes went wide. "Surely you don't mean that platinum blonde in the barely-there thong?"

"That would be the one," I replied without looking away from her face.

"That would explain the daggers she's throwing from her eyes," she said with a small shiver. "Gregory, she was probably trying to flirt with you!"

"She was most definitely trying to flirt with me."

"And you still let her buy my lunch?" she exclaimed. "That's rude."

"I thought it fairly rude of her to be flirting so crassly with someone else's boyfriend," I said, smirking.

"But how was she supposed to know that?" Nikki insisted. "You're devastatingly handsome, remember? She was probably thrilled to find someone in her league!"

"While arguing with the vendor, I used the phrase, 'for my girlfriend' no less than three times, Nikki. She was well aware of the fact that I was taken," I corrected her gently. Then I leaned forward to whisper, "And the only league I'm interested in is yours, so long as you're willing to let me play."

"Oh," she said, a smile gracing her beautiful lips. "Well, in that case," she sat up tall, lifted her pretzel in the air and waved enthusiastically at the poor imitation of human beauty. The peroxide blonde huffed and turned on her heel, bouncing away. Nikki giggled and thoroughly enjoyed the rest of her lunch.

When she was finished, she lay down with her head resting on my stomach, declaring that she couldn't move for thirty minutes while her food digested. I was more than happy to comply. My eyes were beginning to note the difference between wearing sunglasses instead of my usual contacts. I took the insufficient protection off and closed my eyes, putting an arm over my face to completely block out the light for a while. My other hand played idly with bits of Nikki's thoroughly disheveled hair. We were quiet for a time, at peace listening to the sounds of ocean waves and busy tourists around us.

"Gregory?" Nikki whispered, not wanting to disturb our bubble of tranquility.

"Yes, love?" I whispered back without moving.

"What happened at the end of my bedtime story?" she asked. "I only heard as far as them declaring their love in her tent."

"That's where I ended it," I replied.

"I know, but what happened next?"

"You fell asleep."

"I know that," she said, poking my side. "I meant in the story."

"They ran away together."

"And lived happily ever after," she sighed.

"They were disgraced and disowned by their families." *Why am I telling her this?*

"But they had each other," Nikki continued.

"Until she died in childbirth."

"But he could find comfort in the baby," she pressed.

"Until the emperor decided he wanted an heir and whisked him away."

"Did the samurai find no peace at all in his life?"

"In his old age, he was allowed to spend summers with his grandchildren."

"I guess that's something," she said sadly.

We were quiet again, but the peaceful feeling was gone. I felt Nikki sit up and turn toward me. I lifted my arm and replaced my glasses to look at her.

"Don't you know any stories that end with 'happily ever after'?" she asked with a concerned face.

"'Happily ever after' isn't really the end to any story, Nikki," I replied, suddenly feeling macabre. "It's simply a way to avoid discussing the true ending to every story."

"When someone dies," Nikki said quietly.

"That would be when their story ends," I agreed. "But people like you who believe in God, heaven, an afterlife and such have some hope."

She looked at me expectantly.

"Sad endings are only sad for those who get left behind," I explained. Nikki's deep blue eyes were a mirror to the ancient sadness I could feel weighing down my heart.

Suddenly she jumped up, brushed off some sand and held her hand out to me. "C'mon, Mr. Mopey Pants, let's go."

"Where are we going?" I asked, taking her hand and standing up. I felt horrible that I had once again managed to ruin a fantastic time with my personal cloud of doom.

"I have someplace to show you," she replied cryptically with a smirk. I helped gather her things, and we headed back to the little bug of sunshine.

Chapter Thirty-Two

Back at the apartment, it was decided that Nikki would shower first, then finish getting ready in the bedroom while I showered. I only had the clothes from last night, but since I don't sweat, they were still relatively fresh. They just smelled a little like Nikki after being used as her personal mattress. I smiled at the memory as I opened the bathroom door and pulled the shirt on over my head.

"Ready?" Nikki asked brightly from the couch. Her hair was still damp, as her dryer was in the bathroom. She was wearing dark jeans and a cotton shirt with a deep v-neck. The deep brown would normally have accentuated her ivory skin, giving it a healthy glow. But something wasn't quite normal.

"Nikki! Your chest!" I exclaimed, not only sounding like an idiot but pointing as well.

She blushed, but rolled her eyes. "Really, Gregory, it's just a v-neck. You saw me in less at the beach today."

"No, Nikki," I said, still pointing. "I meant look at your chest. It's bright red. I think you missed a spot with your sunscreen." The look of surprise on my face faded into one of concern.

Nikki looked down and gasped. "Oh! I didn't notice while I was getting dressed. It doesn't hurt yet." She touched the angry red skin gingerly. "But it's sure going to."

I watched as she went into the bathroom to assess the damage in the mirror. She winced when she turned on the light and saw just how bad a burn it was.

"I'm an idiot," she said, almost to herself. "I'll be peeling by tomorrow."

I had an idea that brought a smirk to my face, but I wasn't sure Nikki would approve. Perhaps if I worded it just right… "What if I could help?" I inquired.

"With my sunburn?" she asked. Noting the smirk, she raised an eyebrow. "I can put aloe on it myself, thanks Gregory, but nice try."

I fixed the smirk and tried again. "Let me rephrase. What if I could heal it?"

Her brow furrowed in confusion. "What do you mean, *heal* it?"

I took a few steps forward and stood by her in front of the mirror. "I mean exactly that. Heal the burn, make the skin new."

Nikki stared at me. I decided perhaps a demonstration would help. Before she could think, much less move, I swooped down and licked firmly at the base of her throat. I had already moved away again by the time she jumped back, giving a little yelp of surprise. Seeing she was about to reprimand me, I took her chin in my hand and gently turned her face, gesturing to the mirror. There was now a spot of ivory amid the sea of red.

Nikki's eyes grew wide, her hand reaching up to touch the damp skin. She turned to look at me. I was grinning at her reaction. "What? How?"

"Whatever it is in my blood that heals me, be it DNA or what have you, is in my saliva as well," I said simply, glad to have found some way, however inconsequential, that I could be of actual benefit to her.

"Wait, so you can heal people?" she asked, astonished. "Of anything? Cancer? AIDS?"

"Nothing so extravagant, I'm afraid," I corrected her. "Mostly…flesh wounds," I said, pausing awkwardly, not wanting to explain that being able to heal a wound as you made it helped cut down on wasted blood loss. "Anything more substantial would require Immortal blood to heal it, and that would cross the line."

"Because it's 'inappropriate' to heal a human with your blood?" Nikki asked peevishly.

"Because they would cease to be human," I answered quietly.

"Oh."

I watched her for a time, wondering if she was going to panic, or scream, or simply throw me out. When she did none of those things I was slightly encouraged.

"You never answered my question," I finally said, breaking the silence.

"What question?" she asked.

"What if I could heal your sunburn?" I reminded her. "Would you want me to?"

"You don't have to do that, Gregory," she said, searching my face. "It's just a sunburn, and it's my own fault."

"I don't mind," I said, a small smile forming on my lips.

"If it's really not too much trouble," Nikki began. I took her hand and walked her over to the couch sitting her down. "I really hate peeling."

"It's no trouble," I assured her, my smile growing. I reached down and took the edge of her shirt in my hands. She immediately grabbed them with her own.

"What are you doing?"

"I need access to the burn. I assume most of it is covered by your shirt," I said. My tone was casual, but my lips were twitching into a smirk. "Don't you trust me?"

Nikki eyed me skeptically, then sighed. "Of course I trust you," she said, pulling her shirt off herself. She held it in her lap with both hands, blushing furiously.

She was wearing the same purple and teal paisley patterned bra I had seen the first night I started watching her. I groaned, too softly for her to hear, realizing this would be even better, and worse than I thought.

"What?" Nikki asked, knowing something was off even without hearing the noise I made.

"Nothing," I assured her, but she gave a look that let me know she wasn't buying it. "I like your bra," I admitted. Nikki rolled her eyes and pushed on my shoulder.

"What do you want me to do?" she asked, seeming a little self-conscious.

"Nothing," I answered. "Just hold still."

"Yes, sir," she sassed, causing me to chuckle.

I put my hands behind her back, holding her in place. This time I lowered my head slowly to her neck, giving her a small kiss on the spot that was already ivory again. She laughed nervously. I drew my tongue across her fiery skin and her heart rate immediately began to pick up. As I worked my way from one side to the other, I would stop occasionally to plant more chaste kisses. After each pass, I would lower my head further to cover the entire burn. By the time I was done, Nikki was near breathless, her heartbeat hammering in my ears. My own heart had beat twice already and I was trying very hard not to increase my own breath.

"See?" I said pulling away to look into Nikki's blue and presently clouded eyes. "No trouble at all."

"Thank you?" she muttered half as a question, while I smiled down at her. Nikki blinked a few times to clear her head and then stood up and put her shirt back on. "I think we're ready to go now," she said, walking over to get her car keys.

Nikki began mumbling to herself under her breath, "Of course it's 'no trouble' Mr. Immortal-Casanova-with-the-smooth-moves…" but of course, I heard every word.

Chapter Thirty-Three

I was just about to ask Nikki if she was lost, when she stopped the car in front of a dilapidated building surrounded by rundown businesses. What could she possibly want to show me in such a nasty area of town?

"What are we doing here?" I asked. My eyes instinctively took inventory of the humans crowding in around us, my body tensing slightly in case I needed to protect Nikki from one of them. The smell of dirt, decay, and other more horrible aspects of humanity was overwhelming. Nikki seemed completely oblivious.

"This is where I spend most of my free time," she said, taking my hand and smiling brightly.

"Why?" I questioned, a little too loudly. I was horrified by the thought of her coming here alone on a regular basis. I frequently used an alley not two blocks from here to stash bodies. It was that sort of neighborhood.

Nikki kept her smile in place, though she raised one eyebrow at my outburst. Using the hand I had welded to hers, she dragged me through the front door. The inside of the building was in just as much disrepair, and so were the people that seemed to fill it from side to side and top to bottom.

"Who are all these people?" I choked. The ventilation was lacking, and I could literally feel the stench crawling through my clothes and pressing into my skin. I wrapped an arm protectively around Nikki's waist and drew her close to me, using her sweet scent as a buffer.

"These are the people left behind," Nikki said quietly. I looked at her in shock and confusion. Surely she didn't think these occupants were Immortals. "Welcome to The Shade Tree Shelter, Gregory."

Realization finally dawned. "This is a homeless shelter?" I questioned, looking around again. "And you spend time here? Why?"

Before she could answer, we were accosted by a rather large black woman who was literally dripping with small ones.

"Nikki!" she cried exuberantly. "Child, where you been? You know the sun don't shine 'til you come round!"

"I've been busy lately," Nikki replied with a smile. "But you know I can't stay away for long. I'd never hear the end of it from those little ducks of yours!"

"Girl, you know they'd hunt you down," the woman laughed. Then she noticed me standing there, and her entire being changed. She tensed from head to foot and glared at me. I was almost intimidated. "Who you?" she asked crossly.

Nikki released my hand and put her arm around my waist. She put her other hand on my chest and answered for me, "Sharice, this is Gregory. He's with me. He's safe in every way."

The switch flicked and Sharice was once again ecstatic. "Well then! In that case, you can take Henry, he's clean 'nough," she said and thrust an especially small human in my direction before she turned and flounced off. I had no choice but to catch him, or he'd have fallen to the floor. I held him at arm's length and looked at Nikki.

She laughed. Then she noted the stricken look on my face. "Here. Try it like this," she suggested. She moved the boy to sitting on my shoulders. I estimated him to be around two years old, but he was very light. I reassessed and realized he could be as old as four from his frame, but had been malnourished for so long, I couldn't evaluate him accurately.

"Horsey!" the little boy shouted. I winced as he gripped my hair with his grimy little hands. Not because it hurt, because it was disgusting.

I looked at Nikki with a pleading expression, hoping she'd take the child. "He wants you to neigh," she explained. "Like a horse," she clarified at my still baffled expression.

I gave up on being rescued and did as instructed. Opening my mouth I mimicked the sound horses make. A perfect impression, I thought. But it was awfully quiet atop my head.

"That was very impressive," Nikki said. I could tell she was trying very hard not to laugh again. "But I don't think he's ever heard a real horse. He wants you to actually 'neeeeigh.'"

"Neeeeigh," I said dryly, feeling more like an ass than a horse. The little boy squealed in delight and began bouncing up and down on my shoulders. Nikki gave me a smile that made the whole ordeal worth it. "Neeeeeigh," I said again, with a little more enthusiasm.

"Ride horsey!" Henry cried. I looked at Nikki for another translation.

"He wants you to gallop," she said simply. I raised an eyebrow.

"I beg your pardon?"

"I'll show you." She took my hand and pulled me forward while taking jumpy, yet shuffling steps.

I gave her a disbelieving look. Surely she didn't expect me to make that much a fool of myself.

"C'mon Gregory," Nikki whispered with a smirk. "Spread a little sunshine."

I sighed in defeat. We made our way across the room in a loping gallop. By the time we stopped, Nikki and Henry were giggling uncontrollably, and I couldn't help but laugh at their glee.

"All right, Henry," Nikki said as she wiped the tears from her eyes. "You better get on back."

I knelt down in front of a table with benches attached and helped Henry jump down from my shoulders. He thanked me with a grin from ear to ear and scampered off. I turned around to put a hand on the bench and stand up, but froze in place.

"I know you!" I shouted at the man across the table from me.

"No you don't," he replied.

"Yes I do," I countered. It was the vagrant that used to inhabit the corner near my loft. I would recognize the wrinkled brown skin and graying dreadlocks like I would the bricks that covered my warehouse.

"Then what's my name, mate?" he asked. For the first time I noticed his Australian accent.

"I was going to ask you, but you disappeared," I explained.

"You two know each other?" Nikki asked.

"Yes," I said, while he said, "No."

Nikki raised an eyebrow.

"Is this where you went when you left?" I asked him.

"Brother, you had twenty years to ask me questions. Too late to know me now."

"Lucas, this is Gregory. He's with me," Nikki said vouching for me again.

Lucas looked from Nikki to me and back again. A sardonic smirk spread over his face. "Ah, I see. She got to you too, eh, brother? You know I lived on that corner for decades, and then this pretty little bird comes up to me one day and in an hour has me convinced I should be someplace else."

"She seems to have that effect on people," I said with a smile.

"On men especially, I suspect," he added with a wink.

"I suspect so," I agreed.

"All right, enough you two," Nikki said, rolling her eyes. "We're probably needed in the kitchen. See you later, Lucas."

"I reckon you will."

We walked through a swinging door and saw a soft, middle-aged woman. Half of her shoulder-length hair was pulled back, highlighting the streaks of white in the thick black. She bustled from the sink to the stove to the cutting board, trying to do the work of four or five.

"Need a hand, Beth?" Nikki asked brightly.

"Nikki!" Beth cried in delight, turning to gather her in a warm hug. "How is it that you always know just when I need your help?"

"Because you always need help," Nikki laughed. "Though you do seem even more short-handed than usual tonight," she added.

"Don't I know it!" Beth agreed. "I was just about to give up on getting dinner out on time. And you know how it gets around here when dinner is late," Beth stated, shaking her head.

"Heaven forbid," Nikki replied. "Beth, this is Gregory. He's with me."

I was starting to feel a pattern. Apparently Nikki's approval was all it took to be accepted without question. Beth handed me a large wooden spoon and waved toward the stove.

"The sauce is on, the noodles are cooking," she said. I blinked and looked at Nikki. She took the spoon from my hand and replaced it with a large knife. I blinked again.

"Why don't you chop the veggies for the salad?" Nikki suggested pointing to the mound next to the cutting board. "Bite-sized," she instructed. "About an inch," she clarified quietly for me.

I was slightly put out that she thought such exact instructions necessary, but also relieved that she thought to give them. I had no idea what a human would consider "bite sized."

"I wouldn't let him near anything that needs spices. He's got terrible taste," Nikki explained to Beth. "But he's great with a knife." I smirked at her comment and went to work on the food, which had already been cleaned and prepared.

"So I see," Beth said with an awed tone that brought my head around. Over her shoulder Nikki gestured for me to slow down. I did, but only until Beth was distracted checking the bread she was baking. The task was too tedious to do at a human's pace.

The three of us quickly finished preparing dinner and then doled out equal portions to the waiting masses. Once everyone had been through the line, Beth dismissed Nikki and me, assuring Nikki she could handle dishing out the seconds until the food ran out.

"Nikki," Beth said in a scolding tone before we got out the door.

"Beth," she sassed back.

"I'm not having this argument again, miss. Get yourself a plate," Beth's tone left no room for further discussion.

Nikki sighed heavily and did as she was told, though I noticed she gave herself half-portions of everything. I had a feeling this was a long standing compromise between them. We turned to leave again, but Beth cleared her throat loudly and gave me a pointed look.

"He's on a carb-free diet," Nikki explained. Beth pursed her lips in displeasure, but let us go without further comment.

"How do you do that?" I whispered as we searched for a table with empty seats.

"Do what?" she asked. Her eyes lit up as she spotted a place for us to sit.

"Make the humans here look at me like I'm normal," I replied.

We sat down at a table and thankfully I was at the end, so Nikki was the only one I was pressed against.

"The truth is, Gregory, no one here is normal. We're all just freaks in different ways," she said, smiling. I noted that she had grouped herself among the freaks.

As Nikki ate, she made conversation with the humans sitting around us. She knew all their names and stories. I could visibly see their countenances brighten as Nikki interacted with them. I lifted my eyes to scan the rest of the crowd. I could see the smiles spreading out from our table like ripples in a pond. I noted similar reactions coming from areas Nikki had already been, near Lucas and Sharice.

Sharice was surrounded by no less than ten little humans. She fussed over every one and made sure they all ate and that their mouths were wiped.

"Are they all hers?" I asked Nikki, gesturing.

Nikki looked up and smiled at the sight. "No, actually, none of them are hers."

"Where are their parents?"

"Some are around here somewhere." Her smiled faltered. "Some are ... not."

"Why does she care for them, if she's not responsible for them?" It seemed like so much trouble.

"The kids need someone consistently there for them, who loves them enough to cuss them when they need it, and hold them when they're scared," she explained. "Sharice needs someone to love."

I watched the large woman dote on the children that weren't hers, my head tilted slightly to one side, trying to process what Nikki had said.

"Family is more than genetics," Nikki said softly.

"And humans are so desperate for family that they complicate their own survival for it?" I questioned.

"Everyone needs family," Nikki replied, then quickly went on. "Once upon a time, Sharice was a young mother of four. She did what she could, but there came a day that she just couldn't make ends meet. They were evicted. Sharice had no money for a hotel, no money for food. It was the middle of winter in New York. So she found the nearest homeless shelter."

Nikki's beautiful face darkened as she continued her story. "It wasn't the best neighborhood, or the safest shelter. That night, all of their things were stolen and Sharice was … accosted. The next day she fled with her children, vowing never to go back. They wandered around the city, looking for somewhere else to go, begging for money. Night came and there was nothing."

Nikki's eyes began to glisten. "The children were hungry and cold, but Sharice couldn't bring herself to go back to the shelter. They huddled together in an alley, hoping the buildings would keep out most of the wind and snow. In the morning, Sharice woke to find she couldn't feel her hands or feet; she could barely move her limbs at all." Nikki paused, closing her eyes and swallowing before she could continue. "And all four children were dead. Frozen in the night."

My eyes went wide and automatically sought out the woman from across the room. Nikki wasn't finished.

"She had no money for a funeral, no one to call, nothing. She stayed in that alley with them for two days, trying to think of something, anything. In the end, she had only one choice. She left. Once she left the alley, she couldn't stop. She spent the next few years hitch-hiking and walking across the country until she ended up here in California."

Nikki's face softened as she watched Sharice with her little brood. "I think she's trying to make up for failing her own children. She needs to love every bit as much as they need to be loved." Nikki turned to watch me for a moment. "Do you want to know about Lucas?"

"Yes," I said automatically. I searched the overflowing room for him, wondering if I really wanted to know at all.

"Once upon a time, Lucas lived in Sydney, Australia. He was young and ambitious and going places in his company. He met a young woman, fell in love and got married. Soon after, Lucas was offered a very important promotion that would transfer him to the US. Though his wife was somewhat reluctant to leave her family, he immediately accepted. She loved him and so they moved here to San Francisco. Months after they settled in, she found out she was pregnant."

I had found Lucas and was trying to picture him as young and prosperous. It was very difficult. I was also having trouble getting him from such a happy story to such a destitute place as the corner near my building.

"Lucas was thrilled. He doted on his wife and catered to her every whim. Late one night they went out to satisfy such a craving. They went into the convenience store at the end of their block. While waiting in line, a man with a gun stormed in. He was obviously high on something and out of control. Lucas' wife was shot three times and died before the ambulance could get there."

My breath left me in a short burst. Nikki nodded, agreeing with my shock.

"When the paramedics finally arrived, they found Lucas catatonic, covered in his wife's blood. He was institutionalized for months. When he finally surfaced, his wife was gone, her body buried in her home town in Australia. Her family wanted nothing to do with him. He had nothing left to live for, but couldn't bring himself to take his own life. Instead, he just let himself fall through the cracks."

I took inventory of Lucas: the wrinkles in his face, the grey of his dreadlocks, the sagging of his body. If he had been young when this happened, he had been on the street for at least forty years. I shook my head, trying to realign my thoughts. I knew this was the human condition. It was why I had no sympathy for them. Their plight was hopeless. Yet, I had never actually known any of them.

"You don't have to be … like you, to get left behind," Nikki finished softly. "Everyone gets left behind at one time or another."

I turned to argue that she had never been left behind, and saw her fingering the scars on her cheek. "How can you still believe in happily ever after?" came out instead.

"Because, not only the people who leave have hope," she replied. "Look around you again, Gregory. These stories aren't over yet. Life is a roller coaster, and sometimes it turns you completely upside down. You never know what's coming. You only know that things will change. Why not hope that they will change for the better? Life without hope isn't worth living."

I couldn't agree with her more. I looked around the room again and realized what had been spreading through it from Nikki and everyone she had touched. It was hope. Nikki was full of it, and it radiated off her like sunlight lighting every corner of the desolate building. My life hadn't changed in centuries before I met Nikki, but it was most certainly a roller coaster now. And I found that, with Nikki beside me, I couldn't help but have hope that it was only going to get better.

After dinner, we went back to the kitchen and helped Beth clean up. I could feel the grin splitting my face. I had never felt so … human.

"I can't thank you enough for coming in tonight, Nikki. Lord knows you have better things to do on a Saturday night," Beth said.

"You know I love coming here. It's really no problem. Plus Gregory had fun, right?" she asked turning to me.

"Right," I agreed with a salute. Beth chuckled.

"And I know you've been especially shorthanded without Clara," Nikki continued. Her tone became more serious and I watched her carefully.

"I can't believe they haven't heard from her yet," Beth acknowledged. Something began nagging at the back of my mind.

"I know. It's so unlike her to just take off … I'm not sure I believe it," Nikki replied, biting her lip.

"But didn't her roommate say she saw her with some guy at the library?"

The library …

"Yes, but I can't believe Clara would just run off with some guy like that."

Clara. No. Nonononononononono.

The air left my lungs in a rush, and I couldn't get it back. My stomach was suddenly lined with lead, and the room began to spin. I turned and fled out into the back alley. I took two steps away from the building and hunched over with my hands on my knees. My abdominal muscles were clenching, my body shaking as I tried desperately to suck in a breath. I vaguely recognized that I was dry-heaving and insanely wished I had something in my stomach to empty. Finally the violent sickness passed, and I leaned back against the wall, sinking to the filthy ground. If this was guilt, I could understand how it drove humans to insanity. I reached my hands up to rub my face and was shocked to find my cheeks wet. I didn't remember the last time I had cried. I didn't think I could.

Nikki came running out the back door, searching for me. "Gregory?" she called softly when she spotted me. "Are you all right?"

Was I all right? I wanted to laugh. I would never be all right again. I was a monster, a demon. I had to tell her. She began to walk toward me, but I held up a hand.

"Clara isn't missing, Nikki. She's dead." I looked up and met her blue eyes. Determined to see them turn from concerned to horrified.

"You don't know—" She stopped, and I saw understanding come. "Oh, Gregory," she sighed.

"Now do you see?" I shouted, rising to my feet. "Now that I've murdered someone you know, can you finally see me for the monster I am?" I expected Nikki to cower before my misplaced rage.

Instead she took slow, cautious steps toward me, as if she was afraid of scaring me. I searched her eyes for meaning, and to my utter shock I found no terror, no anger, only the deep pools of sympathy I had come to know so well.

She reached out and put a hand to my face. I felt the warmth begin to pour from my eyes again. "If you're a monster for killing in order to survive," she whispered, tears streaming down her cheeks as well, "what does it make me, if I don't want you to stop? How selfish and wrong am I for not being able to want her back, if it means I'd lose you?"

I had no words. I covered her hand with my own. With my other arm I drew her close and buried my face in her neck and shoulder. *Oh, my sweet Nikki, what have I done to you?* She wrapped her arms around me and buried her face in my shoulder as well. The clouds burst open, and we stood together, weeping in the rain.

Chapter Thirty-Four

The air was hot and damp, the darkness complete. I could hear sounds. There was a familiar heart beating with mine. Nikki was near. But there was another sound, the dangerous one. I began to run, pressing through the heavy plants, searching for Nikki, needing to protect her. The noise of pursuit flew up a tree so I followed hoping to find her before it was too late. I could hear his enormous paws cracking branches in the darkness. I held very still. I heard no sound. There was nothing. I opened my mouth to call for Nikki, but I heard an angry roar and saw two glittering eyes soaring at my face and by instinct I reached out. The great cat stopped in midair and I heard its neck snap, its body crash to the ground below. I looked up and saw Nikki, her hands dripping with blood, her teeth sharp under curled lips, breath hissing as she whispered, "What does it make me?"

My eyes snapped open, but it was still dark. I was momentarily disoriented, then heard the soft beating of her heart, felt the warmth of her body against mine. I knew the dream had nothing to do with how I saw Nikki. It was my fear of how she now saw herself. I had done this to her by dragging her into my reality. If I could go back … but no, the truth was I couldn't wish anything different. I was too selfish in my need for her love. And now I could see she was just as desperate in her love for me. We were both truly lost.

Even in her sleep, she clung to me, her legs twined with mine, her arms wrapped around my back and locked into place. The rain had soaked us through, leaving me only boxers to sleep in. Nikki had come to bed in shorts and a tank top. I sensed we each took comfort in the skin on skin contact. Nikki's face was buried in my neck. I tilted my head and kissed her hair. She smiled faintly and squeezed even tighter.

I held her firmly in place with one arm around the small of her back, holding onto her hip. My other hand drifted into her hair and played idly with the ends while I pondered what I could do to show her she was not a monster by association. She was an angel in love with the devil. She was in no way tarnished herself.

An idea began to develop as the sky began to lighten. Eventually the dawn came, bringing a new day. As much as I hated to move, I knew I needed to get up if I was to have a few hours to take care of things at my loft before walking several hours to meet Nikki at her parents'. I began to rub small circles on Nikki's back. She sighed deeply and snuggled against me, nuzzling my neck.

"I love you," I whispered into her ear, speaking the first words between us since our melt down in the alley last night.

She smiled against my skin, then leaned back to look up at my face. "I love you, too."

I smiled back at her, leaning down to reach her lips with mine. Bringing my hand up to cup her face, I kissed her tenderly. When I released her, she smiled again and pressed her cheek to mine, closing her eyes to savor the closeness. I closed my eyes as well, committing the moment to memory, wanting it to last forever. Finally I sighed and spoke again.

"I need to go soon, love."

Nikki pulled back, a worried look on her face. "Aren't you coming with me to my parents' house?"

"I believe the plan was for me to meet you there," I reminded her, smiling. "It will be hard enough for you to convince them I'm a normal boyfriend if we spend more than a few hours there."

"I can see your point," Nikki said smirking. "But they're never going to believe you're normal."

"Why not?" I asked, my brow furrowed. Could they all be as intuitive as her?

"Three reasons," she replied, letting go of me to number them on her fingers. "First, you're in love with me. Second, I'm in love with you. Third, my family is going to love you."

I raised one eyebrow. "And that makes me abnormal?"

"Absolutely," she responded seriously. "Which is good. My family is partial to nonconformists."

Nonconformist. An interesting way to describe my situation. "That explains why you enjoy antagonizing half the English department," I noted.

"Exactly!" she laughed. "Now you get it."

I chuckled and shook my head, kissing her on the nose before I moved to get out of bed. I had to chuckle again at the pout on her face and pulled her up to her knees to kiss it away. She brought her hands up my arms and tangled them in my hair. The sweet kiss quickly deepened into something more passionate. As she became more aggressive, one of my hands slid down to rest on her backside, the other snuck past the edge of her top to caress the smooth skin of her back. I noted there was no tensing or hesitation from her at all. After a few moments, she languidly pulled away with a sensual smile on her face.

"All right, Casanova," she teased. "You better get going before I decide to chain you to my bed."

"Hmmm," I replied, leaning over to kiss softly under her ear before backing away again. "If I didn't have plans, I would have to see if you really meant that."

"You have plans?" she asked, her tone shocked, and perhaps even a little jealous.

"Not to worry, they all revolve around you, of course," I assured her.

"Of course," she replied rolling her eyes, but with a smile.

I dressed and got her parents' address before leaving Nikki with her breakfast, promising to see her soon after lunch.

Back at my loft, I stripped off my now filthy clothes, but decided not to shower until just before I left. Nikki's scent was still clinging to my skin and I wasn't ready to wash it off. Being honest with myself, I was afraid of being overcome by my thirst again. I knew I was pushing my body much too far, but I still couldn't bring myself to feed. I would have to find another way to survive. Surely I could avoid killing. I just needed to get creative.

For now though, I was busy with something else. First, I added a few pages to the journal which used to be only about Nikki, but was now about us. Then I started on the idea that had come to me in the early morning hours. I wanted Nikki to see herself as she really was, so I was going to show her. I found an empty canvas and some paints and went to work on a portrait. This time I would truly capture Nikki's image. A few hours later, I was covered in paint and finally satisfied with my work. I had never spent so long on one project before, but it was perfect. Just like Nikki.

I took a very long, very hot shower, trying to ease my aching body. But the ache was bone-deep and would remain that way until I did something about it. I felt perpetually tired, and while the few hours of sleep I got the night before had rejuvenated my constitution, the dream had left my senses edgy and raw.

I spent some time trying to find an outfit that looked like I was trying to make a good impression, without looking pretentious. Despite Nikki's assurances, I was nervous to meet her family. They meant a great deal to her and I knew their acceptance of me was important.

Finally, I left and started the long walk to see Nikki again. I was moving briskly, anxious to see her, and so was quickly among the Sunday afternoon crowd on the streets. I was suddenly overwhelmed by the smell of their blood, the press of their warm bodies. My breathing picked up speed and my hands began to shake.

So thirsty.

I turned and fled up a deserted alley, hunching by a Dumpster, hoping it would mask the enthralling scent. Taking deep breaths of the putrid refuse, I looked up toward the blue sky, and saw the roofline. I scaled the brick wall and stood atop the building, tasting the air. The smell of blood was still scintillating, but it was muted, blending with the other scents of the city. I could do this. I was not an animal.

In addition to easing the smell of blood wafting up from the humans, keeping to the rooftops also made it possible for me to travel as fast as I wanted to. The trip I thought would take several hours flew by. Once I got to the residential neighborhoods, I had to go back to the sidewalk, but there was much less foot traffic, and I could subtly cross the street to keep from getting too close.

CHAPTER THIRTY-FIVE

I was desperate to see Nikki, and as I pressed the bell by the door, I was momentarily flooded with relief. Until I realized I was about to shut myself in a small room with her family for hours. Before I could panic and bolt away, however, the door opened to reveal the most welcome sight. Nikki stood before me, smiling brightly. I immediately swept her up into my arms, crushing her to my chest, burying my face in her hair.

"Miss me much?" she teased, returning my embrace. I put her back on her feet and looked around, realizing her family could be watching. We were alone in the entry.

"You have no idea," I said, my tone more serious than I had meant it.

Nikki looked at me in concern, took my hand, and noticed the shaking. "Gregory! Are you all right?"

"Yes," I lied. "I've just been away from your scent too long," I finished, hoping the truth would outweigh it.

Nikki looked me straight in the eyes, her blue orbs piercing me straight through and freezing me in place.

"Nikki," I sighed. "I don't know if I can do this." I broke her gaze and looked away in shame.

"You can't be that nervous to meet my family," she insisted.

"I'm—" I faltered. How could I explain? I hated myself, everything I was. "I'm thirsty," I finally admitted. It was barely a whisper.

"And you came here first?" she questioned. I flinched though there was no condemnation in her voice, only the desire to understand.

"I needed you," I whispered pathetically.

Nikki's eyes sparkled and she smiled softly. Taking my face in her hands she drew me forward to meet her lips. My senses were flooded with her scent and taste, with her essence. I closed my eyes in relief, my hands wrapping themselves in her soft hair as my entire being relaxed. After a few moments of delicious heaven, she pulled away. I smiled at her, running the back of my fingers along her cheek.

"Your hands have stopped shaking," she noted.

"I'm filled with you," I replied. She smirked, but raised a delicate brow for an explanation. "The touch of your skin, the sound of your voice, the taste of your kiss, the very smell of you," I whispered against her skin, took a deep breath of her hair. "I'm drowning in you, and it smothers any other desire." Nikki took a moment to lean into my embrace, returning it with her whole being.

"So as long as you stick by me, you'll be fine?" she asked, pulling away to look into my face again.

"Nikki, I don't think—" I started, but she cut me off.

"Nu-uh, Gregory, you're fine. I can see it in your face. Now you're just being chicken, and that's no excuse." She smiled confidently and took my hand, pulling me into the next room. "C'mon, before my family starts wondering why it took me so long to answer the door."

The small living room was … quaint, as Jenny would phrase it. At one end of the room was a large TV that was trying not to be the focal point, but failing miserably. The worn but comfortable looking leather sofa, love seat, and armchair were surrounding a wooden coffee table, but it was obvious they all had a great view of the TV. Lining the walls were bookcases filled with books, though as they neared the TV, they also contained many videos and DVDs. On the coffee table were several boxes of different sizes and shapes. The three people sitting around it were having an animated discussion about which game should be played before dinner.

They looked up as we walked in and then stood to meet me. Nikki introduced me to her father, Tom, who taught history and government classes at a high school. He was tall, with salted auburn hair cut very short to tame the tight curls in it. His eyes were hazel, and I could feel their heavy gaze appraising me. Next to him, on the love seat, was Nikki's mother, Gale. She had thick, golden blond hair that was pulled into some kind of twist, her eyes a gray color that were soft and amused. At the sofa was Nikki's brother, Jack. His hair was a shocking red color that spilled from his head in all directions, with no apparent attempt to tame the curls he obviously inherited from his father. His blue-green eyes were also appraising me, but with a touch of humor as well. They all looked so different, but there was an underlying likeness. They were obviously a family.

After the introductions, Nikki led me to the big armchair and I sat down. Then she sat comfortably in my lap. Her father raised an eyebrow, her mother gave a knowing little smile, and her brother put on a smarmy smirk. Nikki ignored them and turned back to deciding what game we would play. I couldn't help but be relieved that I could keep Nikki this close to me, surrounded by her scent.

We ended up playing a game that had various tasks to choose from each round. I was exceptional at the trivia questions, the language skills, and the art, but was hopeless during the music round, and many of the acting ones. I had no grasp on pop culture. Nikki's family teased me about this, as they had been teasing each other throughout the game. When Jack asked me if I had been living in a cave, but actually sounded half serious, I realized Nikki had avoided telling her family anything about me. I wondered if it was because she didn't know how to explain me, or if she didn't want to lie to her family.

Despite the handicap of having me on their team, Nikki and Jack won, with much bragging and boasting. Throughout the afternoon there had been laughter and jesting. It felt a little familiar, which I found both comforting and disconcerting. Why would I feel at home spending time with a human family?

When it was time to go, they all walked us to the door.

"Are you sure you can't stay for dinner?" Gale asked us, again.

"Sorry, Mom," Nikki apologized, hugging her mother.

To my extreme surprise, Gale hugged me next. She smelled a little like Nikki. "It was good to meet you, Gregory."

"The pleasure was mine, Mrs. Christian," I replied, trying not to look shocked.

"You're cool, man," Jack said as he shook my hand and punched my shoulder. "I guess Nikki can keep you around for now." Nikki laughed and hugged him as well.

"I liked Rich," Tom said abruptly as we got to him.

"Dad!" Nikki scolded.

"Let me finish," he persisted, looking me straight in the eye. "I liked the way he treated Nikki, the respect he gave her. When he looked at her, I could tell he felt like they belonged together."

I was silent. I knew Nikki and I didn't belong together.

"But you," he continued pointing a finger at me, "you look at her as if you know there's no chance in hell you'll ever deserve her."

"Dad!" Nikki interjected again. Tom ignored her, still speaking directly to me.

"Hang on to that attitude and maybe she won't figure it out," he finished, with a smile.

"I can only hope, sir," I replied.

He reached out and shook my hand firmly. "Same time next week?"

"If Nikki hasn't come to her senses yet," I agreed. Nikki rolled her eyes, laughing, and kissed her father on the cheek.

CHAPTER THIRTY-SIX

We had traveled a few blocks in the Sunshine Bug, when I turned to ask Nikki a question.

"Why are you wearing make-up?"

She glanced sideways at me. "I usually do."

I raised a skeptical eyebrow and waited. While she usually wore minimal amounts of eye make-up and lipstick, I had noticed that tonight she was also wearing concealer.

She sighed. "It's just easier."

"I don't understand. It's easier to cover your scars for your family than for strangers?"

She shook her head, curls bouncing lightly. "No, it's easier for my family if they don't have to see them."

I furrowed my brow, still confused.

"My parents know where the scars come from. They don't judge me by them, they judge themselves. They still blame themselves for not being able to protect me." She took a deep breath. "It's easier for us all to pretend this way."

"Do you blame your parents?" I asked.

"Of course not!" she yelled, indignant.

Finally it all clicked into place. "Ah, but you blame yourself for their pain, so you hide your scars so that everyone can pretend no one is hurting."

She gave a mirthless little laugh. I didn't like it. "Yeah, I guess it's something like that."

"Your family seems genuinely happy, Nikki," I noted.

She smiled, and this time she meant it. "We are, really. It was just so bad for so long…so much guilt everywhere. I guess I just don't want to risk opening old wounds."

I let the subject drop. Who was I to tell a human how to interact with her family?

"I told you my family would love you," she said after a few moments of silence.

"Or they were just humoring you until you move on," I suggested dryly.

She rolled her eyes. "I'm serious, Gregory, even my dad likes you. That's saying something."

"Really?" I asked, surprised at the relief I felt.

"My dad has never, not once, invited someone outside the family to our family Sundays. He would usually tolerate people Jack or I wanted to bring along, but never seemed eager to have them come back. Tonight was a first."

I sat quietly with a smile on my face. Nikki's family liked me, and knowing that made me happy. I had wanted their approval. How very odd. I realized it was because Nikki had taken me into the very heart of her world, of who she is, and I *belonged* there. Then it occurred to me that Nikki might want the same from me. I had no family, but I could bring her deeper into my world, hopefully without further endangering her.

"Nikki, would you like to see where I live?"

"Yes, please," she answered eagerly. I chuckled and began giving her directions as she drove.

"Would you like to meet some others?" I questioned, watching her carefully.

She stiffened briefly, then relaxed again. "By 'others,' I assume you mean other Immortals?"

"Yes."

"Who are friendly like you?"

I had to keep myself from laughing at her choice of words. "There are a few Immortals that I socialize with on occasion, who are very anxious to meet you. They are stunned at the effect you've had on me."

She smiled. "When?"

I was suddenly very anxious to introduce her to them. "How about tonight?"

She laughed, but nodded. I borrowed her cell phone and called Jenny. She was surprised to hear from me, but eager to meet Nikki. She agreed to bring Lance and Rob by my place later that night.

"I guess it's good I'm wearing make-up after all, if they're all as beautiful as you."

I rolled my eyes at her comment and realized suddenly I had gotten the gesture from Nikki. It made me smile to think that I was spending so much time with her that she was beginning to influence my behavior.

"You know I think you're the most beautiful creature on the planet," I reminded her.

"I also know that you're biased," she retorted.

Then she was quiet and I left her to her thoughts. I watched her face as she drove. It became increasingly serious. I wanted to ask her what she was thinking about, but was also enjoying simply gazing at her.

"Gregory," Nikki said quietly several minutes later.

"Yes?" I asked, reaching out to stroke her soft hair for a moment. She closed her eyes briefly at my touch, and waited until I drew my hand back to continue. Her next words caused my heart to sink.

"Is there … any chance Clara's family will … find her body?" her voice was barely a whisper.

"Yes," I replied, almost as quiet. "Eventually."

She glanced at me again. "If they knew where to look?"

I watched her in silence, wondering why she was asking these questions. Surely she didn't want to know about what I had done. Suddenly, Nikki swerved to the side of the road and halted abruptly.

"You have to tell them, Gregory," she said passionately.

"That's not how it works, Nikki," I patiently replied.

She rolled her eyes as if I had missed the point. "Obviously I don't mean you tell them everything that happened, but they need to know where Clara is."

"What would you have me do?" I asked, my voice tired. I was already starving to death for the woman. Did she want me in jail as well?

"Use that pay phone to leave an anonymous tip about where to find her," Nikki said, nodding her head at my window. I glanced in that direction, seeing why she had so suddenly pulled over.

"Why?" I questioned, turning back to her. "She won't be any less dead when they find her."

Nikki flinched slightly at the word dead, but quickly recovered. "Her family needs to know, so they can grieve, have a funeral … they need closure."

I cocked my head to the side, considering what she had said. I knew about human rituals for the dead, but it had not occurred to me. There were no such traditions for Immortals. If you died, it was because you were foolish, weak, or had somehow annoyed the Queen. None of these were cause for celebration, and we didn't generally have close relationships with one another. There would be no one needing "closure."

But humans were dependent on one another. Nikki was right, of course. I nodded and stepped out of the car, making the phone call.

"Thank you," Nikki whispered when I got back into the car.

"It was the least I could do," I replied. Nikki didn't ask any more questions and, save for my occasional direction, we drove the rest of the way to my loft in silence.

CHAPTER THIRTY-SEVEN

*N*ikki commented on the corner Lucas used to live on, and seemed surprised when I told her to pull over in front of my building.

"Are we walking from here?" she asked, looking around.

"We are here," I replied. "This is it."

"You live in a spooky abandoned warehouse?" she asked with a smirk.

"It's not abandoned, seeing as yes, I live here," I retorted. "And it's only spooky after dark."

She laughed and shook her head. She was surprised again when I opened the door. "You don't keep it locked? What about your secret identity?"

"There's nothing of value on the first floor." I chuckled and led her into my labyrinth of discarded property. "My lair is upstairs."

She smirked, then gasped as we passed a primitive antique Spanish desk. "Nothing of value? Gregory, that desk must be worth several thousand dollars!"

"I suppose I should have said nothing of value *to me*," I amended. "These are cast offs from earlier eras I lived through. I occasionally sell some of them for the cash, but it all rots away sooner or later."

"Then why keep it around?" she asked, looking at me intently. "If it's only going to rot away?"

"Too lazy to get rid of it, I suppose," I replied.

"Hmmm." Nikki sighed. I felt as though I had missed something. We continued winding our way to the elevator, Nikki occasionally stopping to peer closely or softly touch this item or that. I made note of which she seemed to prefer. There was no reason for her not to have them.

I quickly typed in my security code to call for the elevator. It was upstairs as I usually left through the roof access.

"That's a lot of numbers," Nikki commented.

"It's actually letters."

"That's a lot of letters," she quipped.

"Some of them repeat."

"So the stuff you discard is so worthless it's not even worth stealing, but whatever is upstairs deserves first rate security measures?" she asked dryly.

"My secrets are closely guarded."

"Riiiiiight."

I laughed. "Well, they were, until you wheedled them out of me."

"Wheedled?" She mocked offense. "And here I thought I was bewitching."

She stepped past me into the elevator, crossed her arms and pouted. Unable to restrain myself, I seized her around the waist with one hand, and brought her face to mine with the other hand. I kissed her until she relaxed her arms, then gripped my shirt in her hands. I moved back slightly stroking her cheek.

"You are indeed bewitching," I assured her.

She smiled sadly. "For now."

"For always," I corrected. I would treasure her long after she was gone. Surely she must understand that.

"Hmmm," was all she replied. Before I could push the issue, the elevator opened and she stepped into my loft. "It's very dark," she said into the blackness. I reached around her and turned on the lights. She whistled softly. "Nice place."

"I spend most of my time here. It only makes sense for me to make it comfortable."

"Comfortable, right. Just what I was thinking," she said, bemused.

"You don't like it?"

"No, I do. It's just so … opulent," she replied, looking around. "But comfortable, too."

I wasn't sure what she meant, so I had nothing to say to that. Nikki took a few steps, then noticed something.

"No coffin, eh?" she asked with a smirk.

I smirked back. "Listen."

She was quiet for a long minute. "I don't hear anything."

"Not anything?" I prodded.

"Nothing at all." Then she got it. "Wait, this whole loft is a giant coffin?"

"More like an isolation chamber, but in essence, yes," I replied.

"Okay, now I have to ask some more stupid questions," she began.

"None of your questions are stupid, Nikki," I corrected.

"Yeah, yeah, not stupid, just naïve, I know," she said, waving a dismissive hand. "So, you do need what amounts to a coffin, but you're awake during the day? So when do you sleep?"

"When I get tired," I answered. She smacked my shoulder.

"You know what I mean," she scolded, walking over to my bed. She sat down, and almost fell over when it moved beneath her. "A water bed?"

"It helps with the sensation of being weightless," I replied. "The coffin myth is also based on partial truth. Feeding keeps our blood young and healthy, but our senses are so hyper developed that they can get overloaded. Especially as the world progresses and gets noisier and noisier."

"I've heard progress is hard to sleep through," she noted dryly.

"So," I continued, "we spend a certain amount of time resting our senses, cutting ourselves off from the world. It's like sleep, but not. I suppose it's more like a trance, but just about anything can bring us out of it. The slightest disturbance."

"So, when you stay at my place, you don't actually sleep?" she asked. "You just lie there all night and watch me?"

I chuckled at her expression. Moving to sit beside her, I lay back and spread my arms out. "I thought you liked it when I watch you," I teased. "But truthfully, I've found that your body rhythm is almost better for relaxation than my loft."

Nikki blushed slightly. "My body rhythm?"

"The beating of your heart, the pattern of your breath." I tried to explain. "It soothes me to be near you when you sleep."

She smiled and lay back on the bed, resting her head on my chest. "That's nice."

"Indeed," I agreed.

Nikki noticed my *daishō* above the bed and stood to look closer. I was slightly disappointed she had moved, but was willing to be patient. She peered at the swords, but made no move to touch them.

"Would you like me to get one down?" I asked.

"No, I'm sure I'd only hurt myself," she replied.

"I didn't say I was going to let you hold it," I teased. She shook her head at my comment, but then nodded. I took the smaller sword down and slipped it carefully from its sheath, holding it in the soft light.

"It's beautiful," she whispered. "Is it old?"

"Very," I answered.

"But you haven't abandoned it with the rest of your belongings?" she questioned, looking up at me.

"Some things are worth maintaining," I said softly. This made Nikki smile. "These swords were once the only reason I locked my loft at all. I would be devastated to lose them."

"They're from the Samurai," she realized.

"Yes."

"What did you give him in return?"

"A noble death," I responded, before I could think about what I was saying. I was afraid Nikki wouldn't understand what I meant, what it had meant for him to be dying from old age, But before I could explain, Nikki changed the subject.

"Does that window open?" she asked, nodding to the other side of the room.

"I haven't tried it since I sealed the room, but it should, yes."

We walked over to the window and I slipped several latches, then pushed it open. It was stiff, but not stuck. The sun was setting over the ocean, coloring the clouds vibrant reds and oranges.

"What a beautiful view," Nikki breathed.

"Yes, it is," I said, slightly stunned. I hadn't looked out this window in a very long time. I brought her in front of me and wrapped my arms around her, resting my head on her shoulder. We watched in silence until the sun was completely gone.

"You said the swords were once your only reason for locking your loft. Is there another now?" Nikki wondered.

"Yes," I said smiling. "Now I have secrets that could be exposed should someone find them."

I led Nikki over to my writing desk and handed her one of the two nondescript notebooks. She opened the cover and read the title aloud, "True Stories." She looked up at me. "That night I asked you to tell me a true story to help me get back to sleep."

"Yes, and shortly after I realized I wanted to tell you all my stories. So I began writing them down when I wasn't with you."

"Gregory … wow," she whispered. "Can I keep it?"

"It's not full yet, but when that notebook is finished, I'll give it to you and start a new one."

"I don't know what to say," she paused. "Thank you."

"Most of them are pretty dark," I warned her.

"But they're true," she countered. "I'll take the truth over fairy tales any day."

"The truth is, I love you," I said sappily.

"See? Much better than a fairy tale."

"This book is true as well," I said, picking up the other notebook. "I started it just after I met you. I was hoping to study and analyze you. You were so completely baffling, and annoyingly perceptive. I had to find out what made you tick so I could catalogue and dismiss you."

"Yeah? How'd that work out for you?"

"Once I actually sat down and read it with an objective eye … that was the night I realized I was in love."

"Do I get to see *that* book?'

"Eventually," I said, hanging onto it. "It's not finished yet, either. But I do want to show you some things."

I flipped through the pages and showed Nikki the sketches I had made of her. She stared at them, wide-eyed.

"Is this how you see me?" she asked in awe.

"No," I replied. Her face fell, but I pulled her over to my covered easel. "This is how I see you," I said, pulling away the silk sheet.

Nikki gasped at the painting. She was standing on a background of rich, sapphire blue, which matched her eyes. She was dressed in white robes that flowed around her like clouds, while clinging to her feminine silhouette. Her curls were blown back by an unseen wind, fanning around her like rays of golden sunshine. Her face was radiant, complete with scars and she was wearing the open, inviting smile that had drawn in so many people. Her arms were outstretched, waiting for someone to embrace. Her eyes shone with compassion and unconditional love. I had finally truly captured the essence of Nikki.

"Oh," was all she could say, eyes watering.

"But it's more than that, Nikki," I pressed, wanting her to see. "This isn't just how I see you because I'm biased. This is who you are. To those people in the shelter who know what hope is because they know you, to the people you cheer with a word or a touch, to your family. This is what everyone sees. Everyone who truly knows you."

Nikki wept silently, continuing to stare at the portrait. When she spoke it was so quiet, even I could barely hear her. "I can never go back."

"What?" It was not the reaction I had been expecting, and I had no idea what she meant.

"Gregory, don't you see? Your words, your honesty, your love. You have me almost convinced that really is me! I can't go back to living without that, without you there, telling me you love me." She grasped my shirt in her hands again, her eyes pleading. "I am yours, truly and completely. Tell me you'll keep me forever."

Surely she wasn't asking what I thought. I could wish for forever, but I couldn't do that to her. Not a soul as compassionate as Nikki. I embraced her, stroking her cheek. "So long as you want me, you will not know a life without me."

"Forever," she repeated adamantly. Then her lips crashed into mine with wild abandon, and I was helpless to do anything but react.

Her hands went into my hair, tangling it around her fingers. My hand went into her hair as well, at the back of her head, holding her face securely to mine. With my other arm, I pulled her closer, nearly bringing her off the floor. She leaned even further forward, pushing me back, the chaise lounge behind us hitting my legs. I fell onto it, one leg on, one leg off, bringing Nikki into my lap. She pulled on my hair, bringing my chin up so she could kiss and nip at my neck. I groaned at the exquisite torture.

She smiled against my skin and let go of my hair, her hands moving to my chest to undo my buttons. I leaned back to give her room, but continued to run my hands down her back and along her thighs. As my shirt came open, she trailed kisses over my skin, stoking the flames that were burning me. "So beautiful," she whispered, almost to herself. Once she finished, she made her way back up my torso to my neck.

I became lost in the hummingbird beating of her heart, her gasping breath that matched my own. Her smell was intoxicating me. I had two buttons of her shirt undone before I even realized what I was doing. When I did, I brought my head down to look at her. She looked directly into my eyes, and then started kissing my mouth again, her hands continuing to roam over my chest. I took that as consent and made quick work of the rest of her buttons. Then I gently pushed her back so I could see her.

"It's not my paisley one," she admitted breathily, her face flush.

"It's perfect," I said, taking in the white lace. "You're perfect," I restated. Then I put a hand to her neck and brought her forward to once again taste her mouth. I slid my hand slowly down from her throat, so lost in the sounds she was making that I was just as startled as she was by the rapping on my window frame.

"Enter, my sword is drawn," I called. Nikki went wide-eyed and flushed even deeper. I chuckled, realizing how she might have taken it. She was further shocked when she went to close her shirt only to find I had already buttoned it. I stood, helping Nikki to her feet and walked over to greet our guests.

CHAPTER THIRTY-EIGHT

"Did we interrupt something important?" Rob asked smugly as he climbed through the window, followed closely by Lance and Jenny. I knew he must have heard Nikki's heart pounding from outside. It was only now beginning to slow. And of course, we had both been breathing pretty hard. And my shirt was still open.

"Nothing we can't finish later," I replied, causing Nikki to flush again. Jenny and Rob laughed; Lance was still disapproving. "Come in and sit down."

"Nikki, this is Rob," I began.

"I'm incorrigible," he added with a wink. "Nice to finally meet you in the flesh. I knew you had to be beautiful to get a gargoyle like Greg to take notice."

"This is Jenny," I continued.

"I'm insatiable," she purred. Then she took one of Nikki's hands and sniffed from her wrist to her neck. Nikki froze, holding perfectly still. I glared at Jenny, but she ignored me. "Delicious," she declared.

Nikki blinked a few times. "Thank you?"

"You're welcome!" Jenny laughed. "I like her, Gregory. She's adorable."

"And this is Lance," I finished. He nodded, but remained quiet. "He's only this solemn with strangers."

"Yeah, once you get to know him, he's annoying as hell," Rob agreed, earning a glare from Lance.

"You were just as solemn when I met you," Nikki said to me.

"Yes," I agreed, then turned to Rob. "And you are just as annoying," I reminded him. Jenny nodded.

We all sat down, with Nikki once again in my lap. She smiled timidly at me and kissed my cheek. My heart beat in response to her touch, and the three other Immortals heard it.

"Did she just—?" Jenny asked.

"No way," Rob said in awe.

"Coincidence," Lance said uncertainly.

"What?" Nikki asked. "What did I do?"

"They are a little surprised by the effect you have on me," I replied calmly. "They've never seen me in love before."

"I've never seen any Immortal in love before," Jenny corrected. "Do it again."

"Do what?" Nikki asked.

"Make his heart beat."

Nikki still looked confused. "Remember what I told you about how often my heart beats?"

"Every thirty minutes or so," Nikki replied. Lance gave me a disapproving look.

"And every time you touch me," I amended. Nikki thought about that for a moment. Then a sly smile graced her face.

"I make your heart race?" she asked.

"Of course," I replied. "Much like I do yours."

"Do it again," Jenny repeated.

Nikki shrugged her shoulders and placed her hand on my bare chest, over my heart. It beat against her palm, causing her to smile. She leaned forward, kissed my lips and it beat again, loudly. Three times in five minutes.

"Wow," Jenny whispered.

"No way," Rob reiterated.

"You really are in love with her," Lance finally admitted in awe.

"I told you I was," I replied. "You didn't believe me?"

"Honestly? I didn't think it was possible for us," Lance answered. "I thought perhaps..."

"Perhaps I had simply found a new way to distract myself?" I replied.

"You have been flirting with danger lately," he defended himself.

"You're one to talk, Captain Death Wish," Rob snorted.

"Captain Death Wish?" Nikki questioned.

"Lance is a fan of extreme sports," I explained. "Much like I amuse myself with my writing."

"And I amuse myself with sex," Jenny supplied, causing Nikki to look at her.

"And you?" she asked Rob almost hesitantly.

"I'm mostly just amused in general," he said jovially.

Nikki's stomach decided to remind her that she hadn't had dinner yet, loud enough for everyone to hear. "Sorry," she apologized, embarrassed.

"It's my fault, Nikki. I should have thought to get you dinner before we came here," I said, feeling like a cad.

"Do you like Twinkies?" Rob asked, pulling a couple from the many pockets in his cargo pants.

"Yes?" Nikki said it as a question, looking at me.

"You don't want to know," I assured her.

"I'm sure I don't," she agreed with a laugh. "Thank you," she said to Rob, who gave her a nod and a wink.

While Nikki ate, the rest of us made conversation, teasing Lance about his last sky diving stint and Rob regaling us with his last outing of surfing.

"Rob, is that short for Robert?" Nikki asked when there was a lull.

Lance snorted, and Jenny grinned while she answered, "No, it's short for Robin."

"Wow, not many men with that name these days," Nikki commented casually.

"They won't let me change it," Rob grumbled.

"Do you change your names often?" she asked us in general.

"Not really, no," I answered her. "On occasion a name becomes too outdated and unique, so we change or alter it to avoid attention."

"How can they stop you?" she asked Rob.

"We really only have a certain name because that's what we're called by. It's not as though we have papers or anything else that would be binding to us," he replied testily. "And they refuse to call me anything else."

"Why would you do that?" she asked us, "when Robin is such an uncommon name for a man?"

"Because we can get away with calling him Rob," Jenny answered.

"And it suits him so well," Lance went on. "He is, after all, such a merry little man."

"Wait," Nikki said, holding up a hand. "How long have you had the name Robin?"

Rob eyed her warily. "Since the Middle Ages."

"No way!" Nikki cried, laughing. Lance eyed her as well.

"I told you she was perceptive," I reminded him. He nodded, smiling in appreciation.

"You're Robin, as in Robin of Locksley? As in Robin Hood?" Nikki hooted.

Rob ducked his head uncomfortably. "It was a long time ago, and it's not like the stories say."

"You didn't run around Sherwood forest in tights?" Nikki asked. Jenny snickered.

"Everyone was wearing tights back then!" Rob defended. "The sheriff's men were the best available food source. The peasants were all weak and starving."

"Then how did you get made into a hero?" Nikki questioned.

"I had no need of the gold they carried, and it was heavy, so I left it behind."

"Essentially giving it back to the poor."

"It's not like I was doing it on purpose!" Rob cried indignantly, causing Nikki to laugh.

"Always getting into trouble when you're on your own," Lance chided.

"Because life is so much better when I tolerate living with your condescending ass!"

"Wait, the two of you are … together?" Nikki asked.

"*No!*" They both yelled, while Jenny and I chortled.

"They're more like The Odd Couple than an actual couple," Jenny corrected when we calmed down.

"Oh," Nikki said. Then she grinned mischievously. "Then, if he's Robin, does that make you Batman?" This time Rob joined Jenny and me in laughing heartily. Lance shook his head, but smiled at Nikki's wit.

"It's not like you stay out of trouble when you're on your own," Rob finally said. I gave him a warning glance, not wanting to set Lance off in front of Nikki, but Jenny was already joining in.

"He's been known to stick his sword in places it doesn't belong."

I winced and waited for Lance to get ugly. He simply sat still, all traces of humor gone. Nikki thought for a moment again.

"His sword?" Recognition once again brightened Nikki's face. "Are you telling me you're Lance, as in Sir Lancelot? From King Arthur? He was real, too?"

"Oh, Arthur was real all right," Jenny said quietly. Nikki looked at her in confusion. Jenny looked back at her for a moment, debating, then shrugged her shoulders. "Jenny is a modern form of Gwen."

Nikki's jaw dropped, her eyes going wide. "As in Guinevere? Shut Up! You're telling me I'm sitting in the same room with Robin Hood, Lancelot and Guinevere?"

Jenny smiled at Nikki's enthusiasm. "In the flesh."

"Wow," Nikki replied. "Oh, then does that mean the two of you are together?" she asked Jenny and Lance. I winced again.

"No," Lance said sternly.

"It was kind of a one-time thing, if you catch my drift," Jenny supplied.

"Sometimes Jenny and I are together," Rob volunteered helpfully.

"Sometimes?" Nikki asked.

"When I feel like it," Jenny clarified. Nikki looked at Rob, who smiled and winked at her.

"I see," she said, shaking her head.

"I told you I've never seen an Immortal in love before," Jenny reminded her, "or smelled one for that matter. Now I'll know what I'm looking for, though."

Nikki looked at her funny, but turned her attention to me. "So, who were you in a past life? Prince Charming?" she teased.

"You didn't tell her?" Jenny asked me.

"Tell me what?" Nikki asked.

"I don't remember being anything but Immortal," I answered.

"You were born this way?"

"No. No one is born this way. I just don't remember anything before."

"Surely someone must know who you were," Nikki insisted. "What about the person who changed you?"

"Gregory's an orphan," Jenny said causally.

"What?"

"No one knows where he came from," Lance clarified. "He's older than anyone we know."

"Except The Queen," Rob added. I scowled at him for bringing her up.

"Lance named him Gregory after he stood for us," Jenny continued.

"Wait, if Gregory is oldest, why would Lance have given him a name?"

"Because he didn't have one," Rob said as if it was obvious. "We couldn't just keep calling him 'sir' for the rest of eternity."

"You didn't have a name?" Nikki asked, perplexed.

"I didn't really need one," I replied. "I didn't socialize with anyone regularly, didn't care to know anyone intimately enough."

"But—" Nikki interjected, however Lance cut her off.

"I don't think you understand who Gregory was before he met you, Nikki. He was alone for eons, all but a hermit. Even once he accepted us, we only saw him sporadically. Maybe a few times a year."

Nikki turned to look at me for confirmation. "I told you that you had no idea the power you have over me," I reminded her.

"But to be so alone for so long," she said, shaking her head, her eyes beginning to mist.

"All that matters is that I have you now," I insisted. Nikki kissed me sweetly, then was quiet for a while. The rest of us let her have a moment. Finally she sighed deeply.

"I have to ask," she said quietly.

"Ask away," Rob encouraged.

"Well, here I am with people I thought were myths, but turns out, they're just vampires." She shook her head as we chuckled. "So it begs to be asked … Is Dracula real?" She scrunched one eye and flinched as if waiting for us to laugh. When we didn't, she sat up again. "He is? Was he really Vlad the Impaler?"

"Actually yes," I spoke first. "Dracula was Vlad the Impaler, but he wasn't an Immortal until after his son was born."

"Obviously," Rob rolled his eyes.

"Why obviously?" Nikki asked. The others looked at me as if I should have told her.

"Immortals don't reproduce like humans do," I explained. "Because we constantly regenerate ourselves, there is no biological need to pass on our genes. But in order to continue as a species, we are able to convert others with our blood … and such." Rob sniggered, but my glare was vicious enough to silence him.

"Okay, so Vlad has a son, then becomes Immortal," Nikki prompted.

"Then his wife found out and committed suicide," I continued.

"Because he was an Immortal? That doesn't make any sense," Nikki argued.

"She was a very devout Catholic. She saw him as a demon and was mortally afraid he would damn her, too. She chose certain damnation in hell from suicide rather than being damned to live by his side in his atrocities forever," I explained.

"She hated him that much?" Nikki asked.

"I don't think that was it," Jenny argued. "I think that she may have loved him so much that she overlooked the monster that he was, praying for the day he would return to the Church and repent. When she lost that hope, she had nothing left."

"How tragic," Nikki commented. "Do you all know him?"

"Not anymore," Rob said.

"He's dead?"

"He had a penchant for drama that got him killed," Lance explained.

"I don't understand."

"He was such a terror as Vlad the Impaler that he became too famous. We're not supposed to draw attention to ourselves," I reminded her. "He was forced to fake his death and go into hiding."

"Forced to? By who?"

"Queen Eve, of course," Jenny said bitterly.

"But she didn't kill him?"

"Not right then, no," I replied.

"She appreciated his tastes," Jenny continued. Nikki looked bewildered.

"In torture techniques," Lance clarified. Nikki shuddered.

"But his penchant for being the villain couldn't be quashed, and he ended up starring in a book. Hell, it even bore his name. She couldn't abide that," Lance finished.

"But your latest books are all vampire stories," Nikki said to me. "And now you have me, isn't that extra dangerous?"

"Gregory tends to get away with a lot," Jenny said with implication. "Though I think we'll keep you to ourselves, just in case."

"Does she respect you for being ancient?" Nikki asked innocently.

Jenny snorted rudely. "She doesn't respect *anyone*."

"Gregory's age is actually another example of her lenience towards him," Lance explained. "She doesn't allow most of us to live so long. We become too much of a threat."

"She kills people just for getting old?" Nikki asked.

"She kills people just for being annoying," Rob answered. Nikki blinked. "I generally avoid any contact with her," he added with a wink.

"You could consider her an extreme form of population control," I explained. "If she doesn't think you deserve to be an Immortal, she kills you. If you change someone without her express permission, she kills you. If you challenge her in any way, she kills you."

"If you sneeze in her direction, she kills you," Rob added.

Nikki raised an eyebrow at me. "Which is the real reason you don't all run amuck."

The others chuckled at that just as I had. "I would so rock at running amuck," Rob interjected.

"So why does she get away with it?" Nikki asked. "If she's so horrible, why hasn't someone overthrown her by now?"

"She's too powerful," Lance said. "The older we get, the stronger, faster, etcetera we get. The Queen is the oldest Immortal in existence."

"And she's damn scary," Rob added.

"And her talent is very useful to maintaining power," Jenny went on. "She can sense relationships between people, so she knows who is loyal and who is not."

"And she's damn scary," Rob repeated.

"Do all Immortals have a talent?" Nikki questioned.

"Many of us have a regular knack," I explained. "Like Jenny's sense of smell. It's so strong and defined that she's learned how to smell emotions by reading body chemicals."

"Wow," Nikki acknowledged.

Jenny smiled. "But on a rare occasion, an Immortal is found to possess a true talent. Like The Queen's gift, or Gregory's perception."

Nikki turned to me, and I rolled my eyes. "Jenny is convinced I have some kind of precognition. But as I keep telling her, I'm just old enough that all my senses are heightened to the point that I usually know what someone is about to do, seconds before it happens."

"Wow," she said again.

"Not really," I answered. "I haven't found much use for it. Though, right now it's telling me you're exhausted." As I finished speaking Nikki yawned, trying to hide it behind her hand. We all laughed at her.

"That wasn't fair," she whined. "Of course I'm going to yawn if you tell me I'm tired. I have more questions."

"Such as?"

"Such as … if you're all told to isolate yourselves, then why are the four of you together?"

"Lance turned me shortly after he was turned himself, and then he turned Jenny by accident so he feels responsible for us," Rob explained while Lance scowled. "Acts like an overbearing father a lot, but we put up with him anyway."

"He turned you by accident?" Nikki asked Jenny, probably sensing Lance was already uncomfortable.

"There wasn't exactly a reliable form of protection back then," she said coyly.

"Protection from what?" Nikki asked. Again three pairs of eyes stared at me.

"From being intimate," I whispered in her ear.

"What? Oh. Oh," she stammered, then quickly changed the subject. "And Gregory?"

"Got drawn in when I met them at their first Gathering," I replied with a smile. "Lance had just changed Jenny and found Rob again, when another Immortal found them. They were warned they had better introduce themselves or the Queen would hunt them down. I met them shortly before they were to be presented, and they amused me, so I stood for them."

"Essentially taking responsibility for anything we do," Lance took over. "So he taught us how to behave ourselves and would look in on us from time to time."

"They amused you, huh?" Nikki asked me with a smile.

"They still do, most of the time," I agreed.

"So, most Immortals avoid each other, but you stick together. What does that make you? A coven?" Nikki questioned.

"There's not really an official title, since a group like ours doesn't really exist. What do you think we are?" I asked the others. "A pack?"

"A passel?" Lance suggested.

"A flock?" Jenny tried.

"A gaggle?" Rob offered with a straight face. We all broke down into laughter again.

"I know what you are," Nikki said, watching us. "It's obvious from the way you tease each other, and drive each other nuts, but stick together not because you should, but because you need to."

"Oh?" Rob asked. "And what does that make us?"

"A family," she replied, smiling brightly. We were all stunned silent for a moment. Then there were smiles all around.

"I like her," Lance admitted.

"Most people can't really help it," I replied.

Then Nikki yawned again, but this time it was huge, causing us all to laugh again.

"All right, everybody out," I said standing up to see them off. "Nikki has class in the morning and needs her sleep."

"You look like you could use some rest yourself, Gregory," Jenny noted. "And a meal." I gave her a harsh look to halt any further conversation. We said pleasant goodbyes and I shut the window after them.

"Don't you people use doors?" Nikki teased.

"How boring would that be?" I responded. She yawned again, her eyes already droopy. "We'd better get you home."

"I—" she started, but halted.

"What is it Nikki?"

"Would it be all right if I just stayed here tonight? I really am tired, and I don't want to fall asleep at the wheel."

"I could drive you," I offered. Just because I didn't own a car didn't mean I didn't know how to use one.

"But then when I go to class, you'd just have to get up and come back here tomorrow to get any real sleep anyway," Nikki protested. "But if it would make you uncomfortable…"

I put a finger to her lips. "I'm only uncomfortable when I'm away from you, Nikki. Of course you're welcome here," I assured her. "In my bed," I added, wagging my eyebrows. She laughed, knowing I was kidding considering that she was already half asleep.

Nikki set an alarm on her phone, and washed her face clean of the make-up. I gave her one of my T-shirts to wear to bed. She looked absolutely edible. I stripped down to my boxers before climbing in and she wrapped her arms around me without hesitation. I kissed the top of her head, then reached over to turn out the light. In the complete darkness I floated with Nikki's body clinging to me, her scent and heat drowning me.

"Wow," she whispered. "I'm surrounded by you."

I smiled at her words, and kissed her head again. Then I stroked her hair, listening to her breathing and her heart until she fell asleep. Oblivion claimed me not long after.

Chapter Thirty-Nine

The breeze had been most fortunate for Lazarus tonight. It had kept him downwind and also carried the voices emanating from the abandoned warehouse up to his rooftop perch. Guinevere had most definitely been hiding something from him. Not only had the four Immortals given their secrets to a lowly mortal, but they had betrayed their Queen. To speak of her to one so unworthy! His blood was on fire. He would have swooped down and slaughtered them all immediately, but he had to know more. He had to know if this was truly The Prophecy or simply treasonous Immortals who didn't deserve the blessing of Life.

The fact that Gregory was involved, and that he was personally invested in this mortal seemed significant. Lazarus had never understood why the Queen would dote on him, bestowing him with favor after favor. Perhaps Gregory was worth notice after all. There must be something about him that would entice the Queen so. And this whole unnatural conclave, mortal cow included, was his doing.

After all this time away, Lazarus could spare another day or two to follow him. With luck, Lazarus could tie Gregory directly to The Prophecy and find reason to destroy him, killing two birds with one stone. When he returned home, there would be no division of The Queen's attention.

Chapter Forty

Through the haze of exhaustion, I heard an annoying melody playing. I wanted it to stop. I began to feel the ache in my bones, the weak blood slogging through my veins. It was very unpleasant, and I wanted my oblivion back. The deliciously soft warmth pressed to my side moved away, and I was irritated further. My brow furrowed in displeasure but I couldn't quite open my eyes. I was so tired. Not just over-stimulated or weary, I was physically tired. That wasn't right. I should be concerned about that. But being concerned sounded like such a bother.

"Go back to sleep," a sweetly feminine voice whispered. Ahh, Nikki. Wait, she was leaving. "I'll see you later," she continued, her hand attempting to smooth the wrinkles between my eyes. Right, I'd see her after her classes. After I got some more rest. Her lips pressed against mine gently, and I struggled to respond. She laughed quietly. "You really must be tired."

Then she was gone. I missed the sound of her breathing, the rhythm of her heart. I should have at least seen her to the door. That was rude. I hoped she wasn't irritated with me. Jenny sounded irritated last night when she left. She was reminding me to do something. I didn't need reminding. I was going to get it done today. If only I could remember what it was. This dull pain spreading through my body was so distracting. *I'll feel better after I get some rest.* I was just so very *tired.*

I tried to drift away again, but didn't quite make it. I couldn't let go of the pain I was in long enough, but I couldn't wake up enough to identify it. I was disoriented and confused. I was confused by the fact that I was disoriented. And I missed Nikki. I wondered how long she had been gone, and how soon she'd be back. I tried harder to keep track of the time. I had lost my grip on it. I couldn't pace my breaths, they were shallow and irregular. My heart was beating, but it was weak and sporadic. I was in shock that my biological clock seemed to be out of sequence. Then all at once I realized what was happening.

I'm dying.

As much as an Immortal could die anyway. I had pushed myself too far. I hadn't fed in so long that my body was shutting down. I had meant to find some way to feed without killing, but now it was too late. Soon I would be completely incapacitated. My body would grow thin and wither, my mind slipping in and out of consciousness, aware only of the thirst and the pain. I had seen Immortals the Queen had decided to starve before she disposed of them. It was not pleasant.

How had I let it come this far? How had I missed the signs? I pondered that for a while, my mind rapidly losing the battle for coherent thought. Finally, I touched on the reason I had been denying myself and knew it was the same reason I had missed how desperate my state had been. Nikki. She inspired me to be above murder at the same time she distracted me from the consequences. I had been completely wrapped up in her.

For the first time in my life I had been thinking of someone other than myself. Now it was killing me. No wonder we're selfish by nature, it's a survival instinct. But even as I thought that, it didn't ring true. I had been more alive with Nikki in these past few weeks than I had ever been before. I couldn't regret a moment of it. I only wished I had time for more.

My thoughts grew more vague as the time drifted by. In the silent blackness, I sometimes couldn't remember where I was. Sometimes I lost myself, then I would panic until I could remember who or at least what I was. It seemed like an eternity was passing as I struggled to hang onto something, anything. In the end all I could remember was Nikki. I could see her lips smiling at me, smell her hair and skin. I could even hear her sweet voice calling my name... until I no longer remembered what it was...

CHAPTER FORTY-ONE

A sudden clacking seemed to rupture my eardrums and was followed by a bright light that pierced through my eyelids and rebounded off the back of my skull. My entire being flinched at the intrusive sensations, yet my body didn't react. Another muffled sound assaulted me, bringing me further into consciousness.

My body ached as though I had been tumbled around in a cement mixer full of paving stones. And the thirst, oh god, *the Thirst*. My throat was the nucleus of a white hot star, burning every inch of my veins. Even as I recognized it, I could smell its relief. Blood, fresh, clean, and most importantly, near. The thrumming heartbeat echoed in my ears, taunting me as the blood came even closer. Another sound caught my attention, higher in pitch. My body trembled in anticipation. Surely if it got close enough, I could muster enough strength to attack.

And then it was on me, pressing against my chest, screaming in my face, surrounding me with the scent of life … and almonds … and lilacs?

"Gregory!" Nikki shouted, shaking me roughly by the shoulders. My eyes flew open as the recognition brought me fully conscious. I wanted to hold her close and push her away at the same time. I needed her desperately, but I was in such a state that I didn't trust myself near her. I then realized I didn't have the strength to even warn her. Hopefully that meant I was past being able to kill her as well.

"Gregory, what's wrong? What's happened?" she was nearing panic now. She put one hand to my face searching my slack features, her other hand reached for one of mine. "You're hands are so cold! And you're shaking! Like when …" her voice trailed off as realization dawned in her eyes.

She went to lean closer again, probably thinking her scent would help like it had before. But she was bringing her thick carotid artery too close to my lips. Her heart was pumping wildly, and the adrenaline coursing through her was taunting my thirst to the point of agony. A noise bubbled up from my throat that sounded much like a wounded dog being kicked in the ribs. She immediately backed away. I was relived and disappointed.

"Gregory, what do I do? Please, tell me. Can you talk at all?" as she pled, her hand reached out to stroke my cheek softly. I closed my eyes at the delicious warmth. Then felt a stinging pain as Nikki brought her hand sharply across the same cheek. My eyes flew open in shock again.

"Don't you do that! Don't you close your eyes. You were so still when I came in. I have to know you're still there." I blinked twice, then kept my eyes open. "Thank you," she said, relaxing slightly. She leaned back from me but stayed on the edge of the bed clinging to my right hand with both of hers.

"How long has it been since you fed?" she asked quietly. "You were in trouble when you got to my parents' house weren't you? I should have known. I should have known you were starving yourself after your reaction to finding out about Clara." She watched me for a moment, her eyes desperate and sad.

"What have I done to you?" She closed her eyes and hung her head. She stayed like that for a long time, while I agonized over being unable to comfort her. Suddenly her face lit up.

"That's it!" She jumped up and dug into her pocket, retrieving her cell phone. She pressed a few buttons, searching, then held it up to her ear. The ringing buzzed my sensitive ears and then I could hear a familiar voice at the other end of the line.

"Hello? Who is this?"

"Jenny! Thank God you're there. It's me, Nikki."

"How did you get this number?"

"Gregory used my phone to call you Sunday night. I didn't have anyone else to call. Something is wrong with Gregory. I can't get him to talk to me. I don't think he can move. I don't know what to do!" Nikki was breathless and nearly hysterical with relief at finding help.

"Calm down, Nikki. Where are you?"

"We're here at his loft. I don't think he's moved since I left Monday morning."

"I knew he was in trouble, I just didn't realize how much," Jenny muttered.

"Jenny, can you help him?"

"Yes, I'll be right there. We can bring him back, Nikki, don't worry."

Nikki sighed, her entire body relaxing. "Please hurry."

"I will. And Nikki?"

"Yes?"

"Don't go near him until I get there."

"But—"

"No arguing. If he could, he'd tell you the same thing. Talk to him, keep him conscious, but don't touch him."

"All right."

"I'll be there in ten minutes, Nikki, I promise. Trust me."

"I don't have much of a choice, do I?" Nikki laughed dryly.

"I'm coming," Jenny reiterated, then she hung up.

Nikki looked at me from where she had stopped pacing at the end of my bed. "Jenny is coming to help," she said. She put her phone away and fidgeted with her hands for a moment. "She'll be here soon."

When she finally looked up at me, my heart broke. In her eyes, along with the desperation and sadness, was something I had never seen there before. Fear. Nikki was finally afraid of me.

She filled the air with nervous ramblings about what she had done Monday. How she had been disappointed that I didn't come by, but didn't start to get upset until I missed class. I realized it must be Tuesday night. I'd lost two days.

"I was actually coming over here to give you a piece of my mind," she said with that same mirthless laugh she had used with Jenny. "I thought you were already getting bored of me. It didn't occur to me that you might be hurt. I'm so sorry."

Getting bored of her? Had she not listened to a thing I said yesterday? Or Sunday, rather. How could she have thought that?

Finally there was a pounding on the door that led to the roof. Nikki flew across the room, flung it open, and pulled Jenny through, surprising her with a tight hug.

"Thank you for coming so fast."

Jenny blinked and tentatively hugged back. Then she pulled away and smiled. "That's what families do, right? They help each other."

"Exactly," Nikki agreed, tears streaming down her face.

"Even when it's your own damn fault you're in trouble, you moron," Jenny added striding over to me. "He's been like this since Monday?" she asked Nikki.

"I don't know, that's when I left for class. He seemed sleepy, but I didn't think to worry. I should have come back sooner."

"Wait, you left?"

"I had to go to class. I didn't know he was in trouble. Obviously I would have stayed if I knew. I would have called you then."

"No, what I mean is, if you left, how did you get back in? Gregory's alarm is impenetrable and locks automatically when the door shuts." Jenny's eyes widened. "Did he give you the code?"

I would have if I thought she'd ever need it.

"Well, no," Nikki said, chagrined. "I guessed it when he didn't answer my knock."

At this point Jenny could have caught seagulls, much less flies in her gaping mouth. "You guessed? A thirty digit code?"

How did Jenny know it was thirty digits?

"They're really letters," Nikki informed her. "And a lot of them repeat." *Tomorrow, and tomorrow, and tomorrow.*

Jenny just shook her head. "Whatever. It's good you got in because it would have been months before we realized he was missing, much less been able to get past his security." She looked up at Nikki. "By then it would have been too late."

"I thought Immortals couldn't die."

"We don't, but he would have been past the point of being able to help himself. Beyond you being able to help him."

"There's something I can do?"

"Yes. Do you trust me?"

Nikki hesitated, but answered, "Yes."

Jenny wasn't offended. "I understand. You know very little about me. The real question is, do you trust Gregory?"

"With my life." This time the response was automatic. I realized what I had really seen in her eyes. She wasn't afraid of me, she was afraid *for* me. Ridiculous.

Jenny smiled. "Just what I wanted to hear."

All at once, I knew what Jenny was planning and panic seized my system. It gave me just enough strength to make my wishes clear.

"*No!*" I roared, my head lifting slightly off the pillow before I collapsed again, my breathing ragged.

Nikki looked at me in shock, while Jenny rolled her eyes. "I expected no less from you, the moron who starves himself instead of searching for alternative measures first."

Nikki turned to Jenny. "You ... you want me to feed him?"

"Yes."

"But ... you told me not to go near him."

Good girl. Finally she's got some survival instincts.

"Only until I got here," Jenny explained. "In case he's so far gone that he can't stop himself. Though, honestly, I don't think he could kill you."

Nikki blanched, but nodded and stepped toward my bed. She sat down in the same place she had been sitting earlier. When she reached up and drew her hair back, exposing one side of her slender neck, my eyes widened in horror.

Jenny reached out and put a restraining hand on her shoulder. "Not the neck. You might bleed out before he could stop himself. Try the wrist. He'll have to keep the wound open, and it might hurt a little, but it's safer that way."

Nikki swallowed hard and reached her hand out, stroking my face once before placing her wrist to my lips. I could smell the blood just below her skin. But I held perfectly still, letting my eyes express exactly what I thought of this idea. Nikki stared back at me, anger quickly overpowering the fear in her eyes. We glared at each other until Jenny cleared her throat.

"Maybe if I got it started, he wouldn't be able to resist," she suggested.

"No," Nikki said harshly. She turned to Jenny and her face softened a little. "I appreciate that you're here to help, but the truth is that this is between me and Gregory." She looked back at me, the anger returning. "He has to choose to live."

Jenny looked back and forth between us, then took a step back.

Nikki's eyes locked onto mine like steel beams. "If you think you're going to get away with giving up and dying on me, you've got another thing coming. I'm the one who broke in this time, so it's my turn to be in charge. And I say you have to live, you high-minded, self-righteous, ass of a martyr!"

I continued to stare at her, impassive.

"You said you'd stay with me, that I wouldn't know a life without you in it." Now her voice was giving out, betraying her emotions. "I refuse to settle for anything less. If I have to find a knife and slit my own wrist, I will."

Tears began streaming down her beautiful cheeks again. Damn her, she was winning. "Please, Gregory. Don't do this, don't leave me." She dropped her head in defeat, her voice falling to a whisper. "You said you loved me."

I snapped. With strength that surprised us both, my hand came up, clamping her wrist to my mouth like a vice. I hesitated for one last moment as a single tear, the last moisture my body had left to give, escaped, rolling down my cheek. Nikki gasped, her eyes wide as my teeth sliced through her supple skin.

Then her blood filled my mouth, and I began to drink in earnest. The effect was instantaneous. I was able to sit up and put my free arm around her back, supporting her even as I drained her. She closed her eyes, her face tensing as I had to open the wound again and again to keep the blood flowing. Finally, her face paled and her body became limp, falling against me. I laid her gently down on my bed, continuing to lap at her wrist, helping the wound to close and heal. I was still very thirsty, but I had taken enough from Nikki. It showed through the tears I was now shedding copiously.

"Are you … crying?" Jenny asked in awe. I had forgotten she was there.

"Get out," I answered.

"I knew you wouldn't kill her," she defended. "It wasn't even close."

She didn't understand, but I didn't expect her to. I sighed. "Jenny, I appreciate that you came to help. But please go, now."

"I would like to come back later," she pressed. "I could bring food for Nikki."

I gave in. "Again, I appreciate the help." And with a whisper of sound, Jenny was gone.

I pulled Nikki close and stroked her face softly. "I *do* love you, much more than is healthy, for either of us."

Chapter Forty-Two

After a few minutes, which felt like decades, Nikki began to stir and then blinked open her eyes.

"You look better," she said, smiling weakly.

"That makes one of us," I replied.

"I do feel a little out of it," she admitted.

"I took a little more blood than if you had donated it, but you don't need a hospital," I assured her. She began laughing, and I raised an eyebrow in question.

"I *was* donating," she explained, still laughing as I rolled my eyes. She stopped laughing. "It wasn't as bad as I thought it would be."

"It won't happen again, I promise."

"But if I can help," she began, and I cut her off with a finger against her lips.

"If you're about to suggest some kind of perverse arrangement, save your breath. Even if we were both willing, it wouldn't be enough. I'm still thirsty and I'll need to really feed soon. You brought me back to the point of being able to fend for myself, but only just. Trying to maintain it like this would only keep us both weak."

"Why did you go so long without feeding?"

"Falling in love with you seems to have opened a door I can't close. The last time I tried to feed, I saw your face everywhere. The more time I spend with you, the more I see humanity through your eyes."

"So, what now?" she asked. I sighed and laid my head down on her chest, listening to the steady beat of her heart.

"Now I think of alternatives."

"Could you get blood from a blood bank?"

"Wouldn't that be convenient? I wouldn't even have to screen it for disease. Unfortunately, the anticoagulant they use when collecting the blood makes it indigestible for us."

"Too bad," Nikki sympathized. One of her hands came up to play absently with my hair. I sighed again and closed my eyes. I knew I needed to be seriously thinking about this problem, but I was still so tired, and Nikki was so deliciously comfortable.

We lay in a peaceful silence for a while, then she spoke again.

"I have another 'naive' question, and this one's a doozy."

"Let's have it."

"Well, you can't buy human blood, and apparently can't bring yourself to take human blood," she squeezed my shoulder, "so it just begs to be asked ..."

"What?"

"Does it have to be human?"

My eyes came open, and I lifted my head to look at her.

"Sorry I asked," she said, embarrassed.

"No," I finally replied.

"No, don't be sorry?"

"No, it doesn't have to be human," I said, beginning to get excited. "We've all had to make do with animals now and then, especially back when traveling took months instead of hours."

"You 'make do' with animals?" Nikki asked. "What does that mean, exactly? Are they not as digestible?"

"That's just it. There's nothing wrong with animal blood. We just avoid it unless we're desperate. And I am most certainly desperate. I've never thought about sustaining myself on it before. But it might be worth a try."

"Worth a try? If there's nothing wrong with it, how has it not occurred to you?" she asked, somewhat incredulously.

"It's not something Immortals generally do. It's taboo, actually. We've all had to do it, but no one talks about it."

"You're ashamed to kill an animal, but not a human?"

"Not me, Nikki, Immortals in general," I corrected her gently.

She looked away. "Right, I know. I'm sorry." She turned back to me with a sigh. "It's just hard to relate to a culture so cavalier about taking human life when there's such an obvious alternative."

Although I no longer shared my culture's views, I wanted her to understand where I was coming from.

"How hungry would you have to be before you'd eat a rat?" I asked her. It triggered an immediate look of revulsion to cross her face. "See there? You can't help but be disgusted by the very suggestion."

"It tastes that bad, huh?" she asked.

"No, actually. And that's my point. Rat doesn't actually taste any different than other small mammals like dogs or cats." Nikki's face grew increasingly disgusted. "They're all meat, Nikki, and in some countries it's something humans eat every day. You've just been taught to think it's wrong."

"Tastes just like chicken," she said.

"What?"

"It's a saying about different meats not being so bad if you give them a try," she explained. "Like when you're camping in the wilderness and have to roast a rattlesnake. You convince yourself to do it by telling yourself it tastes just like chicken."

"Exactly. What I'm saying is that before I met you, I had no reason to question my food source. Immortals prey on humans. That's just what we do. It's what is expected."

"And then I came along and convinced you to try the rattlesnake."

"Tastes just like chicken," I said with a smile. "Now I just have to find out if it will sustain me long term."

"Do you want me to come with you?" she asked, moving as if to get up.

"You need to rest, young lady. You're not quite yourself at the moment," I said, holding her firmly to the bed. "Besides, I was hoping to get a little rest myself. It's been quite a day."

Nikki looked at me skeptically. "I'm not sure I should let you go back to sleep."

I chuckled at her concern. "I'm fine, I promise. I just want to hold you while you sleep for a while. I missed you when you were gone."

I could tell I was winning her over, but she still looked worried.

"Plus, Jenny is coming by later to bring you food, so I won't have time for a coma."

"Not funny," she chided, but she also relaxed against the pillows. I reached over and turned off the lights, then drew her close to me. Once I could feel her heart beat against my chest and her breath on my neck, I finally felt like everything was right again.

"Perfection," I sighed. I felt her smile against my skin and then her breathing slowed as she relaxed and fell asleep. I continued to hold her firmly against me until her rhythms lulled me into a dream.

In the darkness I could hear sounds. The damp air was heavy in my lungs as I ran. I was fleeing from something dangerous, following the animals around me. I needed to find Nikki, needed to keep her safe. The birds flew from the trees but I stopped at its base. I couldn't hide this time. I turned to face the terrible monster, knowing if I could destroy it, Nikki would be safe. But there was Nikki behind me, walking beside the great cat as though nothing was wrong. She stopped and smiled, one hand reaching out to me, the other stroking the head of the beast that sat at her feet. "Don't be afraid, Gregory," she whispered. "Everything will be put right; all will be restored."

Chapter Forty-Three

A loud rapping at the door of my roof brought me abruptly back to my senses. Cursing Jenny silently, I eased out from under Nikki, trying not to wake her. Walking swiftly I made it to a dim light near the couch before the rapping came again. Rolling my eyes and clenching my fists I raced back to the door to fling it open just as the rapping sounded for the third time.

"Nevermore," Rob squawked as he sauntered in. I slapped the back of his head.

"Nikki is sleeping, idiot. Keep it down." I gave Jenny an exasperated look.

"Hey, I had to keep myself busy for a few hours," she said by way of explanation.

"And then I decided to tag along," Rob added.

"And I had to see for myself that you hadn't killed her," Lance said as he came in.

I wanted to be offended, but he was right. It was a miracle I hadn't. He looked over to the bed and watched Nikki for a moment. "Are you sure she's just sleeping?"

Before I could answer him or, even better, punch him in the face, Nikki spoke up.

"No, Nikki is not sleeping, but neither is she dead." She sat up and squinted. "And you're a Robin not a Raven."

"And she's still funny!" Rob said.

I went over to the bed and stacked some pillows behind Nikki so she could lean back again. She smiled sweetly up at me, taking my hand as I sat next to her. When I turned back to the others, they were watching me like an exhibit at the zoo. It was both disconcerting and irritating.

"I don't see why it was necessary for all three of you to be here," I said.

"I brought Nikki food for recovery," Jenny reminded me, gliding over and sitting on Nikki's other side. She pulled a large bag into her lap and took out several kinds of juices and a box of cookies. I raised an eyebrow at her choice and she just shrugged. "It's what they have set out everywhere they donate blood isn't it?"

Nikki laughed at that. Rob came over and flopped himself on Jenny's side, his head landing in Nikki's lap.

"And I, of course brought you more tasty cakes," he said, pulling several from his pockets. I wondered how he carried them around without crushing them. Nikki smiled and ruffled his surfer mop, making it an even bigger mess and soliciting a big grin. Then, she looked up at Lance, who was now standing at the foot of the bed.

"I'm glad you're not dead," he said bluntly. Nikki stared at him for a moment, then started laughing again. I sighed, realizing I couldn't kick them all out when they were making Nikki so happy.

"Get used to it, Gregory," Jenny teased. "We're family now."

I closed my eyes and put my head back. I felt Nikki turn in my direction, probably worried about my reaction. At least she cared about my discomfort.

"Gregory's not used to accepting help," Jenny explained to Nikki. "But he can't turn us out because we're not trying to help him, we're helping you." I looked at her just in time to see her stick out her tongue.

"He would really kick you out?" Nikki asked.

"I'm still surprised he let us in," Rob replied. "You've probably been here more than we have."

"Sunday was my first time," Nikki said. Jenny looked surprised while Rob snorted. I gave him a severe look and he let the comment pass.

"We had never been inside before then, either," Jenny said.

"Why wouldn't you let them in?" Nikki asked me.

"I had no reason to," I replied.

"Gregory was a real stick in the mud before he met you," Rob said. "I meant it when I called him a gargoyle—all stony and solemn." He frowned deeply for effect and Nikki laughed again.

"How long are you all staying?" I asked. Nikki pulled on my hand and gave me a disapproving look while the others laughed at me. "I need to hunt," I said by way of explanation.

"I thought you decided to abstain," Rob sniggered.

"About time," Jenny added.

"That doesn't bother you?" Lance asked, watching Nikki.

"Not that kind of hunting," I extrapolated. "I'm going up into the hills."

I got three blank stares.

"I'm going to hunt animals," I said slowly.

"Like humans do?" Lance asked incredulously.

"I suppose so," I answered.

"With a gun?" Rob asked.

"No, not with a gun," I said. By this time Nikki was trying not to laugh at their reactions.

"I want to come," Jenny said, surprising all of us. "I want to see it for myself. If it works, this could change everything," she said.

She had a point.

"Since you're all so eager to help, I was wondering if you could stay with Nikki while I'm gone," I said, finally making the point I had been working toward.

"What?" Nikki asked. "Like I'm some kind of pet that needs to be fed and watered?"

"And taken for walks," Rob added with a serious face. I glared at him.

"That's not what I meant, Nikki, and you know it," I said. I was holding one of her hands and brought my free hand up to her face. "You're going to be weak for a day or two. I want to know you'll be taken care of and protected while I'm gone. If you don't want to spend time with Tweedle Dee and Tweedle Dum, I understand. I'll stay until you feel better."

"I already feel better, and you need to go as soon as possible," Nikki said.

"You haven't tried to stand up yet," I pointed out.

Nikki glared at me and sat up swiftly, moving over to the edge of the bed. Her face paled. She put an arm out to steady herself against my chest as she swayed slightly. I gently grabbed her arm and helped her lay down again.

"Okay, maybe I'm still not quite myself," she admitted.

"I don't think you realize how much blood you've lost," I said.

"You said it was like I'd given blood."

"I said it was a little more than that," I reminded her. "And a lot of humans pass out and are weak for a while after normal blood donation."

Rob laid down on the bed, propped up on his elbows, his chin in his hands. "Don't you want to hang out with me and Lance?" He pouted. Nikki laughed and mussed his hair again. If she didn't stop encouraging him, I'd never get rid of him when I got back.

"At least I don't have to worry about being bored while you're gone," she said to me.

"You better let her get some rest," I warned Rob. He rolled over, putting his hand over his heart and gave me a salute. "And you, please make sure she gets something to eat besides those terrible cakes," I instructed Lance.

"You mean tasty cakes," Rob corrected.

"I meant exactly what I said," I countered.

"When do we leave?" Jenny asked.

"I guess we could go now. If you're sure you'll be okay," I said to Nikki.

"With these two as my protectors? I'll be just fine," she assured me.

"We'll take good care of her, Gregory, don't worry," Lance said.

"Hurry back," Nikki said. She leaned over to kiss my cheek, then whispered in my ear, "I'll miss you."

I pulled back far enough to reach her mouth and kissed her. The moment our lips met I was lost. I buried one hand in her soft curls, opening my mouth to taste her. She responded willingly and we promptly forgot we had an audience, until Lance cleared his throat. Softly ending the kiss, I leaned my forehead against hers.

"I love you," I whispered.

"I love you," she answered.

"Wow," Jenny said quietly. I looked to see the three of them staring again.

"That's going to take some getting used to," Lance said.

"Seriously…weird," Rob agreed.

I was quiet for a moment, deciding whether to be annoyed or not. Then I laughed. "You have no idea."

I stood up and smoothed the covers back over Nikki, leaning down to give her another quick kiss. Then Jenny and I left for our hunting trip.

CHAPTER FORTY-FOUR

"This is pointless." Jenny sulked. We had parked the car at the edge of the wilderness an hour ago and were still meandering around aimlessly.

"We had to get away from the tourist areas first, Jenny. And the animals aren't going to just come out and find us. That's why it's called hunting," I said peevishly. "You didn't have to come along."

"I know." She sighed. "And I do want to see if this will work. I just didn't think it would take so long."

"You've been spoiled by easy prey for too long," I said. She opened her mouth to respond, but I held up a hand to silence her. She gave me a pointed look, but complied. The breeze subtly changed, and suddenly Jenny could smell what I had heard. Her head jerked up and to the south. She looked back at me.

"What is it?" she breathed. "It smells…" She searched for the right word, "feral."

I smiled at her description. "I'm not sure, but I think it's a predator of some kind. It sounds big. I'm going after it." Jenny looked slightly sick, but I didn't give her a chance to argue before I began running south.

Jenny stayed right behind me and within the next two miles I could smell it as well as hear it stalking through the brush. She was right, feral was a good way to describe its scent. It was musky, strong, and wild. Under normal circumstances, I would have turned up my nose. But I was long past normal these days, and the blood was clean, much cleaner than human blood had been for decades.

Now that I could use two of my senses to track it, I ran much faster, without fear of losing it. Jenny began to lag behind. I didn't wait for her. My world opened up on every side. The sky expanded overhead, the trees clear and distinct before, beside, and behind me, the grass and brush rising to meet each step. I came close enough to hear its heart beat. It had realized it was being pursued and was now taking flight. I caught flashes of tan fur on a long body as it raced between the trees. A cougar. Perfect.

The adrenaline pumping through its system called to me as I scaled the rocky side of a hill. At the top I found the beast pacing on a ledge, aggravated and tense. The incline behind it was too steep to climb, too smooth to find purchase. Its only retreat was the way it had come. Straight through me.

It growled and roared at me, body tensing to spring. My body tensed in response, my senses heightened. I snarled back at it. There was a sound from above but neither of us turned to look. We pounced at the same time, and though I was stronger, its claws were thick and sharp and tore through my flesh as we struggled. It was painful and exhilarating. Finally, I got both hands around its neck and twisted sharply. With a snap, it went limp and I sank my teeth into its neck.

For an instant the fur against my mouth was repulsive, but then the blood flowed thick, warm, and sweet. After draining the cat dry, my stomach was full. I turned and went back down the rocky slope. Jenny was at the bottom.

"Bloody hell, Gregory!" she exclaimed, "What did you do, rip it to shreds?"

I looked down at myself and realized I was covered in blood. "I think most of it is mine."

"What? Your blood? How is that possible?"

"It was a cougar, Jenny," I said. "They have lots of teeth and claws."

Jenny just stared at me.

I headed for a river I could hear just beyond the trees. Kneeling down, I splashed the water on my face and neck. I turned back to Jenny and she gasped.

"Gregory! You're bleeding!"

"Didn't we just go over this, Jenny?" I asked, starting to get a little annoyed. "You've seen Immortals wounded before."

"You're *still* bleeding," she said, pointing to my face. I reached up and my hand came away red. "Why aren't you healing?"

I moved the tattered sleeve of my shirt to the side. "This wound was to the bone, but now it's only an inch deep. I am healing, I can feel the skin pulling together. It's just taking longer." I evaluated myself for a moment then added, "Which makes sense."

"How can that make sense?" Jenny asked.

"Because I'm still full."

"I don't understand."

"I'm full, Jenny. I tracked and killed a cougar and it was the most exhilarating hunt of my life. It felt natural, familiar almost," I said. "And now I'm still *full*."

"No Thirst at all?"

"None."

"Good God."

"I'm starting to think so."

A smile spread across Jenny's face. "Me next." She looked me over again. "But I'm finding something with less pointy parts."

I laughed and then watched as Jenny searched the breeze for something to track, we caught the scent at the same time.

"It smells different," she said.

"Yes," I agreed. "I think it's less dangerous."

"How can you know that?" she asked.

"Instinct?" I replied. She raised an eyebrow. "I'm serious. We've been smelling these animals all our lives, we've just never taken notice of them before. It's like you being able to identify emotions by their different chemicals. Something in the back of my mind remembers this scent as docile."

Jenny didn't look convinced, but we tracked the scent anyway. She stalked it much slower than I did, being careful not to make a sound. We came upon a clearing with a herd of deer grazing in it.

I gave Jenny an "I told you so" look while she gave me a look that said she was sure I had been practicing this without her. I held my hands up in a gesture that said it wasn't my fault I was naturally better at this than she was. She scowled at me and pointed a finger, effectively telling me to stay put.

She took a silent step into the clearing. When the deer didn't respond, she took several more. When the giant buck finally looked up, she froze but didn't look away. He had a good two hundred pounds on her and she couldn't have looked very intimidating. Jenny slowly bent forward, lowering her head slightly. The buck returned to its grazing.

To my surprise, Jenny turned and started for one of the smaller does. It looked up at her approach, and she caught it in a penetrating stare. With a coy smile and slow steps she inched her way forward. They came face to face. Jenny actually pressed her cheek to the doe's, stroking her neck softly. I stood there in total shock. A part of my brain disconnected and I could see not Jenny, but Nikki standing there, embracing the timid deer.

I was swiftly brought back to reality when Jenny sank her teeth into its neck and it began to thrash, sending the other deer scattering. She rode it to the ground, keeping her mouth securely attached. Finally, the doe was still. Jenny stood and turned to me, eyes bright, one hand absently rubbing her stomach.

She opened her mouth to speak, but found herself without words.

"Full?" I asked with a smirk.

"Completely," she said in awe.

"Why didn't you go for the buck?" I asked. "He was a much bigger animal, more blood."

"I'm not as big as you, Gregory. I don't need as much to fill me up," she answered. "Besides, did you see the antlers on that thing? Much too pointy."

We laughed together, running back through the forest with wild abandon. I had never felt so free, and found myself once again picturing Nikki, running by my side, her hair flying in the wind. But I shook my head, clearing the vision. While there was much about being an Immortal I wished I could share with Nikki, there was infinitely more I would die to protect her from.

CHAPTER FORTY-FIVE

Nikki's reaction to the sight of me was much like Jenny's had been.

"Good God, Gregory!" she yelled, jumping up from the couch to rush over and take my face in her hands. "What happened to you?"

"Cougar," Jenny answered with a smile. Nikki gasped while Rob and Lance's eyes bugged out.

"It's not as bad as it looks, I promise," I said to Nikki, taking her hands in mine and kissing her forehead.

"A cougar. Really?" Rob asked me. I nodded with a smile.

"Did you have to go after something so dangerous?" Nikki asked.

"I took a deer," Jenny replied. The boys looked at her in shock.

"More like seduced a deer," I added. "She walked right up to it, like she was going to kiss it on the mouth, then went for its jugular."

Jenny smiled wickedly while Lance chuckled at the image and Rob rubbed his throat distractedly.

"So you had fun?" Nikki asked. "And it was a success?"

"A complete success," I agreed. "And more fun than I could have imagined."

"Tell us more about this cougar," Lance urged. Nikki's eyes grew concerned again.

"I'll tell you about it while I get cleaned up," I suggested.

"And I'll stay here and tell Nikki about the deer," Jenny added.

"I don't think Nikki needs all the gory details, Jenny," I said.

"No, actually I want to know," Nikki argued. I looked at her and she continued. "I couldn't and didn't want to know about hunting humans, but I can handle this. My dad goes hunting every year. If he can tell me about cleaning and gutting a deer, Jenny can tell me about nearly kissing one."

Jenny laughed, delighted. I shook my head and kissed Nikki's forehead again. "Amazing," I said softly.

Nikki sat back down on the couch with Jenny while the guys followed me into the bathroom. I turned the hot water on in the shower and stripped off my shredded and filthy clothes. Rob and Lance cringed at the several painful looking scratches I had on my torso.

"Are those all from an animal?" Lance asked.

"This one nearly took my arm off," I said, pointing to the nearly healed wound at my shoulder.

"Really?" He seemed excited by the possibility. I knew he would love the danger. I laughed as I stepped under the steaming spray, then hissed as the water stung my open wounds.

"Wait," Rob said putting a hand up. "You got trashed by a cat?"

I gave him a scathing look. "When was the last time you tried to kill something that fought back?" I asked. "With razor-sharp claws?"

"Point taken," Rob admitted. "I'm not sure I could get into that sort of thing."

"Once I broke his neck, the fight went right out of him," I said, toweling myself off. "You could start with that," I suggested. He thought about it.

"You have to take me," Lance said.

"What?" I asked, walking into the closet.

"You have to take me hunting," he repeated.

"Why don't you just go yourself?" I asked.

"You need to show me where to go, what to do," he insisted.

"It's not as hard as you're making it sound," I replied. "Once you get out there and wrap your head around it, it feels natural. It feels right."

"Please?"

I sighed. "Fine, but you'll have to wait until sometime next week. I don't want to leave Nikki again. We'll go while she's in class."

"Thank you." Lance turned to Rob. "Are you in?"

"I'm not sure it's worth all the trouble," he replied.

"It is," I said with certainty. Rob still looked doubtful.

"I'm full," I said simply.

Rob stared at me, then his eyes widened. I nodded. "I think animal blood is absorbed more gradually somehow. I was severely wounded and I healed, but slowly. I'm only now beginning to feel the first hint of thirst creeping back."

"But you fed hours ago," Rob said. I nodded again.

"No more Twinkies," Lance said, clapping Rob on the shoulder.

"To hell with Twinkies." Rob laughed. "I'm in."

We went back into the main room, and I walked straight to the couch, picking Nikki up in the air and twirling her around before kissing her soundly on the mouth. Then I sat in the leather armchair with her firmly in my lap, my lips never more than an inch from the skin of her neck or face.

"You look much better," she laughed.

"As do you," I replied. "These two rogues behaved themselves?"

"They took excellent care of your pet human," she replied.

"And she wasn't all that easy to take care of," Rob said. I raised an eyebrow in question. "She wouldn't even let me give her a bath."

Though he was joking, I was enraged by the comment. I was going to move Nikki so I could attack, but she grabbed the nearest projectile from the table, which happened to be a Twinkie, and hurled it at Rob's head. He, of course, caught it, which caused her to pout and mutter about unfair reflexes. The humor of the situation finally got through to me, and I kissed her cheek, whispering, "Here, let me."

I then leaned forward, grabbed a large book from the table and flung it, hitting Rob directly between the eyes.

"Ouch! Damn, Gregory!"

Nikki's eyes went wide, but then she joined in the laughter when she saw I hadn't done any real damage.

"That's what you get for trying to pick on me now that my invincible boyfriend is back," Nikki said, wagging a finger at Rob.

"Watch yourself," I warned him, only half-kidding.

The atmosphere was warm and jovial. It seemed we were all feeling that a wonderful future lay ahead. There was only one thing that didn't match the mood.

"Jenny, could you open the window?" I asked, too comfortable where I was to get up. "The air in here has gotten stale."

"And it's such a fantastic view," Nikki added. Jenny glanced back and forth between us, then, with a broad smile, she walked over to the window.

"You're right, Gregory," Jenny said. "It's been far too stuffy in here. It's definitely time for some fresh air."

I knew she was teasing me, but I didn't care. I had Nikki, and I could live without being a monster. I couldn't wipe the smile from my face. Jenny slid open the stubborn widow and the wind from a brewing storm came in, heavy and salty.

Jenny was the first one to smell it.

"Shit!" she exclaimed, making Nikki jump and the rest of us turn to her. "Shit! Shit! Shit!"

"What's wrong?" Nikki asked with concern. Another gust blew in bringing the scent deeper into the loft and the rest of us caught it. Like newborn skin, clear and crisp, with a touch of something that was disturbingly familiar.

"What the hell is he doing here?" I asked, then leapt up and left Nikki on the chair, joining Jenny at the window.

"You know him?" Jenny asked me at the same time Lance and Rob asked us both.

"He's the Immortal who attacked Nikki on campus," I said to Jenny.

"What?" Nikki cried. "Why would he be here? How does he know where you live?"

Those were very good questions. "There's no time," Jenny said as I opened my mouth. "We need to get Nikki out of here, now."

"There are four of us, Jenny. He wasn't that powerful before, if we stay here, he'll have to come through all of us to get her," I said logically.

Jenny's eyes looked panicked. "Gregory, I have no time to explain this better. You have to trust me when I say that the only reason you and Nikki survived your first encounter with Lazarus was that he didn't know who she was." She glanced at Nikki and started pacing. "Now he does and we need to get her away."

I didn't understand, but I wasn't willing to bet Nikki's life on it. "The roof will give us the most room to maneuver," I suggested. Jenny nodded quickly and pulled a still stunned Nikki to her feet. Grabbing my swords off the wall, I led the way up the stairs to the roof access, Nikki right behind me, followed by Jenny, Lance, and Rob.

I opened the door to the roof and led them out onto the flat asphalt surface. "Which way, Jenny?" I asked hurriedly.

The clouds burst open, the storm beginning to rage in earnest.

"Too late," Jenny whispered, staring over my shoulder. "Too late."

I whirled around, and though the combination of deep night and obscuring rain had probably rendered Nikki nearly blind, I saw the dark figure across from us on the rooftop. He reached both hands up and back. I heard the soft whisper of swords being drawn. His lip curled up into that same smug sneer. I growled low and fierce and stepped in front of Nikki. "Get her back downstairs," I hissed. Rob was the first to spin around and try the door.

"It's locked!" he cried.

I reached back to the keypad, only to find it had been completely destroyed. I spun back around to face the dark assassin. It was a trap, and we had walked right into it.

CHAPTER FORTY-SIX

"No need for this to get messy," the assassin's soft voice carried to us on the wind. "Just hand over the mortal and I'll be on my way."

"Never," I said fiercely, taking a step forward.

"I was rather hoping you'd say that," he replied.

The assassin Jenny had called Lazarus flew at me from the roof's edge. I freed my swords.

"No!" Nikki cried, but Jenny instantly grabbed her, clamping a hand over her mouth to keep her from distracting me. I opposed the violence she did it with, but was relieved to be able to concentrate.

We met in the air midway across the rooftop, our swords sparking off one another's like the lightning, and landed in opposite positions from where we had started. I quickly lunged at him, forcing him to move as I worked my way back, putting my body between Nikki and this demon. His blades were both long and thin. Lazarus was fast, but I managed to dodge and parry his strikes.

"Such effort to protect a mere mortal," he laughed. "I wonder what it is that makes her so special? What could make her worth feeding on *animals?*"

How could he possibly know that?

"She's mine," I said by way of explanation. I took a step back, deflecting a blow with my long sword, then brought my shorter sword forward, surprising him. My blade sliced through his black trench coat and I could smell fresh blood. His face lost all its joviality. I had finally gotten to him.

"Now I'm going to make you suffer, my privileged brother," he snarled. His blows began raining down with increasing speed and velocity. Soon, it was all I could do to defend myself.

"Concentrate, Gregory! Use your damn gift!" Jenny screamed at me. Lance and Rob started forward. "No!" Jenny and I called in unison. I was beginning to understand her fear of this Immortal. I didn't want anyone else to be at risk. Jenny was right. I had been focusing on my own fighting. I needed to focus on him. I took a deep breath and opened my senses. I had never tried it under such circumstances, but if I ever needed to know what was about to happen, it was now.

Time slowed. I watched the rain drops bounce off every surface of the roof. I perceived the hundreds of tiny water particles explode as each drop made contact. My family seemed to stand still, almost motionless. I could hear each of their hearts beat and could distinguish them from one another. All this I took in as if through peripheral vision. My true focus was on Lazarus.

Hearing the fabric of his coat rustle, I stepped sideways, matching his movements. The muscles in his forearms gave away the direction he was swinging his swords. His heart was beating faster than I had ever heard an Immortal's beat before. It sounded almost human in its report. As I concentrated on him even harder, our deadly dance became more evenly matched, and then I began to advance. The ring of steel on steel became a nearly constant echo as again and again we traded blows.

We had each drawn blood several times, though I couldn't see his wounds beneath his thick clothes. Finally, I got the opening I was looking for. Spinning fully around I brought my long blade across the top of his shoulders neatly severing his head.

But something was wrong. I had ended my spin facing away from him, so I could not see what my senses were frantically trying to warn me about. As my blade had passed through his neck, it had made too much noise. I heard his spine, each tendon, and every tissue separate as it was parted by steel. However, it sounded like everything had been separated twice. I shrugged off the warnings. He was dead. I let my senses return to normal. I stepped back to watch him fall. As I turned my head, his boot met the bottom of my chin. My mouth snapped shut, my teeth made a terrible *clack* sound. I nearly bit my tongue off. He started to laugh.

It was high-pitched and maniacal, a sound I would never forget. He brought one hand up and wiped the back of it along the red line on his neck. The blood came away, revealing perfect, whole skin. I was frozen in shocked horror. I had decapitated him. That should have ended it. For him to survive that, his neck would have had to heal instantaneously while my sword sliced through it. Those sounds I heard were not his neck separating the second time. His body had rejoined as quickly as it had been severed. But that was impossible.

He lunged forward and I jerked back to my senses in time to avoid being beheaded myself. After a few half-dazed parries and attacks, I realized I had to drastically change my fighting strategy. I could not destroy him. The best I could hope for was incapacitating him.

I raised both my swords over my head and rained blows down upon him. This forced him to retreat a few paces. I pursued him with almost animal abandon, and while I was faster, he refused to allow me access to his heart, taking several unnecessary wounds to avoid exposing it in any way. I became desperate to end the fight, no matter the cost.

I extended my arm as far as I could and forced my sword into his chest. A scream of rage and frustration tore from my throat as I missed his heart by less than an inch. I twisted my wrist and pushed my body in an arc over his head and he raised his blades into my body. I could feel and hear his weapons dig deep into my own chest, one digging from my left shoulder down to my right hip, the other making a deep gouge at the base of my neck. Before my mind registered the pain, I felt the tiny electrical pulses travel up my nerves. They were almost as painful as the signal my brain received.

I finally snapped, dropping my elbow into the base of his skull, and I heard his neck break. Then, I extended my arm, driving my long sword through his kidney and stomach. I withdrew my other blade from his chest, allowing me to twist my body. As luck would have it, he turned his head just in time for my knee to connect with his face. I felt his cheek bone shatter.

It all happened in an instant. I was again standing, waiting to see what damage my attack had wrought, when he turned around. It was a sight straight out of one of Rob's horror movies. One eye was swollen shut. His symmetrical anatomy was horribly disfigured as half his facial structure curved inward where it once curved outward. On the other half of his face, he sported a smile.

His shirt had a large tear and I could see blood gush out of his open wound. The flow slowed, until it stopped. Then, I watched as his cheek realigned itself and the swelling in his eye disappeared. He smiled broadly, revealing two rows of perfectly straight teeth.

My attack did not end the fight as I had hoped, but it was worth the cost. His face had healed only after his organs did. While his body could handle one, terrible wound, it could not as quickly regenerate from multiple ones. If I could not deal a single lethal blow, I needed to overwhelm him with enough wounds to keep him from healing so fast. I could feel my senses fading. I had lost a lot of blood and I was still healing slowly. I had strength only for one more attempt.

I slowed my pace and went on the defensive, paying close attention to how Lazarus moved. I listened to how he breathed, to his muscles tighten and twist. I watched his eyes, how they darted back and forth. The details gave away his every move. Once I felt confident in reading him, I made my attack.

I sprinted towards him, one blade extended forward, the other behind me. He brought his swords to the ready, his eyes focused on my hand. That was it. He was going to attempt to block my extended blade with both of his. An instant before our blades connected, I quickly swung my arms, switching their positions. As I brought my back arm forward, I released my grip on my long sword, flinging it into the air. His eyes left me for a moment, watching the unexpected ascent of my blade. They returned quickly to me, but it was already too late.

I turned sideways, slipping in between his blades. With my now-free hand, I grabbed his wrist, twisting with all my might until I felt his bones and sinews snap in my hand. I continued twisting his hand until his weapon pointed downwards and then quickly raised his limb before thrusting down. I could feel the deep crunch as his blade penetrated his knee and ran the length of his tibia, snapping it in half. The tip exited through his heel and entered the rooftop.

I used my forward momentum and slammed my forehead into his face. My face was immediately drenched with blood exiting his broken nose and open mouth. With his foot anchored to the ground, he lost his balance and fell over backwards. As he fell, I wrapped my arm around his elbow and pulled. With a loud pop, I heard his shoulder dislocate from its socket.

I loosened my grip, allowing his limp limb to slide away from me. Then, I dragged my short blade along his arm and severed the tendon in his wrist. Plunging my blade deep into his other shoulder, between his clavicle and scapula, I separated the two bones.

His body continued to fall, now parallel with the ground. I pulled my arm back as if to strike, even though my long blade was not in my hand. I did not have to look. I could hear it as it cut through the rain in its heavenly descent. The hilt found my hand, and I thrust forward. My sword penetrated his body, just above the pelvic bone. It pushed through, piercing first his kidney, then his lung, then his heart. It continued up through his neck, and into his brain. It exited through the crown of his skull, the hilt of my blade flush with his skin.

With a primal roar, I savagely freed my precious swords from the broken body, and staggered back, my chest heaving, heart pounding. The rooftop was covered in blood and gore, and so was I. It was a gruesome sight, even for an Immortal. The rain continued to fall and I turned my face up into it, washing it clean of Lazarus' blood.

It was over. I had never seen anything like him in all my years.

"Gregory, you have to get Nikki and run, now," Jenny called to me. Turning my back on the corpse, I looked at her in confusion.

"What are you talking about? He's dead." I stated the obvious.

"Lazarus doesn't do 'dead,' Gregory. Now come get Nikki and get the hell out of here!" Jenny insisted. I was about to argue again when Lance, who was staring in awe at the macabre scene behind me cried out.

"Gregory, look!" I whirled around, bringing my swords back to the ready. But Lazarus was still and unmoving. I shook my head and turned to stare at Lance, confusion written on my face. "His hands! Look at his hands!" he insisted.

I turned back and looked at the bloody hands lying against the asphalt roofing. I stared, seeing nothing. Then the fingers twitched. My eyes opened wide and I began backing away. What kind of madness was this?

"There is no time!" Jenny screamed at me. Finally accepting the incomprehensible truth, I turned and ran across the roof. In seconds I had Nikki gathered into my arms.

"Keys!" I called and Lance tossed his to me. I snatched them out of the air.

"Let's go," I instructed my family. Rob took a step toward me, Lance and Jenny each put a hand on one of his arms.

"Take Nikki and keep her safe," Lance said grimly. I opened my mouth to object.

"Go, Gregory, we will be all right," Jenny assured me. I shook my head, but then the monstrous assassin began to rise.

"You will explain this to me later, Guinevere," I said, using her proper name, indicating there would be no alternative.

"Yes, yes, just go!" she pleaded.

I turned with Nikki clasped firmly to my chest, and stepped off the roof. She screamed all the way down until we landed smoothly on the concrete walk. She swallowed hard and glared at me. "A little warning when you're going to do that would be nice next time."

I couldn't help myself and chuckled despite the situation. "Yes ma'am," I said.

"Why aren't we taking my car?" she asked, still dazed and probably in shock at what she had just seen me do to another living creature. I had shredded him like a cheese grater; she must have been horrified. And I had managed to smear the mess all over her clothes. I wondered for an insane minute if it would make her feel better to know most of the blood I'd gotten on her was mine.

"Because we're in a hurry," I replied, keeping her in my arms as I ran to Lance's sedan. I unlocked the doors and put Nikki in the passenger seat, clicking in the seat belt.

"I could have done that myself," she muttered as I fastened my own.

I didn't respond. Instead, turning the key, I hit the gas and peeled away from the curb. We wove in and out of traffic, speeding toward the freeway. I didn't know where we were going, but we would get there fast.

"Slow down, Gregory. It won't do us any good to get there fast, if we get there dead," Nikki chastised me.

I turned to make a reply, but my words died in my throat. An enormous, black Hummer was running its red light as I was speeding through our green one. There would not even be time to hit the break before we collided.

"Nikki!" I screamed above the sound of breaking glass and screeching metal. She covered her face with her hands, but was sprayed with glass from the windshield and her window. I watched in horror as her door crumpled in and Nikki was crushed against the dash. I heard innumerable sick crunching sounds from her fragile bones. As the cars slid to a stop, I could see she was bleeding from a gash on her forehead as well as several cuts covering her hands and arms.

I could taste my own blood in my mouth and my shirt had been shredded further by the flying glass. Kicking open my door, I flew around the car to Nikki's side. "Nikki!" I cried again. "Nikki, look at me!" She didn't respond, but straining over the tumult of sound around us, I could hear her heart beating faintly. I wasn't sure how to get her out of the car without doing more damage to her poor, broken body. Then I could smell the gasoline and it didn't matter anymore.

I ripped her door off its hinges and flung it away. She was pinned under the dash. Bracing my feet against the floor board, I pried up with my hands and was able to widen the gap enough to pull Nikki free. Slicing through the useless seatbelt with my teeth, I pulled her small, limp body from the car and turned to run from the wreckage.

We were only a few yards away before a fiery explosion threw us another four feet. I curled my body around Nikki's as a protective shield from the heat blast, and then from the asphalt, as we hit the ground and rolled.

We came to a stop, and I sat in the street, rocking back and forth with Nikki in my arms. The rain poured down on us, mixing with the tears streaming down my face onto Nikki's pale features.

"Please live, please be okay. Please. You can't leave me now, please come back. I need you. Dear God, please," I rambled on and on until the ambulance came and the paramedic tried to pry my hands from her. Unthinking, I growled and snapped at him. He jumped back in surprise.

"Look, Mac, I don't know how you managed to save her from the fire, but if you don't let me at her now, it won't matter," he said urgently. I blinked, coming partially back to myself, and stood up with her.

"She's mine," I whispered weakly. The tech looked at me for a moment.

"Bring her over here and lay her down," he said, allowing me some control of her. I nodded and placed her on the gurney he indicated. I then latched onto the steel bar of its side with one hand, indicating I wasn't letting her out of my sight. He nodded to me, and we got into the back of the ambulance. He started firing numbers and letters into his radio as his partner took Nikki's vitals. Less than thirty seconds after the back door shut, we were speeding to the hospital, the siren giving voice to the scream tearing through my heart.

Chapter Forty-Seven

 was entirely unprepared for my first visit to a human hospital. The small room was full of loud machines and even louder people. They fluttered around the edge of her bed, shouting and stabbing her with needles. Ripping open her shirt, a small woman used brute force to jab a piece of steel into the side of her chest initiating a puff of air followed by a long hiss. I was standing helplessly in the corner, wrapped in a blanket trying to keep my injuries hidden. By standing perfectly still, I was able to remain unnoticed amidst the chaos.

Nikki's heart stopped beating at 10:08 p.m. Instead of the silence I expected at death, the room erupted further. A shrill and constant beep began to sound and one of the doctors began pushing on her chest with both hands. When there was no change, he grabbed part of a machine that came off in both hands, still shouting numbers I didn't register. A different woman stripped Nikki of the last of her dignity by slicing apart her bra and pulling it away from her breasts. Somewhere in my mind I recognized what they were doing, trying, in their way, to bring her back, but it was all so brutal. Then the man bellowed "Clear!" and for the first time since we entered, everyone in the room took a step back from Nikki. He put the flat panels against her chest and pressed a button. Nikki's entire body reacted, arching up before flopping back onto the cot. I gasped loudly enough for the woman nearest me to look in my direction. Before she could address me there was another "Clear!" and her attention was forced back to Nikki, as was mine. Again her body threw itself up from the table only to have gravity pull it down again. I finally managed to close my eyes, but the image was burned into the back of my lids. They tried three times to bring her back before officially declaring her dead. Then, without the decency to remove anything they had done to her, they covered her from head to toe. At least someone had turned off the blaring noise.

Just after they cleared the room, Nikki's family arrived. Gale rushed through the door, followed closely by Tom and Jack. With one look, they knew the awful truth. Gale collapsed against Tom, sobbing hysterically. Jack sank into a chair, his face slack. Then, he set his features into a determined mask and stood up again, reaching for the sheet covering his sister's face.

"Don't," I warned him. Through his tears, Tom found me still cowering in the corner.

"What happened?" he choked.

"I killed her," I replied.

"They said it was a car wreck," he responded, confused.

I knew I could never explain to these good people how entirely responsible for their daughter's death I really was. "I was driving," I tried lamely.

"I meant, what happened in the wreck?" Tom explained. "How are you still standing?"

I realized he was really asking why I wasn't dead as well. I should be. I wanted to be. "A Hummer ran a red light, hit the passenger side. I was speeding; there was no time to react." Even for me.

Jack stood up from his chair and walked over to me. I thought he was going to scream at me, hit me, strangle me even. Instead, he wrapped his arms around me and hugged me tightly. "I'm sorry," he whispered.

My heart broke open again and a sob tore from my throat, the tears flowing anew. Sympathy from her family? Could it be possible to feel more guilt?

Jack walked me over to the chair and I sank down, burying my face in my hands. "I'm so sorry. For everything."

"You can't blame yourself for this, Gregory. It was an accident," Tom insisted. Gale composed herself enough to look up and speak. "She loved you. Very much."

"I know."

This time it was Gale who reached for the sheet. "Please don't," I begged. Her hand hovered, I could see the desperate need in her swollen eyes. "She doesn't look like herself," I tried, desperate myself not to see the reality of what I could never erase from my mind.

"I just need to see her again," Gale whispered, then collapsed again into Tom's arms while their weeping started anew. At the sight of his broken mother, even Jack began to sob, wrapping his arms around her back, hanging on to both his parents.

A nurse came in and sheepishly said she had some paperwork for them to fill out when they were ready. Tom nodded, wiping his eyes. I could see the physical effort he was making to try and hold it together for his family. Putting his arms around them, he started toward the door, then hesitated, looking back at me, inviting me to go with them.

"I'd like to stay here a few more minutes," I said. He nodded in understanding, and they left, Gale's shuddering sobs echoing down the hall.

It had all happened so *fast*. All I wanted was some time. I just needed some time alone in the now silent room. But I wasn't alone. I was with Nikki, *my* Nikki, my love, my life, my everything. I forced myself to her bedside and took her slender hand. It was still warm. I would miss that warmth when it faded away. Suddenly unable to bear the thought of her turning cold in my grasp, I dropped her hand back to the bed and returned to my corner, sinking disconsolately into the chair.

Jenny came rushing into the room and stopped abruptly when she saw the telltale sheet.

"Where are Lance and Rob?" I asked before she could open her mouth. I didn't want to talk about Nikki. I was selfishly unwilling to share my grief. "Are they all right? Is Lazarus dead?"

"They're fine," she assured me. "And I told you, Lazarus doesn't die, but he is gone."

"Who is he, Jenny?" I demanded. "How do you know about him?"

"Does it really matter anymore?" she asked, looking over at Nikki's still form.

"It sure as hell does!" I yelled, coming up off the chair, my sorrow suddenly finding a new outlet. "He came after us! He knew everything! He may as well have been driving the damn car!"

"You were driving the car," she said quietly. I clenched my fists to keep from striking her.

"You don't think I know that?" I cried. "You don't think I know this is *all my fault?!*" I took a step toward her, and she cowered back. Then, I fell backward into the chair again, my rage dissipating as quickly as it had flared. "She's gone, Jenny. If you won't help me get revenge, I have nothing left."

"Getting Lazarus to kill you won't bring her back," she replied.

"Killing him might make me feel better," I lied. Nothing would ever make me feel better.

"No it won't," she insisted. "You should have turned her, Gregory. You should have changed her the moment you knew it was love."

"That's exactly why I wouldn't change her, Jenny." My voice was rising again. "My life before her was hell, and it wasn't just because I didn't have her, it was because I was an Immortal. I wouldn't have damned her to that."

"Did you even give her the choice?" Nikki asked, her voice rising to meet mine.

"Of course not!" I yelled. "She was so young, Jenny. Of course she would have wanted it! And we would have been happy for a while. Then she would have had to watch her family grow old and die. A hundred years from now, two hundred years from now, would she still have been glad I did it?"

"Yes!" Jenny screamed stubbornly.

"You can't know that!" I yelled back. "Not even Nikki could have known how she would feel in a thousand years!"

"But it was love!"

I took a deep breath to add even more volume to my argument when something happened that froze my every thought. Looking at Jenny, I saw my shocked expression mirrored on her face. I turned to the clock on the wall.

10:27. I watched as the hands crawled around in a circle. A minute went by, five minutes, ten minutes, twenty minutes. At 11:00 I heard it again, the most beautiful sound in the world, a faint thump emanated from Nikki's chest. Jenny and I gasped in unison, our first breath since the last beat of Nikki's heart.

Falling to my knees, I didn't know whether to laugh or cry. I was torn between the joy of knowing Nikki was still alive and the grief that I had somehow done the unthinkable.

"How did this happen?" I asked quietly.

Jenny was laughing. "You were wounded in the fight—" she suggested.

"—And in the accident, and it started to rain ..." I added.

"Washing your blood into hers," she finished.

We stood for a moment just looking at Nikki.

"C'mon, get up," Jenny said, smacking my back as she passed me to get to the bed. She began pulling off the covers.

"What are you doing?" I grabbed at the blankets.

"We have to get her out of here!" she said, yanking them back. "Her family could be here any minute!"

Her family. Suddenly I had a new purpose. Nikki may never forgive me for what I'd done, but starting now I was going to do everything right. The way she would want it.

"No," I said, taking Jenny gently by the shoulders and moving her away from the bed. She looked at me like I was mad. "Think about it, Jenny. Nikki was severely injured in the accident, massive trauma. With so much blood lost, it will take days for her body to learn how to heal itself."

"So we leave her here?" she asked incredulously. "Gregory, they're going to take her to the morgue. Even if they don't do an autopsy, she's going to be embalmed."

"Not if we take care of things," I replied, my mind beginning to work quickly now. "We bribe the coroner, the funeral home, the grave digger, anyone and everyone we need to."

Jenny was shaking her head. "The risk you're taking…"

"Is exactly what Nikki would want," I insisted. "Her family wasn't here when she died. They need closure, they need to say goodbye. Please, Jenny, I've made the biggest mistake imaginable, let me do this one thing right for her."

Jenny pursed her lips. "It wasn't a mistake, Gregory. It was a miracle."

I knew it wouldn't help to argue. "Please."

"Fine." She sighed, giving in. "How do we do this? What if she wakes up?"

"One of us will stay with her at all times. You go tell Rob and Lance what's happened. We'll work out some kind of schedule. I'll talk to Nikki's family and convince them to let me help with planning the funeral. Then no one will wonder why her grieving boyfriend is talking to the funeral director in hushed tones," I explained rapidly.

"I hope you're right," Jenny said, shaking her head.

"I hope so, too," I replied. "Meet me back here later, and bring plenty of cash."

Nikki's family returned minutes after Jenny left. They didn't question for an instant my desire to be involved. In fact, I was welcomed with open arms, which made my tasks easier while adding nearly unbearable amounts of guilt. I knew after the funeral I could never speak to them again.

Rob and Lance were both as thrilled as Jenny that Nikki would soon be joining us and, between the four of us, she was never left unattended. Because I had to do so much healing of my own, I fed on a few stray dogs to avoid leaving her side for too long. I did what I could to speed things along, not knowing when Nikki would begin to wake. Any moaning or stirring would certainly ruin the façade of her death.

Even with monetarily lubricated wheels spinning, it was still three days before we stood in the viewing wing of the funeral home, waiting for the funeral to begin. At her mother's insistence, I stood with Nikki's family and accepted condolences from people who had no idea who I was. Hundreds of people had come to share in the grief.

Beth came through with Sharice, Lucas, and several other people obviously from the shelter. They each embraced me. "Gotta keep troopin' on," Sharice said through her tears. "It's what Nikki would want." Lucas, however looked like his family had died all over again. Seeing his haunted eyes nearly did me in. I wanted to shake Nikki awake, show them all that she was fine. She could go on loving and helping them. But I didn't. I couldn't. She would bring as much danger to all these people as I had brought to her. It had to be this way. The truth is often painful.

As the crowd thinned and headed into the main room, Rich walked through the door. My body tensed instinctually. Gale noticed and followed my gaze. Reaching out, she took my hand, squeezing gently.

Rich went through the line shaking hands with Jack and Tom, and hugging Gale. Then he turned to me.

"What are you doing here?" he asked. He looked like he was trying to decide whether to spit in my face or break my jaw. I hoped he decided against both. I didn't want to hurt him in front of Nikki's family.

"We asked him to be here," Tom spoke up.

My throat tightened.

"He loved Nikki," Jack added, moving to stand at my side opposite his mother.

"I . . ." Rich started, but changed directions. "A lot of people loved Nikki. He barely knew her," he finished, pointing a finger at me.

"He's family," Gale said firmly, squeezing my hand again.

I closed my eyes. I had never been stood for. Here I was, primarily responsible for Nikki's death, and her family was trying to protect me. I would never be able to put this right. I could never give Nikki back to her family. But I could watch over her for them. I would do whatever it took to protect her, for their sakes. And I would never forgive myself for taking her away from them.

Rich saw that he faced a united front and tactfully decided this was not the place for the conversation he wanted to have with me. He decided to ignore me completely instead so he turned to Gale.

"It just seems so wrong for her to be gone," he said. "I can't believe she's really dead."

"I know, son," Tom said, putting his hand on Rich's shoulder. "We all feel that way."

"It just isn't right," Rich muttered. He was quiet for a moment, then looked up again. "The picture you have on display is beautiful. It looks just like her."

"Gregory painted it," Gale informed him. "He wants us to keep it," she broke off, overcome by emotion. Rich looked like he'd swallowed something rancid.

"I'd better go find a seat," he said, and walked away.

I was left alone with the family. While I was sorry Nikki wouldn't have a chance to say goodbye, I was grateful she wasn't aware of their grief. Only her occasional heartbeat and nearly imperceptibly slow breaths had assured me she was still there. She hadn't stirred at all.

"Your sister's here," Jack said, motioning with his head.

I looked up to see Jenny standing in the doorway. It had been easier to introduce her than to keep her a secret during the last few days, so we had told them she was my sister to easily explain our relationship.

"They're ready for you," Jenny said.

Tom said a prayer and shut the lid to the casket. The family started to walk away, but I hesitated. "I need another minute," I said when they turned back.

"Take your time, son," Tom said. I didn't miss that he had used the same term with Rich.

"Thank you," I replied.

"They're coming for the casket any minute," Jenny reminded me.

"I know," I said. Then I surprised her by taking her hand. "Jenny I need you to help me."

"What else have I been doing these last three days?" she asked tenderly. "What do you need?"

"Nikki can't wake up alone in that casket."

"You want me to steal her body?" she asked. "How would I get out of here without being seen?"

"You wouldn't," I agreed. "I want you to take my place as pall bearer."

"What? Why?"

"So the others won't notice the extra weight."

She looked at me a moment, then nodded. "All right, Gregory, whatever you think is best for Nikki. What do I say to her parents?"

"Tell them I was overcome, that I couldn't bear to sit through the speeches and eulogy."

"Okay," she said, placing a hand to my cheek. She could see I was telling the truth. "I'll dig you up as soon as I can."

"I know you will."

I opened the coffin back up and carefully moved Nikki so she was lying on her side. I moved the book her mother had tucked in with her to her feet to make more room. It was a leather bound copy of Romeo and Juliet. How very ironic. I climbed in and wrapped my arms securely around her, knowing this may be the last time she allowed me to be this close to her. But she would know she wasn't alone if she woke up in the dark. Jenny leaned down and kissed Nikki on the cheek.

"See you soon," she whispered, then closed the top.

The seal was tighter than I had expected. I lay in the dark, clinging to the warming body of the woman who had taught me to love, to live. Our chests pressed together in the confined space, hearts beating in sync. I closed my eyes and allowed myself to drown in almonds, jasmine, and an overwhelming and continually building amount of guilt.

Chapter Forty-Eight

heard the slight change in Nikki's breathing with her pressed so tightly against my chest. I fervently hoped that she was finally starting to wake up. She'd been asleep for three days before the funeral and now we'd been in the ground another twenty four hours. I had quit breathing twelve hours ago to prolong the already thin air for Nikki. I was getting unbearably stiff from laying in the hard casket for so long, but more than that, I was beginning to worry something had gone wrong with her change. It wouldn't have been the first time someone didn't quite make it to the other side. Nikki had been so damaged by the car wreck, and then the literal shock of attempted resuscitation … three times. I reflexively closed my eyes against the unwelcome image that sprang forth at that thought. The tension was getting unbearable. And where was Jenny? Then came the sound I'd found comfort in for the last ninety six hours—the unison beating of our hearts. I rolled my shoulders, trying to will myself to relax. I would need my wits about me if—*when* Nikki came to.

"Gregory?"

It was the whispered voice of an angel, a miracle that flooded my system with relief like rain through the cracks of a sun-baked desert.

"Yes, Nikki, I'm here. You're not alone. You're safe, you're alive," I whispered as well, though I wanted to shout, I wanted to sing. Then, I noted how quiet Nikki was. Something was … off. Of course something was off. We were laying here, buried alive because everyone she'd ever known and loved thought she was dead.

"Why wouldn't I be alive?" she asked.

Had the head trauma from the wreck done irreparable damage? It seemed unlikely, but I'd never heard of anyone being brought over in such devastating circumstances.

"What's the last thing you remember?" I asked, trying to gauge her response time.

"I remember meeting your family," she said, and I could hear the smile in her voice, "then…" Perhaps she didn't remember the worst of it.

"Oh, Gregory!" she suddenly cried in horror. It stabbed me straight in the gut. She remembered…but what? The fight, the wreck? Please, not the hospital…

"Are you all right? Jenny? Rob? Lance? What happened? Where are we?" She was clearly beginning to panic, and yet her first thoughts were of the others. Before I could calm her down, I needed to know how much to explain.

"What do you remember?" I asked again. I was trying very hard to keep my voice steady.

"I remember jumping off the roof," she replied, then added, "Let's not do that again." I couldn't help but smile at her capacity to make a joke even now, but it was very brief.

"Then what?" I prodded gently.

"Then…nothing," she answered. "Just waking up here, with you. Where are we, Gregory?"

She gripped my shoulders and I was taken aback by the strength of her hands. I tightened my grip on her waist, as if to keep her from pushing me away when I told her the truth.

"Nikki, I'm so sorry," I whispered pathetically, hoping she could someday forgive me.

"What happened? Where are we? Where are the others?" Her questions were asked rapid-fire, her voice rising in pitch and panic. I tried to explain myself as quickly as possible.

"Nikki, I'm sorry, but there was an accident…you were…killed," I stumbled.

"What? I'm dead!" she cried, hysteria closing in. "What about the others, are they dead too?"

"No, Nikki. The others are fine. No one is really dead," I said, cursing myself for my awkward words. My presence was supposed to be making things easier for her. "I meant to say, you were assumed dead. Your family even had a funeral."

My poor choice of words broke the last of her resolve and she began to thrash about, screaming in earnest now.

"We're in my coffin?! Buried?! Gregory! What are you doing here? If they thought I was dead, why would they have buried you, too? I don't understand!"

My guilt consumed every nerve as I felt and heard her crumble in front of me, her tears soaking my shirt.

"Jenny and I realized you weren't dead, but your family needed closure," I began to explain, but I couldn't bring myself to finish.

Nikki's hysteria was quickly escalating, and she seemed to be having trouble breathing in the thin air. "I'm … so … sorry," she gasped.

"Nikki," I said a little too harshly. "You have nothing to be sorry for. You've done nothing wrong." She couldn't begin this life thinking any of it was her fault. It was all *my* fault.

"This is all my fault! I'm so sorry, Gregory. I've been nothing but trouble since you met me. I should have just left you alone," she began to babble.

I couldn't help but laugh at how her manic words were becoming a perverse mirror of my thoughts.

"What's that? What's happening?" she screamed, as we began rocking back and forth. Her new strength was beginning to crush me as she grabbed at me in panic.

"It's Jenny," I tried to soothe her, letting her know she would shortly be free of me. "She's digging us out as we speak."

"We're not trapped?"

"Of course not, Nikki." I was now certain my idea of sharing a coffin with her was not one of my best.

"Why did they assume I was dead? Why did you go along with it?" she asked, her voice shaking with dread.

"Nikki, I'm sorry, it was an accident, but my blood was everywhere … and you … you're Immortal now," I blurted. Again I cursed whatever fatal flaw it was that caused my talent with words to fail me every time I really needed it. I was making a mess of this whole situation. Not that there would have really been a pleasant way to wake up dead, so to speak.

Suddenly, I realized how eerily quiet it had become. "Nikki!" I called, panicking, "Nikki, breathe!"

Instead of the deep, calming breaths I was hoping for, Nikki began to giggle, but it was a horrible twisted version of her normally wonderful laugh.

The coffin settled roughly on the ground and the lid was thrown to the side. Her laughing only got worse.

"What the hell?" Jenny asked, from above us. I sat us up as Nikki continued laughing wildly. Jenny found the clarity I lacked and gave Nikki a sharp slap. My guilt finally overcame me completely

"I'm so sorry!" I cried. Nikki's sweet voice matched mine, words, pitch and all.

Jenny was utterly astounded.

"I'm sorry," Nikki whispered again, then sank into a soft chant that echoed my anguished thoughts. "I'm sorry, I'm sorry, I'm sorry."

Jenny looked at the two of us and took a deep breath through her nose. She blinked. Then she sampled our individual scents.

"You," Jenny said harshly to me. "Get out. Go wait in the car."

"Jenny, I'm not just going to leave her here like this," I argued.

Instead of arguing back, Jenny simply took my shirt in her hands and tossed me away from Nikki. I stood up, ready to get equally violent, when I noticed the immediate change in Nikki's condition.

"See? She's already better," Jenny said, stating the obvious. Then she continued, "You're drowning her with your guilt."

The awful truth of her words was like a dagger to my heart. I tried not to believe, but then Nikki spoke.

"I'm so sorry, Gregory," she whispered, confirming Jenny's accusation. I was doing this to her. I was hurting Nikki with my very presence.

"I will explain later. For now, go lock yourself in the car with the windows up," Jenny said. A long, agonizing moment passed before I could tear my eyes away from Nikki's tear-streaked face. Then I turned away, moving toward the rented sedan. Each step felt like I was somehow giving up, giving in to losing Nikki. But what choice did I have? I sat in the driver's seat and locked the door as Jenny had asked.

How could I hope to help Nikki in any way if she couldn't even stand to be near me? I collapsed in utter defeat against the steering column, weeping bitterly for what might have been. What should have been. I had secretly wished for an eternity with Nikki, and now I had it. I had succeeded in damning the most perfect angel to an eternity of hell.

After some time of wallowing, I pulled myself together and looked out the window to see that Jenny had indeed managed to calm Nikki down. They were deep in conversation.

"Gregory!" Jenny called. "Roll the window down a bit!" I did as she requested, wondering what she was playing at.

Nikki immediately took a step further away from the car, mumbling something I couldn't hear.

"Roll it up again, please," Jenny called after a short exchange. I did as I was told, beginning to rankle at the fact that Jenny seemed to know what Nikki needed better than I did. Nikki's eyes went wide with some understanding. Maybe she was finally realizing what a mistake it was to let me love her. I wished they would speak up, but they continued to speak in hushed tones and I couldn't hear them from this distance through the window.

Finally, after a lengthy discussion and much gesticulation, they walked to the car and Jenny motioned it was all right for me to get out.

"I'm sorry, Nikki," I said, carefully keeping my distance. I didn't want to do any more damage.

But Nikki reached out and touched my face. It only made me want to touch more of her, which in turn made my guilt even worse.

"Please don't, Gregory," she whispered, as if reading my thoughts and agreeing with my shame. "I'm sorry," she finished. My only thought was to beg her not to shut me out completely.

"Gregory!" Jenny's shout was even louder after Nikki's soft plea. "Get a hold of yourself!"

"What exactly would you have me do, Jenny?" I asked, my temper lashing out.

"I don't know," she retorted, "but until you can get yourself under control, you have to stay away from Nikki."

"*What?*" I yelled, knowing that would be impossible. Then I realized Nikki had joined in my outcry. Could it be possible she still wanted me?

"Look, I know this is hard, but it's for your own good," she said softly to Nikki.

Jenny then turned to me. "Nikki is an empath. She can see and feel all the emotions around her. Apparently yours are a little too much for her right now. Give her some time to sort it out."

Of course. Suddenly it all made sadistic sense. I smiled at my angel. "It looks like you kept your gift."

"I'm sorry," she replied, my guilt still poisoning her. I took a painful step further away.

"No really. *I* am sorry," she insisted. "It isn't fair that you should be inconvenienced by my freakish nature."

"Nikki Christian," I chastised harshly. "You are not now, nor have you ever been, a freak." A goddess, an angel, a miracle … "You're gifted," I reminded her.

"Thank you," she said timidly.

"All right," Jenny said, opening the passenger door and gesturing to Nikki. "Let's go."

"What about Gregory?" Nikki asked. "We can't just make him walk from here."

After all she'd been through she was still concerned for me. Perhaps there was hope. I laughed at myself. With Nikki, there was always hope.

"I've walked much further than I will tonight, Nikki. Please don't worry about me. You already have enough to worry about." More than enough to worry about, thanks to me. If only I had left her alone. But no, even now I couldn't truly mean it, which only made me that much more the monster. "I'll see you soon," I said, knowing I couldn't stay away for long.

Jenny shut the door between Nikki and me and got into the driver's seat. I stood there, watching as they pulled away. Not until long after they had passed through the iron gate did I turn and begin to fill in the now empty grave.

EPILOGUE

Queen Eve stood gazing out a narrow window, not seeing the green sea of jungle spread out below her. Her nails against the cement sill were making sharp clacking sounds that echoed into the room. When her phone rang, she immediately withdrew it from the folds of her gown. Then, getting control over herself, she let it ring several times before she answered it. Even her son should know his place.

"What news?" she asked without preamble.

"Most Beloved Queen, I desire your permission for a thorough cleaning," came the familiar tenor voice.

"You know my mind and my heart," she replied. "Why do you ask permission for what needs to be done?"

She could hear the quiet joy her response had brought through his voice; she hoped it would hurry him along. "There are unusual circumstances," Lazarus said.

"Such as?"

"There is a member of the Inner Court involved," there was a short pause, "and Gregory."

She could not help but snort at the name he had allowed himself to be called. Then the meaning of Lazarus' words came to her. "Involved how?"

"He took particular interest in a female human, so much so that he told her the truth. He has betrayed even you, my Queen."

There was silence.

"Kill the human bitch," Eve ordered. "Slowly."

"I would find great pleasure in it. Unfortunately, she is already dead," Lazarus replied.

"How?" She hoped it was painful.

"I defended your honor, but I underestimated Gregory, and he was able to escape momentarily with the human. While fleeing, Fate stepped in and eliminated the threat on your behalf. The car they were driving was hit by another large car, then exploded."

Silence filled the air again. The Queen was disturbed both by Gregory's involvement and Lazarus' choice to use the word "Fate."

"They are both dead?"

"Gregory lives," he said. "Which is why I seek your permission to clean out his entire following."

The Queen blinked. "He has a following?"

"The Immortals he once stood for were all involved in betraying you and protecting the human. They spend a great deal of time together. He has spread many unnatural habits."

"Such as?"

"He and Guinevere feasted on <u>animals</u>."

"And how does Gwen defend herself?"

"She claims that she did not know the extent of Gregory's betrayal until it was too late. And that she humored his indecent excursions in deference to you."

"She is a crafty one."

"That she is. I don't trust her."

"Nor do I; however, she is also extremely valuable. And her fear of me is complete."

"What is your will?"

"The mortal, you are sure she is dead?"

"I stand watching as they lower the casket into the ground."

"And Gregory is there?"

"He is not. I don't know where he is at present."

"No doubt he has moved on already. He pursues the most disturbing amusements," the Queen mused, pacifying herself.

Lazarus was not so convinced, especially since Gregory's subordinates were all present, including Guinevere. He knew better, however, than to contradict the Queen. He would continue to watch this group. Guinevere had assured him he could leave, which meant he should surely stay.

"Lazarus, my son, come home," Eve said, breaking into his thoughts.

"You think this could have been what we were trying to prevent? Has Fate taken care of The Prophecy for us?"

"I think you have been away for too long. After a brief visit, you will be once again in tune with my will and be able to more effectively serve on my behalf."

"As you wish, Beloved Mother." Lazarus closed his phone, his body already beginning to tingle with anticipation. All thoughts of Gregory and his aberrations were lost, crushed by thoughts of love for Mother Eve, Queen of Immortals.

The Queen turned away from the window and crossed to the stone table. She looked down on the now gaunt face of her Seer. Reaching out, she stroked the pale face softly. She considered freeing Cassandra. If this incident did relate to The Prophecy, it may have given her clearer vision. The Queen reached out and grasped the wooden stake lodged in the Seer's heart. But her hand began to tremble and instead of pulling the stake free, she turned angrily away and went to once again stare out the window. For the first time, the Queen was not only afraid of the unknown, but of knowing the truth.

ACKNOWLEDGMENTS

I have a lot of people to thank, first and foremost, my mom, who got this novel finished by starting and ending every phone conversation with "Don't you have some writing to do?"

A big thank you also goes out to my brothers: Mikey for being willing to read and edit, and to Jason whose mad skills with capturing gore in a poetic light made the fight scenes much more than if I had been left to my own squeamish devices.

Also, thanks to my editor, Jennifer DeLucy, who helped me take this novel from "good enough to share with my family," to "so great I can't wait to share it with the masses." And, of course, thank you to Kimberly Myers, Jeffery Hoyle, and everyone else at Omnific Publishing for taking a risk on an unknown and helping me bring forth the best possible product I could offer.

ABOUT THE AUTHOR

KC Randall inherited her wit from her father, her imagination from her mother, and her love of reading from pretty much everyone she's genetically related to. Her family used to tell stories to pass the time on long road trips because they were more entertaining than anything on the radio. From this, she learned to love playing with words.

It was not until she was almost thirty and reading a ridiculously popular young adult novel that it finally occurred to her... "Hey, I could do this." So, she set about writing her first full-length novel. Once she started, she realized it was actually hard work, and that she couldn't stop. Now she deals with countless stories boiling around in her head, demanding to be told.

While trying to type these stories into submission, she also plays the roles of wife, mother, and elementary school teacher. She currently resides in a small town in Arkansas with her husband, two sons, daughter, and Thomas, the imaginary guinea pig.